Since 2004, international bestselling author **Sherrilyn Kenyon** has placed over fifty novels on the *New York Times* bestseller list; in the past two years alone, she has claimed the No. 1 spot fifteen times. This extraordinary author continues to top every genre she writes within. Proclaimed the pre-eminent voice in paranormal fiction by critics, Kenyon has helped pioneer – and define – the current paranormal trend that has captivated the world and continues to blaze new trails that blur traditional genre lines. With more than twenty-three million copies of her books in print in over thirty countries, her current series include: the Dark-Hunters, League, Lords of Avalon, Chronicles of Nick and Belador Code.

Visit Sherrilyn Kenyon's websites:
www.darkhunter.com | www.sherrilynkenyon.co.uk

www.facebook.com/AuthorSherrilynKenyon |
www.twitter.com/KenyonSherrilyn

Dianna Love is the *New York Times* bestselling co-author of *Phantom in the Night*, *Whispered Lies*, and *Silent Truth*. She is a national speaker who started writing while working over a hundred feet in the air, creating marketing projects for Fortune 500 companies. When not plotting out her latest action-adventure, she travels the country on a motorcycle to meet fans and research new locations. She and her husband live near Atlanta, Georgia.

ALTERANT

SHERRILYN KENYON

AND

DIANNA LOVE

BOOK 2 IN THE BELADOR SERIES

PIATKUS

First published in the US in 2011 by Pocket Star Books
A division of Simon & Schuster, Inc.
First published in Great Britain as a paperback original in 2011 by Piatkus

A CIP catalogue record for this book
is available from the British Library.

ISBN 978-0-7499-5468-0

Printed and bound by CPI Group (UK) Ltd, Croydon, CR0 4YY

Papers used by Piatkus are from well-managed forests
and other responsible sources.

MIX
Paper from
responsible sources
FSC® C104740

Piatkus
An imprint of
Little, Brown Book Group
100 Victoria Embankment
London EC4Y 0DY

An Hachette UK Company
www.hachette.co.uk

www.piatkus.co.uk

We'd like to dedicate this book to Cassondra Murray, whose attention to detail has made all the difference in early reads of many of our books.

ACKNOWLEDGMENTS

FROM SHERRILYN AND DIANNA

Thank you to our family, friends, and fans. We love you all and couldn't do this without you! You rock!

A special hug to our husbands, whose endless support means the world to us. They tolerate the chaotic lives of two authors who are constantly typing and traveling. A special thanks goes to Cassondra Murray and Mary Buckham for beta reads and terrific feedback, plus being major support at any time, day or night. And thanks to Debbie Kaufman, another early reader, who read in the midst of celebrating her first sale. I also wanted to thank Wes and Ann Sarginson for their help in researching Costa Rica with me (Dianna).

A major thank-you to Louise Burke, a publisher whose passion for this business is clear in all she does, and thank you to our talented editor Lauren McKenna, whose spot-on editing makes the creation process a pleasure. We have to send a high-five to the Pocket Art Department, who has once again outdone themselves on giving us a cover to die for. And we so appreciate the brilliant job Robert Gottlieb of Trident Media Group does of guiding and managing our careers.

Last, but never least, we want to thank the readers who come out to see us in every city, send encouraging messages that touch our hearts, and read our stories so that we may continue doing what we love most. You mean the world to us. We love to hear from you anytime, at authors@ beladors.com, or stop by www.SherrilynKenyon.com and www.AuthorDiannaLove.com

ONE

What's a girl to wear to spend eternity in prison?

Evalle Kincaid would rather fight a pack of demons alone than face the Tribunal at midnight.

Seventy-two minutes from now.

She *might* walk free tonight . . . *if* the Tribunal took into account that she'd spent the last forty-eight hours protecting humans from an eight-hundred-year-old warlord instead of mounting her defense.

Like it was her fault she'd been born a half-breed Belador? An Alterant. The only one not dead or caged. The others had *killed* humans. Taking the Belador oath at eighteen had kept her free of persecution . . . until now.

One thing at a time, like getting dressed. She had to show up in more than a bra and panties.

She pulled out her favorite cotton shirt, a vintage piece, from her antique chest of drawers. Stepping into jeans and boots, she shoved a couple of lug nuts in her pocket and froze.

Her apartment was too silent.

Not a lot of noise reached two levels beneath downtown Atlanta when you lived in the equivalent of a concrete bunker.

But this stillness was a something-must-be-up quiet.

She headed out to investigate and had just reached

the hallway when a harsh blowing noise roared in the kitchen.

It sounded like . . . a giant blowtorch.

Grace be to Macha, *no!*

She broke into a run and swung through the kitchen doorway as another blast rocked the air. *"Feenix!"*

Her two-foot-tall pet gargoyle stood facing the open oven with fire shooting from his snout. He stopped blowing flames and cut his big round eyes up at her in a sly "who me?" innocent look. "Ye-eth?"

If she laughed right now he'd never learn that he couldn't shoot flames in the apartment. But she kept her voice calm and curious. "What are you doing?"

That must have been the right question. He turned to face her and started dancing from side to side on fat little four-toed feet. *"Thurrr-prithe!* Peetha. Peetha." He clapped his pudgy-clawed hands and chortled.

She stepped further into the kitchen and bent down to see one of her frozen pepperoni pizzas charred beyond recognition on one side.

He'd cooked for her.

Her heart climbed into her throat. How was she going to live without him if they locked her away? He was the reason her heart sang every morning when she opened her eyes. She'd find him plopped on the bed next to her with his pet alligator tucked under his arm and a gap-toothed grin on his face.

She closed the oven and smiled at him. "It's perfect. Thank you for cooking me dinner."

Feenix flapped his wings, flying up to eye level. Two

little overbite fangs pointed down past his lower lip. She opened her arms and he floated into them, tucking his wings, which were soft as bat skin.

But it was the sweet way he said "Mine" that threatened to fold her at the knees.

She couldn't let on how hard it was going to be to leave him tonight or he'd fret the entire time she was gone. Fear of losing her might cause him to regress into the fire-breathing little animal who hadn't even been able to communicate when she'd first brought him home. If she didn't return after tonight, and he got out, someone would kill him for sure. He deserved better after escaping the crazy sorcerer who'd created, *then* tortured, the poor thing.

No way could she lock him away somewhere.

She wouldn't do to him what others wanted to do to her.

Nothing would stop her from coming back to Feenix . . . except two of the three Tribunal deities ruling against her. Even then, she wouldn't go down without a fight. She didn't care if they could smoke her where she stood.

That left her one choice—to gamble on her chances of convincing the Tribunal she would not shift, involuntarily or otherwise, into her Alterant beast form and kill humans.

Vegas would laugh at her odds of winning.

She swallowed the lump threatening to choke her.

Feenix leaned back. "Peetha?"

"You bet, baby." She hugged him, inhaling his warm, leathery smell, then lowered him to sit on the island counter.

The uncharred half of the pizza tasted better than it looked. And she'd have made all the same *ooh* and *ahh* comments even if it had been a mud patty.

"Nutth." He opened his mouth wide.

She tossed him the two lug nuts from her pocket.

He caught the steel snacks with his tongue and chomped them like M&M peanut candies.

She eyed her watch. Time had a grudge against her.

Delaying the inevitable wouldn't make walking out that door any easier. And arriving late for a Tribunal meeting would be considered an insult—a guaranteed thumbs-down. She washed her hands. "I have to go out for a while, so don't cook anything else while I'm gone, okay?"

"Yeth." He watched her from his roost on the kitchen island, eyes beaming pure happiness.

"You're the best." She touched his wide nose with her finger, smiled, and headed for her bedroom.

The sound of Feenix's wings flapped behind her.

Ten-foot ceilings allowed him to fly over her head in the hallway and reach the bedroom before her. When she strode into the room, he was perched in the center of her bed.

Feenix said, "You come back?"

The million-dollar question, but he asked the same thing every time she left. "As soon as I can."

"What ith thoon? One, two, five, theven, eight?"

Did he mean minutes or hours? He'd just learned to count to eight. Time was a whole other concept. She was thinking more in terms of years, but rather than stretch the truth any further, she changed the topic. "How's your counting coming?"

"Good."

"Count for me."

He bent his legs and leaned over to count each toe around his potbelly. "One, two . . ."

She picked up her dagger off the nightstand and slid it inside her boot. She didn't walk the streets unarmed.

When Feenix stopped counting at eight, because he had eight toes, she told him, "Thought we were working on nine and ten this week."

"What ith nine ten?" He looked up at her with big orange eyes full of curiosity.

"I'll tell you on the way to the door." She headed to the door in her living room that opened into the exit tunnels.

Feenix needed a reason to count more than his toes. She told him, "Your horns are nine and ten."

He grunted unintelligible happy noises as he thumped down the hallway at her heels.

When she reached the door she turned around. "Are you going to practice?"

His eyes rounded as he realized he had new information. "Yeth, dammit."

"No cursing." She wanted to blame Quinn, one of her two closest friends, for irritating her to the point she'd said that word in front of Feenix, but the fault was hers.

"Thorry." He smiled, tongue poking out one side of his mouth.

"That's okay. I know it was an accident. Promise to be good and practice counting while I'm gone and I'll get you a hubcap."

His scaly forehead wrinkled with confusion.

She explained, "A hubcap is like a silver pizza."

He waddled in a circle, clapping and fluttering his wings, making happy sounds. She'd make sure Tzader, the other person she trusted most in this world, brought Feenix a hubcap if she couldn't.

She could if the Tribunal cut her some slack tonight and treated her equal to everyone else.

Was that asking too much?

Just one time she'd like to be judged on her own merit and not her tainted blood.

She had to go now or she'd never leave. Bending down, she gave Feenix one tight squeeze and said, "Where's your gator?"

He looked around and spied his favorite stuffed toy, then flew to his beanbag. After settling into the cushy bag he cuddled his stuffed alligator.

That was the picture she'd take to her grave.

"Bye, baby." Shutting the door quickly, she hurried through the concrete hallways to her garage area. No point in taking her GSX-R motorcycle out tonight. She had almost an hour to make the twenty-minute walk to Woodruff Park, where she'd get teleported to the meeting.

She hated teleporting almost as much as she disliked Sen, the liaison who would escort her to the Tribunal, but that was life in her world.

Walking across the garage, she used her kinetic power to access the elevator that took her up two floors to street level. She stepped out and scanned the pitch-black area through special sunglasses that protected her ultra-sensitive vision even at night. Similar to looking through night-vision goggles, she'd been born with vision that perceived the street and surrounding area in shades of blue-gray. Her strange DNA had gifted her with a deadly reaction to sunlight as well.

Sunshine wasn't an issue this close to midnight, but preternatural creatures could hide in the dark jungle of steel and concrete she'd have to traverse between here and Marietta Street. Quinn owned her building and didn't like charging her rent, but she insisted. She'd live life on her own terms.

Independence meant something different to everyone.

Unless someone had lived trapped in a basement the first eighteen years in this world, she doubted they could understand what independence meant to her.

She paused. Had she felt energy skimming through the air?

Or was she just jumpy?

Nothing stirred this late on a Thursday night except weeds withering in the August heat. Patchwork concrete and gravel stretched ahead of her, running beneath the street-level parking deck that fronted CNN. Tourists rarely wandered down here, where a ten-foot-high chain-link fence protected parked cars from vandalism.

Prime area for something nasty to wait for prey.

Bring it. I've got time to wash blood off my boots.

Or at least she'd die doing something for the greater good versus dying because of being born part Belador, part beast.

She swept a suspicious gaze from side to side and kept moving toward the dimly lit area, but not even a roach crawled in this sweltering weather. Sweat trickled along her cheek. Loose tendrils from her ponytail clung to her neck.

She'd miss Atlanta if she didn't return, especially being able to ride her motorcycle throughout the winter.

Would the Tribunal send her somewhere hot or . . .

The humid air skimming her arms changed with a prickling of awareness. Her boot heels tapped softly across the rutted pavement. No other sound filled in the gaps.

She opened her empathic senses . . . then wider.

Another presence moved toward her.

Human? She didn't think so.

If someone or something tangled with her right now it had better have a death wish. Tzader and Quinn would be waiting at the park to see her off, and she wanted to see them.

A male voice close behind said, "You're hard to find, Miss Kincaid."

Definitely not human.

TWO

Evalle swung around to face her stalker. "I'm not hard to find if I *want* to be found. How'd you know where I live?"

"You forget that VIPER hired me as a tracker?" Storm asked.

No. She just hadn't thought about him using that skill to find her apartment. She should be annoyed at his invading her privacy, not secretly thrilled at seeing him before she left.

Silly, but she *was* glad he'd shown up unexpectedly.

She'd only known Storm for the few days he'd been assigned to be her partner at VIPER—a coalition of powerful beings who protected humanity against supernatural predators. But the time they'd spent together had been intense while they'd hunted the Ngak Stone, an ancient and powerful relic. She'd fought demons and Kujoo, enemies of the Beladors for centuries who had escaped their cursed life beneath a mountain and traveled through a portal to Atlanta with apocalyptic plans.

She still nursed wounds from those battles.

Storm stood three steps back with thumbs hooked in the belt loops of his nicely broken-in jeans. A casual stance to those unaware. What lurked beneath that tranquil pose could change into a deadly black jaguar. Not a lycanthrope but a Skinwalker. Straight hair the color of midnight fell around his shoulders with rebel intent. His open-collared shirt blended with the obsidian night. Brown eyes with thick lashes took in every whisper of movement and punctuated a face cut of sharp cheekbones and a square jaw.

He'd been brought into VIPER for his ability to track supernatural energy.

She had one thing in common with Storm. He was a mixed bucket of powers, too, part Navajo and part Ashaninka.

Cocking her chin up in question, she asked, "What's up?"

"Came to tell you something," Storm murmured, distracted.

He stepped closer to her. His gaze roamed over the side of her face where a bruise was just getting ripe at twelve hours old. His eyes lifted to hers. "Too bad we sent the Kujoo back eight hundred years. I'd like another shot at that warlord."

"I could have done without him coming here the first time."

If she hadn't been busy fighting the Kujoo, she wouldn't be facing the Tribunal empty-handed. She made a show of checking her digital watch. "If this is about agency business, save it for later or email me."

"This isn't about VIPER, but it's important. I know you're on a tight schedule. That's why I've been waiting out here for over an hour."

Storm had waited an hour to talk to her?

That was . . . nice.

She could afford a few minutes to find out what he had to say and still make it to the park on time.

He eased forward, reducing another slice of space between them. His dark eyes stirred with interest that would cause another woman with her sordid history to retreat.

Not her. She cowed to no man and, deep inside, she believed Storm wouldn't try to harm her. And she wasn't a vulnerable fifteen-year-old girl anymore but a twenty-three-year-old woman with Belador powers.

He hooked one long finger under the string of leather tied around her neck. "You're still wearing the amulet."

She blinked at his change of topics and looked down to where a silver disk the size of a half dollar hung from a leather thong tied around her neck. An intricate pattern had been inscribed inside the pentagram center. Nicole, a white witch friend, had placed an invisibility spell on the amulet before loaning it to Evalle for Storm to wear during a mission.

Even though the spell had run out last night, this thing had to be valuable.

"Glad you reminded me," Evalle said. Dipping her head down, she reached up to untie the leather thong. "I need you to return this to Nicole."

Storm's fingers curled around her wrists, heating her skin.

She froze at the contact. Her pulse rocked with awareness that excited her . . . *and* raised nervous hairs along her arms. No matter how strong she'd become in the past five years, some things from her past would haunt her forever.

Without moving a muscle, she met his gaze with her unyielding one. "Don't."

He swore softly and released her wrists, muttering, "When are you going to trust me?"

Not in this lifetime.

Storm deserved *someone's* trust and had earned a little from her in the past few days, but she didn't know how to give it freely to men other than Tzader and Quinn who wanted nothing but friendship from her. Her biggest problem with them was when they acted like overprotective brothers.

She couldn't fault Storm for stirring an unnatural reaction born of hideous memories.

Was she attracted to him? Yes.

Was she comfortable with that attraction? No.

His next words came out as a vexed sound pushed through gritted teeth. "I'm not taking the amulet."

That ticked her off, and she could deal with anger better than desire. She retied the leather thong, dropped her arms and raised her head until their noses were an inch apart in a battle of wills. "Why not? You could tell Nicole thank you while you're at it, since this kept *you* from being seen in public last night as a jaguar."

"The only reason you want me to take that now is because you think you won't be coming back after the Tribunal meeting. And, as far as Nicole goes, I sent her flowers and a thank-you note."

Really? I've never gotten flowers. She frowned and backed up two steps before she could stop the reaction, a ridiculous one at that because she appreciated what he'd done for her friend.

Storm missed nothing. Like now, when he studied her as if he'd just noticed something that surprised him.

He had better-developed empathic senses than hers plus the ability to tell a lie from the truth. No point in wasting her time trying to convince him she believed differently about her chances with the Tribunal.

"Okay, fine." She'd give Tzader the amulet when she saw him at the park. "So why're you here?"

"Two things. First—do you know about the latest Alterant attacks?"

"No." Was this her week or what? More attacks would not aid her case one bit.

"One in San Francisco this morning. Three more up the West Coast in Portland yesterday."

"*Four?* What the—" She stopped short of cursing, since Brina, the Belador warrior queen, hated for her Beladors to curse and Evalle wanted Brina in an accommodating mood tonight. She would need Brina's help to swing the Tribunal's decision in her favor. But what was up with so many Alterant attacks in just twenty-four hours? She'd thought the last two in less than a month had been unusual. "How'd you find out?"

"I talked to a VIPER agent earlier tonight who had caught a few details. He said our agents on the West Coast heard about a family of five found slaughtered around their campsite and the authorities couldn't figure out what had attacked them, because it hadn't killed like a bear, a mountain lion or a wolf. They're waiting on a bad fog to lift before they try tracking."

Evalle felt sick. An Alterant had killed a family. Anything

that murdered deserved to die, but she asked, "Did they capture the Alterants?"

"By the time VIPER's team found the beasts another group had them surrounded. Five human men in black-ops-type camo gear were closing in on three Alterants. Casper said the beasts attacked the men as if out of their minds."

"And the men in camo had megaweapons they used to blast the Alterants to pieces," Evalle finished.

This only got better.

Four more Alterants. Multiple attacks in less than a day.

Storm cocked his head, thinking. "You know who those black ops guys are?"

Sounded like Isak Nyght's men, but she didn't want to get into that right now. "Maybe. Have to tell you about it later when I'm not in a hurry. What about the Alterant in San Francisco?"

"Killed a man and his wife on a pier. Authorities have no idea what happened because the only thing they found besides the mutilated and half-eaten couple was the nude body of a man floating in the water nearby. The nude guy had chunks of human flesh in his throat."

Gross. "So the Alterant maybe fell into the water, drowned and shifted back to his human form?"

"That's what VIPER thinks. They stole the body and disposed of it. I hate to give you bad news going into this meeting," Storm said, "but I didn't want you blindsided either."

She nodded, noticing the concern behind his words. "Thanks. I'm not in a hurry to face the Tribunal, but I can't show up late, so what else did you have to tell me?"

"I need you to do something for me," Storm said.

Was he serious?

But Storm had helped her last night by shifting into a jaguar—a form he hated taking—to track someone for Evalle. He'd also brought an army of Beladors to where the Kujoo had held her captive.

And had rushed into battle, wielding a sword to free her.

She pointed out, "I'm not in a position to be of much use to anyone right now."

"Hear me out. I left South America six months ago to find someone, and that trail went cold two months back. That's when I had a vision that you could help me find this person."

Storm had visions about me? "Who are you looking for?"

"It's not safe to speak her name."

Her? A flare of jealousy that was as unexpected as it was uncomfortable jolted Evalle.

Storm's gaze glinted with a hint of surprise that vanished in the next blink of his eyes. A smile touched the corner of his mouth.

If she survived the Tribunal meeting, she was going to start playing cards with Tzader and Quinn to improve her poker face.

Men. "I'm a little *busy* to help you find women, Storm."

"Talking to you is more challenging than petting a porcupine." He lost his smile and scrubbed a hand over his face, then seemed to regroup. "This is serious and I'm only asking you to help me find one woman, who's responsible for my father's death. And she has something important that belongs to me."

Oh. *Add socially inept to my list of flaws.* Evalle didn't care for the porcupine comment, but she'd let it pass this time. "*If* I come back, I'll try to help you."

"There is no *if* to it." Storm's jaw hardened with determination. "There was another part of the vision where I'm tracking you after the Tribunal meeting."

"Are you insane? If they lock me away and you come after me"—which sort of made her happy when she thought about it—"Sen and the Tribunal would fight over who could kill you first for daring to defy them."

"I won't defy them."

She rubbed her forehead, pulling away fingers damp from perspiration as she tried to process what he was saying. Pacing helped Tzader think, so she started walking in a short circle and muttered, "I don't understand."

"To be honest, neither do I, but I trust my visions because they led me here . . . to you."

She stopped walking and turned to face him. "What?"

"Yes. The vision I had two months ago showed me working with a woman riding a motorcycle, but I couldn't pinpoint her location. I could only tell it was in a city in the United States. When I got an offer to work with VIPER I knew it would lead me to her. I started having visions again the night we met. You may be my only hope to find the woman I'm hunting."

Like I don't have enough riding on my shoulders? Evalle doubted Storm was searching for just a human female. "If you can't tell me her name, then what *is* she?"

His gaze trailed past her shoulder as if he was working something out in his mind, then he gave a shake of his head. "I'll tell you more when the time comes, and I won't let her or anyone else harm you in the meantime."

"I can take care of myself but I don't think I can help you, Storm."

"Because you don't expect to come back?"

Like she needed to be reminded of that? Again. "That's a distinct possibility. And you don't need to come after me."

He made a sound that came out part growl and part frustration. "The Tribunal is judging *you* unsafe because *other* Alterants have shifted into beasts and killed humans. Are you willing to spend the rest of your life locked away for a sin you haven't committed?"

That struck at the heart of what she'd been trying to avoid thinking about. Day after day, year after year, she'd lived in a twenty-by-twenty underground space as a child. The aunt who'd "owned her" had used the threat of sunlight harming Evalle as an excuse to lock her in a basement with no windows because she'd hated Evalle, her own brother's bastard child.

Living imprisoned again would be a death sentence.

If Evalle lost her case with the Tribunal, the Beladors had to stand by that decision. Any retaliation or failure to support the ruling would breach the agreement between the Beladors and the VIPER coalition. If the Celtic goddess Macha, who ruled the Beladors, backed out of the VIPER coalition because of Evalle—*okay, cue up wild laughter at that possibility*—Beladors across the world would become enemies to be attacked without retaliation. Bloodbaths would erupt between pantheons, and the world would turn into the battleground Beladors had spent hundreds of years trying to prevent.

No one would go to war for an Alterant.

But if she could prove VIPER needed an asset with her powers she might earn a reprieve from what she considered a death sentence.

Evalle conceded Storm's point. She would not willingly accept being put away for a sin she hadn't committed. "You're right. I'd rather die than live out my life in a cage, but your life would be forfeit as well if you try to find me."

"My life was forfeited a long time ago. It's my father's death that matters."

She couldn't untangle what he meant by that statement, which was clearly Storm's intention. He wasn't sharing a thing with her yet that he didn't have to, and he didn't give her a chance to question him on it when he threw a new worry at her to juggle.

Storm said, "If the Tribunal locks you away, you do realize Tzader and Quinn will not stand by quietly either. Do you want them to come after you?"

"No." She hadn't considered that. "They'd have to break their Belador vows to go against a Tribunal ruling. That would be suicidal." She could never live with either of them paying the ultimate price for her. She'd do the same for them, but Tzader was the Maistir who led the North American Beladors, and Quinn had family, plus he was one of the financial geniuses that managed the holdings of Beladors around the globe.

They were needed. She was not.

But Storm was right yet again. Tzader and Quinn were born to protect others and would not leave her locked away.

They knew she had no one else in her corner.

Except Storm, it seemed.

And he must have a major reason for putting such a low value on his life. That didn't mean she could live with *his* death on her shoulders either, even if he did have a personal agenda. "I don't want anyone coming after me."

"You don't have a say with me. If you aren't back within two hours after you leave, I'm tracking you down."

"Time in the Nether Realm runs at a different speed than here. The last time it took me five hours to get back."

"Two hours. That's my deadline. I'm coming for you whether you help me or not."

She wished she had time to consider how that warmed her heart, but Storm couldn't go against the Tribunal and win. "No matter how you paint it, coming after me will end in your death."

"That's my decision to make and I've already made it."

She couldn't stand here and argue anymore. If Storm wouldn't be deterred, she might as well find out what he had in mind. "How would I help you?"

"By making it easier to track you."

She shook her head at his lack of logic. "I don't see how you can do that. Sen will teleport me from the park to the Tribunal meeting and wherever they send me after that. You said you couldn't track someone's energy through teleportation. How do you expect to find me?"

"I have a way . . . but you have to agree."

"Agree to what?"

"To let me use my majik on you."

Use majik on an Alterant? Who knew what might happen? "I can't do that. If I lose control and shift into my beast form, the Tribunal would have all the evidence they need to bury me."

He gave her a steely look that accepted no excuses. "You're out of time, Eve. You have to get off the fence and make a decision. You don't trust the Tribunal to give an Alterant a pass and you won't put Tzader or Quinn at risk. It's me or them, because they *will* come for you. And when that happens, I'll still find you. What's it going to be?"

THREE

Evalle made a habit of not lying to herself. The downside was disappointment, and the upside?

There wasn't one on days like this.

She had no choice, really. Not if Storm intended to come after her if she didn't walk away free from the Tribunal meeting. She had to prevent Tzader and Quinn from risking their necks to find her.

Her arms prickled from a sizzle that raced over her skin.

Energy radiated off Storm, pulsing with fury.

She lifted her eyebrows at him. "I didn't say no yet. What's got you cranked?"

A humorless laugh escaped his lips. "You." He shook his head and looked at her as if she missed the whole point. "The only reason you're considering my proposal is to save your two Belador watchdogs. *Your* safety and life are important, too."

She could kill a demon in three moves, but she had no skill for handling a man who said things that gently squeezed her heart. She'd only known Storm a few days, but in that short time he'd come through for her more than once. Enough that she owed him some form of trust, but she'd learned at an early age the dangers of trusting too easily. Her abused heart might want to open the gates for him, but her mind protected that fickle organ behind a fortress of suspicion.

Rather than address his last comment, she said, "Let's say I agree to do this. How does your majik work?"

"Can't share that."

"Can't or won't?"

He didn't answer, which was an answer in itself. Storm had his own trust issues, with that woman behind his father's death most likely at the center. Evalle doubted he'd share any more about that than he'd tell her how his majik worked.

Still, without getting all the facts she couldn't allow him to turn her into some kind of spirit transponder. "If you do manage to find me and we both escape alive, what exactly will I have to do to help you find this woman?"

"Like I said, I'll tell you more after the Tribunal meeting."

"You want me to agree to something without knowing all the details?"

He crossed his arms. "Tick tock. What's your choice?"

She didn't have one and he knew it.

Rolling her shoulders back to vanish any look of a caught animal, she finally gave in. "I'll take your deal, but I have the option of changing my mind *before* you do anything to free me if I lose my fight with the Tribunal."

He struck a thoughtful pose, then nodded. "I'll go with that."

Eyeing her watch quickly—forty-six minutes, still okay—she glanced around once more, then gave him an impatient lift of her chin. *Please tell me I'm not going to shift and kill him.* "Let's get twitching or chanting or whatever you do."

"I need you close for this to work."

"How close?" Call her jumpy, but this whole majik thing had destroyed any comfort zone.

He sighed at some silent thought. "Close enough to put my hands on your shoulders. I'm not going to hurt you."

She knew he wouldn't harm her just like he knew that if he did, she'd make him pay dearly. Standing inside Storm's personal space didn't bother her, not really.

Not if she didn't look at his mouth and think about how she could still feel his lips from when he'd kissed her yesterday.

"You're running out of time, Evalle."

Handing over control of her body—an Alterant body—to anyone with powers or majik had to be a bad idea on so many levels. She'd been forced to do this recently with a Sterling witch named Adrianna and hadn't liked that one bit.

But Storm wasn't Adrianna.

She stepped up to him. "Let's do it."

His hands settled on her shoulders with a firm but gentle grip. "Shut your eyes."

"Why can't I watch?" Her pulse strummed wildly enough without the thought of doing this completely blind.

What if she had a reaction? What if . . .

"You've got twenty minutes before you have to leave for Woodruff Park if you don't want to run, and I need eight of those to work my majik. The faster we get this done, the sooner you get moving. What's it going to be?"

"Sure you can do this without turning me into a toad?" she grumbled.

His eyes twinkled with a smile. "If I do, I'll kiss you and turn you into a princess."

She had no clever comeback. The only time she'd spent with men had been fighting alongside them or battling an evil one.

Until Storm.

All her worst fears surfaced. She might snap and turn into a monster if she allowed him to do this. If that happened, she could kill him in seconds. He knew that, but he just watched her patiently with no more concern than if he faced a meter maid.

She gave up and closed her eyes.

His fingers started massaging her neck and shoulders. "This will go quicker and be easier on both of us if you don't fight me."

She let out a long breath and nodded her agreement.

When Storm spoke again his voice came out low and husky with words she didn't recognize. The cadence rose and fell gently. His fingers moved in rhythm with his voice, weaving touch and sound. Her muscles surrendered every knot. His voice filled her mind and curled around her until her skin tingled as if tiny stars danced along her exposed arms. Needle-sharp points of pain and pleasure pricked her spine too quickly to be defined separately.

Vibrations from his voice smoothed out and spun

into a web of sound that wrapped around and around her until she floated within a cloud of his presence . . . of him. Above the world, surrounded in a warm cocoon of his voice and scent.

Protected.

The rhythm of his words began to fade. She felt his knuckles skim her collarbone when he lifted the amulet.

Was he taking it with him after all?

"Evalle?"

She mumbled, "Huh?"

"I'm done. Open your eyes. You have to leave. The Tribunal meeting."

Tribunal . . . gods and goddesses . . . midnight. That's what she had to do.

She opened her eyes and realized she no longer stood an arm's length away in front of him. He held her against his chest, rubbing her back lightly.

Heat spread from every place he touched her, warming her skin from the inside out. She shivered at the intimate feel, surprised at how much she wanted to stay here in his arms when she'd barely tolerated any touch in the past.

Was that a side effect of his majik?

What else had happened?

She pushed up from his chest and shook her head. That cleared some of the haze in her mind. When she stepped out of his arms, Evalle blinked until she could see clearly again.

Good news? She hadn't killed Storm.

Hallelujah for that, but he studied her with worried eyes.

Not the expression she wanted to see after playing voo-doo doll for him. "What's wrong?"

"That shouldn't have happened," he mumbled to himself. His cell phone dinged with a text message.

She asked, "*What* shouldn't have happened?"

His face closed down as tight as a bank on a holiday. "Hold on." He looked at his cell phone. "They need me at Brookwood Station to track something."

"You're not going anywhere until you tell me what happened."

"We're all set. I'll be able to find you."

She'd held a tight leash on her anxiety for hours now and had no patience left for vague answers. "You know what? I don't feel any different, so I doubt your witch-doctor majik took anyhow."

That got his attention. "Oh, it took, Eve."

"My name's Evalle. Not Eve." *Eve* meant "life" in Hebrew. What a crock, since everybody who mattered thought *Alterant* meant "death" in any language. Crossing her arms, she told him, "Fine. If you're not going to tell me what's not right, then don't expect my help later on."

She turned to leave.

"Wait." He hooked his fingers around her arm, turning her back to him, then pulled her hands up to his lips and kissed her fingers. "Nothing went wrong with the majik. You have to know by now that I would never harm you."

She wanted to think her heart beat like a jungle drum because he'd annoyed her with being evasive and not from a crazy vibration of current that jolted her when his lips touched her skin. He still had explaining to do. "So why did you say, 'That shouldn't have happened'?"

His gaze swept over her head and around her shoulders. "The majik affected your aura."

She didn't see auras because her DNA had failed to offer that option, but she'd recently been told that hers was silver. She hadn't realized Storm could see hers. "What? Is it brighter or something?"

"Bright would be a fair description." He gritted his teeth as if he suffered a moment of pain.

"Are you okay?"

"I'm fine." He drew a sharp breath that made her think he'd hurt himself somehow. He gritted out, "You need to get moving."

But now she'd have to walk into the Tribunal meeting shining like a chromed-out Harley. "How long will this shiny stuff last?"

"I'm not sure. I'll try to have an answer when I see you again."

That could be never. "Don't you mean *if* you see me again?" No matter how exceptional Storm was at tracking, she couldn't bank on anyone saving her.

Storm's thumb stopped stroking her knuckles and his fingers tightened on her hand. "I *will* come for you."

"I got it. You need help tracking this *important* woman."

A woman he'd risk his life to find again.

What woman could have been close enough to Storm to have held that kind of power over him in the past and drive him to this point now? A past lover?

And why did knowing that he only wanted to find Evalle for that one reason feel like a paper cut doused with lemon juice?

Because her brain had wandered off into Stupid Land. That had to be the only explanation for this ridiculous feeling of aggravation about what this woman meant to him.

Evalle would thump herself if her hands were free.

She wasn't dating Storm.

She didn't date anyone.

He smiled at her. "There is one more reason I have to find you."

She gave him an incredulous look. "Do I look like one-stop shopping for solving your problems? I'm running out of patience faster than time, so this better be good. What *else* do you need me to do?"

He let go of her hands, then cupped her face and lowered his head. "This."

Then he kissed her. He didn't touch her anywhere else except her face and with those amazing lips.

She'd thought yesterday's kiss had been pretty spectacular. This one topped that one hands down. And she had a strange feeling he could move into another level that would melt her where she stood. Her thoughts scattered under a deluge of emotion from surprise to hunger to happy. She'd keep happy.

Kissing Storm made her feel like a weed that had never known anything but drought and his lips were a summer rain, flooding her with a life energy that pushed her to grow.

He made her want more, made her want to feel more.

His mouth took her places she'd never visited with a man. She had little to compare kissing him to, but this man could probably win a trophy with his lips.

Hunger for something she didn't want to name crept through her. He held her mouth captive, her lips unwilling to escape.

Then he lifted his head.

For a fleeting moment, she wanted to ask him to do that again . . . until she met his eyes. Dark embers burned hot with desire to do far more than kiss her.

His cell phone buzzed again and he released her face. "You better leave now, while I'll still let you."

His gaze dropped to where she twisted his shirt in her grip.

She let go and jumped back. The blasted meeting! Had the majik he'd used on her wiped out brain cells?

To be fair, even *she* couldn't blame her lapse of attention on the majik. "If I'm late—"

"Don't be," he warned. "You can make that mile in plenty of time."

Fast as her heart slammed the wall of her chest she should have been able to take a giant leap and land in the park, but she didn't have that ability either.

Storm walked with her to the stairs that led to the upstairs parking deck facing the CNN building. He told her, "See you soon," and took off up the steps, disappearing into the dark.

Evalle continued on in the opposite direction. She had nineteen minutes left to cover the length of the parking deck, cross the tracks and reach Marietta Street, then zip down to Woodruff Park . . . in the opposite direction.

Piece of cake. She could make it easily without breaking a sweat because of her Belador speed, but she'd have to be careful not to allow a human to see her.

She'd still arrive in enough time to see Tzader and Quinn.

Frigid air rushed past her face and arms. Out of survival instinct, she paused to determine what energy had approached her.

Unintelligible words murmured and hissed through the chilly whip of air.

Ah. A Nightstalker trying to make contact with her.

One she didn't know. These ghoul informants traded intel on supernatural activity for ten minutes of human form. All it took was a quick handshake with someone who wielded power, like her, for the ghoul's form to solidify.

But this one hadn't yet mastered basic communication skills without being in a corporeal form. Evalle could burn twenty minutes she didn't have just trying to figure out how to communicate with the ghoul.

A sense of duty thumped at her conscience, but she said, "I can't help you right now, but I'll send someone else soon who can."

The minute the energy quieted she took several steps and hit another wall of cold air.

This Nightstalker swirled around Evalle's face, temporarily blurring her vision. He whispered in a wobbling voice, "I have a warning. Shake now."

She hated passing up a chance for information if something significant was going down in Atlanta.

Especially if they knew anything about another Alterant turning from human to beast.

But even an experienced Nightstalker could take time she no longer had to share. That's why she liked to work with one Nightstalker named Grady, whom she could make get to the point when necessary.

But Grady hung out over by Grady Hospital, the origin of the nickname she'd given him, and she could *not* shake hands with him anytime soon again.

Not after helping him out last night.

What could have the ghouls down here so stirred up? This couldn't wait, but she had no business slowing down to spend time on something she had no control over.

She'd tell Tzader.

Pushing past the cold zone, she called him telepathically. *Z? You at the park?*

Where are you? he snapped at her. *You got something more important to do than make this meeting? You know how close you are on time?*

Yes! Give me a little credit.

Silence filled her head. Tzader had a way of making loud statements without a word. *Do you really think I'd risk ticking off a Tribunal?*

Not intentionally. The wry chuckle in his voice softened his dig. *What do you need?*

Freedom and peace of mind, but someone else had gotten that fate. Two people cared what happened to her, Tzader and Quinn. Well, three, if you counted Feenix.

And what about Storm?

That was complicated. She knew he cared, but she didn't know why.

She told Tzader, *I'm walking past a lot of agitated Nightstalkers in the lower parking deck near my apartment. Something's up.*

Don't slow down over there.

She caught the warning in his voice, which had more to do with her safety than being late. *I'm not exactly defenseless, Z.*

Quinn and I wish you'd realize you're not exactly indestructible either. I'll check out the Nightstalkers after you get to the park.

What if it's important?

It'll wait until I know you're at the Tribunal meeting.

No point in arguing with Tzader when he clearly had his mind made up. *I need you to do me a favor and return the amulet I have to Nicole.*

Tzader grumbled something low and dangerous, then said, *You making out a will, too? You are coming home after this meeting. Brina will be there for you and she'll make this right.*

I know. Not really. Evalle had her doubts about their Belador warrior queen convincing the Tribunal to leave even one Alterant free to roam the streets. Rather than address that, Evalle told Tzader, *Taking the amulet off my hands would make facing them easier if I'm not thinking about anything else.*

The amulet warmed against her skin. She glanced down to see it glowing in the shadowy darkness.

What was up with that?

Another Nightstalker wavered in and out of form, trying to waylay her. What threat had entered the city?

Tzader relented with, *Fine. Just get here.*

I'll be there soon, but what if . . .

What if what?

This Nightstalker activity has to do with an Alterant attack, like the ones on the West Coast?

I was going to tell you about that when you got here. Where'd you hear?

She hesitated at the idea of punking out Storm, but then she remembered where he'd gotten the intel. *Storm told me. He heard the news from VIPER. Think the Nightstalkers are worked up over another Alterant in the city?*

We've got everyone on alert and no one has heard of any Alterants shifting here yet.

Okay. I'm on the way.

One more thing, Evalle, since we won't have much time when you get here. Do us both a favor and don't give Sen any grief tonight, okay? It won't help your case.

I hear you. I'll be the perfect little prisoner.

She could have sworn she'd heard Tzader sigh, but she didn't need a reminder tonight.

If she wasn't standing in that park when Sen showed up to escort her to the meeting, she was toast. As the VIPER liaison, Sen would teleport her from Woodruff Park in downtown Atlanta to the Nether Realm, a parallel universe where the Tribunal convened. He'd like nothing better than for her to step into the park five seconds past midnight.

He hated her.

Right back at ya, Sen. Although hate required an emotion. He was more like a boil on her life she'd like to lance with a sledgehammer.

He was dreaming if he thought she'd miss this meeting.

A cry ripped through the air.

Evalle had just crossed a section of the old railway tracks covered by the parking structure. She slid to a stop and turned in the direction of the shout. Several box trucks had been left in the bottom level of the parking area near loading docks.

The scuffling of soles against gravel reached her. It sounded as though two people fought.

A sharp scream cut off midstream raised gooseflesh on Evalle's arms. If not for her exceptional vision, she might have missed the brief image of two figures struggling.

Was that a pair of drunks settling a dispute, or was it gang related?

Evalle opened her senses. No unusual energy wafted through the air. No preternatural creature involved.

Instinct to protect a human pushed her to step that way before she stopped. She couldn't get involved. Not tonight. If she called Tzader, he'd send the police to deal with the two humans.

Someone else would have to save the world tonight.

Turning away, she started to call Tzader when a pain-filled, high-pitched wail wrenched her attention back to the fight.

This time, she saw the smaller figure more clearly.

A woman . . . being beaten by a large man.

Evalle glanced at her watch. She had fourteen minutes.

She could pass up intel from Nightstalkers and give up time to see Tzader and Quinn, but she could not allow some monster to hurt a defenseless woman.

Not after what a man had done to her at fifteen.

Evalle took off toward the pitiful whimpers and begging of a woman under attack. Adrenaline surged through her blood at the memory that sound raised, a dangerous thing when handling humans. She'd just have to be careful when she kicked the attacker's worthless butt, because she was not letting him harm that poor female.

Worst case, she might only lose a minute or two dealing with a human. That still wouldn't put her late reaching the park.

Dealing with a human male would be quicker than hitting speed dial on her phone.

Calling the police, or even Tzader, would be futile. Evalle doubted this woman would survive the wait for police to arrive, and Tzader would order Evalle to leave while trying to convince her he could get here in time.

As she rounded the corner of the chain-link enclosure beneath the street-level parking deck, she passed through an open gate. A crack of flesh against flesh rocked the air when the behemoth of a man slapped the woman. He dragged her toward one of the delivery trucks.

Evalle gritted her teeth to keep from throwing a blast of kinetic power at that two-legged snake, but he'd end up in a thousand pieces if she did.

A bright spot in her day, but VIPER agents weren't allowed to play smash-a-rama with humans.

She ran forward, wishing she could do more than knock the guy away long enough for the woman to escape. Evalle had nothing to tie him up with to leave him for the police.

Too bad she couldn't give him a dose of her cure for jockstrap bullies. That bastard was lucky she'd sworn an oath to Macha not to use her powers to harm a human, or Evalle would hand him his head while he was still talking.

The closer she got to the altercation, the stronger the female victim's fear reached out, begging for anyone to save her. Fisting her hands, Evalle forced calm into her voice as she closed the last fifty feet.

She called out, "Let her go and I won't hurt you." *Much,* she should have added.

The bastard laughed. "Come on, sugar. I can handle two wildcats."

Oh, yeah? Can you handle a beast? She wished.

Twenty feet out, she slowed to a walk but kept moving forward. Could she get away with crushing his knees so he could never get to another female?

Keeping his eyes on Evalle the whole time, he swung the woman in a backhand motion against the truck. Her head bounced with a sickening crack. Knocked her out cold. He grabbed his crotch and gave Evalle a smile lacking upper teeth on one side of his mouth. "Keep coming, sugar. I'll make you beg for it."

Evalle fisted her hands so hard the burn of cartilage rippled along her forearms in advance of shifting into battle form. Beladors stopped changing at that point, but for her battle form was just the first step in morphing into the Alterant beast state. *Can't do that.*

She had to calm down and not let him bait her.

She held all the power cards. He was just a human.

With one deep breath, she pulled her body back under control and gave him a cocky lift of her eyebrow. "No, I think I'll make you beg for death instead."

His kneecaps would be the first to go. That should slow him down for the police.

He continued grinning at her as if she was the idiot here. "Not the way I see it. They said I could—"

The guy's eyes bulged and he doubled over, mouth sucking for air, then he collapsed on top of the woman.

Heart attack? Nice to have some good luck for once. She muttered, "Adios, you miserable excuse for a human."

Now she could leave this for Tzader to handle.

Something dropped over her head and shoulders.

Everything went black. The stench of rotten limes clogged her next breath. Noirre majik.

Ambush.

FOUR

Evalle struck out at the spongy sack that covered her head and shoulders. Worming her forearms up to her chest, she pushed her hands out, shoving whatever covered her away from her body.

The sack stretched but didn't loosen.

What was this stuff that wouldn't rip or break?

With Noirre involved, she had the freedom to shift into battle form with some cartilage and muscle change that would allow her more strength. But as an Alterant she'd have to take care not to just keep on changing until she turned into a ten-foot beast with fangs and claws.

Nonhumans had ambushed her. Gut feeling? Medb, the Beladors' most fierce enemy.

She called forth her Belador warrior form and clenched her fists against the pain as cartilage jutted a high ridge along her forearms and back.

Wait until this bunch got a load of what they'd caught.

Clenching her jaw, she put the brakes on any further change.

"Well, well, well," a raspy male voice said, his words getting louder as he approached. "That cloaking spell was worth the money, wouldn't you say, boys?"

With her senses wide open, Evalle picked up on each of the "boys" as they moved toward her, like reading incoming enemy blips on a radar screen. Her empathic ability had been inconsistent at times, evolving, but right now it kicked into high gear. She detected three emotions—one cold as a dead fish, one trying to hide his terror and one excited, lusting for a kill.

"Gotta make sure we got the right one before we hand her over," the same guy said, the one she'd figured out had the cold soul. Must be the leader. He added, "If she's the one, we're set for life."

Evalle needed the blades hidden around the soles of her boots, but she'd have to cover the noise of releasing them when she stomped her feet. She taunted her kidnappers with, "Only a coward would be unwilling to fight me fair and—"

A boot slammed her in the stomach.

She sucked air for a moment, but grunting and stepping back to keep her balance gave her the perfect cover for stomping her boots against the pavement.

Two men chuckled. One smelled of tobacco and breathed like a winded racehorse.

The web sack hugged her body to her thighs. Did they think they could contain her in a bag?

As if.

Although, technically, they had.

"Okay, boys," the leader said. "Let's get her out of here and collect."

Anger fed the rippling across her arms and up her neck.

No one touched her. No one.

They'd trapped her like an animal, but none of them had the jewels to get close to her. She should just stay still and force them to move.

Crud. The Tribunal. She didn't have time for this. She tried to call out to Tzader telepathically. The minute she sent, *Tzader, I'm caught . . .* her head ached with sharp stabs of pain. Her eyes watered.

Blasted Noirre majik was jamming her telepathy.

"Go get her, Tagot," the cold one ordered.

Bunch of mercenaries without a kinetic ability among them or they wouldn't risk coming near her.

Tagot must be the one lusting to kill her, because that's what she picked up moving toward her with deadly intent.

Evalle focused on the movement. When he got within a couple of feet, she stepped forward quickly, then threw herself backwards, kicking her booted feet in his direction. The drag of a blade through flesh and a howl of pain told her she'd made contact. She fell all the way back and landed with her shoulders against the pavement.

Chaos broke loose with all three men yelling at each other.

She took advantage of that and used her momentum to flip on over backwards.

Landing on her feet in a crouched position, she got her hand on the dagger in her boot. This dagger came with a little extra mojo because Tzader had gotten a friend to have the blade made especially for her. It wasn't sentient, like the two blades he carried, but this one was wicked enough to cut through a Noirre-infested sack.

Grasping the edge, she sliced the front open, snatched it off and slung the slimy thing away. The wad of rotten-smelling goo smacked a wall.

She used her kinetics to kill all lights in the area.

As her night vision took over, colors muted into shades of blue in total darkness. The three men had bright hair, maybe red, and wore dusters. Even the one screaming and writhing in pain as he tried to stop the blood from gushing out of his thigh.

She'd hit a femoral artery? *Sweet.*

But she still had to get that woman to safety.

With no humans present and conscious, the gloves were off. She raised her hands and shoved a kinetic blast at the men.

They stumbled back several steps, but not as far as she'd expected. The stone-cold leader with spiked hair and tats across one side of his face whipped out an evil-looking machete that sizzled with majik.

Where on earth had these mercs gotten all these majikal toys?

The Medb.

She should be able to reach Tzader now, but before she could send a telepathic message his voice yelled in her head, *Get your butt over here, Evalle! What are you doing?*

Got caught in an ambush. Need help. I'm over on—

Machete guy swung the blade back and forth as fast as an airplane prop. Maybe he wasn't a stupid merc after all.

She shut off her telepathy and sent all her energy into raising an invisible shield at the moment her attacker swung a high arc.

He brought the sparking blade down fast to cut her in half.

The strike hit her force field so hard that it jarred her teeth.

She spared a glance at the other goon to make sure he wasn't coming after her with a weapon, too. He pulled an oversized handkerchief out of his coat pocket and dropped it over the bleeding guy, who howled one time and glowed like a stoked coal in a fire, then turned to ash.

What kind of hanky was that?

Tattoo face swung again.

Her shoulders took the brunt of the constant attack from the machete. She braced one foot behind her and pushed forward, but she was losing ground.

Could he cut through her wall of power?

Tzader shouted, *Can you run?*

No. He'll kill me if I drop my defense.

Where are you? Tzader said in a voice charged with fury.

*Still under the parking deck at—*Another barrage of blade attacks beat her backwards several feet.

Was she out of time? Would the Tribunal understand if Tzader reached Brina before the meeting and explained?

Tattoo face kept coming at her with the machete. Evalle strained to give everything she had to hold her protective wall, but he'd break through soon.

That blade had serious juice.

Power surged through the air and shocked her skin.

Light exploded, flashing against the walls of the dark buildings.

Her attacker and his buddy took one look, turned and fled.

Evalle lowered her arms, now aching from the pounding they'd taken. She drew a long, hard breath, pulling her body back into its normal form. Pain shot through her chest and legs. She had no idea how Z had found her or gotten here so quickly or what he'd done to scare off that bunch, but she was ready to hug him when she turned around.

Ah, crud. Could her night get any worse?

Sen stood with arms crossed and a look of disgust on his face that rivaled his usual hate-filled welcome for her.

His being here explained how someone had shown up so fast. Sen had the ability to teleport anywhere he wanted. He must have been in the park when Tzader had called to her.

She couldn't believe she had Sen to thank for getting her out of that fix.

Standing much taller than her and twice as wide, he was dressed in gray T-shirt and black jeans. He wore his hair skinned short today, but it could be down to his waist tomorrow. Would be nice to know what he was or where he'd come from with those diamond blue, almond-shaped eyes. Or who had the power to force him to be the liaison between VIPER and the preternatural beings that were agents for the VIPER coalition.

A job he obviously loathed.

Tzader had warned her to play nice, so she said, "I can't believe I'm going to say this, but I'm glad to see you."

A muscle in Sen's jaw flexed in and out. "You waste good oxygen just by being alive. Don't think this little theatrical act fooled me."

"Act?" Couldn't he smell the Noirre majik? She sniffed and looked around. Where was that sack? Nothing smelled like Noirre majik now, but she couldn't back down. "I was tricked into an ambush. They attacked—"

"Yeah, right. Tell it to the Tribunal." He waved a hand.

She wrapped her arms around her stomach as it tightened from the first stage of teleporting. Couldn't he at least say *Ready?* before doing that? There was no way to reach Tzader once Sen had her in transport.

Had those three men been trying to trap anyone with powers, or her specifically? What had the leader meant when he'd said they had to make sure they had the *right one?*

The right Belador? The right Alterant? The right VIPER agent?

Or the right something else?

She had to tell Brina about the attack *if* she was allowed a moment before the Tribunal meeting started. Much as Evalle detested Sen on every level, at least he'd come looking for her rather than waiting at the park.

Not because he gave two hoots about her being late, so he must have had orders to deliver her on time. Whatever the reason, she was glad for it right now.

Sen's superior tone ghosted through the swirl of colors and spinning sensation, but she couldn't see him. "One more thing, Alterant."

"What?" she said nicely, or at least she tried. Hard to be civil when her insides were coming apart.

"I was at the park on time," he said, then paused to let his point settle in. "Once you were late, I had no choice but to pick you up. You're a minute late according to time among the humans, but in the Tribunal's world time flexes. You're already forty-five minutes late."

FIVE

Once the vertigo from teleporting ended and her next breath tasted ancient and dangerous, Evalle knew exactly where she was—the Nether Realm. She held her head in her hands, fighting nausea. Screw Sen. She would not give him the pleasure of watching her barf in front of the Tribunal.

She opened one eye to peek.

When she'd last visited the Nether Realm, she'd stood on grass that had covered a circular plane the size of a city block. This time, her feet had landed on a rocky surface that glistened lavender and silver. She looked up further to locate the dais in search of the two gods and one goddess who would preside over this meeting.

The Tribunal was indeed in progress, and no one was happy to see her, not even Brina.

Especially Brina, whose holographic image, with her waist-length flaming red hair and vibrant green gown, sung with tense energy.

Silence hung like a guillotine awaiting a neck.

The trio on the dais glared at her. Pele, the Polynesian goddess, wore a swoop of deep pink and purple flowers across her breasts. More flowers wrapped her lower body as a floor-length skirt. She stood between Ares, the Greek god of war, decked out in his battle attire, and

Loki, the Norse god of devilment, who showed off his massive naked chest by wearing only blue silk harem pants.

Stars crowded the black sky stretching from one side of the Nether Realm to the other, the perfect backdrop for glowing entities.

Pele's exotic eyes studied Evalle with the same consideration an exotic bird might ponder the merits of a slug. She spoke in a voice crafted of honey and gold. "You have delayed this Tribunal, Alterant. Why?"

Evalle made the mistake of taking a second to decide how best to answer, which allowed Sen to speak first.

"She has no excuse, Goddess."

"Wait a minute," Evalle snapped, spinning on Sen. "She asked me."

Sen lifted a negligent shoulder. "You won't like what happens if you lie during a Tribunal meeting."

Loki had been spinning a ball of power between his hands. The sphere rumbled and flashed with a kaleidoscope of colors inside. He paused to interject, "The body of one who tells an untruth here will glow red."

Evalle hadn't planned on lying now or any other time in a Tribunal meeting because she figured they'd just *know* if she told a lie.

But this was the first she'd heard about glowing red.

Ares leaned forward, squinting. "Was not your aura silver the last time you were here, Alterant?"

Everyone gawked at Evalle.

Brina's lips parted in surprise.

Evalle considered his odd question. He hadn't said

anything about her aura being brighter. She answered truthfully. "As far as I know, yes."

Ares scowled at her. "Then why did you change it to gold?"

Gold? Storm changed her aura to gold?

Evalle would kill him if she survived this. How was she supposed to answer that and not tell this bunch about Storm using his majik on her? What *had* he done to her? "I didn't change my aura. I can't see auras and don't even know how to change one."

That didn't soften Ares one bit.

Evalle added, "I'm around a lot of different beings, and one of those must have affected mine somehow."

Her skin didn't light up red, so tiptoeing around the truth seemed to work. She let out a strained breath.

Loki juggled two balls of power and sighed loudly, clearly feeling put upon to be here. "Gold, silver, whatever. This is not why we are here."

Evalle took that cue to change the topic back to smoothing things over. Submissive had never been part of her makeup, but she gave humble her best shot when she spoke.

"I have the greatest respect for the Tribunal members and Brina." Yes, she'd intentionally left Sen out of that lineup. "I apologize for arriving late, but while going to the aid of a human in danger I was ambushed by three men wielding Noirre majik and was fighting for my life when Sen arrived to escort me. As a member of VIPER, I swore an oath to protect humans first even at the risk of my own safety."

Evalle caught Sen looking at her with a curious expression. *Surprised I didn't light up like Rudolf's nose?*

She gave a quick check of Brina, who stood ahead of Evalle and to the right, between her and the dais. Brina hadn't been happy at first, but now her eyes registered . . . pride?

That breathed life into the hope clamoring inside Evalle's chest.

The Tribunal must have been appeased by her explanation, because Pele moved on. "When last we met, you were told of a pregnant Alterant female who shifted into a beast and killed a human. Until then, the only Alterants who had shifted and killed were males. You were given a chance to produce proof that humans are at no risk from you as an Alterant. Where is this proof?"

Evalle didn't have said proof. She'd gotten sidetracked helping VIPER save the world.

Brina asked in her Irish lilt, "Might I have the floor?"

Loki spoke up. "By all means, anything to move this along and spare me from spending any more of eternity here."

That drew a gritty snarl from Ares. "If being immortal is an inconvenience, I am willing to end your suffering . . . now."

Loki leaned forward to speak past Pele. "I would find that amusing for the few minutes it would take to destroy you."

Pele lifted her hand and flicked her fingers. Lightning shot from her fingertips and spread across the sky. Thunder rolled around the Nether Realm. "Enough!"

Evalle held her breath. Just her luck she'd have the Tribunal meeting where a god went postal. That'd end up being her fault, too.

As if nothing had happened, Brina calmly launched into what she had to say. "There are still questions we have not answered about Alterants—"

What? Evalle could hang herself without Brina's help.

"—but Evalle has proven to be a valued member of the Beladors. She's put mankind and our tribe ahead of her own needs, which impaired her ability to deliver tangible evidence for you. As we are living proof of the intangible within the world of the humans, can we not accept her actions as intangible proof of her reliability?"

Way to go, Brina. That's more like it.

Brina wasn't done yet. "Evalle was also part of the VIPER team tasked with finding and returning the Ngak Stone before daylight in Atlanta yesterday morning. She acted selflessly, risking her life to stop the Kujoo warlord *and* at one point when she took possession of the Ngak Stone—"

A collective gasp erupted on the dais.

"—Evalle voluntarily handed the stone over to be placed in the VIPER vault," Brina continued. "Might I point out that many of our kind would not have relinquished an artifact so powerful? As warrior queen of the Beladors, I consider her one of my best."

Really? Evalle couldn't believe her ears, but Brina's voice rang with sincerity and passion. Tzader had stated over and over that Brina was always ready to stand up for her Beladors. All of them.

Ares appeared unmoved by Brina's declaration. "What of the seven Alterants that shifted and attacked humans in recent days?"

Seven? Evalle spoke to Brina mind to mind. *I just heard about the attacks on the West Coast. Now is not the time for them to lock me away with a surge in Alterant attacks. I know the Tribunal won't see it this way, but I could help with this outbreak. Beladors are the strongest arm of VIPER, but they can't link their powers to face an Alterant, not after what happened in Charlotte.*

Two months ago, nine Beladors had linked to stop one Alterant. They should have been able to contain him, but he'd shifted and ripped the head off one of the Beladors before any of them had a chance to unlink.

When linked, if one warrior died, they all died.

I agree. Brina addressed Ares. "With these new Alterant discoveries, we need Evalle's abilities in VIPER more than ever."

With one disgusted snort, Ares gave his opinion of how much he thought of Evalle as an asset.

Pele and the gods spoke among themselves for several minutes, but Evalle started to feel optimistic about being returned to VIPER long enough to help them deal with this problem. Maybe she'd been worried unnecessarily.

Worried sounded so much better than terrified.

When the trio of entities finished talking, Loki leaned against one of the columns that decorated the dais, and Ares tapped his fingers on the hilt of the sword sheathed at his hip.

Pele paid no attention to the gods when she spoke. She

had a soft voice, but power surged beneath the feminine tone. "Evalle has committed a larger transgression."

What the hell? Evalle got an air cuff upside her head kinetically from Brina for cursing. *Sorry.*

Brina asked Pele, "What transgression?"

"When we last met, Evalle was told not to associate with another Alterant. We have learned that while hunting said Ngak Stone she communicated with the escaped Alterant Tristan."

That blasted Sen must have ratted her out even though he knew the circumstances. She'd also sent Tristan back to his spellbound cage in South America with him begging her to kill him instead.

She'd hated doing that to him. Tristan had only wanted what she wanted, what any person wanted—to be free. Death would have been more humane, but neither could she have killed him in cold blood.

Tristan would gut her if he stood before her now, and she couldn't blame him, even if she had been doing her duty when she'd sent him back.

Pele asked Evalle, "Do you deny communicating with the other Alterant?"

Evalle said, "No. I did speak to him, but doesn't the fact that I returned Tristan to captivity count for something?"

Ares pointed out, "We let you live."

Brina kept her hands linked in front of her, docile to an untrained eye, but she wasn't a warrior queen in title only. When she spoke her words rang with authority. "Evalle communicated with Tristan only to gain valuable information that was key to getting the Ngak Stone away from a dangerous predator. Had she not, the Kujoo might have destroyed much of the human world. Due to Evalle's efforts the stone is now secure in the VIPER vault."

Ares crossed arms bulging with muscles and dismissed Brina's explanation. "No provision was made at our previous meeting when this Alterant was ordered not to associate with another Alterant. She should have asked for an exception to the terms before agreeing, and that is but the least of her charges. Any aid she gave to recovering the Ngak Stone does not justify her part in releasing deadly Alterants in the human realm."

I did not release Alterants, Brina, Evalle sent to her queen mind to mind.

I believe you, Brina replied, then addressed the Tribunal. "What evidence is used to charge Evalle with this?"

Still amusing himself by tossing miniature fireworks the size of a baseball from the palm of one hand, Loki said, "Let us get to the point. You told Tristan you wanted to see Alterants freed."

"Tristan said that. I didn't," Evalle argued.

Brina swung a look at her that promised retribution if Evalle had just fed her a bunch of hooey.

Evalle shifted her hands to open palm out at her sides. *Do I look like a glowing beacon in the red light district? I never told him that.* Sen had obviously given his own version of what had happened that night, editing at will.

Pele asked Evalle, "What *did* you say to Tristan about the Alterants?"

Anything less than truth would burn her. Evalle said,

"I told him I wanted to help Alterants so we wouldn't have to be locked up or destroyed."

Loki interjected, "I see no difference."

Ares' voice boomed. "Guilty as charged."

Evalle argued, "No, there is a difference, because it was taken out of context."

Shaking her head at Evalle, Pele said, "Context doesn't matter. In our world, words are as dangerous as any other weapon and should be wielded with care."

Loki said, "She influenced the Alterant Tristan, who released three others from captivity. Now we have even more beasts shifting and killing humans. It appears this could be part of a plan by this Tristan to turn Alterants loose on the world."

Un-freaking-believable. Forget being locked away. They could dust her if they thought she played any part in the Alterants that are now shifting and killing. "If that's the case, why don't you bring Tristan in for questioning?"

Pele glared at Evalle, power blowing across Evalle so sharply that it bumped her back a step. "Macha ordered the Alterants caged. We do not have Tristan's location."

Evalle tossed a look of question at Brina, then swung her attention back to Pele. "I asked the Ngak Stone to return Tristan to his original prison."

Pele picked up on Evalle's glance. "Brina is under oath to her goddess. She can only divulge information voluntarily."

Brina gave a brief shake of her head. "Unfortunately, I can share nothing about the captured Alterants, O Goddess."

Pele told Evalle, "We cannot locate Tristan without Macha's assistance, which she is not offering. Since Tristan does not fall under the jurisdiction of a specific pantheon that is a part of the coalition, we cannot demand his presence."

In other words, Tristan was safe from the Tribunal.

For now.

Chills skittered along Evalle's spine, but so did a hot streak of anger over the injustice of twisting her words to make her responsible. Without thought to ask for permission first to speak, she said, "So Tristan commits a crime and doesn't even have to answer for it, but I do?"

Don't push this, Evalle. You're not helping your case if you annoy them.

I have to push this, Brina. Humans are dying and I have a bad feeling that something is happening for so many Alterants to shift at one time. We need to know why, and I'm the best one to put in the field to find out. But I can't get that information or help anyone stop these attacks if the Tribunal is going to drag me in here every time there's an attack.

Ares' booming voice shook the ground. "Insolence is not tolerated here, especially from a beast."

I got your beast in my boot. Evalle kept her hands at her sides, when she wanted to shake her fist at the god. "*I* didn't change and kill a human. And *I* didn't release the three captured Alterants. And *I* have nothing to do with the ones who are shifting and killing now. Why am I being held responsible for the actions of others?"

Brina started, "My apology for her disrespect—"

Pele lifted her hand in a signal the floor was clearly hers.

She silenced Ares with a severe glance, then addressed Evalle. "A fair question. Alterants are an unknown element in our world and not a recognized race. Until someone can determine their origin or they are accepted into a pantheon, their status will not change."

Evalle deserved credit for not rolling her eyes. What deity was going to invite Alterants into a pantheon where the god or goddess ruling it would be responsible for powerful beings that might shift involuntarily into beasts and kill everything in sight?

Ignoring Loki's drawn-out sigh, Pele continued, "When other Alterants have shifted and killed, they were captured or destroyed. You are the only Alterant we have allowed to remain with the Beladors rather than cage you as an undomesticated beast."

Anger clawed up Evalle's spine at being compared to a rabid animal.

Without pausing, Pele said, "You were permitted a great deal of freedom for the past five years because you were the only female Alterant identified until this new one was discovered. Her pregnancy raises the possibility that male Alterants are seeking females for breeding. That alone is reason enough to require placing you in a secure location."

Schooling her face to neutral took some effort once Evalle caught Pele's point that she would now be a magnet for rutting male Alterants. She'd happily offer to neuter *those* Alterants, but Pele wasn't finished.

"Are you being held accountable for the actions of others? Perhaps. Associating with an escaped Alterant this week and indicating you would like all Alterants to be free lays the responsibility of the three escapees and the more recent Alterant shifting at your feet."

That pretty much killed any chance Evalle saw for walking away from this free.

She spoke to Brina. *I live with the proverbial axe swinging over my head every day because, fool that I am, I protect humans when my life counts for nothing.*

Not true! Brina shouted in Evalle's head, this time with a thicker Irish brogue. *You are Belador and we will find a way to take this mantle of burden from your shoulders.*

Evalle maintained her blank expression when she answered, *I appreciate your sincerity, but the only way to do that would be by defying this Tribunal. I would never put the entire Belador tribe in conflict with VIPER or a Tribunal decision, so I'm stuck answering for the crimes of others until I can figure out where Alterants came from . . . but know that if they try to lock me up I will not go quietly.*

Brina spoke to the Tribunal. "I believe Evalle is not just safe to walk among humans but that they need her now. She is an asset both VIPER and the Beladors cannot afford to take out of active duty. Not with this new threat having surfaced."

Evalle wanted to smile and give a shout with a fist pump for Brina, but keeping her mouth shut and showing no emotional reaction would better aid her warrior queen.

Ares stepped forward, his standard grim expression twisted with irritation. "An impassioned statement in favor of the Alterant to be sure, but if we allow this Alterant to remain free, will you pay the price of this Tribunal's judgment if you are wrong?"

His blatant challenge struck Evalle with a cold fist. Ares dared Brina to put her neck on the line with Evalle, but the Belador warrior queen couldn't make that commitment because—

"I will," Brina confirmed.

Evalle shouted into Brina's mind. *No! You can't risk the future of the Beladors on me.*

Will you not uphold your vows?

Of course I will, but I'm, I'm—

What are you, Evalle?

A bad gamble.

No, you are a Belador who has sworn to protect your tribe, just as I have. I vowed to protect every Belador, too, which includes you. Even if this Tribunal will not recognize you as one of us, we do. I do.

Evalle swallowed hard at the gift of Brina's faith, but that was even more reason to accept that she'd been cornered. She told Brina, *I'll . . .* Evalle drew a breath, determined to get the words out. She could not put the most important person behind the future of the Beladors at risk. *I'll let them lock me up.*

You. Will. Not. I will not allow it.

Evalle would never doubt Brina's support again and she would not let her warrior queen down, starting with trying to convince the Tribunal not to place Brina in jeopardy.

Ares said, "I admire your loyalty to the Alterant, Brina of Treoir, but that does not mean she is safe to move among humans."

"May I speak again?" Evalle asked Pele.

Ares ignored the direction of Evalle's question and snarled at her. "Speak one last time and be done with it."

Brina's shoulders moved as though she'd taken a breath, preparing to intervene once more, but Evalle answered first.

"Is there not some way to clear my name once and for all? I only ask for the same chance any of you would want if you stood in my place today."

Fury rolled through the air, and Ares' formidable gaze turned black. He warned Evalle, "Do not compare yourself to me. I am a god."

Evalle saw her last chance slip away with his anger.

Loki stopped playing with his tiny fireworks and glanced over at Ares, who didn't notice the sly smile that lit Loki's eyes. "I say we grant the Alterant's request."

Evalle's mouth slipped open at the unexpected support from Loki's corner, even if the real reason behind his comment was only to poke at Ares, who reached for his sword.

As moderator of this Tribunal, Pele took a step back, placing herself between the two gods once again. Addressing Loki, she said, "She must first answer for the three escaped Alterants."

Loki nodded. "Agreed. Let the one who returns the three escaped Alterants to VIPER be cleared of prior transgressions. That would stand as proof of her safety to humans and solve the missing Alterant problem."

That was *an* answer, if not *the* answer, to Evalle's problems. How would she find the escapees? And if she did find them, how could she condemn someone to life in a cage when she would fight to the death to avoid the same thing? "About those three—"

"Silence!" Ares shouted.

"Let the Alterant speak," Loki said in the most gracious benefactor voice anyone had ever heard.

Evalle knew better and attributed the intervention to Loki yet again antagonizing Ares, but that was Pele's problem, not hers.

Pele nodded. "You may speak."

Ares sent her death looks. *Not getting any yea votes from that corner.*

Evalle said, "Thank you. If the three Alterants come with me willingly, I'd like to ask for a provision that they have a chance to plead their cases to a Tribunal court."

Brina didn't move, but her posture stiffened.

Ares said, "No."

Loki beamed a rich smile. "I see no problem with that."

"This is not a vote," Ares argued.

"Oh, but it must be," Pele said, stepping in before things heated up again. She turned her back on Brina, Evalle and Sen to confer with the two gods. Ares glared the look of death at Loki, who grinned nonstop.

Evalle told Brina, *The only way I'll bring back three Alterants, if that's even possible, is if Macha will guarantee their safety while they are waiting to speak to the Tribunal and not just toss them back in a prison. And if any of those three killed in self-defense I want them freed.*

Your freedom is in question at the moment, Brina reminded her.

No one's freedom is worth more than mine. I know Alterants have just killed in the last two days without cause, but that doesn't mean they are all insane murderers. If an Alterant stands in this court and says he fought to defend his life and doesn't turn into a red lightbulb, he's telling the truth and deserves to be protected.

Brina nodded slightly. *I will allow an Alterant his freedom if the Tribunal finds him innocent of murder and he swears loyalty to the Beladors.*

Evalle released her breath. Her chances of finding the three escaped Alterants would be minuscule if she didn't have her Belador buddies and Storm to help her.

When Pele turned around, she addressed Evalle. "We have reached an agreement and support Loki's offer."

Only by one vote, based on Ares' steaming frown.

Evalle had already been burned by not clarifying the rules of engagement last time. "Is there anything I can or cannot do while searching for the three missing Alterants?"

Brina would know where the three had been before they'd escaped, since she was the one who'd ordered them caged. If Evalle asked to be sent to the locations with Storm, then he could track from there.

Evalle brightened at that thought until Pele said, "You may not request help from anyone with VIPER, as the escaped Alterants are not their problem and their assets must be used to defend humans against the current problem. Neither can you ask Brina to share what she knows, as she is under an oath of silence regarding the Alterants."

"Then it's an impossible task," Evalle murmured,

though Brina and the entities missed nothing spoken in this realm.

Sen stood close enough to hear, his mouth curving with undisguised delight.

Loki lifted a finger, as if he were Aristotle instructing students. "Not so. We give you three gifts, as long as they are used with the explicit intent of returning the Alterants. If not, the power will turn on you. Each gift must be unique and cannot be duplicated once requested. You may not use any of these gifts to kill unless you have no other option."

Evalle frowned. "What are the three gifts?"

"That will be for you to decide as the need arises," Loki answered. "To call upon a gift, speak the words 'By the Tribunal power gifted me, I command' what you need. You may only use these gifts for fulfilling your agreement. If you misuse a gift, there will be a severe penalty."

It would take a magician to unveil the truth beneath words spoken by a god or goddess. Evalle banked the three gifts mentally and started to ask about how to get help when Loki added one more caveat.

"And you may ask one person *now* for help. Is that not generous?" Loki smiled, supremely pleased with himself.

Talk about a trick question.

Ares held his hand out, and an elegant gold-and-black hourglass appeared in the palm of his hand. "When I turn this over, you have until the sands run out, then we will send Sen for you. When your time is up, the hourglass will take Sen to wherever you are. If you fail to deliver the missing Alterants, we will turn every asset at VIPER loose to hunt down *all* Alterants and destroy them."

That would include me, Evalle acknowledged silently.

She got it. Ares had no intention of spending another minute hearing further arguments on her behalf. Evalle couldn't gain anything more right now. She had no choice but to get moving and figure out her next step—*if* she could actually find the escaped Alterants.

And there was only one person who might know where the other three Alterants were. Since she'd been told she could ask one person for help, maybe Tristan could be brought here.

That seemed fair. That way Brina wouldn't have to divulge his location and she could send him back to his cage after he answered Evalle's questions.

What were the chances of Tristan answering truthfully?

Pretty good if he lit up bright red every time he lied. No one could defy a Tribunal but a god or goddess and that would end in bloodshed.

And Tristan can't attack me here.

This had potential.

"I understand," Evalle said, then added, "but how long does it take the hourglass to empty?"

Loki said, "More than a day and less than a lifetime."

Not helping. She gave up on that and moved on to something she might be able to get straight. "I wish to carry full responsibility for the success or failure of this on my shoulders, not Brina's."

Ares barked, "Denied."

Brina's words came to Evalle's mind on a whisper. *Do your best. I expect no more.*

The power of that faith hit Evalle squarely in her chest. She couldn't speak for a moment.

Brina whispered quickly in Evalle's mind, *The Tribunal is not as informed as they'd like to believe. There have been sixteen Alterants that have shifted and attacked in the past forty-eight hours. Those have killed seventy-six humans. But sharing that with a Tribunal convinced that you are at fault for this outbreak will not free you sooner.*

Are all the Alterants dead?

No. Eight are still loose.

Ares turned the hourglass over and sand began to spill down in a thin stream.

Brina spoke even faster in Evalle's head. *You are right about the danger of Beladors linking to fight Alterants. I can't share much about Alterants because of my oath, but I can tell you that you are unlike any other and the most powerful of the Alterants we've encountered so far. I need you here to figure out what is causing this and to help Tzader understand how best to defend against this outbreak.*

You need me to hunt my own kind.

Yes.

Now Evalle understood why Brina would agree to guarantee the safety of those three and ensure that they got a fair hearing with the Tribunal.

Evalle cleared her throat. "The one person I'd like to ask for help is Tristan. He might know where the Alterants went after they escaped." Now to see if Brina would work with her by teleporting him here. "If Brina could—"

In a cheerful voice, Loki said, "Granted. Brina, teleport her to Tristan."

What? Evalle looked at Sen, who couldn't have been happier if the Tribunal had struck her down with a bolt of lightning.

Brina swung to face Evalle, panic and worry laced in her eyes.

Loki ordered in a booming voice, "Do it *now!*"

Evalle shook her head, saying, "Tristan will kill meeee—"

Lights blurred and the world spun into a thousand colors that turned her stomach inside out. She was already winging her way to some unknown location.

Facing failure sickened her more than vertigo, especially if she landed right in front of Tristan. She'd fought him once and walked away, but that had been because he'd wanted her alive.

He'd want her in pieces this time.

Brina's voice whispered to her. *I have only seconds until the Tribunal calls me back. Do not use your powers in Tristan's cage or they will backlash against you twofold. I believe in you.* Then she was gone.

Death awaited her at the end of this trip . . . but what fate would befall Brina and the Beladors if Evalle failed to return with the escaped Alterants?

SIX

Bracing for the role of doomed messenger, Kizira swept through the arched hallway that led to Queen Flaevynn's private chamber in the realm of TÅμr Medb. As one of the most powerful witches in the Medb coven, Kizira should be walking in with the Alterant Evalle Kincaid, not empty-handed.

But using those mercs to kidnap the Alterant had not been Kizira's lame idea . . . it had been Flaevynn's.

Pointing that out would not spare her.

As for lame ideas or private thoughts that might betray her, it was time to mentally tuck away anything she didn't want discovered by an unwelcome telepathic intrusion.

The queen enjoyed snooping through the minds of her underlings.

The simplest way Kizira had found to protect her innermost secrets had been to push out all her real thoughts, then flood her mind with a fictional tale of her everyday life and false memories she'd begun creating thirteen years ago.

With an ease born of constant practice, Kizira hardened her eyes to those of an enforcer who carried out her queen's orders. She let her pseudo-persona take over, the one in which she was proud to be the premier Medb enforcer and a loyal servant of the coven, content to fulfill her role with no aspirations of ruling this evil . . . oops.

Try that one again.

. . . with no aspirations of ruling so vast a kingdom or, in this case, a queendom.

When Kizira neared the gilded doors, the guard never met her eyes or moved a muscle, and he had plenty to move. He wore only a gold chain-mail skirt that stopped above his knees and allowed quick access for the queen's whims. Flaevynn chose her guards for their beautiful faces and powerful physiques, as well as their prowess in bed.

They were unfailingly loyal.

If a guard's gaze strayed to another woman, the queen would blind him and then banish the man to live among humans.

But if the guard was fool enough to touch another woman, the queen would cut off his fingers and string them as a necklace he'd have to wear while chained and forced to watch her have sex with another guard.

No threat here for you, young man. Kizira had known the best of men, and no one could walk in Vladimir Quinn's shoes.

She bit the inside of her cheek at that slip.

Quinn was *not* part of her make-believe world. She couldn't risk Flaevynn finding out what had happened between him and Kizira thirteen years ago.

To keep that secret safe, Kizira had to concentrate. Taking a few breaths, she slipped deeper into her imaginary world. She sharpened her focus and repeated silently that she cared only for protecting the Medb coven empire. Her greatest wish was to see Cathbad the Druid's curse upon the Beladors come to fruition, for Kizira to hand her queen Treoir Island, the seat of Belador power.

That would be the curse uttered by the first Cathbad, who had lived two thousand years ago, not the current Cathbad sitting in the TÅµr Medb dungeon.

Flaevynn argued that it was not a curse upon the Beladors but a curse upon Medb queens and, granted, she had a valid point. As a result of the power behind the curse, each Medb queen lived only six hundred and sixty-six years.

Not a day more or less.

Flaevynn had railed endlessly about not knowing if Treoir would be captured during her life or the next Medb queen's rule. The tightly guarded specifics of the curse had been passed down only from one Cathbad the Druid to another. Flaevynn's anger had turned volcanic a year ago when the current Cathbad had once again refused to share what he'd known.

She'd imprisoned him until he'd agree to reveal all.

She wanted Treoir *now*, but the dangerous game she'd launched over the past few months to speed up a timeline set thousands of years ago tampered with fate.

Kizira would ruthlessly support Flaevynn's drive to take Treoir and gain immortality for one simple reason—Kizira planned to take the Belador island and castle for herself. Gaining immortality, the Belador power, and all the Medb power before Flaevynn could do so was Kizira's only hope for sliding out from beneath Flaevynn's thumb and protecting those she loved . . . even the one who was her sworn enemy.

Two steps from the entrance to Flaevynn's chamber, Kizira silently ordered the doors to open and passed through as they swung wide.

What a welcome relief to find the queen's chamber free of naked men chained to her throne like rutting dogs waiting for her to demand service.

Queen Flaevynn stood to the side of the room with arms raised, chanting softly as she faced a towering wall of precious stones that formed a dazzling backdrop for the water cascading down. From diamonds to emeralds to rubies and not a stone smaller than Kizira's fist. Light from a hundred tapered candles surrounding the room glanced off the sharp cuts and angles to send a kaleidoscope of color across Flaevynn's pale skin, waist-length black hair and sheer iridescent gown.

Few women in this otherworld realm equaled her beauty, especially when the queen put to death any female who might.

When the chanting ceased, Kizira took a breath and prepared to face Flaevynn's wrath for her failure, but the doors burst open.

Gruin, the ranking elder, barreled into the room, knee-length white hair flowing behind him, his grizzled face mottled with anger. "What's this I hear of the myst being released?"

Flaevynn spun around on a bed of air. Purple eyes sparked with bright orange flames. "Take care with your tone, elder." Shifting her gaze to Kizira, she demanded, "Why are you dressed like a common wench?"

Kizira didn't see where her black jeans and deep blue

silk shirt were wench clothes, but she shrugged and answered, "I find it easier to move undetected through the human world when I wear their attire, Your Highness. I'm willing to dress however is necessary to serve you best."

Gruin strode past where Kizira had paused two steps inside the chamber. He cast her a dark look, fingering her as the one who had actually released the sentient fog in the human world.

Like I have a choice when Flaevynn compels me, old man?

Dismissing Kizira with a jut of his bony chin, Gruin pulled up short in front of the queen's throne. His abrupt stop sent the hem of his cherry-red robe whipping around his skinny ankles. "Is it true or not?"

Flaevynn now lounged on the onyx and gold chair carved in the shape of a dragon. Her eyes gleamed with a predator's confidence and her voice dropped low with threat. "You know the answer to that or you would not be here. As you can see, my enforcer waits to give her report. State your business and be quick, elder."

His mouth pinched tight as a raisin. "This realm exists to shield us while we fulfill our duties according to the timeline set forth. The hostility myst was not to be used this soon. You endanger all of us by rushing ahead without knowing the entire prophecy."

"It's a curse, not a prophecy," Flaevynn snarled at him. "I will not sit quietly as my death approaches and condemn yet another queen to my fate."

Kizira doubted any altruistic intentions on Flaevynn's part about future queens.

Undeterred by Flaevynn's caustic bite, Gruin argued, "I am your advisor—"

Flaevynn cut him off with, "I don't recall asking for your advice, old man." She pointed a long black finger-nail sprinkled with diamonds at him.

He backed up a step, then froze as if his feet wouldn't move. "I'm an elder . . . protected by Cathb—"

Flaevynn swirled her finger in a tiny circle.

Kizira had never heard of an elder being killed, as the punishment for harming one was severe, but with Cathbad in the dungeon there was no one else powerful enough to intimidate Flaevynn.

Gruin's lips yanked open. He started gagging as his tongue slid out, stretching until the pink flesh narrowed to the thickness of a pencil. A strangled cry squealed from his throat when his tongue began looping into a knot. From nowhere, a thin metal spike appeared and drove down through his tongue between the knot and his mouth.

Blood from the wound ran down his chin, spiking the air with a coppery scent.

He fell to his knees, fingers gouging his throat. Tears streamed down his wrinkled cheeks. A pitiful sound streaked past his constant gagging. His face turned deep red before he fell forward on the marble floor and stopped moving . . . or breathing.

Kizira felt Flaevynn's eyes on her, observing . . . judg-ing. The queen punished weakness. Any aid Kizira might offer would only make this worse for the elder as well as herself.

Tapping into the role she'd created so long ago for survival, Kizira smiled at Flaevynn when she remarked, "I hadn't considered the spike. Effective and brutal. Nicely done."

Flaevynn appeared satisfied, almost smiling. She glanced down at the inert form, made a sound of disgust and snapped her fingers.

The elder jerked, then started gasping and coughing. He struggled to his knees, breathing hard through his open mouth now that his tongue had been released. Blood coated his thin lips.

Flaevynn told him, "I allow you to breathe again so that you can take my warning back to the other elders. Do not interfere where you are not needed or invited." She looked from him to the entrance, where two guards built like ancient Spartans stood. They each hooked one of the elder's arms and walked out carrying him between them.

Flaevynn moved her hand to the right of her throne and held it there until a young man with black hair and a perfect body appeared. He wore leather chaps and a silver choker. The punishment collar consisted of spiked links that would stab the man's neck when anyone yanked on the braided silver rope dangling from the choker.

The queen gave the rope a light tug, and the collar pricked bloody spots on the young man's skin.

He didn't so much as flinch, and, like a well-trained animal, he turned his body to face her throne.

Flaevynn believed that a constant supply of young men in her bed would keep her beautiful and desirable, but she had no control over aging . . . or the last day of her predestined life.

Not without conquering Treoir Island first.

"You've returned sooner than I expected," Flaevynn said, releasing the leash. She ran her hand down her mantoy's sculpted abs. "Since you didn't take time to change into a proper robe to meet with me I can only assume you rushed here with good news. How many Alterants are left to retrieve?"

Kizira stepped forward until she stood upon a white tiger rug with her booted feet apart and hands clasped behind her back. She couldn't put this off any longer. "We still have to locate and capture all five Alterants."

Fury burned through the queen's gaze. "What happened, Kizira? You said the bounty hunters we gave the spell to could bring in the female Belador Alterant."

No, I said the ambush was a gamble I didn't recommend and the men weren't qualified. But someone had to be blamed for the failure. "They lost her."

"Lost? As in misplaced an Alterant? How does one do that?"

Kizira held her calm. Flaevynn's anger could cower an army of guards, and she would only grind someone harder if they showed any vulnerability. Feeling the expected mental nudge from her suspicious queen, Kizira filled her mind with distress over having disappointed her sovereign.

Revolting, but effective, because the intrusion disappeared.

Kizira gave up a commiserative sigh, explaining, "Our

hunters almost had the female Alterant overpowered, but the VIPER liaison Sen teleported her away. We had the best bounty hunters available, but nothing like Dakkar's. We would have used his if he hadn't turned down the contract."

"Offer him more."

"I tried. He refuses to even discuss it."

Flaevynn slapped her hand against the arm of her throne. "What kind of bounty hunting operation does he run to refuse *us*?"

"He will not jeopardize his standing with VIPER."

The queen hissed. "VIPER is only as powerful as those who support it. When Brina of Treoir falls, so go the Beladors, their power *and* the backbone of VIPER. *Then* we'll see who rules this world. None of this would be my problem if you'd brought me the Ngak Stone."

Another risky project Kizira had warned against. "The Ngak Stone is known to direct its own destiny and to be highly unpredictable. If you had taken possession, the stone could have turned on you and perhaps . . . killed you."

The only reason Kizira actually regretted losing the stone.

Kizira refused to pay attention to what the queen was doing to her manservant. She turned her gaze to the gleaming yellow eyes of the dragon's head that hovered above Flaevynn as if daring anything to touch her. "If there is nothing else, Your Highness, I shall leave you alone."

"You're *not* dismissed yet," Flaevynn spat at her. "How do you plan to capture the Alterants? I gave you permission to release the fog that would force them to change into beast forms. What more do you need?"

Permission? She'd ordered Kizira to release the fog, an ancient myst with sentient quality that turned anything it touched hostile. But contradicting the queen might end with worse than having her tongue tied and staked.

Kizira said, "The fog is only making the Rías shift." Rías changed into beast forms similar to the way Alterants shifted, but Rías lacked the Belador blood that carried powerful abilities. Using the fog now was a mistake. One of the few specifics Cathbad had shared about the curse was warning them to wait until five specific Alterants were located before releasing a fog to intentionally force Rías to start shifting in advance of attacking Treoir.

Kizira reminded Flaevynn, "According to Cathbad's curse, we should wait—"

"Shut up!" The room shook and the water at the base of the waterfall boiled with Flaevynn's rage.

An invisible force struck Kizira behind her knees, buckling her legs. She dropped to the floor, clamping her teeth hard to keep from cursing Flaevynn over the pain scorching her thighs.

One day . . .

Holding on to her temper with a tight grip, Kizira swallowed a snarl and concentrated on humility. Sweat sheened over her skin in seconds. This was more like the Flaevynn she knew and the reaction she'd expected, which was why Kizira had worn pants and a shirt instead of a bulky robe.

She squared her shoulders and straightened up.

The queen pointed a finger at Kizira. Her black nail lengthened two inches as she spoke. "I told you we do not have to wait any longer. The time has come to end this stupid curse. All you need to concern yourself with is locating the five Belador Alterants."

Kizira lowered her head, more to keep from exposing how she gritted her teeth. "I understand, Your Highness. I did not mean to challenge you."

Yet.

"Have you conjured the fog in all the cities we discussed?"

Did she really think I'd come back here without doing that? Raising her chin, Kizira said, "Yes."

"Are you sure you made no mistake in execution?"

"I followed your instructions exactly. I generated hostility fogs scented with sulfur to mask the Noirre origin. The first cities infiltrated were along the coast in areas where that type of atmospheric condition already existed to hinder VIPER in figuring out too soon that the fog is behind the Rías shifting."

"VIPER has no way to dissipate the myst without Medb help."

That's what we think, but there is always the unexpected in our world. And the ancient spell could only be used once, but that mattered not to the queen either. "Of course not, Your Highness, but it benefits us to impede their progress in defending against our attack any time we can."

"Has the fog reached Atlanta, where the female Alterant is?"

Kizira nodded, enjoying a brief fantasy of Flaevynn being drawn and quartered. "It will soon. I conjured the myst in areas north of the city this morning. This will allow the haze to finger into Atlanta rather than originate there, which would alert VIPER too soon. I'm concerned about turning so many Rías that it will draw the attention of the entire North American VIPER resources."

Rías were the name given to descendents of a beast-line traced back over a thousand years to the famous warrior Cú Chulainn, who'd had superhuman abilities, as demonstrated by his *ríastrad*, a berserker-like battle mode during which he shifted into an unidentifiable monster that killed everything in his path.

Flaevynn scoffed as though VIPER was no more than an inconvenience. "The Rías are not a concern as long as the Alterants are exposed when the sentient myst forces them to shift into their beast form."

Kizira warned, "VIPER and the Beladors believe *all* human forms that shift into beasts are Alterants. If Rías continue to shift too soon, you will not have an army of them when you're ready to breach Treoir Castle."

"That's ridiculous. Why not?"

"Because VIPER is killing Rías as soon as they are discovered and VIPER is not the only force capable of destroying them. A group of humans with high-powered custom weapons is blowing up the beasts, too. They may kill the Alterants we seek before we locate them."

Shaking her head, Flaevynn chuckled. "One would think the lack of glowing green eyes would be a clue the Rías are not Alterants." She sighed. "Beladors are not the brightest beacons in the night."

Only a masochist would correct the queen, but Kizira

would argue the Beladors were their most dangerous enemy and not one to underestimate. Flaevynn hadn't left TÅμr Medb since Kizira had been handed the role of enforcer at eighteen, or she'd realize that.

Flaevynn almost frowned, but wrinkling that perfect skin was out of the question. She murmured, "The fog should cloak the Rías."

Kizira clarified, "The fog *is* cloaking the beasts until they walk out of it."

"Don't bring me problems," Flaevynn cautioned. "I want those Belador Alterants. Now. Create a wider band of the myst, do something, but deliver them to me or I will find someone else who can."

Like who? Kizira clamped her mouth tight to keep from shouting that. Flaevynn had no one with Kizira's level of power to send out to do her bidding. At least no one Kizira had ever met. Flaevynn's panic over facing impending death had turned her crazier than usual. If Flaevynn did have someone else to fight her battles, she would order Kizira to remain in TÅμr Medb.

Kizira couldn't risk that, not when the safety of another life depended upon her ability to come and go at will.

Stop! Do not think about . . . Kizira flushed her mind, returning to her mental calm. She was Flaevynn's most trusted enforcer, who worshipped her queen.

Schooling her face to passive, Kizira said, "I *will* deliver the five Alterants."

"Then do it. You have forty-eight hours to hand me *two* Alterants. I will not suffer failure again. There is plenty of room in the dungeon with that druid."

There was Kizira's opening to lobby for a meeting with Cathbad. "I understand, Your Highness. Speaking of Cathbad, might you allow me to speak with him to see if he could enlighten me on how to locate the Alterants more quickly?"

Flaevynn's face twisted with hatred. "You think he will tell you what he refuses to share with me? His own wife!"

Hard to understand why a man locked in a dungeon by his wife while she had sex with every penis in this realm would feel the least bit vengeful, huh?

Kizira forced devout sincerity into her reply and tried to sound as though she feared Cathbad. "I'm willing to risk meeting with him if it will benefit you, Your Highness."

That soothed Flaevynn, who sat back and smiled over at the young stud next to her. Her hand drifted down along his abdomen to . . .

Kizira could not stomach another minute of this. She gritted out, "The sooner I see Cathbad—"

Flaevynn yelled, "Go!"

Before Kizira could form a thought the room vanished from around her. Hallelujah. She spent a moment suspended between time and reality before her feet settled on a stone floor. She'd have preferred to teleport herself, but she couldn't reach the dungeon without going through Flaevynn. The queen had imprisoned Cathbad by convincing him she'd sent Kizira to the dungeon. When he went to the dungeon to see Kizira the queen locked him inside a warding she held the power over.

When the room came fully into focus, Kizira faced Cathbad the Druid . . . the fifth to carry that name.

Appearing closer to a human age of midthirties than he did to six hundred years old plus, he sat in calm repose in a padded desk chair. Far from an archaic dungeon cell, his accommodations had plenty of candles for light but no windows to see the outside.

What would he have seen in this realm anyhow except the greenish-gray myst that enveloped TÅμr Medb, the Medb Tower?

Bookshelves lined one wall of his cell, displaying precious tomes that had been passed down from the original Cathbad the Druid. An armoire held two more robes identical to the black one he wore. She knew this because she'd been the one to bring him those two robes the one time she'd been allowed to visit him when he'd first been imprisoned.

He swiveled sideways to face her and scratched his neatly trimmed black beard, considering her with hawk-like eyes. Wavy black hair touched his shoulders. "'Tis good to see ya, child."

"Hello, Da."

"I'm surprised Flaevynn allowed you to visit. Something change between you two?"

"No. She still hates me as much as the day she bore me."

SEVEN

Kizira faced her usual dilemma with Cathbad—should she hug him or keep as much distance as possible between them? Unlike with Flaevynn, she felt a bond to her da and danced along a fine line between care and respect, careful not to step on the wrong side of all that lethal power.

Just as a baby shark should respect the jaws of a parent that might consider the newborn food under dire circumstances.

She smiled at him, ignoring his teeth for now. "I had to convince Flaevynn that I would risk my life to face you to help her. You are still not in her good graces."

"And will no' likely ever be again," he said in a brogue as old as the Irish brews he loved. His handsome blueish-purple eyes twinkled with a conspiratorial smile when he shrugged. "She hates me more than you for impregnating her to fulfill the curse, but she should be thanking us both. Failing to have a child would have prevented her from gaining Treoir Castle."

More riddles about that damned curse. "Why?"

"Ah, child, you know I will no' be sharing more than necessary about the curse, no' till it's time. But I will tell you that had she no' birthed you, she would ha' no chance at gaining Treoir atall."

"But Flaevynn thinks birthing me put the first nail in her coffin. That she would be immortal if not for me."

"She's a hardheaded woman who must accept that her fate is no different than that of any other female born to marry a Cathbad. Had she no' married me as directed in the curse, she would no' ha' lived this long, but a *geasa* set into place along with the curse protects her . . . for just a bit longer."

Kizira smiled, asking him, "You're *sure* Flaevynn will live for only six hundred and sixty-six years?"

"Yes. This is her last year as Flaevynn the Medb queen, whether she wishes it to be or no'."

Kizira had two words for the day Flaevynn spewed her last bit of venom: Party time.

Once that happened, Kizira would be free to visit . . . she skittered sideways mentally, to thoughts of the curse, before a face and name could take shape in her mind. "Flaevynn thinks that if she escalates the plan you laid out to us for this year she can gain Treoir before her time runs out."

Cathbad scoffed under his breath.

Moving over to where he sat, Kizira pushed herself up onto the desk and looked down at her da, whose attractive profile could rival that of human men who modeled designer clothes. He was the closest she'd ever had to a real parent, but the druid would use her, too, if it benefited his cause. Life as a Medb priestess came with few moments of free choice. But he embodied her best hope for one day having control over her future, a normal life away from all this.

Normal? What would that be like?

A life such as the humans enjoyed with loved ones . . .

And thinking about that risked opening the gates to her thoughts. She slapped up mental walls and got back to her task with the one person who might be able to help her.

Right now she was Cathbad's only hope for escaping this dungeon, and, like him, she would use that to her benefit if need be. Kizira gave her da a sympathetic look. "I'm sorry Flaevynn locked you in here when I failed to deliver the female Alterant the first time."

"I told you before, 'tis no fault of yours." He watched her carefully. "She blames me for sending her son with you. I know you did your best to protect him."

She hoped it wasn't her fault that her half brother had died when she and her warlocks had trapped those three Beladors in Utah two years ago, but she didn't miss the sexual deviant who had been her mother's child by another man.

When she said nothing one way or the other that might trip her up, Cathbad said, "Flaevynn believes I will tell her all the curse if she leaves me here, but she plays her hand poorly in this game. Speaking of bein' here, much as I'm glad to see ya, I'm thinkin' ya got troubles."

"Flaevynn is upping the time frame for finding the five Alterants. She's running me crazy with hunting them and has forced me to release the hostility myst."

Cathbad covered his eyes with one hand and leaned back. "I ha' warned her repeatedly that if she alters the curse in any significant way it can change the outcome.

She guesses at the rest of the curse rather than free me and agree to do as I direct her. She risks ruining her chance—and *mine*—to gain Treoir Island."

"If you'd tell me the entire prophecy wrapped around the curse I could help you. Help us."

He leaned forward, propping his elbows on his knees. "'Tis my blunder in revealing too much too soon that caused this problem. I was sent to Flaevynn when hair had just begun to grow on my chin. I thought myself quite the man but was no' prepared for one as powerful, or sexual, as Flaevynn."

"Please, no details." Kizira would need to acid wash her mind if he said more.

He chuckled. "I am only sayin' we would no' be havin' this trouble if she had no' searched my mind when . . . er, my guard was down and found out her true birth date. She should be thinkin' she has a few more years to live and no' be facin' her last year."

"That's why she's always been obsessed with the Beladors, but even more so now."

"In part," he murmured cryptically. "Trouble with the Beladors goes back to Queen Medb's time. Like every other queen descendant, Flaevynn is born with a deep hate and the duty to regain the island that was once Medb property."

"Really? Treoir belonged to the Medb at one time?" Kizira knew more than most about Medb history, but the Cathbads held tighter to information than a predator did to captured prey. When he nodded in answer, she asked, "Did the Medb live there first?"

"No' exactly, but the Medb have no other place to live safely outside this tower until we take control of that island."

She could see how wars would be fought over a treasure such as Treoir, which was reputed to be one of the most magnificent places in all of the hidden realms. This would explain thousands of years of bad blood between the Beladors, who sought to protect Treoir, and the Medb, who were just as determined to possess the powerful island. "How did my ancestors lose it?"

"'Tis a twisted tale I spend my days unwindin' to understand and ha' no' yet woven the threads into a full tapestry. I believe there is somethin' more powerful at stake than merely gainin' that island."

"And Flaevynn doesn't know what that might be?"

He sighed. "No. She cares nothin' for history, only for today and her immortality. I traded her another part of the curse for my Cathbad library. I ha' never studied as much as while down here. I am piecin' together what happened in the past in hopes of understanding the truth of what will happen in the future."

"Why didn't your ancestors tell you everything you needed to know when they passed down the curse?"

When he smiled, the flat planes of his face softened with human warmth that disarmed those foolish enough to be sucked in. "We Cathbads are no more trustworthy than the Medb queens. I, too, wish to see Treoir taken in my lifetime, but I will no' make Flaevynn's mistakes. If she would heed me, we would take Treoir Isle, the Belador power, and then kill them all once they are vulnerable."

Kizira clutched the edges of the desk but masked the

stab of pain at the possibility of killing one particular
Belador. "But Flaevynn fears you'll outmaneuver her and
steal all the power, then kill her."

"True."

"How do we get around her to free you and save this
realm before she destroys all of us?"

"I do no' ha' that answer . . . yet. I keep ponderin' on
why a powerful druid would place a curse to unfold over
so many years. I feel close to findin' out."

"What's your guess?"

He propped an elbow on his desk and supported his
head with his fingers. "I believe every generation of Cathbad druids and Medb queens ha' become more powerful
than the one before based upon journals of former Cathbads, and that may be at the center of the mystery. But 'tis
a mystery that needs more time than you ha' today. You
still ha' yet to tell me why you're here besides to brighten
an old man's day."

Kizira's lips curved at the "old man" comment. "The
hostility fog is forcing Rías to shift into their beast forms
in the human world. VIPER and some paramilitary
bunch are killing the beasts when they shift. I'm concerned there may not be enough Rías for an army of them
when the time comes."

"Oh, there will be more than enough," Cathbad said
with so little concern that Kizira's skin chilled.

She had no intention of living out her life here or
on an island. What if there were so many Rías turned
that eventually not even the Medb would be safe in the
human world?

He scowled. "But you should no' be releasing the fog now."

She bristled. "It's not like I have a choice when I'm compelled to do her bidding . . . and yours."

"Och, child. 'Tis better that we take the power from you to refuse our biddin' or Flaevynn would kill you for sure if you balked. You were born with more heart than any Medb I've ever known."

Her skin quivered with warning. Did he know she'd spared a life she should have taken? She might think that flaw had come from Cathbad if not for what she'd seen of his merciless side.

If anyone stood in her way they'd find out just how merciless she could be as well.

He sighed at her. "Compassion 'tis a dangerous flaw to ha' in our world."

Tell me about it. Kizira had waited until the last minute to conjure the myst near Atlanta, where it might have risked hurting Qu . . . shit. She repeated silently to herself, *I don't care what happens to anyone in Atlanta or anywhere else in that world. I have no one to protect or care for.* Getting back on topic, she said, "I tried to talk Flaevynn out of releasing the fog so soon and suggested the five Alterants could be *anywhere* in the human world."

"That is no' the case."

"Why not?"

"The curse says *those* five will arise in a human land protected by a giant brown bird with a great beak and a white head."

"The North American bald eagle?"

"That fits. Specific things must happen for us to reach Brina within Treoir Castle." He held up a hand to stall her question. "Do no' ask me for more than I give ya. I told Flaevynn she must wait until all five Belador Alterants were captured before she created chaos among the humans with the fog. There will be plenty of Rías, but the point is to use them in a surprise attack once we ha' *the* Alterant in place who can triumph over Brina."

"How am I supposed to appease Flaevynn when I don't know what I'm up against or any of these rules?"

"Does no' matter. You can no' refuse to act when Flaevynn compels you or you die."

True. In fact, Kizira faced the same consequence if Cathbad compelled her and she didn't comply. She had come from seriously whacked-out breeding stock. "At least tell me what it's going to take to pacify her."

He lowered his arm to rest upon the desk and tapped a finger. "Flaevynn wants only to take Treoir so she can bathe in the pool of immortality that runs beneath the castle."

"Can she swim? Maybe she'll drown before the immortality kicks in."

Cathbad grinned.

Kizira thought for a moment. "That's why the Medb are rabid for that island. No queen has been immortal since Queen Medb herself, and even she eventually died."

All humor fled Cathbad's face. "But *I* am the one who must succeed above all when the time comes or the curse *will* be reversed. If that happens, we could all be destroyed."

More riddles. No wonder she'd grown up hating puzzles.

Kizira just wanted all of this to end. She wanted the power to have a life away from the poison she breathed every day, but she'd never see that life if Flaevynn became immortal. Kizira would never have battled to earn her place as the most elite Medb priestess had she known she'd lose her free will, bound to the ruthless queen for as long as Flaevynn lived.

The queen had tolerated Kizira this long only because Cathbad had convinced Flaevynn that Kizira played a vital role in destroying the Beladors.

She just didn't know her entire role. Yet. And she couldn't live with herself if she destroyed Qu—.

She would not think about that. Not here.

Cathbad's gaze swept over her with a pained expression. "I know you think I only use you as Flaevynn does in all this, but 'tis no' true. I care about what happens to you, girl. The less you know the safer you will be."

She ignored the way her heart clutched at his claim of caring when she had no doubt he'd play her like a favorite instrument. And she'd be compelled to dance to the music.

The Medb Coven was no place for the vulnerable or the meek. She asked, "Where's the logic of keeping me in the dark all the time when I'm the one being sent in to face Alterants, Beladors and every other being out there with a grudge against the Medb? And don't tell me it's for my safety."

"'Tis."

"Right. Flaevynn just stuck me with me a deadline to

find two of the Belador Alterants in forty-eight hours. That's *two days* or she'll lock *me* up down here! The best shot I had at catching one Alterant this morning slipped through the fingers of bounty hunters I hired. How am I supposed to find two anytime soon?"

He sat quietly, thinking on something, then whispered, "'Tis dangerous to care deeply for someone you fear losin'."

"I learned that at my mother's knee when she found my pet rabbit and gave it to the cook." Anxiety rippled across her neck again, but no one knew who she protected. She repeated silently, *I have no one to lose. I only care about serving the Medb. I have nothing that matters to me.*

"So you have no one to protect?" he asked in a way that challenged her to lie.

Panic flared, threatening to take hold.

He couldn't know.

She flooded her mind with everything from happily serving the queen to thanking the day she'd been born Medb. "No, I have *nothing* to protect except you, and you have more power than me."

He slapped his knee and grinned. "Alright, now. I know who can help you locate *three* Alterants."

Kizira perked up. "Three? Really? Who?"

"The Belador you saved when you were eighteen."

Her chest muscles constricted and her grip on the desk tightened. He couldn't know about Quinn. If he did, that meant he knew . . .

Cathbad's brown eyes narrowed with shrewd understanding. "You know the Cathbads are gifted with sight. I saw you meet him in a vision. Saw how you stopped our warlocks from killing him, then this Belador risked his life to save you from the warlocks. 'Tis why I think your heart is soft."

Oh, no, no, no. That was exactly what had happened when she'd met Quinn. She'd been sent out on her first task to prove she was worthy of becoming a priestess. Her Medb warlocks had attacked Quinn so quickly that he'd had no chance to defend himself. But when the warlocks had started torturing him instead of taking him captive, she'd intervened to stop them.

And they'd turned on her, accusing her of high treason by protecting an enemy—an immediate death sentence for any Medb.

Badly wounded, Quinn had struggled to his feet. He'd used his powerful mind and the element of surprise to kill the warlocks.

Cathbad knew . . . but he'd obviously not told Flae-vynn. Kizira asked, "Why didn't you tell the queen?"

"Because she would no' ha' understood that even a Belador plays a role in fulfillin' the curse. If you wish to hand the queen at least two Alterants in forty-eight hours, you will need this Belador's help . . . and mine."

She'd seen Quinn only in rare situations since that initial brief affair, and every time they'd been adversaries. There was no way he'd help her locate the Alterants, especially Evalle, whom Quinn watched over like a younger sister.

Kizira shook her head. "That Belador will not help me capture the female Alterant Evalle."

"He will once I tell you how to persuade him."

"What if I can't persuade him?" She wouldn't put Quinn at risk, no matter what. But if she didn't play this out with Cathbad he'd know he could use Quinn against her.

"Then you risk Flaevynn learnin' the truth behind this man."

She stared silently. He could not know *everything*.

He nodded and answered, "Oh, but I do know everything. I know you care for him, which is why you will do as I compel you if you wish him to live."

Welcome to life as the lowest pawn in a deadly game.

EIGHT

Evalle stumbled forward, tripping over a bulging root covered in ferns. Her vision cleared from teleporting.

But not the urge to upchuck the pizza she'd eaten.

She held her forehead for a few seconds until the nausea passed, then she turned slowly to assess her surroundings.

It looked like she'd been dropped in a jungle that smelled of damp earth and decaying vegetation constantly composting. Water drizzled over her face and streaked her sunglasses.

If not for her unusual optics, she'd have been blind in this almost-total darkness. That meant her twenty-minute visit to the Nether Realm hadn't lasted five hours in the mortal world this time, or she'd have been facing sunshine.

But how long would a day or "more than a day" in the Nether Realm translate into human time?

Or had Loki meant one day in the human world?

Who knew, but she had to get back to Atlanta—with three escaped Alterants in tow—and help stop an Alterant massacre.

At least she could offer the three Alterants she took back a chance at real freedom.

She used a finger to squeegee water off her forehead.

Warm water soaked her shirt. Glancing up, she couldn't even make out cloud cover through the thick canopy of hardwood trees and tropical palms. Hidden somewhere up there were critters that chirped, screeched and chattered.

So this was where Tristan lived, *if* she'd landed in his spellbound prison. When she'd first met him in Atlanta, he'd said his cage was in a South American jungle, but not the specific location.

And that had been when they'd been on speaking terms, before she'd used the Ngak Stone to return him to captivity.

A tingling warmed the skin on her chest. She looked down.

The amulet still dangled from her neck.

Thank the goddess she hadn't lost it. She always worried about losing some part of her clothing or her sunglasses in transit, but she instinctively put a hand on her glasses to hold them when she teleported. If the leather thong holding the amulet had come loose while teleporting, would the necklace have landed at her feet or ended up in another part of the world?

She didn't know. Now the thing was heating up even more.

Just like it had before she'd been ambushed in Atlanta.

The jungle stilled. Not a chirp to be heard.

She didn't have to be hit over the head to figure out this silver disk was acting like some kind of warning device, but why? Nicole's spell on the amulet was long gone. Opening her senses wider, Evalle tried to determine if the danger approaching was of this world or preternatural.

No energy touched hers.

That ruled out preternatural.

Regardless of where she'd landed, she couldn't use her supernatural powers to harm a natural creature of this world.

She needed a defense plan or someplace to hide if she didn't find Tristan soon.

What did he use for shelter here?

She suffered another swipe of misery at sending him back to isolation in this place. From her perspective, living in a jungle beat being confined in a basement for eighteen years, but she doubted Tristan would see it that way.

She couldn't blame him.

Loss of control over your life sucked even if you lived trapped in a castle, like Brina.

Poor Brina could never leave the Isle of Treoir except in a holographic image. Doing so would put the whole Belador tribe at risk of destruction.

Hair stood up along Evalle's arms.

Two bright eyes, probably yellow, peered at her from between wide palm fronds and froze the blood in her veins.

She could tell it was a large jungle cat but not much more.

For a moment, her heart leaped to the hope that the animal stalking her might be Storm in his black jaguar form. But even if he could track teleportation he couldn't have found her in another country—and on another continent—this quickly.

She'd probably never see him again and wouldn't be able to help him find the woman he was hunting either. If she didn't satisfy the Tribunal's demands, the list of people she'd let down would continue to grow.

The animal watching her didn't blink.

Running generally excited a predator, but she couldn't stand here all night. She had to find a hiding place before daylight, too. With her deadly intolerance to sunlight, she'd fry faster than fish in hot grease the minute rays hit her skin.

And end up just as dead as being eaten by a three-hundred-pound, four-legged killing machine.

Evalle took a step back, then one more.

Another set of predatory eyes with narrow black centers appeared several feet to the right of the first cat. A hunting party, or just taking advantage of a snack dropped in front of them?

Both cats moved forward at the same time.

Game on.

She swung around and dove headfirst into the jungle, swatting low branches and thick undergrowth out of her way. Thorny vines clawed at her clothes and arms. Her boots sucked in and out of wet bogs of mud. She felt as though she ran against a current of energy, like swimming in a resistance pool.

Even her natural Belador speed was useless here, which pretty much confirmed she was inside Tristan's enclosure. She couldn't see any other reason she'd slow down to the speed of a human.

She could hear the snap of twigs and rattle of vegetation as the cats stalked her at a steady pace. She hurried ahead, willing herself to outrun them in spite of her mind arguing that was unrealistic.

When she entered a moonlit clearing, she stopped in the center and turned slowly.

Three more sets of yellow eyes faced her from the other direction.

Now she got it. The first two cats had been herding her.

The amulet around her neck warmed and glowed again.

Great. Like these cats needed help finding her in the dark?

All the cats converged at one time.

Golden jaguars. Must be a mother and her grown cubs.

Evalle fisted her hands and crossed her arms in front of her like an X, prepared to block her face and eyes. She couldn't even use her dagger because the blade was flush with supernatural power. For a moment, she considered shifting into her beast just to frighten them away, but that would probably backfire here even if she didn't have to worry about having to face the Tribunal again.

The largest cat, likely the mother, started moving in a fast stalk and prepared to leap off the ground to attack.

Evalle braced herself for sharp claws and fangs ripping into her body.

The roar of an animal that sounded much larger than any of these cats shook the trees surrounding her clearing.

Power burst into the open space, flowing between her and the closest cat, and shoving the attacking feline back. The other jaguars perked up at the noise, alert to a new player.

She'd have liked to mark that as a positive sign, but the sound of heavy footsteps bearing down on her warned she had something far deadlier than these animals to face.

Someone who wanted more than her death.

Tristan would want to see her writhe in pain.

A giant beast shoved small trees aside with no more

effort than if they had been saplings. He stood taller and greater in bulk than her Alterant beast form and stomped forward on feet twice the size of a human's. Forty feet away, he paused and dropped his head back, roaring a long, guttural sound.

Chills crawled up and down Evalle's spine in spite of the damp heat.

The jungle cats skulked away unharmed but clearly intimidated by the beast in ragged jeans that actually fit his huge legs. Where had Tristan gotten clothes?

He stood with hunched shoulders, cracked lips pulled back to show uneven, razor-sharp fangs. Long arms dangled at his sides, fingers tipped with curled claws. Shaggy locks of matted, dirty-blond hair hung in clumps between scaly patches and leathery skin that covered the vicious angles of his face. Beneath a jutted forehead, a broad nose flared and black eyes glowed hot in the darkness.

Black? Not bright green?

A terrifying creature for anything or anyone to fight.

But Tristan hadn't let the jaguars rip her to pieces.

Could that mean he would give her a chance to talk before he killed her himself?

She had little time and a tiny hope that she could convince him to listen to her. "Hi, Tristan. I know we parted under less than ideal circumstances."

He pulled his lips back in what she thought might be his version of a smile or a grin. Maybe he was glad to have company. She would be.

For lack of a better response, Evalle smiled, too. "Speaking of that—"

He lifted his head and released a more terrifying roar than the last one.

The entire jungle fell silent as a tomb.

Bad analogy.

When Tristan looked at her this time his eyes bulged with the need for retribution. He growled and his fangs dripped saliva.

Her empathic senses picked up energy coming from him that dispelled her previous ideas. She'd completely misread his expression. He had been smiling all right, but not because of the chance to entertain unexpected company.

He wanted blood. Hers.

She spun around and took off the way she'd come, running in one direction, then another.

Pounding stomped the ground behind her with amazing speed.

He could use his power within this cage, which meant he could kill her with a strike. Why hadn't he?

Because a quick kill clearly wouldn't appease his need for revenge.

Evalle had covered a mile of running and fighting her way through areas strangled with dense growth when she caught the toe of her boot and fell to her knees. Mud splashed her face and arms. The palms of her hands burned raw from scrapes.

The steady pounding of footsteps gained on her.

She shoved up and shot forward again, breathing hard without the benefit of her Belador endurance.

But she was far from beaten.

She battled her way through the undergrowth. The

jungle's teeth scratched her arms and dragged at her clothes. After stumbling into another clearing wider than the last one, she bent over to catch her breath. Human weakness sucked.

The thud of footsteps slowed, then stopped.

She heard him breathing close by, waiting for some reason.

He wanted something . . .

Lust washed over her skin.

There was one thing worse than death, and she would risk supernatural power backlashing in this domain before she'd submit to that.

She turned to face him and leaned to pull the dagger from her boot. If using the power ricocheted back at her, she'd just have to end up cut. She would not give up without drawing blood, too.

Tristan pushed his monster-shaped hands together in front of him then opened his arms, parting the overgrown jungle to accommodate his girth as he stepped into the clearing with a thump, thump, thump.

"I may not be able stop you from killing me to get your pound of flesh, Tristan, but touch me—" She let her gaze drop to the bulge in his pants and spun the dagger in her hands. "And I'll get my own pound of flesh with one swipe."

The only part of him that retained any human quality was his black eyes as they studied her quietly.

His eyes were . . . sad.

Had she misread his lust?

She wished she had a better grasp on her empathic abilities, but they were constantly developing.

Besides, how could anyone tell what an Alterant was thinking or feeling in beast state when no one had observed them in a natural setting?

Wait a minute. She was standing here talking to a shifted Alterant.

She tried again. "I want to help you, Tristan—"

Her dagger flew up out of her hands and landed halfway between them, stuck in the ground.

He crossed beefy arms and angled his head. His mouth pulled tight on one side in what she supposed could be considered a smug look.

This might be her best, her only, chance to plead her case to him. "Hey, I'm only here because you turned loose the other three Alterants and the Tribunal thinks I told you to, which we both know isn't true. I just want to help—"

His snarl clawed her nerves.

That might have been the wrong tactic.

He growled and stomped his foot. The ground vibrated with his fury. Teeth bared and claws extended, he lunged for her.

Evalle backpedaled ten fast steps and lost her footing.

All her attempts to regain her balance and race away ended with her feet coming out from under her. She fell, but she arched to land as far away from him as she could.

When the beast rushed her, he slammed to a stop two steps away, his body plastered against an invisible wall.

His cage.

He rammed the wall over and over again, pummeling the boundary of his prison. He beat the enclosure so hard with his fists that she felt the concussion like multiple blasts of a bomb.

She covered her ears against his howls that were equal parts mournful and furious.

The desperate sound struck her heart sharp as an ice pick.

She'd put Tristan back in there when all the reasons had weighed in favor of that decision. He'd sided with the Kujoo who had helped him escape. He'd helped the Medb priestess capture Evalle. He'd tried to keep the Ngak Stone to use for his own benefit.

But seeing him now in this pain, her heart argued that anyone stuck here for years would have accepted the Kujoo's help. That Tristan had intervened, or tried to, when the Medb witch had started torturing Evalle. That he'd only wanted the Ngak Stone's power to guarantee freedom for himself and other Alterants.

How could she fault him when he'd offered that same freedom to her and she'd turned her back on him to stand with the Beladors?

And she couldn't leave now.

Even if she managed to find her way out of this jungle alive, she had no one but Tristan to point her toward the escaped Alterants.

With every minute she lost, Brina's safety hung in the balance and with it the fate of every Belador on earth.

And her only weapon was stuck in the ground on the wrong side of that wall.

NINE

If Macha finds out what I agreed to at the Tribunal meeting, she may finally grant my wish to leave here . . . in a casket.

Brina paced the stone floors of the castle her ancestors had built thousands of years ago as a haven for the Treoir family.

She'd once loved life in this castle.

That had been before she'd lost her entire family and become the sole guardian of the Beladors. Supernatural power of all Beladors existed only as long as a Treoir remained physically inside this castle on this island.

As the only Treoir left alive after Medb warlocks had murdered her da and brothers four years ago, she was, for practical purposes, imprisoned here forever.

Really. She was immortal.

And Macha wouldn't kill her.

Not until Brina bore an heir to the dynasty.

She didn't particularly want to end her life at twenty-four, but living meant more than breathing, and that's all she'd been doing for a long time.

A warrior queen should be out on the front lines with her tribe, especially with Alterants now shifting faster than Macha changed her hair color.

Something had triggered these changes. Who or what?

The Medb topped her list of suspects.

Belador warriors were battling the beasts while Brina sat in this hollow castle.

No more.

She'd avoided discussion of the Treoir heir for four long years here, but she couldn't put it off any longer. Every time she left the castle, even in holographic form, she put the Belador powers at risk if the Medb figured out how to capture her holographic image.

She shuddered at the mere possibility.

The time had come for an heir.

And it was *high* time that Macha listened to her if the goddess wanted that heir in the near future.

Brina flopped down on a sofa carved from the trunk of a tree. It had Celtic designs scrolled along the edges and was padded with down-filled cushions. Her favorite place to strategize.

Her da had been a brilliant strategic planner.

Now she needed her own battle plan.

One that provided for a husband who could pass through the castle warding. Not just any man but—

The ward protecting Treoir Castle shivered with the introduction of power. Massive power.

"Must you always sulk?"

Brina sighed at Macha's husky voice. Had she called up the goddess by thinking about her? Unfortunately, when Brina's father had warded the castle against any other immortals, he'd made an allowance for the Celtic goddess to pass through unharmed.

He'd believed Macha would watch over his only daughter.

He'd never considered how a goddess could turn eternity into a living nightmare.

Brina lifted her gaze to where Macha now lounged above the giant stone mantel that spanned a fireplace two brawny warriors could stand inside. Waves of tawny hair spun with sunlight floated past Macha's bare shoulders and covered the arm she was using to prop herself up. Today she wore a dazzling white gown created with thousands of perfect pearls. She turned her luminous hazel green gaze downward toward the fireplace grate and logs appeared. Flames blazed to life.

Macha's attempt at being hospitable.

Or she was in one of her decorating moods.

Brina appreciated the gesture, but she would not accept being reduced to the level of a child. "Wee ones sulk. I am contemplative."

"Ah, yes, semantics, as mortals like to say." Macha waved long fingers glittering with jewels and rare metals carved in intricate designs.

"I'm glad you've come by," Brina replied. The only reaction she received was a glint of curiosity in Macha's eyes.

Brina went on. "I feel it's time we discussed an heir."

Macha brightened at what had to be an unexpected topic. "I have been so patient, allowing you to adjust to this life."

Is that what Macha thinks I've been doing for the past four years in this place? Adjusting?

Brina forced her hands to remain at ease and not flinch with anger. She'd learned long ago that showing any emotion handed the goddess ammunition to use at a later time. Not that Macha was a cruel or unfair goddess, but like all deities she used everything within her power to get her way.

"Why must you keep this place so gloomy?" Macha glanced around the room.

Candles flickered to life, dancing soft light against the stone walls. A wicker basket filled with dried flowers and spices appeared on the smooth wooden table her father had crafted with his own hands, right down to the inlaid Belador Triquetra emblem. Her father had sat on that stout table facing her the last night they'd spoken.

Six nights later, Macha had informed Brina that her father and brothers were dead and that Brina could not leave the castle. Some memories were best left unbidden.

The goddess kept dabbling until the room changed from dark and lonely to toasty and . . . suspicious.

Watching Macha decorate picked at Brina's limited patience.

When Macha spoke, her vibrant voice smoked through the room with purpose. "I'm pleased to find you ready to do your duty to secure the future of the Beladors."

As if I have ever shirked my duty to the tribe. "Do allow me to point out their future is why I'm here. Every. Day. Forever."

And alone, because Macha professed she could not remove the cursed warding.

Macha made a clicking sound of reprimand. "Insolence is unattractive, unproductive and . . . unwise."

Not like she's going to kill me, but she could make life

more miserable than it is, though that would be hard to imagine. "My apologies."

The goddess stared up as if studying the cathedral-high ceilings, then lowered an unreadable gaze. "I know you're lonely here and we must continue your family dynasty." She smiled. "Marriage would be good for you."

Brina couldn't prevent the sudden joy that flooded her face. Had she gotten lucky enough to catch the goddess on one of her more benevolent days? Macha knew who Brina wanted, the man she craved every waking hour. "I completely agree and—"

"You will choose a mortal Belador to wed, one who can enter the castle."

Stunned, Brina lowered her bare feet to the rug-covered floor and stood, all ability to shield her emotions gone in the face of what Macha was suggesting.

Not suggesting. Ordering.

Brina said softly, "You *know* Tzader and I have been practically betrothed since childhood. He is the *only* man I want."

The only man she'd ever loved.

"I'm sorry, but I cannot deliver you Tzader," Macha said with such heartfelt sadness that Brina was tempted to believe her.

But facing the loss of the only person she wanted, the one person she lived for, caused her to speak without guarding her words. "Who can? Is there one more powerful than you?"

The air crackled with sparks of electricity, a prelude to real anger from Macha that could make the heavens plead for peace. "Stop longing for what you cannot have and act as an adult! As an immortal, Tzader can never pass through this warding."

"He could if you would help us."

"I gave my promise to uphold the warding around this castle *and* to assure Tzader's immortality indefinitely. You expect me to break vows to both of your fathers?"

Brina should tone down her words, but she couldn't. "I'm asking why you can't right a wrong. Or won't. Our fathers had no idea what they were doing to us. My da would *never* have created a ward that barred Tzader from the castle. He didn't know Tzader's father was going to ask you to pass his immortality to his son if he died fighting alongside my father and his men. And *nobody* expected our families would be wiped from the earth that day."

Except maybe Macha.

Had she helped her da place this ward?

Brina hoped to never find out any of that was true.

Macha shrugged her indifference. "True, but it changes nothing. You will produce an heir in one year—"

Wait a minute. How had this gotten so far off course? "Or what? I do believe killing me would defeat the purpose."

"Spare me the melodrama and the sarcasm." A mild reaction flowed over Macha's face that shouldn't be mistaken as encouraging. She was a female, and a deity, at her best when she had everyone who served her squirming. "I will do whatever it takes to ensure the safety of all Treoir heirs as well as protect my warriors from losing their powers. This castle can never fall to the Medb. The human world would face destruction like never seen before if the Beladors are conquered."

That was well understood. But Beladors around the world weren't the only ones at risk if the Medb killed Brina and took control of Treoir.

Macha drew power from the Beladors loyal to her. Take out the Belador power base and Macha became vulnerable. She'd always been a fair and compassionate goddess, but where was her compassion now?

When the goddess angled her head in a show of patience, her hair lifted, darkened to a deep chestnut color, and adjusted back into place around her shoulders of its own volition. "You don't understand, do you?"

That might be possible if Brina could get an unclouded answer from Macha, but gods and goddesses spoke in circles. Doing so allowed them to wiggle out of a tight spot verbally.

Brina tried to sound sincere and open-minded when she said, "Please enlighten me, Goddess."

It must not have sounded as sincere to Macha, who shot her a testy look. "I have been remiss in allowing you to wait so long to produce an heir, but . . . I could not ask that of one so young as you were when your family was killed. But you've indicated you're ready and will take a mate."

"Not unless it's Tzader."

"Why do you make this so difficult, Brina? You will either willingly choose a mate who can pass through this ward, or you will no longer leave this castle in any form and I will not allow Tzader to speak with you again."

What? "I'll go mad if I can't at least travel in hologram or never see Tzader again."

"Must you always think only of yourself?"

An unfair accusation, but it still nicked Brina's pride. "I have done my duty as a Treoir descendant since birth. How can you accuse me of being selfish?"

"Oh, you have never failed your tribe, but what of Tzader? Do you expect him to wait forever on a woman he can never have?"

Yes. No. Brina didn't know. *I dream of him every night, holding me and making me laugh, just like when we were teens.* She missed his smile, hadn't seen it in a long time.

That gave her pause.

Was his unhappiness her fault for holding him to a teenage vow? *Was* she being selfish, expecting him to live alone in the mortal world just because she was stuck in this grand prison?

She would wait until the end of time for him, but she'd never force that on Tzader. His happiness meant all to her.

"You care for him," Macha continued. "But he grows closer to another woman, the Alterant Evalle."

The ugly sting of jealousy creeping up Brina's spine was as full of blarney as the goddess. Tzader and Quinn both treated Evalle as no more than a younger sister. "Tzader would never choose Evalle over me."

She hoped.

"Then why does he always defend Evalle, when the Alterants are an unknown element in our world? His allegiance with the Alterant presents a danger to you. The castle was warded against immortals, which Alterants don't appear to be, which means they can breach Treoir's defenses. They may be half Belador, but what about the unknown half?"

Brina puckered her forehead in thought, arguing, "Our warriors have overpowered the Alterants in their beast state, and Evalle has proven herself a loyal follower."

At least Brina hoped she hadn't misplaced her faith in Evalle, since the Tribunal would hold her responsible if Evalle failed to find the three escaped Alterants.

No time to worry about that right now.

Macha's voice hardened with censure. "Alterants are shifting into beasts *everywhere* in Tzader's territory."

"The ones in the past two days don't have green eyes," Brina pointed out, though it meant little in the face of so many deaths. But she had a feeling the eye color was significant.

Macha admitted, "Our warriors are destroying these new beasts, but we have lost Beladors to the green-eyed Alterants in the past, and they still pose a threat. Have you considered that the green-eyed ones may be connected to the traitor that eludes our warriors?"

"Why do you say that?" Brina asked, surprised at the direction of Macha's thinking.

"When Tzader and Quinn were captured by the Medb in Utah two years ago with the Alterant Evalle, the traitor was involved. Just a few weeks ago when an Alterant shifted and killed nine Beladors in . . . what do the humans call that place?"

"North Carolina."

"Ah, yes. When our warriors died there, word of the traitor surfaced again. Consider the first Alterant that shifted and attacked Beladors six years ago. Tzader believes the traitor Larsen O'Meary was the Belador who had called members of our tribe to confront the beast."

Aware of the past, Brina had no argument. Thankfully, Tzader and his team had survived that first meeting with an Alterant.

"Even though Larsen O'Meary is presumed dead, a traitor still walks free," Macha pointed out. "Have you forgotten how one treasonous Belador helped the Medb destroy your family and put you in this situation?"

"Of course not."

"Then why have you not ordered the only O'Meary descendant to go through a mind probe?"

Brina tried to form words to answer the ridiculous question. "Because we have no reason to doubt young Conlan O'Meary's loyalty just because his da was rotten to the core."

"Then there should be no issue with having Vladimir Quinn probe all areas of Conlan's mind, right?"

How could this woman suspect the O'Meary boy? But Brina knew which battles to fight, and this was not one. Macha clearly wanted Conlan investigated. "I shall see it done."

"That sounds more like a Treoir leader."

Brina heard the warning and realized she had to prove to Macha she would always put the future of the Beladors first, even ahead of her own happiness. To prove she thought as a leader, Brina said, "I believe the humans suddenly turning into beasts and killing are not the same as our green-eyed Alterants."

"Why?"

"Because neither Tristan nor Evalle shifted and killed humans." Brina risked bringing up a sore topic. She'd argued against imprisoning Tristan the first time, but the goddess had implied she'd been doing it for his safety. Then Macha had forbidden Brina from speaking about his capture to anyone.

Waving a hand as if to quash the discussion, Macha said, "Only time will tell with the green-eyed ones, but we must find out why these new beasts are surfacing all of a sudden. Instead of searching harder for the traitor who presents a weakness in your defense, Tzader worries too much over Evalle Kincaid. Which gets us back to the problem at hand."

"I don't understand what you're saying." Because following Macha's train of thought was akin to tracing the journey of a raindrop in a bowl of water.

"Tzader's a man with needs," Macha told her as if Brina needed to hear that. "You think he's been celibate all this time?"

Brina forced her hands to remain still and not cover her ears against words that gouged her heart. Had Tzader taken another woman in the past four years? The night she'd given her virginity to him he'd sworn his love for all time.

Their fathers had died before Tzader had been given a chance to ask for her hand in marriage.

Brina shook her head. "I don't believe you."

"Me? I never accused him of anything. I'm only infusing logic into this discussion. So you would force Tzader to go on for years with no one to love if you can't have him. You think love is so selfish?"

Put that way, Brina flinched at the possibility that she was being unfair to him, but . . . she knew the truth in her heart. "Tzader would never walk away from me."

"No, he won't as long as you continue to encourage him. He's a man of honor. Where is your honor? Don't you care about his happiness?"

"Of course I do."

"But not enough to free him to choose another?" Macha shot back at her.

"I—" Brina swallowed, trying not to choke on the words honor forced to her tongue. "I would do anything for him . . . even set him free if that was what he wanted."

"Then prove it by allowing him the chance to decide without the guilt of hurting you. You're the one who brought up the issue of an heir. Were your motives pure and in the best interest of the Beladors, or only for yourself?"

Who would have thought that immortals got headaches? Brina did, and the one coming on felt as though it might lay waste to her brain.

She lifted her fingers to her temples and rubbed. Of course she wanted to ensure the future of the Beladors, but give up Tzader? Her stomach ached as if two brute hands twisted the muscles. Was Macha right? *Would Tzader move on with his life if he thought that was my wish? Could I speak the words over the shouting of my heart—the words that would free him to choose?*

Guilt splashed her anger with cold reality.

Her da and brothers had died defending the Belador legacy and future. Could she not be as selfless with less whining?

She'd accepted her responsibility many years ago.

But she'd always thought the children she bore would have Tzader's brown eyes and heartbreaking smile.

Not to be ignored, Macha interrupted Brina's thoughts with soft words of advice. "We face a growing crisis with these Alterants and leave the future of our tribe in jeopardy with each day you delay producing an heir. I am not without compassion for your situation and have a proposal."

Brina listened with a guarded ear, but she would make any concession for the possibility of having Tzader. "I'm listening."

"Convince Tzader you are no longer interested in waiting for him. Give him a chance to decide his future without any burden of guilt. If, once he truly believes marriage to you is no longer an option, I am convinced he still persists in wanting you, I would be inclined to reconsider my position on this matter and entertain possible solutions."

"Really?" Brina hesitated to believe Macha's words so easily. The goddess wouldn't blatantly lie to her, but she could turn words into a thousand different shapes and meanings.

"Do you question me?" The goddess stilled.

The fire beneath Macha blazed and grew in fullness.

"No, Goddess," Brina quickly amended. "I was merely

surprised . . . and overwhelmed." Could she break up
with Tzader and stand quietly by if he walked away and
never came back to her? "But why can't you simply ask
him the truth?"

"Because he would cut his arm off before he'd hurt you."

Brina enjoyed a thrill at Macha's having to admit just
how much Brina meant to Tzader.

Macha added, "And I believe he would relinquish
immortality without a second thought to be with you."

"Then what is the problem?"

"If he has suffered a life-threatening wound from
Noirre majik while immortal, the majik may still linger
in his body. If so, and I remove his immortality, he may
suffer the aftereffects of that wound, possibly even die
immediately."

Brina couldn't speak. Breathing hurt.

Tzader had fought countless battles against the Medb
and been wounded more than once in the past four years.
He'd almost died when the Medb had trapped him,
Quinn and Evalle in Utah. A Medb warlock had stabbed
Tzader with a spear tipped with the only substance that
could kill him.

The thought of Tzader risking death just to be with her
sickened Brina.

"But," Macha continued, "let's say he survives becoming mortal. Then he has to give up being the North
American Maistir to live here, which sounds like a nonstop honeymoon, but eventually a warrior needs to battle
because that is who he is."

Macha sent her a pointed look and continued in lecture

mode. "If he manages to get through all of that, Tzader would then face turning old and dying while you age in tiny fractions of the same time, still looking young and beautiful when he has one foot in the grave."

Brina had considered many possibilities, but in the back of her mind she'd always thought they'd end up immortal together. "You paint a sad existence for us."

"I only wish to know for sure that what you two have is more than a passing infatuation before I irrevocably change Tzader's life. And if he did give up his immortality, it would be permanent. Can you in good conscience ask him to make that choice never knowing whether he could be happy without you?"

Brina fought a trembling chin and watched her dreams crumble beneath Macha's onslaught of reality. She clamped her jaw and stiffened her resolve to find a way to make this work.

First, Tzader deserved to have a choice.

But now that Brina had said she was ready to have a child, Macha would not let that pass. There was no going back. Brina told the goddess, "I accept your proposal. I could never ask Tzader to make a life-altering decision without allowing him the opportunity to choose without limitations. I will set him free."

Macha's lips curled pleasantly and the fire around the grate settled down.

For the first time in three years, Brina smiled in earnest. When Tzader had first found out he couldn't pass the warding and she couldn't leave Treoir, he'd told her nothing would stop them from being together.

She believed in the depth of his love and in their ability to find a way to make this work, but right now Brina hoped she could depend upon Tzader to forgive her later on for the pain she would cause them both by accepting Macha's offer.

Macha moved faster than a thought, one minute atop the mantel and the next standing in front of Brina. Pearls sparkled across her breast and twittered in delight all the way down to where the gown swished around her bare feet. "As part of this agreement, you will end this relationship today."

"Why today?"

"Because he is on his way to see you."

Now? The goddess had dropped an impossible choice in her lap only moments ago and now expected her to be prepared to face Tzader this minute?

"Are you already reconsidering your agreement, Brina?"

Brina knew better than to break a deal with Macha. "Of course not."

"Good. In the interest of producing an heir within a year's time, you have two moon cycles to choose a suitable husband."

Huh? "Sixty days?"

"Dragging this out will make it more difficult for both of you."

Macha vanished before Brina could say another word. How could the goddess expect her to select a husband when she'd had no chance to mourn losing her soul mate?

If she lost Tzader.

Macha's voice ghosted through the room. "Once Tzader

leaves today *and* believes you are no longer interested in him, he has the same time to convince me he will have no other than you even if it means remaining alone. If you give him any hint of our discussion, this deal is off, and if you fail to end this today, don't bring his name up to me again."

Brina glanced around, anticipating Tzader but not ready to face him yet. Her heart thudded, anxious at the possibility of winning him and frightened she'd never see him again.

Brina, I need to talk to you, Tzader said telepathically in her mind.

Her heart burst with a sudden rush of happiness at being alone with him for the first time in so long.

Not truly alone, since Macha had just made it clear she intended to observe the meeting.

Brina closed her eyes, searching for the strength to do this. Could she push Tzader away and risk losing him forever?

Brina? he persisted.

She believed in him. Believed in them.

Much as Brina hated to agree with the goddess, Macha had a point in that Tzader deserved a chance to make a decision that wasn't based on a teenage vow. If he still came back to her, then Macha had to uphold her end and consider a solution to their problem.

But Brina would not leave everything up to fate.

A warrior always had a plan.

Tzader couldn't enter Brina's realm without an invitation and had to leave if she rescinded it.

She answered, *You are welcome to enter, Tzader Burke.*

And there he was . . . in hologram form. Still, Tzader's presence overpowered the vast room, intimidating and protective all at the same time.

Black-brown eyes sharp with intelligence and a warrior's keen gaze peered from a face so rich a shade of brown that his skin rivaled varnished mahogany. She missed running her fingers over his smooth bald head. He wore his usual black jeans and a gray short-sleeved T-shirt over muscular arms that hung loose at his sides with barely contained power. His fingertips dangled near the sentient blades hooked in his belt, but none of that could touch her when he was hologram.

His worry touched her, though.

For any hope of succeeding at Macha's challenge, Brina couldn't let Tzader know how much she missed him. She sucked her emotions in deep where Tzader wouldn't discern them with those gorgeous eyes that took in everything.

Thankfully, neither he nor Macha could lift her thoughts.

She couldn't read his either. Not since he'd become immortal as well.

Brina turned her back on him, stepping over to warm her hands by the fire. "What brings you here today?"

His confusion whipped around her, brushing her skin. She managed not to flinch when he said, "Aren't you glad to see me?"

To empty her voice of any emotion, she drew on the frustration she felt each time Macha visited her. "Depends on if you're bringing me a new problem or not."

The hairs on her neck rippled at his silence.

Had she angered him? She kept her head turned away, afraid to see hurt in his eyes instead of anger.

When he spoke again, he asked, "What happened to Evalle?"

She allowed the flicker of jealousy over Evalle's bond with Tzader to aid her, even though she knew Tzader's interest in Evalle was no more intimate than Quinn's. Brina drew herself up and turned slowly, determined to rip the bandage quickly and get this done one time and limit the pain.

She met his eyes with a passive gaze born of years practicing in front of Macha. "I can't share any details of the Tribunal meeting with you, and Evalle is not your problem. I don't wish to hear her name brought up again unless it's to explain why Alterants are overrunning the human world."

Her heart broke as all happiness to see her fled his face.

TEN

Stunned speechless, Tzader searched for the meaning behind Brina's caustic attitude.

She acted as if this visit imposed upon her time. Why wasn't she thrilled to see him when they hadn't been alone like this in . . . months? He could only enter her castle in holographic form, but he was here, dammit, and had busted his back end to free up this much time.

And what had gotten under her skin about Evalle? Returning to his point, he argued, "Evalle *is* my problem. Where is she?"

When Brina spoke, her words tumbled out as flat and lifeless as the expression on her face. "As the North American Maistir, you have higher priorities than one Alterant, especially with close to a hundred more beasts having shifted, as of the last count I received."

Tzader started to snap back at her but stopped. Brina had a temper, too. He wouldn't find out what was going on with her by putting her on the defensive. "I have teams out investigating the humans that are shifting into beasts. I know my position and duties, neither of which is more stressful than yours. What's wrong? Talk to me, *muirnin*."

Her gorgeous green eyes quivered at his endearment. There was his girl, the woman he loved beyond all reason.

The brief emotion vanished from her gaze just before

her face shuttered again. She pulled her shoulders back in the rigid stance she normally took to address her warriors. "Since you know your job, you shouldn't waste your time—or mine—unless you have something more important to discuss."

This couldn't be happening. Not one to dance around a target, he finally asked, "Have your feelings for me changed?"

Waiting for her answer took an eternity according to his heart, which slowed to a painful thump . . . thump . . . thump.

She looked through him and plainly stated, "You can't pass through this warding and I can't risk leaving. We have . . . no future."

What had crawled up her backside since the last time they'd talked? "We have nothing *but* future. We're immortals. We have forever to figure a way around the obstacles our parents accidentally put in our way. They *wanted* us together. *I* want us together." He stared at her, willing her to show him more than that dead gaze. "Do *you* still want us together?"

The question hit a nerve, if the tiny muscle that jumped in her neck was any indication, but her words held no emotion for him. "You have time to wait, but I must produce an heir—"

"Not right this minute," he muttered.

"—to ensure the future of our tribe," she finished. "You want to know what the Tribunal said? That Evalle is not to contact you or anyone else. As for doing your duty, you should be working harder to find the traitor."

First she rags him about the Alterants shifting and now the traitor? She was just pissing him off. He didn't need anyone to remind him of his duties. "We *are* working to find the traitor."

"Doing what?"

"You know what, Brina. You want a rundown of everything we've been up to for the past three months?"

"I want to know the identity of the traitor."

"We all do." Tzader clamped his jaw tight enough to crack the bones. He and Quinn had gotten close several times in the past couple years, but they had come up empty. They'd spent any free minute searching for the individual who had more than once put Beladors in danger through information that only a Belador should have known. Brina had been kept abreast of all this. "I obviously don't have a name yet, but—"

"But you have time to devote to one Alterant? What about the rest of our tribe, Tzader? We cannot afford to overlook the safety of the entire tribe for *one* Alterant."

"Now wait a minute." He had never put Evalle's interest ahead of other Beladors.

"What about O'Meary?"

"Last I checked, Larsen is still dead," Tzader said more clipped than he'd like, but what was going on with her? Why was she asking about that traitor?

"He's not the only O'Meary."

It took Tzader a minute to follow her abrupt switch to talking about the current O'Meary generation. "What about Conlan O'Meary? He's shown us no reason to suspect him. What are you saying?"

"That when there are two Beladors in a family like that there's a strong connection between father and son."

"Larsen O'Meary abandoned Conlan when the kid was seventeen, or did you forget why we brought Conlan in early to train?" What the devil? Larsen had been the Belador traitor who'd lured Brina's father, her brothers and Tzader's father to their deaths at the hands of the Medb Coven. O'Meary's son Conlan had been born with Belador powers and a few unusual gifts.

Larsen had supposedly died in battle, but Tzader doubted a traitor would actually step into danger, so he speculated that the Medb had killed him once they'd been done with him.

Tzader put his personal issue with Brina's attitude aside and got down to business, since that seemed to be all she wanted from him today. "Conlan has proven himself to be trustworthy and an asset."

"Then he should be willing to have his mind probed for buried memories or a connection to his da. Macha wants results, and so do I."

"What do you expect to find from having a druid probe his mind when Conlan hardly even knew his father?"

Brina's gaze belonged to everything but him. She said, "I'm not talking of using a druid. Have Quinn do the probe. We know Quinn can tap anything Conlan's father might have sent telepathically to him . . . or might *still* be sending him."

"Still? You think Larsen is alive?"

"I would have expected you to consider that possibility, since we've never seen a body."

"But we did have a druid search for Larsen's spirit. The druid said the spirit was no longer functioning in a body in the human world."

"All the more reason to have Quinn probe Conlan for any repressed memories that may aid us in our search or information deep in his subconscious that might be shielded from the young man's consciousness. I don't like to do this either, Tzader, but we need to find out if Larsen is truly dead and, if so, Quinn can reach out from Conlan to tap Larsen's spirit."

"To go that deep would risk harming Conlan *and* Quinn if Quinn runs into something unexpected in Conlan's subconscious mind . . . like a trap."

Brina lifted her hands to her waist, heat searing her gaze. "First you defend Conlan as a loyal follower, then you suggest he *could* be a threat. Which will it be?"

He had no reason to suspect the young man. "I just disagree with putting Quinn or Conlan through this without being convinced it's necessary."

Brina crossed her arms and really looked at him this time, but not with love in her eyes. "You come here asking for information on the Alterant who has me spending more time at Tribunal meetings than taking care of Belador business, but you hesitate to pursue a danger to the Beladors . . . and me?"

How had she mangled his words to make him sound as though he was letting her down? "My first concern is always to protect you and our tribe."

"Then consider this. The Alterants are an unknown entity. Almost a hundred have shifted into beasts in just two days. Does this sudden change, or what is causing the change, not concern you?"

"Of course it does, and I expect a report by the time I return to VIPER headquarters, but it's unfair to point suspicion at Evalle when none of the beasts seen so far have green eyes. And we've even heard of one Alterant intervening to save a teenager's life. If Evalle was here she could help us."

Brina's gaze narrowed in doubt. "You're sure? How do you know whatever is causing this outbreak wouldn't affect her ability to control herself?"

"Because I know Evalle. She can control her beast."

"Are you allowing your relationship with her to blind you to a potential threat from Alterants as well?"

"Of course not." Was he? No. He didn't think so. He asked, "What does all this have to do with the traitor?"

She lifted a hand, counting off fingers with each point. "You believed Larsen O'Meary was involved with the first Alterant incident. You met Evalle when the traitor tricked you into a Medb trap. You got a tip on the traitor because of the Alterant who shifted in North Carolina nine weeks ago."

"I'll concede that you have a point, but why are you so angry with me? What do you want from me?"

She scowled. "What do I want? For you to carry out my orders for the mind probe and deliver me the head of that traitor. And for you to accept that I have a responsibility to the Beladors. It's best we stop pretending that our relationship will ever work out so that we may both move on with our lives."

He heard her message loud and clear this time, every word slashing what they'd shared in the past to pieces.

"You got it, Your Highness." He couldn't enter without her invitation, but he could sure as hell leave without her permission. He lifted his hands and withdrew his hologram from the castle in the brittle seconds before she could dismiss him.

ELEVEN

S he should have let Tristan kill her.

Evalle sat on the fern-covered ground, knees propped up, facing the tangled jungle growth ten feet away that had been ripped to shreds and beaten to pieces by a beast. Tristan. The same Tristan-beast that stood glaring down at her with the promise of reprisal in his hollow black eyes.

The only thing preventing him from killing her was that invisible spellbound wall between them, which he'd failed to destroy in the past three hours.

Sunrise had to be coming soon, even though it was hard to tell with this dense cover of greenery and thick clouds constantly shedding rain and holding the dark close. At this point, she honestly didn't care if her skin fried.

Like fatback on a hot skillet, as her Nightstalker buddy Grady would say.

Evalle had no way back to Atlanta, no weapon and no ally here.

Tristan turned away and made two steps when the air around him distorted, the way heat warped away from an explosion. His body started changing, shrinking from the ten-foot-tall creature to a just-over-six-foot human, arms and legs returning to normal size.

Which meant his jeans no longer fit.

They fell down around his feet, then he stepped out of them and walked away as naked as the day he was born.

She stretched her neck, looking for him, then gave up. Why would he come back, when he couldn't get his hands on her? He'd left her dagger right where he'd kinetically stuck it in the ground—inside his protected area.

Probably using her dagger as bait to lure her back inside.

Evalle dropped her head onto her arms, which were crossed over her knees. Failure would be easier to accept if no one else paid the price but her. She didn't want to be locked away like Tristan, but at this point she'd accept that over leaving Brina to face down the Tribunal.

Not to mention disappointing the entire Belador race, including Tzader and Quinn, who had to be out fighting Alterants.

Now she was letting down all humans as well.

"Thought you wanted to talk."

Tristan? Evalle jerked her head up and there he was, still inside his area, but now he wore a pair of khaki shorts with pockets everywhere. His body was clean, his blond hair slicked back as if he'd taken a quick dip in water.

And his eyes were chameleon green again.

"Yes, I do want to talk." She pushed to her feet, dusting off her mud-crusted jeans. Something bit her neck. She slapped at the bug and brought back a bloody smudge on her palm.

Just great. Vampire bugs.

Tristan moved forward and she took a step back.

But this time he didn't ram his body against the invisible force keeping him walled in. He sat on the ground and leaned against a gigantic tree that appeared to be growing half in and half outside his prison. His left arm pushed against a flat surface she couldn't see, which must be the wall of the enclosure.

If he wanted to kill her, he could have done it inside his area. Maybe he wanted some company after all, but she wasn't stepping back inside with him to test that theory.

In a show of camaraderie, she eased over and slid down on the left side of Tristan against the same tree. But she kept a few inches of separation from him even if he couldn't touch her.

What do you say to a man you'd sent back to hell? "How you doing, Tristan?"

He ignored her, looking up into the canopy of tree cover. His lips moved with whispered words she couldn't hear. She waited for him to say something to her next, but he sat quietly for a few minutes, then a monkey high above them screeched.

Tristan couldn't leave his area, but any animal could.

She tensed and glanced up in time to see a yellow bomb falling at them.

Evalle dove away to her left.

Tristan didn't even flinch.

He caught a large bunch of bananas that filled his hands. Snapping one free, he placed the rest of them on his right and said, "So what do you want?"

Could he direct an animal on her side of the wall to do his bidding, too? Like sending a predator to get her?

She sat back up and kept an eye on her surroundings while she considered how to answer him. What was the point in searching for a diplomatic way to put this when she'd already told him the same thing once? "I was sent here to find the three escaped Alterants."

Tristan bit the banana and smiled briefly around each chew. "You ask Brina where she had them caged?"

"No."

"Why not?"

Evalle could see no reason to shade the truth, not if she had any hope of Tristan answering her questions honestly. "Because the Tribunal forbade my asking her and she's sworn to secrecy about the Alterants for some reason."

"Doesn't matter. Brina doesn't know where those three are right now anyhow," Tristan said, smug with knowledge. He finished the last bite of the banana and tossed the peel aside.

Then why ask me if Brina knew? Evalle would not lose her temper with him. "But you know where those three are, right?"

"Yes."

"Would you tell me?"

"Why would I do that?"

"I know you're not going to see this my way at first, but give me a chance to explain."

Tristan snorted and broke off another banana. "The same way I got a chance to explain before you used the Ngak Stone to send me back here?"

"I didn't want to do that—"

"Tell it to someone who'll listen."

She was tired of constantly taking the blame for everything. He had some responsibility in all this. "You were the one who sided with the Medb and Kujoo. If you had helped our side I might have been able to talk Brina into not sending you back."

"Right. Brina sent me here the first time before I ever shifted into beast form. I'm sure she'd want me walking around telling everyone how she'd screwed me from day one."

Evalle drew her knees up and dropped her chin down. That was what Tristan had said the first time she'd met him, and she could tell he believed what he said, so had Brina really put him away without reason?

"I understand, Tristan, but I wasn't there when she sent you to this prison, so I can't argue with you. I do know other Alterants have killed humans and Beladors after shifting into beasts. Maybe Brina was trying to get ahead of the problem before you shifted. I don't have answers for any of that."

"Then why didn't they lock *you* away?"

The shade of hurt in his voice caused her to lift her head so she could look at him when she answered honestly. "I spent my entire life in a basement because I have a lethal intolerance to sunshine. An old druid came to me there when I was eighteen and told me of my destiny to be a Belador warrior. He didn't know my eyes were an unnatural Alterant green because my eyes are so sensitive I always wear sunglasses, even in the dark."

"But you could leave the basement at night, that's more freedom than I've had here."

She never talked about her life growing up, but Tristan had seen his own share of misery, and he *was* talking to her.

"No, I couldn't leave that basement. I was adopted by my father's sister, who kept me locked up. If I can believe anything that hag told me, when my mother died in childbirth and I had a severe reaction to sunlight the hospital ran tests that exposed that I was not her brother's child."

Tristan didn't look at her, but the stern angles in his face softened some. "What'd your father do?"

"Basically, sold me to my aunt, who believed her brother could do no wrong. She offered to be the martyr and take me on. She didn't want some mutant child to embarrass her beloved Army officer brother, so she legally adopted me, but, as she once put it, I was her retirement nest egg."

Ironically, the hag died before she could retire.

Tristan asked, "What happened when you met the druid?"

She'd never been much for dredging up old pains, so she was glad to move on past family hour. "He offered me a chance to train as a Belador if I was willing to swear an oath to uphold their code of honor. I would have signed on with the devil to escape that basement and my aunt, but I *am* loyal to the Beladors."

At that she got an eye roll from Tristan, but Evalle finished explaining. "By the time the Beladors got a look at my bright green eyes, I was already training with them. They figured I might be different because I'm a female Alterant. That I might not shift involuntarily."

She wasn't sharing the fact that things had changed a few days back when another female Alterant had surfaced and killed humans. That was more of a need-to-know detail.

Tristan said, "I never saw a druid. Never got an offer to choose my destiny."

"That just means you weren't expected to be a warrior. Trust me, it's not all fun and games."

"Neither is this place."

What could she say to that? Nothing.

She had to move the conversation back to finding the Alterants. If those three were together, she'd risk burning one of her Tribunal gifts to find them, but not if they were separated since she could only use a gift one time. "Are the three Alterants all in the same place?"

"Maybe . . . maybe not." Tristan shrugged. "Tell me about Beladors. What made them send a druid to you?"

"They didn't specifically send one to me. The way I understand it, Belador warriors are born under a star called PRIN, but I know nothing about astrology. A druid meets a child around age five to make contact, then goes away until that person turns eighteen. The druid that appeared in my basement said he was Breasel and that he'd met me when I was a kid. I told him I didn't remember meeting him, but the weird thing is that I did recognize him when he spoke to me in an ancient language. He said he'd told me the same words when I was five."

"Was it Gaelic?"

"Sort of, but older than that, a secret druid language. That's when I recognized him as the guy I'd seen working in my basement on a hot water heater or something when I was little. I watched him from where I hid in a corner and remembered him talking some foreign language out loud, then leaving. When he offered me a chance to

escape that basement at eighteen, I was in. I'd been afraid
for years—"

Tristan cut his eyes at her, which she ignored, because
she was not sharing why she'd lived in terror for three years.

"—but I had this moment of knowing for sure that old
druid was no danger to me. I told him I'd go anywhere to get
out of there but I couldn't be exposed to sunlight. He smiled
and said to hold his hand and close my eyes. Next thing I
knew, I was in Alaska, wearing animal skins and heavy boots
with a group of new Belador recruits being trained.

"We lived in a barn with little heat during the shortest
days of the year, which worked for me. We had to fend
for ourselves and learn how to live off the land in a frigid
climate, but for the first time in my life I was free to go
outside whenever I wanted."

Tristan said nothing, just stared straight ahead.

She searched her mind for a way to find common
ground with him. The more she learned about him and
how they were possibly connected as Alterants, the better chance she had of proving Alterants were more than a
bunch of mutant mutts.

That we deserve to be a recognized race.

She asked, "How did you know you had Belador blood
if you didn't meet a druid?"

His smirk tilted arrogantly when he shook his head,
refusing to answer her. He spit out bitterly, "I don't think
having Belador blood counts for shit."

"It might if you'd help me figure out what else plays a
part in our genetics. You told me in Atlanta you had an
idea what had bred with a Belador to make an Alterant

and what we have in common with the other three Alterants." Her stomach growled loudly.

Tristan arched an eyebrow at her.

She hadn't realized she was hungry until he'd started eating, and her mouth had watered at the smell of fresh bananas.

Breaking off a banana, he held this one toward her in offering, but not close enough for the fruit or his hand to pass through the barrier.

She'd passed through once, so she should be able to put her hand back through.

Evalle reached over and took the banana. "Thanks."

He grabbed her forearm.

Every muscle in her body tensed, ready to fight.

She stayed very still, watching the fingers of his free hand slide down to curl around her wrist snug as a handcuff. He turned her arm toward him and gently lifted a leaf-shaped bug off her skin, placing the critter safely on the ground.

Then he released her arm.

She expelled a breath she'd caught in her throat and started peeling the banana. *Act calm, as if nothing has changed.* "You were going to tell me what else you were besides Belador."

"No, I wasn't. I'm not sharing anything I know about our origin as long as I'm stuck in here."

Who could fault him for holding back? In his place, she'd have done the same, which meant she had to offer him something he might be willing to trade for.

A chance to fight for his freedom.

Evalle weighed everything and believed Brina could hold her own if what Evalle suggested came to pass. "I got the Tribunal to agree to let the three missing Alterants plead their cases."

His eyes flicked with surprise, but he only said, "If you find them."

She sighed and moved on. "You said you were unfairly caged. I won't make promises I can't keep, like saying I can get you out of here, but if you'll help me I will promise to ask the Tribunal to let you plead *your* case directly to them, too."

First, she'd have to get Brina to ask Macha to allow Tristan to be released, but one step at a time.

He polished off another banana, asking, "Why would you try to convince Brina to do that?"

"I took an oath of honor, and I consider that an honorable choice. If Brina had good reason for having you sent away—which I'm giving her the benefit of the doubt about as well—then she'll have no problem explaining her actions. I'm going to let truth play out." And hope like the devil Brina did have a sound reason for locking Tristan away.

"But you said you couldn't ask Brina about the location of the Alterants."

"If we can hand Brina the origin of Alterants, I think she'll talk to Macha about giving the Alterants who have their beast under control a chance to join VIPER, and maybe the Beladors."

"I don't know." Tristan scratched his shoulder.

"VIPER and the Beladors need us right now. Alterants are shifting all of a sudden everywhere."

Tristan cracked a smile. "No kidding?"

"Not funny. People are dying."

He rubbed a hand over his chin, losing his smile. "Let's say I consider what you're suggesting. What did the Tribunal offer in return if you brought in the three missing Alterants?"

He wasn't going to like her answer, but then neither did she. "My freedom."

"Guess you didn't come with a conscience, huh?"

Guilt hammered at her soul every time she considered taking those three back with her, because she didn't trust the Tribunal. But she believed in Brina, who had promised that those Alterants would get a fair hearing while being held under Macha's protection in the meantime.

"Of course I have a conscience. Did you not hear me when I told you I got a deal for each of them to prove their innocence? If those three can stand in a Tribunal meeting and truthfully say they did not murder anyone, then I believe the Tribunal will release them to work with VIPER, like I'm doing. I have Brina's word that they'll be safe until they meet with the Tribunal."

"I can't hand Brina that kind of trust."

She understood, but Tristan needed to know all the possible pitfalls if the Alterants he shielded remained on the loose. "If I don't return with those three, the Tribunal is going to turn VIPER loose to hunt down and kill *all* Alterants on sight. No chance to plead their cases. No chance for real freedom."

Tristan grew still at the news of all Alterants being hunted.

"You may not like being here, but if they're out in the world on their own, they're vulnerable."

"And you think they'll be safe walking into VIPER?" he asked with no small amount of sarcasm.

"I'll be perfectly honest, Tristan. If any of the Alterants have killed an innocent human, they have to pay the price, but if they killed in self-defense, that's a different story. With so many Alterants shifting everywhere in the past twenty-four hours, me, you and those three may be the only ones who have a chance to survive." And if this worked out, Evalle wouldn't be dragged in every time an Alterant committed a crime.

"What do the Alterants that are changing look like?"

She lifted her shoulders. "I guess like us. I haven't seen any of them . . . which reminds me. Why were your eyes black earlier when you were, uh, shifted?"

"Think it has to do with being in here. I thought black eyes were normal as a beast, because I'd always seen my eyes that way in water reflections, but they stayed green constantly once I left here the last time. Now they're back to black when I shift in here."

"Oh." That wasn't helpful.

Tristan nodded to himself and stared off into the jungle as if he pondered what she'd told him. "Gods and goddesses are sneaks," he said under his breath. He glanced at her. "You sure if you return the three Alterants they'll let *you* walk away?"

His question surprised her, especially since he'd asked in a civil tone lacking ridicule.

She answered carefully. "That's what the Tribunal

told me, but I'm not walking away unless those three do, too. Convincing them to come in with me would beat them having to live with targets on their backs. And as soon as I return with them I'll lobby for you to plead your case."

She swatted a fat mosquito drawing enough blood off her midriff to feed four normal-sized mosquitoes back home. That was saying something, because Georgia grew hefty insects.

"I don't know. What *exactly* did the Tribunal say?"

"Let me think," she grumbled. She hadn't taken dictation, for crying out loud. "The Tribunal said, 'Let the one who returns the three escaped Alterants to VIPER be cleared of prior transgressions.'"

Tristan listened, interest growing visibly in his face until he finally said in a lighter tone, "Sounds like you're right. I know where the others are. Help me get out of here and I'll show you."

Help him escape so she'd have to recapture *four* Alterants? Was he crazy? Well, maybe. Who wouldn't be after living out here alone all this time, but still . . . she hadn't lost *her* mind. "I can't do that, Tristan."

"Okay." He stood up with what was left of the bananas and dropped the bunch where he'd been sitting. "That should hold you for a while." He pointed past her. "North is that way."

"You can't be serious."

"I am. The last time I trusted someone's offer of freedom, it backfired."

"That was the Kujoo, not me."

"Why should I believe someone who sent me back?" He strolled away, pausing in stride to pick up her dagger.

"Tristan!" Evalle pounded the ground, then jumped to her feet and stepped tentatively inside his area. "Tristan. Come back and talk to me."

Blond hair disappeared into a wide swath of green.

She slammed her fist into the palm of her hand. If she lost him now, could she find him again?

Not a chance.

Evalle raced after him, shoving branches out of her way, and picked up his tracks. Energy inside his prison bogged her down once more, as if she swam against a current. When she'd followed him a hundred yards deep into the middle of nowhere, his tracks disappeared. Pausing to look up, she heard a rattle of noise off to her right, caught a glimpse of blond hair and took off again.

After a couple of hours of trying to catch Tristan every time she'd chase a glimpse of him moving through the jungle, she finally lost him for good. She ended up wandering back into the original clearing where they'd talked.

The bananas he'd left had been hung on a broken branch since she'd last seen them. As a peace offering?

Maybe that meant he *would* come back.

In the meantime, she was still hungry and reached for the only food in sight.

Monkeys chattered and shook the trees overhead, drawing her gaze up and up. The noise increased, but they didn't seem upset. They were just making a racket.

When soft footsteps raced toward her, she realized too late why the monkeys were raising a ruckus.

Evalle yanked her arm down and turned to meet her opponent, but not fast enough to get out of the way.

Tristan raced forward, grabbed her against him and leaped airborne for fifteen feet, propelled like a human missile. He yelled a curse. They hit the ground as one big thud in a tangle of arms and legs.

Her chin bounced down, up and back down again.

She saw stars, lots of them.

Breathing hard and still dazed, she pushed up and squinted to clear her vision in order to figure out what had happened. Then it registered how she'd ended up sprawled on the ground.

She turned back around and looked down. Not the ground.

Her hands pressed against a wall of chest muscles.

Tristan lay beneath her, unconscious after taking the brunt of their landing.

She could live with that.

Wait a minute.

She glanced around again. *No, please, no.*

But there stood the tree that had been half in and half out of the spellbound walls.

Based on the proximity of that tree, Tristan's prone body had crashed on the wrong side of the invisible enclosure.

Another Alterant had escaped.

TWELVE

E valle scrambled up from where she'd landed astride Tristan. This capped a crappy day so far.

He hadn't roused yet from hitting the ground so hard.

Good. She needed a minute to think. Blood and adrenaline pulsed through her veins with enough force to send a rocket into space.

That would have come in handy if she'd been able to strap Tristan to the rocket. She had to get him back inside the spellbound cage even if doing that a second time twisted her gut. The Tribunal would not show mercy on him if they found out he'd escaped.

Using her kinetics to carry him back inside might kill both of them the minute her power crossed the barrier. And what if he came to in the middle of her moving him?

Having him wake up on this side would be worse.

Holding her hands out toward him, she drew on her kinetic ability and lifted his body. Tristan's entire length hung limp in the air. When she had him a few feet from the barrier to his prison, she tried to throw him back inside the cage with a hard shove.

He smacked the wall of invisible energy and bounced backwards, landing on the ground.

Oops . . . my bad. She cringed at the painful sound that slid from his throat.

Tristan's chest moved when he drew a breath. He groaned on his exhale, but he was still out cold.

Served him right for pulling that stupid stunt. Had he thought he could go airborne like an out-of-water porpoise and land on hard ground without having the air knocked out of him?

Of course, slamming him against the equivalent of a steel wall hadn't helped either. Or the fact that he'd taken the brunt of the fall with her on top when he'd jumped out.

Had he landed that way intentionally?

Maybe, maybe not, but he no longer needed her now that he'd escaped.

But she needed him.

She tensed, ready for battle the minute he opened his eyes.

How had he gotten out of the spellbound enclosure? *Worry about the mechanics of his jailbreak once he's back on the other side.*

She had three gifts from the Tribunal and no clue what they were other than she could not ask for a gift unless it was being used specifically to fulfill her agreement to return the *other* escaped Alterants.

Technically, putting Tristan back inside his cage would not meet the criteria, since he would refuse to help the minute he was in captivity again.

Would have been nice if the Tribunal had given her an operation manual for her so-called gifts . . . one with a troubleshooting section.

Tristan groaned louder and rubbed his head. One eye

slid open and peered over at her, then he pushed up on his elbow.

She kept very still, watching for any aggressive move. "How'd you get out of there?"

He smiled. "You broke me out."

"No, I didn't." She hoped.

"Oh, yes, you did. Remember when I held your arm to take off that bug?"

"Yes," she answered warily.

"I shoved my foot past the barrier while I was touching you and I broke through to my ankle, then it stopped me. I figured if I could do that while holding your wrist I should be able to push my entire body through if I was holding all of you." He rubbed his head. "Wasn't quite as simple as I thought. Damned near killed myself finding out."

She was a dead Alterant the minute the Tribunal found out about this.

Tristan chuckled. "Looks like the worm has turned, eh?"

She wasn't sure what powers he possessed or how strong he was out here, but as of now her powers were locked and loaded. "I don't know about the worm, but your being out here puts us both on a level playing field."

He stopped rubbing his head and looked at her. "You think?"

"You might kill me, but you'll crawl away missing vital parts."

"Fighting each other would waste time we could use finding those three Alterants."

She paused. "You're going to work with me?"

"Isn't that what you wanted?"

Sure, but his easy compliance reeked with suspicious intent. "Why're you willing to help now that you're free, Tristan?"

"Let's just say I believe you're telling the truth about getting me an audience with the Tribunal. I don't think you can corral the three missing Alterants without me, and I don't want them killed. I'll help you, but you can't hand them over until I get to see the Tribunal."

She'd offered to *request* a meeting for him. She hadn't said she could do it for sure, but mentioning that right now would not be the best way to move ahead with a potential alliance.

A shaky one she didn't trust one bit.

He rose to his feet and took a look at the ground where he'd been lying, then cut his eyes to where the invisible barrier would be. He licked his lip where blood trickled and scanned the area between them, asking, "I should be over where you're standing. How did I end up here?"

Probably the same way you got that busted lip when I tried to throw you back into your cage. "Majik and aerodynamics . . . hard to say. I landed over here."

He lifted an eyebrow, so not believing her.

She took in his jeans, jungle-camo T-shirt and hiking boots, which he hadn't been wearing when he'd eluded her in the jungle. She used that to change the subject. "Where'd you get the clothes?"

"When the Kujoo broke me out the first time, they gave me a witch highball spiked with Kujoo blood. I can conjure a few things like clothes when I need them." He shrugged, indifferent to how that put him in another category from her.

So now he was what?

Part Belador, part Alterant and part Kujoo?

Plus Medb witch?

She didn't want to think about that possibility.

He lifted an arm and pointed in the direction he'd earlier said was north. "There's a town about sixty kilometers that way."

She did the math in her head to convert kilometers to miles. Thirty-six miles through rough terrain with an escaped Alterant she didn't trust, deadly animals and poisonous reptiles.

Lucky her, huh?

Travel guides called this extreme adventure.

And people paid to put their lives at risk.

If she had to trek through this jungle, she didn't want to do it without her dagger, especially since that blade had an extra kick of power. "I want my weapon."

"No." Tristan slicked blond hair back off his face with both hands and bent down to retie his muddy hiking boots. "Don't worry. I won't let anything eat you either."

"Oh, really?" she said dryly. Why did men assume a woman needed their protection? "I can take care of myself with or *without* a weapon." But she'd have to deal with the sun in another hour if that soft glow tinting the edge of the darkness meant morning was coming. Dense clouds still hovered so close to the ground that a white haze smoked around them.

How long had she been here? Five . . . six hours? Her cheap watch hadn't survived being slammed to the ground with Tristan when he launched them out of the enclosure. "When's sunrise?"

"Soon." He finished tying his shoes and stood up. "We're going to be in this heavy moisture for most of the trip. I'll give you a heads-up before the sun breaks through."

But would he give her a heads-up ten minutes before sunlight stabbed through the thick shield of moisture protecting her skin? Or ten seconds?

Oblivious to her dilemma, Tristan started past her, then paused and dropped his head close when he spoke. "Just so you know, when they gave me the witch's brew I picked up a few special tricks. If I want to kill you I can do it out here just as easily as I could have in that cage, and with little effort."

Having said his piece, he struck out.

If what he said was true, she was safer sticking with him.

If it was true.

Evalle kept pace, but only because she could match his long strides and because she'd stayed in shape walking plenty of miles in Atlanta. The mideighties temperature here would feel no worse than a warm summer day back home, but even Georgia couldn't match the humidity in this rain forest.

She kept waiting for the sun, expecting that death ball of fire to burn off the clouds with a minute's notice, like after a foggy morning in Atlanta. But the air remained bloated with moisture that fell in a constant drizzle. Wet hair plastered her neck and shoulders, the rubber band that had been holding her ponytail long gone from Tristan's acrobatic escape.

If he really intended to work with her, he should be willing to share some information. "Where'd you grow up?"

"Everywhere."

"Come on, Tristan."

He paused at a downed tree, squatted to lift one end, then shoved the twelve-inch-thick trunk off their trail.

She noted that he hadn't used kinetics. What exactly had that witch juice done to him?

When he started walking again, he said, "I lived in five different foster homes."

Crap. "So you don't know who your parents are either?"

"I didn't say that. The last place I lived was near Chattanooga."

"Who are your parents? Do either of them have powers?"

"You want information, but what have you got to trade?"

She'd already offered to talk to the Tribunal. With Tristan free she had even less to barter with than she had before. "You know what I have."

"Then we're through talking until I know for sure there's something in it for me."

Except for occasional stops to drink from a coconut or eat fruit, she trudged silently through vegetation so thick that getting through felt like wrestling a gorilla. Now she was slogging through a muddy path cut along a mountainside.

Something bit her.

Again.

For like the hundredth time.

She'd had survival training, but give her the city anytime. Even with Atlanta traffic, she'd take the smell of a fresh night sizzled over hot pavement after a summer's day. Civilization.

After five hours—or had it been six yet—of feeling like the food source for every bloodsucker smaller than her fingernail, she started thinking fondly of nights spent tracking preternatural predators . . .

The amulet around her neck heated up.

Her skin prickled with awareness and a sense that she'd missed something important.

In the city, she stayed on constant alert.

Out here, she'd gotten lax, assuming Tristan knew the land better than her, since he'd hiked out of here with the Kujoo last week.

But she still should have been paying more attention, because something was following her with deadly intent.

Her heart double-timed with a jolt of fight-or-flight adrenaline that spread through her limbs at the hint of battle. Speaking out loud to Tristan would alert the enemy, but could she reach him telepathically?

Tristan, can you hear me? She waited for some sign from him, but he never paused his stride ahead of her. She'd give it another try. *Something or someone is following us. It's dangerous. I don't want to harm an animal, but I refuse to be anyone's dinner.*

I hear it, he finally said. *Stay close.*

She took stock of her surroundings. They'd been gradually descending for the past half hour, and the land had become more rolling than downhill. Tangled vines and a healthy crop of branches forced Tristan to break open the path on occasion, but there had been a few clearings like the one with the lake and waterfall a hundred yards back . . . until now.

The trail had narrowed with sides formed by thick undergrowth.

Sizing up the ambush potential , she rated the terrain directly ahead of and behind them a high nine on a scale of one to ten.

The jungle had been alive with sounds moments ago.

Everything quieted.

A twig snapped, then leaves shuffled.

That hadn't been by accident. Whatever stalked her was unconcerned about her hearing its approach. She picked up a ripple of power emanating from the woods behind her and to her left. Several origins.

Predators for sure, but not of the human world.

Tristan paused and dropped to retie his hiking boot.

Did he sense anything?

He turned toward her when he stood, eyes alert.

Demons, whispered through her mind. *They're drawn to our power. Link with me if you want to live.*

Linking took absolute trust among Beladors. Plus, she had no clue what might happen if two Alterants linked together.

Evalle? You with me or not?

THIRTEEN

Can't link with you, Tristan, Evalle sent back telepathically. She kept glancing around for the demons closing in on them.

Tristan sighed and shook his head. *And you want me to trust you?*

The first beast attacked, diving at Tristan from out of the trees. Too massive to be a wild dog and not quite wolf, with bared fangs and spiked claws extended, its red eyes burned with the urge to kill.

Tristan moved as a blur, fast as lightning, whipping his arm around to slam his fist between the animal's bright eyes.

The demon went flying up and back into a wad of saplings, then rebounded to his feet and charged again.

Evalle had already turned to cover their backs. Noise crashed toward her from the force of a massive body wrecking everything in its path. She raised her hands to shove power at the next animal when two exploded out of the jungle.

She knocked one demon back against the trunk of a hardwood tree so large her arms wouldn't reach around it. The other demon dodged her kinetic shot at the last minute, diving to the side, then rounding behind her. She whipped a blast of energy at him and rammed the demon into the base of the same tree.

He fell into a motionless heap.

The urge to shift fully into a beast coursed so strongly through her veins that she hesitated to risk even the small change into Belador battle form.

She might not be able to stop at that point.

Why hadn't Tristan taken on his beast form? He had no one to answer to for anything he did out here. *Shift, Tristan!*

Can't.

Why not? But talking would distract both of them. From the corner of her eye, she caught him fighting the first wolf-demon he'd hit, plus a new one.

She expected the demon she'd stopped with her first shove of power to attack again, but when he regained his senses he started climbing the old hardwood tree with humanlike ability. Once he reached twenty feet up, he climbed out on a limb and stalked her from above.

The other beast at the base of the tree began to rouse.

One glance up confirmed the tree-climber was actually waiting on his companion to wake up to attack as a team.

Something behind her screamed with pain. Maybe Tristan did have some super-charged powers without shifting into his Alterant state. Not fair since he had her weapon, too.

Her weapon. *Tristan, throw me the dagger. I've killed demons with it.*

No power to . . . reach it.

She risked a look and lost hope of surviving this.

Tristan was the one on the ground, struggling. A

demon had his upper arm locked in his jaws, ripping muscle and bone with each jerk of its head.

The other animal Tristan had fought lay headless.

But the one chewing on his arm appeared to be weakening Tristan. His movements were sluggish.

A throaty growl above rattled the bones in her spine. Evalle looked up as the wolf-demon above her hunched his body, preparing to jump.

She ripped her attention back to the other monster on the ground, now up on all four legs and snarling.

Those two demons must have figured out she couldn't hold the wall of power in front of her and above her at the same time. The one perched overhead jumped as the demon on the ground attacked.

She changed her hand positions and shoved her power straight up, making a fast plan. When the flying monster hit her force field she would heave that animal at the one coming across the ground.

Her plan might have worked, but the one that landed on her field of energy hit and bounced off, smacking a pine tree that hadn't been thick enough to do any damage.

And the demon on the ground had anticipated her move.

He jumped sideways.

Then slashed back at her before she could swing her kinetic power to stop him.

Fangs bared, he lunged for her knee.

His jaws crushed bone with the first bite.

She screamed at the pain. Claws tore at her thigh, ripping skin and muscle. Blood gushed down her leg and over the demon's muzzle. She beat his head with her fists.

Cartilage shot up along her arms. Energy racked her body with the impending change.

No. Not the beast. She couldn't trust Tristan not to rat her out if they faced the Tribunal together, and she'd glow red if she lied about shifting.

But dying would negate all of that.

Her fingers elongated with clawed tips. She clenched her teeth, shaking hard with the force of holding off the change.

The demon's teeth ground into her knee. Blinding white pain burned through her leg, up into her abdomen and chest. The impending change had given her a weapon she wouldn't waste. Cocking her arm back, she shoved the sharp claw on her index finger into the creature's eye.

And kept shoving.

Bone gave as she pushed the stake deep into his brain.

His other eye rolled up in his head. His jaws loosened.

She pulled back and swung her fist like a sledgehammer, driving it down on the animal's head. Its head broke away from her knee. Two fangs buried in her muscle snapped at the skin line.

The haze surrounding her glowed so bright that it practically blinded her sensitive eyes. When had she lost her glasses? She groped around, found them and shoved them back on her face.

Dizziness assailed her.

She couldn't focus her vision. Something attacked her body almost like a poison, draining her power. She yanked out the broken fangs and gasped for air. Blood shot from opened arteries with each pulse of her heart. Pain screamed through her.

She was going to lose that leg . . . if she didn't die first.

Her arms felt heavy. She was light-headed. What kept depleting her energy beyond the blood loss?

Greenish-yellow liquid mixed with blood streamed down her leg.

The demon's saliva.

Maybe that's what had weakened Tristan. The demons' saliva had to be attacking their blood.

The tree-climbing demon that had bounced off her kinetic power shook his head and gained his feet, facing her with dead eyes. He wobbled when he took a step toward her.

With her power dwindling, she had one shot left.

She threw a blast of energy at the tree ten feet up, severing the trunk and sending a ton of wood down to crush the demon's backbone.

Now she didn't have enough kinetic energy to snap a toothpick.

Tristan bellowed in agony.

She twisted around, clenching her teeth against the throbbing pain. The creature still had what was left of Tristan's mauled arm locked in his jaws. He used the bloody stump to shake Tristan's entire body back and forth.

No point in being quiet now, she yelled, "Where's the dagger?"

"Right . . . boot," he croaked out in a voice wrought with pain. Blood covered his arm, his body and the ground.

Dragging her bad leg, she crawled to his side and lurched for his boot, unable to stop a cry of anguish at banging her crushed knee.

She reached inside his boot and curled her fingers around the handle of her dagger.

Energy wicked up her arm.

With the last surge of strength in her body, she lunged for the demon's head, driving the dagger between its eyes. That had worked on demons in the past and, hallelujah, this one burst into an explosion of light, then turned into gray powder.

Tristan fell back with a pitiful howl.

Nothing alive should sound like that.

She shoved the dagger into her boot and climbed over him. Flesh and muscle hung loose from his shoulder, his arm a mangled mess. He wouldn't survive that any more than she was going to survive a crushed knee that was bleeding out.

"Have to . . . heal," he rasped out in a pain-drenched voice.

She'd healed some wounds quicker than a human would be able to but not an injury like this. "Tristan, my knee is destroyed. I don't have the ability to heal this kind of damage."

She rolled off his body so he could move. He drew a couple of hard breaths and pushed up on his undamaged arm. His sun-kissed skin had turned a sickly gray.

He wheezed out, "Go to . . . the lake."

Like water was going to fix their ravaged bodies? "How will that help?"

"Have to wash away . . . saliva . . . it's attacking our blood."

"That might stop the power loss, but—" She took a couple of breaths to keep from throwing up. "Unless that lake has majik in the water . . . not going to fix mangled bodies. It's too late . . . saliva's draining us."

He gave her a look of confusion, then got to his feet with a great deal of grunting through clenched jaws. He extended his hand to her. "Too much . . . to explain."

She couldn't push him to say more when every word obviously took a toll on his waning energy. "Go ahead if you think you can do something. I can't walk."

"Up." He kept his hand out.

Too exhausted to argue, she grabbed his hand with both of hers and let him pull her to her feet. She sucked in a sharp breath. Tears threatened at the surge of blistering pain. The minute she balanced herself on one leg he let go of her. "What the—"

Before she could fall, he scooped her fireman style over his good shoulder, then started walking. He was headed in the direction of the waterfall they'd passed earlier.

"Put me down. You're in no shape to carry me."

He said nothing, just plodded along like a man who had been beaten with a club.

Struggling would only hurt both of them, so she kept still.

Time in the universe of pain moved at an excruciating pace. Every misstep over the rugged terrain jarred her leg and brought tears to her eyes. There was no way she'd cry out or complain, when he had to be hurting just as much.

He muttered something and plowed on.

She couldn't pay attention to his words past the mind-numbing ache. The sound of rushing water got louder and louder, then she saw the lake and waterfall out of the corner of her eye.

He walked into clear water that wasn't cold, but cooler than the sauna they'd been trudging through.

Everything below her waist had turned into one gigantic, infected throb.

Tristan held her with his one arm and sunk to his neck. He whispered words that sounded like a chant.

She asked, "What are you doing?"

He just kept murmuring strange words.

"Are you trying to put a spell on me?"

He paused from chanting. "If I did . . . it would be . . . to shut you up. Trying to draw out . . . the saliva. Water helps keep the wound clean . . . while the saliva seeps out."

She believed him. "The burning from the saliva is going away, but I'm still getting weaker."

The next time he spoke, his voice came out more even. Not so tight with pain. "I don't think I can pull the saliva out of you the way I can do it on myself. You're going to have to help with that."

"Guess this isn't a majik pond after all." Her knee had quieted to a dull thrum of hurt that still pulsated in time with each heartbeat. She couldn't see past hair that had fallen into her face. She tried to push it away with one hand.

"Hold your breath," he said right before he lowered her beneath the surface.

She sucked in a lungful of air just in time. He kept her against him, tucked within the grasp of his healthy arm. Beneath the water, she watched him go into a Zen-like state, eyes shut. Slowly, he moved his damaged arm away from his body.

Her stomach clenched at seeing his mangled arm in vivid detail.

He continued doing something, because muscle snaked around bone, straightening the arm as it floated.

The blood stopped oozing from his wounds. Loose muscle continued inching back into place. Bone extended, connecting broken pieces, all of it smoothing into normal shape.

She opened her mouth in shock and sucked in water, choking.

He lifted her up until her head broke the surface. She gasped for air, hacking up water.

Tristan snapped out a curse. "Thought you could hold your breath longer than that."

She coughed again. "How'd you do that?"

When he didn't answer, she turned to face him. He was staring at her with indecision at first. "You really don't know how to heal yourself?"

The last thing she wanted to do was admit a weakness to another person, especially a male, but he was insinuating this had to do with being an Alterant.

Tristan used his now-healing arm to wash the last of the mud still clinging to her hair.

She'd normally mouth off at him for acting as if he could do as he pleased with her, but she didn't have it in her to care at the moment.

Her entire body was ravaged and exhausted from the fight.

The demon's saliva continued to drain her life energy.

Her knee felt as if an elephant had stepped on it and she had the headache of death.

She heaved a sigh. "No, I have no idea how you healed yourself. And why didn't you shift to fight those demons?"

"Had to save my energy for . . . later." Tristan hoisted her into his arms, which were now both functioning.

Shifting into his Alterant state drained his energy? Interesting. He must have believed he could beat those demons without shifting and hadn't planned on the saliva killing his supernatural energy.

But what did he plan to do that was important enough for him to weigh saving his power for later?

She could ask him questions once they got out of here. Saving her leg came first, and he was still healing. "What are you doing to fix yourself?"

"If you really don't know how to heal yourself, we need to get busy. The longer that saliva is in your system the harder it is to draw out."

If she hadn't seen the repair to his arm with her own eyes, she wouldn't have believed him. "So how does this work?"

"I'll show you."

Wasn't that what Storm had said when she'd asked how the tracking majik worked?

Why couldn't men just give a straight answer once in a while? She didn't like the idea of trying something unknown, but she couldn't walk out of here.

"Show me," she told him.

"Hold still for a minute. I think I can finish drawing the saliva out of your leg now that I'm getting stronger. The rest is up to you."

Once the burning from the saliva eased, he stopped whispering his chant and walked to the bank. He sat on the ground, dripping water everywhere, and lowered her carefully to his lap.

She stared in awe at the amazing change when he flexed his damaged arm, where new skin had begun skimming over the once exposed muscle.

Tristan said, "I know it hurts, but you need to straighten out your leg."

She nodded, then sucked up her courage and slowly stretched out her leg, gritting her teeth and shaking with the effort. The bananas she'd eaten wanted to join the party, but she kept her mouth shut until her throat cleared. "Now what?"

"You know how to release your inner Alterant, right?"

"I've been forbidden from shifting." That was a safe answer. She was not telling him anything he could use against her at some point.

"I don't mean to change all the way to your beast state," Tristan qualified.

She gave him a look that suggested the demon saliva had reached his brain.

His eyebrows climbed his forehead. "How many times have you shifted?"

Once, all the way, but she wouldn't share that experience with anyone except Tzader and Quinn, since they were the only ones who knew. And she'd risked shifting that one time only to save all three of their lives. Those two Beladors would take her secret to their deathbeds.

She answered, "I just told you I'm not allowed to shift."

He shook his head in disbelief. "You don't know squat about being an Alterant, do you?"

"How am I supposed to know anything when the only person who might be able to tell me a few things won't?" she snapped.

"I can't help it if Brina kept us apart."

"We're together now," she pointed out.

He could have asked her for anything in trade at that moment and she would have been hard-pressed not to hand it over in exchange for her leg.

But he didn't try to barter, which surprised her almost as much as his not shifting into a beast earlier.

He explained, "I had a lot of time to experiment while stuck out here. I found stages of change from minor altering all the way to full beast state, but there's an initial phase of tapping power you can use and still not change into a beast."

If she said she wasn't curious she'd be lying. "How do I tap into that power?"

"You call up the Alterant beast slowly and feel the power seep into your blood and muscles and bone, stopping it short of the physical change from human to beast. If you do that, you can cure damn near anything. How do you think I survived living here? I was bitten by a fer-de-lance."

"What's that?"

"A huge pit viper with upper and lower fangs. The venom can kill within minutes of striking its prey."

She glanced around, now adding giant snakes to the list of nasties to watch out for. Should she trust anything Tristan was telling her, especially about tapping her inner Alterant?

He hadn't walked her into sunlight, and he hadn't taken advantage of her incapacitated position. Oddly enough, she wasn't freaking out about being held by him, which could be due solely to the shock of a crushed knee, almost dying and low blood pressure.

Opening her senses, she searched Tristan for some emotion, anything that might hint at his motive for trying to get her to risk changing into a beast.

Tristan hadn't survived all this time by being stupid. He would use any edge he could get in their alliance.

The minute she opened up to him a flood of reaction hit her. Spurts of anger . . . and frustration . . . that was understandable. He wouldn't have gotten over being furious at her . . . but . . . that wasn't all of it.

His central emotion came clear all at once.

Anger and frustration emerged from a ball of worry.

About her? Yes. Concern over her leg and her pain. Why would he care about a woman who had sent him back to prison?

"Evalle, the longer you wait the more difficult it will be to repair your knee." The grim set of his mouth said he meant that the longer she waited the more painful the repair would be. "If you're vacillating over trusting me, keep in mind I have nothing to gain by healing you and plenty to lose."

With her gut and her empathic side in unison, she

could only hope he was right about her doing this without shifting. "Tell me what to do."

"Close your eyes and think about the center of your body. It's a volcano that can erupt and destroy everything or just bubble up and pour streams of lava down the sides. That's what you're going to do with your power."

She listened to the cadence of his voice and focused on calling forth the power deep inside her.

Her beast roused.

She panicked and shut down the call, opening her eyes. "I can't do it. I'll change."

"So I'm that much better than you at being an Alterant?"

That just pissed her off. She didn't care if anyone heard her curse mentally. She clamped her eyelids shut and slowed her breathing. He started talking again.

She withdrew inside herself until she could feel the bubble of energy within her body.

Focusing on that, she started calling up her Alterant softly, willing her beast power to grow very slowly.

Warm fingers of strength began to ooze through her, just like a lava flow, easing out and touching the bruises on her chest and arms. They ached, but in a positive way. He instructed her to direct her energy down to her leg.

She did as he said and felt the stream slide along her thigh, then circle her knee, building up in that one spot until . . .

Evalle tensed against the burst of heat that seared her knee. She yelled when it wouldn't stop burning her flesh, and she fisted her hands, clinging tight to her sanity.

The white heat engulfed her until she was sure she'd

disintegrate like the demon she'd killed. But slowly the glowing white turned into a soothing fog of coolness she could breathe into her dry lungs again.

When she opened her eyes she had Tristan's healthy forearm in a grip tight enough to break a human's arm.

Sweat rolled down the sides of his face and veins corded his neck with strain.

She finally realized her knee had downgraded to a mild ache. Relaxing the muscles in her hands, she let go of his arm, where she'd left red marks that were sure to bruise. "Sorry. I didn't mean to . . . didn't know I was . . ."

"It's okay." He shook his arm as if to help circulation return.

She started to put her foot down and get out of his lap, but he stopped her. "Give it a couple minutes for the bones to finish bonding and you'll be able to put weight on it. Won't be strong for a little while, but you should be able to limp along without hurting yourself."

But now that excruciating pain no longer sidetracked her brain, she wasn't comfortable sitting in his lap.

A throaty growl from the encroaching jungle wiped away all her discomfort.

She looked up to see a pair of gold eyes staring at them from where the animal stood just inside the dark cover of thick vegetation.

She couldn't fight anything with claws and teeth yet. Tristan was likely in the same shape until he fully healed.

She whispered to him, "I say we risk me standing unless you can do your monkey whisperer thing with what's staring at us."

Tristan spoke loud, not even trying to shield his words. "There's nothing I can say to deter a demon."

Another demon? She couldn't prevent the tremble that shook her body at the idea of facing another fanged demon in her weakened state.

The golden eyes narrowed, then a black jaguar stepped into the clearing and raised up on his hind legs as energy shed across his body. He shifted into a man.

"Storm?" She couldn't believe her eyes or stop the quick smile that touched her lips.

No doubt about it. A naked, and furious, Storm.

He crossed his arms over his chest, not the least concerned over his lack of clothing.

Tristan's body tensed. His grip tightened.

"It's okay. I know him," Evalle mumbled to Tristan, a bit distracted. She tried not to look at Storm's profile, but her eyes had a mind of their own and kept wandering below his navel while she struggled to push up off Tristan's lap. Working part-time at the morgue in Atlanta, she'd seen plenty of male bodies, but not one so well . . . packaged. Literally.

Black hair fell dangerously around the copper skin covering wide shoulders. Bunched muscles curved and cut the lines of his chest where he crossed his arms, and more rippled along his abdomen when he breathed down to where . . . a loincloth appeared?

Storm glanced down at the brief length of what looked like buckskin covering his lower parts, then glared at Tristan. "Naked doesn't bother me at all. But I can see why *you* would be uncomfortable with the comparison."

Evalle looked back and forth between the men. Had Tristan put that loincloth on Storm?

Tristan helped Evalle to her feet and shrugged. "It should worry you to walk around naked . . . with so little to show."

Storm took a step toward Tristan, who turned toward him. Both bodies pumped with aggression.

Evalle had endured all the fighting she could for one day. "I'm in no mood to watch you two play mine's bigger."

Tristan smiled. "It's not necessary. I already know which one's bigger."

Storm stopped, but countered with, "Must be true what they say about the strides they're making with implants."

Before that got out of hand again, Evalle broke it up. "I say we get out of here before anything else attacks us."

Storm asked in a wisecracking voice, "What? Didn't enjoy the way he was mauling you? And who let him out of his cage?"

"He wasn't mauling me . . ." Her voice fell off when she caught the cold fury in Storm's eyes. She wasn't about to admit she had unintentionally helped Tristan escape. "We were on our way back to Atlanta and—"

"I was protecting her." Tristan moved closer to Evalle.

Storm eyed her knee where skin hadn't covered all the raw areas still healing. "Impressive job of protecting her. If I hadn't shown up she'd have been dead before she reached the next town."

Tristan hooked his arm around her in a possessive way that slid under her skin like sharp needles.

Unable to move away, she hissed at him, "Let go of me."

"No."

"Let go of me or I'll hurt you," she whispered.

"You didn't mind me carrying you into the lake for a bath."

She couldn't believe Tristan had said that and clearly for Storm's benefit. If she hadn't still been so unsteady on her one leg he would be sprawled on his butt. "Get your hands off me."

"Do as she says," Storm warned.

"Or you'll hurt me?" Tristan chuckled.

"I won't hurt you." Storm smiled with evil intent. "Well, maybe when I snap your neck, but you won't feel it for long."

A strong emotion from Storm reached her. He was angry . . . no, not exactly.

He was . . . jealous? Really? That brightened her day.

The stupids must have set in again.

Tristan grinned, taunting Storm with, "Come on. I'd like a jaguar rug for my next apartment."

Evalle jerked away from Tristan, keeping herself turned slightly away from Storm or she wouldn't be able to think. "I don't have time for a testosterone battle. And neither do you, Tristan, if we're going to find those three Alterants."

"So you're working with him now?" Storm asked.

Tristan's smile widened.

Evalle glared at Tristan to cut it out, then looked over her shoulder at Storm. "We have an agreement."

The look of disappointment on Storm's face crushed

her. He had come for her just as he'd promised, but would he understand why she had to stick with Tristan?

"Not so fast," Tristan told her. "We had an agreement that did not include him."

She swung back around. "What do you mean?"

Tristan raised his hands, palm out. "If that tomcat found his way here, then he can find his way to the next town. Storm goes or I go."

Storm said nothing, which worried her a lot more than his anger. What did he think? That she'd been allowing Tristan to touch her body . . . *that* way?

As if.

Evalle couldn't afford to lose Tristan, but neither would she abandon Storm after he'd come all the way down here to find her. She told Tristan, "You're not going anywhere without me if you expect me to speak to the Tribunal for you."

Tristan's eyes moved from Storm to Evalle, making a decision. "Remember when I told you gods and goddesses could be tricky? You said Loki's exact words were 'Let the one who returns the three escaped Alterants to VIPER be cleared of prior transgressions.' I don't need you to talk to the Tribunal. All I have to do is show up with those three to negotiate for my freedom. And finding them shouldn't be a problem, since I'm the one who told those three where to hide in Atlanta."

Tristan was going to snake her deal with the Tribunal. "You son of a—"

He shook his finger back and forth. "Uh-uh. Brina doesn't like her minions to curse. Make up your mind if it's me or him if you want to continue our partnership."

"It's not technically a partnership," she said for Storm's benefit. "Just an agreement."

Tristan wouldn't relent. "You with me or him?"

"You know I need your help." The disgusted sound that erupted behind Evalle lowered her expectations of smoothing this over soon with Storm. Surely he realized she would not leave him here. Nobody was going anywhere until she got things straight with Storm first.

Not that she should care what he thought with so much at stake, but she did. His disappointment ate at the happiness that had bloomed over seeing him here.

She said in a firm voice, "I'm not leaving anyone here."

"Can either of you teleport?" Tristan asked.

"No," Evalle snapped, losing patience. "What's your point?"

"I can." Tristan vanished.

"Blast it!" She turned to Storm, saying, "I can't believe he can still tele—"

Storm was gone, too.

FOURTEEN

Evalle shut her eyes, then opened them again, willing Storm to still be standing there.

Nope. No Storm. No Tristan.

Nothing but vine-strangled jungle surrounded the small clearing near the lake where she stood.

Where had Storm gone? Had Tristan taken him . . . or harmed him?

Nobody could have luck this crappy but her.

She raised her fist to the heavens. "I have had it! Just kill me now and spare me all this crap!"

"What's your problem?"

She jumped and lowered her arms to find Storm standing right in front of her. Pain, aggravation and frustration balled in her chest. He'd just made her crazy by disappearing. "Where in the blazes did you go?"

"To put on real clothes. I had a canvas bag I can hook my neck through to carry clothes with me for shifting back into human form." He wore a pair of faded jeans and a dark brown T-shirt.

Her heart did that weird dance it had been perfecting every time this Skinwalker was around.

Which she was not letting him know after he'd glared at her and acted as if she'd allowed Tristan to grope her. What had all that posturing between him and Tristan been about?

He was *still* glaring at her. "Back to why you were asking to be struck down where you stand? What's your problem?"

"I'll tell you what my problem is, Storm. First you change my aura to gold, then you act like I was committing a crime with Tristan."

"Letting him out of his cage *and* allowing him to touch you *are* crimes." The fierce edge in his voice had a ring of possessiveness.

The steamy air between them shuddered with awareness.

She'd consider how she felt about that later when she didn't have to find a way back to another continent. "I didn't let him out, not intentionally." She was not going into detail about how Tristan had grabbed her and lunged through the invisible barrier. "Tristan had agreed to help me."

Storm made a sound that couldn't have been construed as flattering. "Help you do what? Practice for a wet T-shirt contest?"

Out of a knee-jerk reaction, she looked down to see her soaked shirt clinging to her breasts. Her nipples puckered. She crossed her arms over the damning mammaries and glared at him.

She refused to feel guilty about any of this. "Demons attacked us. One of them ripped up his arm." That didn't faze Storm, whose eyes still narrowed with dark thoughts. She added, "And they crushed my knee. Tristan carried me here with his only good arm so we could wash the demons' saliva out of our wounds."

The swift change in Storm's face from anger to concern trimmed the edge off her irritation, but his face closed down again just as fast. He eyed her leg suspiciously. "Doesn't look crushed."

"That's what I've been trying to tell you. When you walked up, he was showing me how to heal myself."

"What *exactly* did Dr. Tristan show you?"

Sarcasm did nothing to improve her mood. She should be getting frostbite from his cool reserve, but Storm didn't seem as angry as before.

She huffed out a long breath and tried once more to clear up Storm's misconception. "Tristan has more experience than me at being an Alterant and knows how to control the change to his beast. He taught me how to tap levels of power before shifting so I could heal safely."

Feet apart and arms crossed, Storm might as well have had a Not Sold sign hanging from his neck. "So you shifted."

"No, of course not. That's the great part. I only *drew* on my Alterant powers." She couldn't get past his stony exterior. Or that suspicious glint in his eyes. "What's with you? Ten minutes ago I faced losing my leg . . . and probably my life. Never mind."

She took an angry sidestep and grimaced at the pain still streaking up her leg.

Concern broke through his hard gaze. "Your leg was really crushed?"

"Yes."

Storm squatted down, studying her exposed knee and bloody jeans where claws had clearly ripped open the material. He lifted shredded flaps of material aside and touched the swollen skin gently until she hissed. "How bad is it?"

"Tolerable, but it's healing by the minute." She avoided putting more weight on her leg, and shrugged. "It's sore, but I can walk through the pain."

His shoulders relaxed when he stood. He lifted his fingers to her face. "I don't like seeing you hurt."

Her heart squirmed under the look he gave her, as if he wanted to maim anyone who harmed her. "I need to get moving to figure out where Tristan went. How'd you find me?"

He scanned around them while he answered. "I had some help. I gave it an hour once I left you around midnight, then I contacted Nicole and asked her to locate the amulet."

Evalle hadn't wanted to involve Nicole, especially since Nicole's life partner, Red, didn't like Evalle and hadn't been happy about Evalle bringing Storm in jaguar form around Nicole two nights ago. "You woke up Red? She'll give Nicole grief over this."

Storm's gaze stopped wandering around and met Evalle's. "I'd have dragged Sen out of bed to find you if I'd thought I could make him tell me anything."

How was she supposed to hold onto any anger when he said things like that? "But Nicole only put a temporary invisibility spell on this amulet when we borrowed it. I don't understand."

"I put a protection spell on the amulet the last time I saw you."

That's why the thing had been warming and glowing right before something had attacked her. Storm had been trying to protect her from a distance. "But how did Nicole determine where I was this quickly?"

"She used a scrying bowl to narrow the location of the amulet to this region, and I had access to a private jet."

Who did he know with a private jet? But she didn't want to waste time by interrupting.

Storm shrugged, saying, "I grew up in Chile and roamed all over this country. Once I got here it was just a matter of tracking you by the majik I used on . . ."

When his voice drifted off, his lips tightened into a frown of remorse.

But she'd caught his slip, which reminded her that she had a serious beef with him. "Speaking of the majik that changed my aura—what'd you do? It's gold!"

He heaved a sigh. "I don't know."

"Wrong answer. Fix it."

"Not sure I can, but you don't have time for that right now anyhow if you intend to find Tristan. I'm assuming you had some plan in mind while traipsing around with him."

That blasted Tristan.

Sure, he'd patched up her leg, but he could have teleported the whole time they'd been together. If he'd spirited them away from the demons, she wouldn't have suffered a crushed knee.

And he hadn't shifted. Had he been saving energy to teleport?

She let that go in favor of getting on the move. "Tristan

knows where the other Alterants are in Atlanta and agreed
to help me locate them."

"He was lying to you."

"Maybe about helping me, but I believe he was telling the truth about the Alterants being in Atlanta." Even
though Tristan had lied by omission he hadn't taken her
dagger again or left her stranded, when he could have.
She hadn't figured that one out. Why had Tristan stayed
with her? No time to waste on that right now. She glanced
around, defeat closing in on her with too far to travel in
little time. "Any chance you've figured out how to track
teleporting?"

"No. If he was headed back to Atlanta, call Tzader or
Quinn so they can start looking for him while we head
back."

"I can't ask anyone for help, especially them. The Tribunal
forbade it." Then a thought struck her.

She hadn't tried any of the gifts because she could only
use them for the explicit reason of finding the escaped
Alterants and bringing them in.

"What, Evalle?"

"The Tribunal gave me three gifts." She got excited. "I
think I know how to track Tristan." In her mind, she had
to find Tristan to locate the missing Alterants, therefore
she could call upon a gift.

But if her reasoning was wrong, she had no idea what
the fallout would be.

"Then do it," Storm encouraged.

Using one gift now left just two for capturing three
Alterants *and* dealing with Tristan at large.

She had no choice, but that didn't make her happy about what she had to do. "I can't believe I'm going to burn a gift on this," she muttered.

"On what?" Storm stepped close to her.

"Teleporting. And I don't know how to do it, so I'll probably throw up the entire way and . . ." She lifted her gaze to him. "I can't leave you, but I might do something wrong and hurt you if I don't do this right."

Storm pulled her into his arms.

She sank against him, enjoying the feel of his body next to hers.

He lowered his head and told her, "I'll keep you from getting sick. Call on the gift."

She opened her mouth to speak, but his lips covered hers.

Since meeting Storm she'd come to realize that kissing cured a lot of ailments.

His mouth managed to suck all the fight out of her. His hands tucked her closer, but carefully. As if he knew just how far to test her ability to be touched. She'd never let anyone kiss her or get close enough to touch her since escaping that basement.

Not until meeting Storm just a few days ago.

He paused and lifted his head. "Teleport us now or we won't be leaving here for hours."

It wasn't what he said so much as the serious intent in his voice and stark hunger turning his eyes black that got her moving.

She didn't hesitate. "By the Tribunal power gifted me, I command that Storm and I be teleported along the same path as Tristan."

The world started spinning as a thought hit her.

What if Tristan teleported somewhere dangerous that he was prepared for, but she and Storm would not be? What if . . .

Storm folded her close to him and kissed her again, pushing thoughts of anything but him from her mind.

An unfamiliar need coiled hot and urgent inside her. His lips caressed hers, his tongue playful. Fingers slid down to her hips, gently moving her snug against him.

Heat rippled through her abdomen.

He whispered calm words between kisses pressed along her neck. She shivered, longed for what his kiss promised. Her body urged her into his touch.

This was the only way to teleport.

He kissed her cheek once, twice.

She leaned back against his arm and turned her head, sucking in a breath when his lips caressed her throat.

All at once the swirling colors melded into distinct lines.

The ride was almost over. Too soon.

She smiled when Storm paused then kissed her again.

Did he do everything with this intense focus? As her feet touched solid ground again, Storm's chest expanded with a deep breath. He released a groan as if he was just as disappointed as she was to realize their trip would end soon.

He cupped her face and whispered, "Welcome to Air Evalle. Coffee, tea . . . or this." He kissed her again, murmuring, "Keep your eyes closed."

She smiled around his lips and followed his advice.

One day when this was over, maybe she would . . .

Day.

A new worry hit her with brutal swiftness. If Tristan had teleported to Atlanta, that's where she and Storm were landing.

It would be . . . afternoon. Right now.

What if the sun blazed overhead?

Still clinging to Storm, Evalle opened her eyes to a glint of brilliant light.

FIFTEEN

Tzader paced the boardroom on the eighteenth floor of Quinn's building, one of several he owned in downtown Atlanta.

His gut said not to do this, especially to Vladimir Quinn.

Not that Tzader wanted to risk destroying *any* person's mind, but Quinn and Evalle were his closest friends.

Next to Brina.

He stopped pacing. How could Brina think he didn't put her safety first? What was going on with her?

She was his world.

Her idea of searching Conlan O'Meary's mind had some validity. A slim possibility of gaining information, but enough that Tzader couldn't refuse in good conscience.

And Quinn was the best they had at navigating a mind.

Quinn's dry Oxford tone broke into Tzader's thoughts. *I'll be up in a moment. I took care of Evalle's job at the morgue on my way here.*

Where do they think she is?

On personal leave. She may not like my interfering, but she's getting my help this time whether she wants it or not.

Leave it to Quinn to pull strings to ensure that Evalle still had her grunt job once she appeased the Tribunal.

She put a higher value on independence than an asthmatic put on oxygen.

She'll appreciate that, Tzader said.

Perhaps. Then Quinn was gone.

The antique clock on the side table dinged softly five times. This late on a Friday afternoon, rush hour traffic heated tempers in any city, but if that sulfur fog descended on the streets of Atlanta this evening the highways would turn into bloody battle zones.

Quinn entered the conference room on a calm stride, but tension lined his forehead. He punched buttons on his smart phone. His cinderblock gray European suit fit his athletic build with a precision only the best tailors could offer. Women seemed to like all that fancy trimming and upper-crust British accent, one of his finer qualities acquired *after* early years spent in Russian ghettos.

Tzader stopped pacing and glanced at the door. "Where's Conlan?"

"Our young O'Meary is on his way here. Then he'll have to be cleared through building security."

When Tzader quirked an eyebrow in amusement, Quinn chuckled and shrugged. "I must keep up appearances at all my corporate properties."

Metal detectors couldn't detect a weapon warded against view, like the two sentient blades hanging from Tzader's belt. The blades had snarled at the security personnel when Tzader had passed through the scanner, but they were invisible to human eyes and machines when he needed them to be.

Quinn stopped fiddling with his phone and slipped it into a pocket inside his jacket. "I heard about beast attacks on my flight back from D.C. I assume these are Alterants, based upon the lurid descriptions. What's going on?"

"I just left a meeting at VIPER. There's a mysterious fog that hovers close to the ground around all these attacks. Has a sulfuric odor and causes everyone it touches to turn aggressive and mean, instant road rage mentality. Bad as that is, this fog appears to be a catalyst for forcing Alterants to shift. We're up to a hundred and thirty-four that we know about that have shifted in different parts of the country."

"I saw a low-hanging haze that covered a massive section of Virginia we flew over. A dull yellow color."

"That's it."

"What—or who—is causing the fog?"

Tzader rubbed his chin and let out a weary breath. "I'd say we don't know, but some people are jumping to conclusions about Alterants in general."

Quinn made the mental leap Tzader expected. "Any word on Evalle?"

"Yes, but what Sen told me after the briefing isn't good."

"Let me guess. Mr. Charm wanted to gloat over Evalle being outside our reach right now?"

"I wish that was all. He said Tristan has escaped again." Tzader had barely restrained himself from wiping the smile from Sen's face.

"The Alterant we just put away *yesterday*? Whose bloody fault was that?"

"According to the Tribunal, Evalle is behind the escape."

Something vile and Russian hissed from between Quinn's lips, sounding as deadly as Tzader's thoughts. Quinn crossed the room and stopped next to Tzader where he stared out the window.

No yellow haze had formed in Atlanta. Yet.

Tzader told him the rest. "The Tribunal believes Evalle and Tristan could be connected to the fog, that they're trying to build an army from the shifting Alterants."

"That's absurd."

"It's absurd that *Evalle* would do this, but Tristan's a wild card," Tzader said. "However, none of the Alterants currently shifting have green eyes that we know of."

"Then how can they tie this to Tristan and Evalle? Maybe these things aren't Alterants. That's like saying anything with a mane, four legs and a tail is a horse, but not distinguish that a zebra or giraffe might be different."

"I agree, but the Tribunal isn't making that distinction," Tzader explained. "Sen indicated the Tribunal sent Evalle on a task with a time limit. Once Tristan escaped, the Tribunal issued a decree to kill *all* Alterants on sight, regardless of the color of their eyes." Just saying those words out loud froze the blood in Tzader's veins.

"Bloody hell. Why don't they send Sen after her? Even if *we* don't know what he is, the Tribunal must, and he's pretty damn powerful. He could find her before anyone else."

"Sen says he's been given parameters for bringing her back that he can't discuss, and the Tribunal won't touch her until her time is up. Even if Sen could go to Evalle, do you really think he wouldn't take advantage of a shoot-to-kill order?"

"The one time Captain Dickhead could really help," Quinn ground out. He backhanded his fist into the window frame, denting it. For someone who prided himself on maintaining control, Quinn still had a temper. "Why is VIPER letting this fog still spread?"

"Because no one, not even the deities associated with VIPER, can stop it."

"With all the power we control in the coalition, we can't stop this? Why not?"

That was what Tzader had been asking everyone at VIPER for the past hour. He'd even contacted Macha, who'd been unable to affect the stinking fog that continued to leach through coastal states only. "No one knows for sure, but VIPER resources are speculating that it might take either the person who created the fog or someone who can wield the same majik to influence it."

"The fact that this fog can cause immediate aggression in humans and trigger Alterants to shift into beasts would suggest that it's sentient."

"That's what I'm thinking," Tzader agreed. The fog had taken on a living quality.

"We've got to find Evalle before someone cuts her down."

"I know, but no one is telling us anything, including Brina."

Quinn's expression offered consolation. "And you don't want to press her until we have something on the traitor to give her?"

"Not with Brina on a tear right now. Evalle needs

Brina on her side, since she's the most powerful person allowed to accompany Evalle in the Tribunal meetings. I figure if we can convince Brina that Conlan's not a threat, and show her we're doing all we can to find the traitor, she'll support helping Evalle." And maybe realize Tzader put Brina's safety first above everything.

He'd intervened to protect Brina many times since meeting her when she was fourteen. He'd lost his heart the first time he'd heard her laugh. The sound had stayed with him like a favorite song playing over and over in his mind. She'd been laughing at how he'd missed a bull's-eye by an inch with his knife, but she hadn't known that he'd been practicing with his nondominant hand. He'd been so taken with her that he'd let her believe she'd out-matched him when she'd tossed her dagger and stabbed dead center.

Her father had warned Tzader long ago that she'd heel to no man's command except the Treoir patriarch, and at times she tested limits even with him. Tzader had smiled, thanking her father for his advice and more determined than ever to win the heart of the Treoir jewel.

Both of their fathers had wanted this union. Everyone had.

None as much as Tzader.

Had Brina really stopped loving him?

Something must have changed. She'd made it clear she wanted to break off their relationship.

Quinn spoke, pulling Tzader back to the issue with Evalle. "The Tribunal might forbid us from contacting Evalle—"

Tzader interrupted. "The Tribunal has ordered her not to contact us."

"That would explain why we haven't been able to reach her telepathically, and Brina would have to support a Tribunal declaration."

"I'll stand down from going after Evalle if Brina can explain how leaving Evalle to be hunted like a dog by VIPER is honorable."

Quinn curved his lips in a grim reaper smile. "In other words, we begin searching by sunset."

"Right."

A voice came into Tzader's mind, asking, *Maistir?*

Tzader answered, *Yes?*

Conlan O'Meary reporting in. I'm entering the building now.

Tzader sent back, *Very good.* He said to Quinn, "Conlan said he's on the way in. Sure you still want to do this probe?"

"We all do things we'd rather not, including Brina. Perhaps she is more objective than you or I. However, I feel the need to point out that Conlan had an alibi for the night the traitor lured us into that Medb trap in Utah."

Tzader had also considered what had happened two years ago. He owed his life to Quinn and Evalle, who had been linked to him when they'd battled the Medb to escape. He'd suffered a fatal wound, which he'd survived only because neither Quinn nor Evalle would unlink even though they could have died with him.

Nodding, Tzader said, "I've thought about that. Conlan has the ability to split his image. He could have left a lifelike replica at his home while he traveled to the Salt Flats the day we were captured by the Medb. The only way we'd have known was if we'd sent someone capable of telling the difference to interact with the copy at his home. None of us suspected him of anything back then, so that didn't happen."

"Good point."

Tzader wished he had Quinn's mind lock ability so he could be the one taking the risk. He'd been hunting the traitor every minute he could spare from his Maistir duties. When he did find that rat bastard he was going to make him regret the day he was born.

Quinn flexed his hand. "It's been a while since I probed someone's subconscious this deeply, and, if you recall, the last time ended in less than ideal results."

"That's a diplomatic way to say the guy stroked out during the session," Tzader joked. "He was a troll convicted of eating a human family. If you hadn't gone that deep we'd have never found where his sidekick was hiding. Saved a pile of lives with that get." Tzader scratched his chin. "And imploding his brain wasn't your fault either."

"If I hadn't opened a path for the demonic spirit hunting the troll to reach through and take control of his mind, the troll would have survived."

Tzader started to question his friend's barometer for justice when Quinn added, "Don't get me wrong. I have no sympathy for a psychopathic predator. I just believe he deserved a far less humane punishment than a quick death."

But something had Quinn more contemplative than usual. Tzader asked, "You think something is hiding in Conlan's subconscious?"

"Not really," Quinn said, still sounding distracted. "He's a decent man and a loyal Belador. He's . . . I don't know. Just thinking out loud."

"I know. I don't like either one of you doing this." Tzader turned to peer out the window at people scurrying along Peachtree Street, oblivious to the potential threat. He hated not being able to warn the public, but humans couldn't contain the fog if VIPER couldn't.

Panic would only add to the crisis.

If the traitor was tied to the Alterants in any way, Brina was right to push for an answer now, but Tzader wanted to give Quinn one last chance to step aside. "It's your decision, but keep in mind that I need you out in the field helping us fight this fog and beasts more than I need you in here taking this gamble."

Quinn held up his hand. "I couldn't allow someone else to try this. We've never had a druid who can match my ability to mind lock. And even if a druid searched Conlan's mind first and didn't find anything, I would still have to probe a second time. That would force Conlan to endure the mental plundering and risk twice. Besides, there's only danger if we're wrong about his being innocent."

Tzader understood all that on a logical level, but the "what if" factor still hung in the air. Evalle wouldn't forgive him if Quinn came out of this with scrambled brains . . . or dead.

And he wouldn't deserve forgiveness.

Thinking of her, Tzader asked, "Have you heard anything on Storm once we split up last night?"

"Can't be found."

Tzader cut a sharp look at Quinn. "You mean like not-in-the-city gone?"

"Yes. You said Evalle learned about the Alterants shifting from Storm. I'm thinking they spoke on her way to the Tribunal meeting last night. I touched base with Devon Fortier this morning before I left for D.C. He's investigating a troll operation tied to the local sting I'm running and had a team following a lead at the Amtrak station last night. They needed a tracker. He tried reaching Storm for almost two hours before Storm appeared close to midnight."

"Any chance Storm mentioned seeing Evalle, or if he knew about her being attacked on the way to the Tribunal meeting?"

"I did inquire. Devon said Storm tracked down one troll in record time, then disappeared. Storm didn't say a word about anyone. No one has seen or heard from the chap since."

Tzader slammed his fist into his palm. "That had to be why Evalle was running late coming to Woodruff Park. She probably got waylaid by him."

"True, but she's a big girl even if we think she's still that skinny little warrior we had to force to stop using a storage room as an apartment."

"She's naïve when it comes to men."

"Inexperienced, maybe," Quinn argued, then his voice dropped into a solemn tone. "But I doubt she's naïve."

Tzader understood Quinn's meaning. Having observed Evalle for the past couple of years, they'd agreed that she might have suffered beyond being locked in a basement for eighteen years.

Someone had harmed her physically.

She was powerful enough to defend herself against any human, but humans weren't his concern at the moment.

"I see your point," Tzader admitted, grinding his fist harder. "But that doesn't mean she's ready for someone like Storm."

Quinn gave a bark of laughter.

He spun around. "What?"

"You sound like an overbearing father. We can't protect her from everything."

Tzader muttered, "We can from a few hard tails—"

Quinn turned serious. "I've watched him the few times he's been around her. I think the greatest danger is to someone who threatens her. Which reminds me, did Sen indicate he knew anything about the attack on Evalle, since he had to have shown up at the same time?"

"No, the prick stonewalled when I asked. Said he couldn't discuss Tribunal business."

"One of these days . . . ," Quinn started, eyes thinned with malice.

A knock at the door turned Quinn's attention. "Come in."

Conlan O'Meary entered the room, first nodding at Tzader, then noticing Quinn. The young man had filled out his lanky frame with whipcord muscle. His half-inch-long light brown hair stuck up on top, similar to styles on most of the young businessmen Tzader had passed coming into the building. Wireless glasses warmed his gray eyes and toned down the lethal air he'd exhibited in training.

Right now those eyes were doing a jam-up job of hiding the debate that had to be going on inside Conlan's mind at his realization that no druid was present.

Any Belador would expect a druid to normally perform a mind probe, but druids could occasionally be fooled.

Not Quinn.

With a hint of regret in his voice, Quinn offered Conlan, "You may withdraw your consent to do this if you'd like."

But all three of them knew that would mark Conlan as highly suspicious.

Shaking his head, Conlan broke out a grin that screamed innocent. "I got nothing to hide. Knock yourself out."

Tzader hoped he was telling the truth and was not the same type of brilliant actor Conlan's father had been for all those years. So brilliant that no Belador had realized he'd been selling out his people to the Medb.

SIXTEEN

Storm wanted the ability to teleport. Evalle had never been this responsive or allowed him to hold her so long. Good thing the spinning was ending and their feet touched solid ground. He couldn't keep his body from reacting when he had her in his arms.

If he had any doubt about when she transitioned back to reality in Atlanta, Evalle cleared that up when she shouted, *"Suuunnn!"*

He twisted his neck to see what was behind him.

Her sensitive eyes hadn't adjusted as quickly as his. That bright light bearing down on them was not the sun, but almost as bad. *"A train!"*

He shoved her up against a concrete wall seconds before a MARTA subway train barreled through the narrow tunnel just inches behind his back. The wheels clacked against the tracks in a deafening roar, and a torrent of wind sucked in behind when the last car whizzed past.

But, hallelujah, they had arrived in a dark tunnel. Underground, where the sun couldn't harm Evalle.

Might take a few minutes to get his heart back under control, though.

He should have been prepared for landing in any location. Like broad daylight on a Friday afternoon *or* in the middle of a train track.

She'd distracted the hell out of him, but catching her with her guard down long enough to taste those sweet lips had been . . . damn fine.

Her hands came up between them so fast that Storm didn't have a chance to move before she shoved hard enough to send him flying across the tracks.

His back slammed the concrete wall on the far side and he slid down. Out of fighting instinct, he landed in a crouch. He twisted his head back and forth to clear the stars in his vision and groaned.

She was damned strong when she drew on her powers.

He shook off his aches, stood up and headed back to her.

"Uh, Storm, that was sort of an accident." She didn't move, but she'd also taken a battle stance and had her fists cocked.

Always expecting to fight.

He kept coming at a steady pace, but he dropped his hands loose at his sides to show he was no threat.

Her wary tone switched to the angry one she pulled out whenever he made her nervous. "Served you right, though. If you didn't want to get hurt, you shouldn't have pinned me down."

He could sense a lie faster than any man-made device.

She'd just told the absolute truth.

Someone had pinned her down at one time . . . and hurt her.

His jaguar roused, ready to hunt. Storm forced himself back under control, but if he ever found out who had hurt her, he would . . . what?

He knew what. That person would only live long

enough to beg for her forgiveness. He had a connection to Evalle he didn't understand beyond the fact that she was under his protection for as long as he could stay.

When he reached the other side of the tracks, he stopped in front of her, heartened to see she didn't back away. Her pride wouldn't allow it, but he hoped that also meant she knew he'd never harm her.

His past could hurt her, though.

The woman he hunted still presented a deadly threat to Evalle if his visions were correct. They'd never been wrong yet. He intended to keep Evalle close while he found a way to stop that bitch who had killed his father.

Lifting his hand slowly to Evalle's face, he ignored the surge of hostility that sheared off of her. He understood defense mechanisms a person turned to for survival. Sunglasses hid her green eyes, but he'd seen the glittering jewels set in an exotic shape. Makeup had probably never touched her honey-colored skin, and she didn't need any. Straight black hair slid along her shoulders and halfway down her back.

And don't get him started on her soft lips.

A natural beauty, but prickly as a cactus.

Carefully placing his palm on her cheek, he barely touched her.

That took the steam out of her hostility and replaced it with a blanket of confusion. Better. He liked her to be a little out of step at times, but he hated to see that haunted look in her eyes. "Sorry I crowded you. No harm done. Besides, you can't hurt me."

"What are you . . . bulletproof?"

"Maybe."

"You might be bulletproof, but are you *Alterant* proof?" she tossed back.

Hearing her sassy confidence back in place gave him the opening to spin her off balance again. "The only thing in question is whether I'm Evalle proof."

Her lips parted and curiosity skittered through her eyes before she clamped her lips together.

Smiling right now would probably get him knocked back over the tracks.

He didn't care. He grinned.

She gritted her teeth then crossed her arms, tapping her foot. Thoughts pummeled her face, shifting her eyes with something she finally accepted with a shrug. "I get it. You're being nice to me so I'll help you find that woman."

His throat muscles tightened against a growl of irritation. He *had* used that reason to convince her he needed her help. He did have to find the Ashaninka witch doctor who'd killed his father and still possessed both Storm's and his father's souls. His ability to determine if someone was lying or not originated with his Ashaninka roots.

The counter side of that gift was incapacitating pain that would stroke through his whole body if *he* told a lie.

He'd learned to be clever about his words when stuck between telling the truth and withholding information, such as a few days ago when he'd had to report to Sen about Evalle while they'd hunted the Kujoo . . . and this morning when she'd asked about her aura.

Shading the truth still hurt, but he could hide those aches. Blatantly lying brought on excruciating pain.

She looked up and down the dimly lit tunnel. "I've got to get rolling. Oh, crap!" She grabbed her head.

"What's wrong?"

"Nothing . . . give me a minute." She gasped short breaths for a few seconds, then slowly lowered her arms. "I should have thought about how bad this would be in Atlanta."

"What happened to you?"

She rubbed her neck. "Telepathy. Tzader probably has everyone trying to reach me. I had my mental shields up even in South America, but Trey just tried. He's like a mega-powerful telepath to begin with and just had his power ramped up so high his call to me was like having a loudspeaker shouting next to my ear. Even with my shields beefed up to where I won't hear anyone else, Trey's voice feels like the constant thump of a bass drum."

"Did he realize you were here?"

She shook her head, then stopped with a grunt of pain. "I don't think so. Can you track Tristan?"

"I can now." The residue from that Alterant had been stinking up Storm's nasal passages since they'd landed here. He pointed to his right in the direction of the train that had just passed them and started walking. "We're going to have to get through this tunnel quickly—between trains."

Evalle fell into step with him, quiet at first and staring ahead. She finally asked, "I said I'd help you and I will. What's the deal with finding that woman?"

That woman. Storm enjoyed a moment over her little bout of jealousy. It soothed his own from earlier with Tristan. "She's not a problem right now. I've got some time until I need to hunt for her."

He expected Evalle to press him over not answering her question, but she trudged along with her own thoughts while he tracked. He *had* told Evalle the truth about seeing her in a vision with the Ashaninka woman, but he hadn't explained why he needed Evalle's help to locate her.

In his vision, the Ashaninka witch doctor intended to kill Evalle.

Not as long as there was breath in his body.

Storm just couldn't pinpoint when to expect the witch doctor because his visions had no time element. Sometimes a vision would be realized within hours and other times it could take weeks or months.

When he'd had the latest vision just hours before Evalle had been on the way to meet with the Tribunal, Storm had come up with the only way she'd permit him to use his majik on her. He'd had to convince her that *he* needed *her* help or Evalle wouldn't have agreed to let him use majik for her benefit.

She'd go to her death protecting the world.

He'd have hunted her down no matter what.

She'd raided his dreams every night since he'd first set eyes on her, to the point he woke up exhausted. His body searched for her when he was awake. Thankfully, she'd allowed him to mark her with his scent, though she hadn't exactly realized what he'd been doing with the majik.

But why had the majik altered her aura from silver to gold?

Gold, silver or no aura, she was . . . exceptional, a fiery emerald you found tucked into a tight spot.

A gemstone that had to be lifted gently and held carefully, but when it glowed there was no equal.

He could accept lusting after a woman, but wanting more with any woman wouldn't fit in his plans. Not with his unfinished witch doctor business.

But he'd be lying to himself if he called this intense desire for Evalle merely physical.

And if she knew how much he wanted her she'd run faster than a gazelle chased by a lion.

She tapped one hand against her thigh in a sign that she was churning mentally on something that aggravated her. "You never answered my question about this woman you're after."

Guess he'd have to give her something.

"My father met her when he went to South America to help remote tribes, sort of a Navajo missionary, if you will. He was a shaman, but he felt many in his tribe had abandoned the old ways and lost touch with their rituals. He wanted to help other tribes preserve their ways."

"Why did he choose South America?"

Storm mentally picked through how much to share. "He had a friend who had started outreach-type programs for more primitive tribes to show them how to hold onto their culture while accepting aid to survive. My father decided to try it for six months, but he ended up staying. The Ashaninka welcomed him and treated him well . . . all but one. The woman I'm searching for repaid his kindness by stealing from him and causing his death."

She'd tricked his father and stolen his soul, then killed him. When Storm had found his father's cold body, he'd been out of his mind with wanting to find the killer. She'd used Storm's grief to convince him she could show him the face of his father's murderer.

She had, right before she'd taken control of Storm's soul.

But he was more powerful than his father and had attacked her before she'd been able to turn him into her personal demon. She'd escaped, but he would find her.

How would Evalle react if I told her I had no soul? The few who'd known that about Storm back in South America had called him a demon and tried to kill him.

"What did this woman steal?" Evalle asked.

"We both have secrets. I don't push you to share yours," he said as gently as possible. When Evalle nodded, he changed the subject. "Let's find your three Alterants, then we'll look for my target."

"*Four* Alterants now that Tristan is free."

"He might not make it back to a cage," Storm added darkly.

She cut eyes loaded with warning at him. "He's the only one who knows where the other three are hiding. You can't kill him."

Yet. Storm nodded his understanding, not his agreement.

He held Tristan responsible for the trouble Evalle was in with the Tribunal. Tristan clearly intended to use what she'd shared about her chance for freedom to cut his own deal with the Tribunal. Tristan should have thought about his future when he'd teamed up with the Kujoo.

Storm tracked Tristan's scent up and down the tunnels. After a while he started thinking Tristan had taken precautions in case Evalle had found a way to follow his teleporting. By late afternoon Storm was sure of it. He literally hit a wall in tracking, a concrete one where Tristan's trail ended, meaning he'd likely teleported away or to the other side.

Why had he spent the time leading them on a chase? Why hadn't Tristan just teleported again in case he could have lost her at some point?

"That's it for his scent," Storm announced. "What do you want to do?"

She brushed loose hairs off her face with an absent-minded move. Her sunglasses hid any signs of exhaustion in her eyes, but no matter how often he'd adjusted his speed for her, she'd limped and lagged behind most of the last hour.

She finally admitted, "I'm beat and hungry."

"There's a service exit up ahead. The last two we passed were locked. Think you can open that one?"

She gave him a sly arch of her eyebrow. "I'm insulted you have to ask."

At the exit door, she raised her hands and moved her fingers in the air. A click on the inside of the door sounded, then the door swung open to expose a long hallway.

He followed her inside, noting how she closed and locked the door kinetically without even turning around. After passing through another door, they mingled with a crowd headed toward the wide concrete stairs that led to street level.

Putting his hand out, he stopped her, pretty sure he'd heard an encouraging sound upstairs. "Give me a minute."

"For what?"

"To see what the weather looks like up there. The sun hasn't set yet."

"Oh, that's right. My body clock is way off."

He ran up the steps, glad to see dark clouds to go along with the thunder he'd heard rumbling. Hurrying back down, he snagged her arm. "We're good. Bad weather coming."

"I feel guilty about being glad when it's going to make traffic worse," Evalle said. Her torn jeans received several double looks before being dismissed with pity reserved for the destitute.

Once he reached the sidewalk along Peachtree Street in downtown Atlanta, he casually offered, "We could go to Six Feet Under for a quick bite, and you can crash at my place if you don't want to run into Tzader or Quinn."

The hard part of having Evalle that close would be not touching her, but he'd do whatever it took to keep her safe.

She stepped out of the foot traffic and turned to him with suspicion riding the frown on her face. "Did someone tell you Six Feet Under is my favorite restaurant?"

"I had an idea it might be one of your favorites."

"How?"

"When we were searching Piedmont Park for the Ngak Stone, I asked Quinn for a place to eat. He said you and Tzader liked that restaurant, which means—now that I think about it—you being out in the open isn't a wise idea. We could go somewhere else like . . . my apartment. I could order something delivered."

She chuckled. "Your apartment? Right. No. I need to stay out of sight, and I've got to head home for a bit."

He didn't like the idea of her being alone for even a few hours. Not that he'd expected her to say yes to going home with him, but it had been worth a try. "Why don't you let me grab some food and meet you at your place?"

"Let me think about that?" She tapped a finger against her cheek and looked up, mocking him. "Uh, no." She checked her watch. "Can you meet me in three hours back where we teleported? Inside the North Avenue Station?"

"Sure, but you look like you need more rest than that."

"You know what they say about getting all the sleep you need when you're dead. If I don't find Tristan soon I'm guaranteed plenty of rest," she said around a yawn. "And don't say anything to Tzader or Quinn about me being here or what I'm doing, okay? The Tribunal said I couldn't ask anyone from VIPER for help. I'm hoping they won't construe your help in any way to get you in a jam, but I didn't ask and I couldn't stop you."

She had that right. "I understand." His cell phone had been vibrating since he'd returned. If he answered any of the calls, he'd either have to abandon her or lie to the caller.

He'd just as soon not inflict pain on himself by lying, and he had no intention of leaving her.

Before she turned to go, Storm stopped her with a hand on her shoulder. When she didn't react to his touch, he lowered his head as though he had something to tell her and whispered, "Sweet dreams," right before he kissed her.

Her muscles beneath his fingers tensed until his lips touched hers, then she actually moved into his kiss.

Damn, he loved the feel of her in his arms.

He wanted her thinking about *him* when she closed her eyes.

When she didn't pull back, he let the kiss go a few seconds longer than he'd originally intended, but he could spend hours tasting her. She softened, fitting against his chest. Feeling her slowly open up to him was addictive, but the longer he let this go, the harder it would be to let her go.

Through sheer willpower, he lifted his head.

Her lips were still parted, as if she was not quite ready to end the kiss. Hell, he wasn't finished either, but another minute so close to her and he wouldn't be able to walk without limping.

He pulled his hands back. "Better get going. See you in three hours."

"Right. See you." She blinked, glancing around as if worried someone from VIPER or the Beladors might recognize her, then took off down Peachtree Street.

Following Evalle could be tricky.

Storm allowed her a head start so she wouldn't notice he was tailing her. He kept her in sight for a mile and a half while she wove her way to Marietta Street via cut throughs.

She headed straight to where he'd seen her emerge from that abandoned building this morning.

He'd bet she lived there belowground.

The tang of sulfur kept invading his nose everywhere he walked, but he had a jaguar's sharp sense of smell that could pick up scents from far off at times. Sirens wailed in the distance. Now that he thought about it, he'd been hearing those for a while, too. Could there have been a huge tanker spill of something sulfuric on the interstate?

He stopped at the corner, since Evalle would be alerted to his presence if he followed her to within the last quarter mile to her apartment. She was as safe as she could be for the next three hours. He headed back into the city.

Evalle needed more help locating Tristan than Storm could offer. She might not be able to ask anyone, but he could. A witch would be his first choice for scrying where Tristan, and possibly an Ashaninka witch doctor, might be hiding in the city.

Evalle would be upset if he involved Nicole.

And Nicole was a white witch anyhow.

To fight fire with fire, he needed someone from the dark side. VIPER had brought in a Sterling witch named Adrianna to help locate the Ngak Stone before the Kujoo.

Of course, Evalle didn't like Adrianna, especially when the witch openly flirted with any VIPER agent. Storm had no sexual interest in Adrianna, but he could use her skills . . . depending on what she'd want in trade.

And he hadn't promised Evalle he wouldn't hunt Tristan on his own while she rested.

As for the Ashaninka witch doctor, better that he found her before the witch doctor found Evalle.

SEVENTEEN

Thunderstorms were building outside the conference room, where a different kind of tension vibrated inside these walls.

Quinn used his kinetics to dim the lights in the boardroom and to draw the blinds tight. He wanted no distractions once he started probing Conlan's mind.

Tzader had been stalking the room, checking the door locks and practically rattling the walls with his anger until Quinn sent him a telepathic message to chill out. He'd reminded Tzader that the entire floor had been secured. In buildings scattered across this country, as well as several others, Quinn maintained a perpetually vacant floor at specific locations, such as this one.

An area available only via keyed elevator access explicitly for Belador use.

Having withdrawn to a corner, Tzader became as still as a stone, if one could image a stone blazing with energy.

Perspiration danced across Quinn's forehead, a rare reaction for him, to be sure. Did he want to tamper with the mind of someone he considered innocent? No, but Tzader had returned from his meeting with Brina looking kicked in the proverbial nuts. Something had gone terribly wrong. If it took a mind search to appease her demand for action, then Quinn would do this for his friend and his warrior queen.

"I'm ready," Conlan said quietly, as though intercepting Quinn's reluctance. He sat on a plush office chair with his eyes shut and his back to Quinn, who stood above him.

Conlan's next breath came out hard and shuddering.

Time was wasting.

The sooner this was done, the sooner they could find Evalle before she walked into a fog and shifted. Even if she controlled her beast not to kill, someone would kill her.

Quinn spoke in a hypnotic tone. "Focus on wherever you go to find peace and this will be easier for you." Then he laid his hands on Conlan's head and closed his eyes. Touching wasn't necessary to tap a mind, but touch enhanced his ability to delve into the subconscious more quickly.

And possibly with less disruption to Conlan's brain.

When Quinn began to roam the young man's mind, he felt his way past areas that were like doors he could open and see into—past and present.

Quinn usually avoided anything in the future because the future didn't come fully formed the way current or past events were revealed. The future held unknown elements, and knowledge gained from those excursions could change events.

Not always for the best.

If he found something to prove Conlan's innocence, Quinn would be spared having to find a link to Larsen O'Meary's spirit. Perhaps the good news was that if O'Meary had truly died, there would still be a link between father and son because both were Beladors.

Unusual for two Beladors in one family to be born under the PRIN star only, and only one generation apart. Little was known about those connections.

Opening the passage to Conlan's present, which covered anything since he'd last slept, Quinn found nothing damning or helpful. When he moved beyond that to Conlan's past, he tapped a flood of misery that washed through Quinn. He saw a grieving Conlan struggling to accept his father's betrayal and death.

Conlan's mother had abandoned the child early on, leaving him to be raised by their father.

Having been informed by a druid of Conlan's powers, and after Conlan's father had been revealed as a traiter, the Beladors brought the seventeen-year-old boy into their fold to train and protect.

The time had come to specifically dig for any hidden connection to the Medb, something that might remain as a shadowy image or telepathic conversation Conlan tried to keep to himself. Quinn searched for any memory the young man had of using his gift for splitting his image so he could travel—similar to an out-of-body experience. Quinn found nothing more than a few experiences from training exercises.

Memory after memory passed in front of Quinn's eyes without a glimpse of even one impropriety. He slowly released a breath over the confirmation that this O'Meary was proving to be the upstanding Belador Quinn and Tzader believed him to be.

But with no irrefutable evidence of his innocence, Brina would expect a full report, including a search of the precognitive area of Conlan's brain. Conlan had shown signs of precognitive ability several times in training, but no special gift with it as yet.

This area of a mind was where Quinn had connected to a spirit once before . . . by accident.

An encounter he didn't want to repeat, but this area also gave access to the future and his report had to include a review of that as well.

Swallowing against the dread that crawled up his throat, Quinn felt his mind settle completely into Conlan's and spread out to mentally finger one spot after another until he entered the zone for the future where one dark spot pulsed with energy.

Quinn hesitated, but he wasn't surprised to find that energy in this murky area. Resigned to his mission, Quinn called out to Larsen O'Meary.

Nothing happened at first, but he hadn't expected the spirit to just be hanging out waiting on him either. All at once, he could feel the temperature flash hot, then cold.

The spirit was reaching for the connection.

Powering up his energies, Quinn extended further, touching the connection.

He'd expected something bright and strong, but this felt cold and dead, disturbing. The last time he'd tried something similar, the spirit had connected back to the host mind, which would be Conlan's, in this case.

This was where Quinn had to decide if he was going to release his spirit to travel to another dimension through the connection in Conlan's mind.

A dimension that opened a path to any images Conlan might harbor of the future.

Quinn's palms were damp, but he couldn't back out now and clear Conlan completely. When Quinn released his spirit to travel, he felt light as he floated forward. He encountered muddled blobs of color.

Sounds warped in and out. Shapes shimmered in a kaleidoscope of psychedelic patterns.

He reached out to Larsen's spirit twice but fell short both times. When Quinn gave his spirit an extra push forward, the spinning shapes and colors tossed him back, as if he were a polar opposite. He realized he'd have to drop his mental shields to go farther.

This was the real test of whether he believed in Conlan's innocence, which he did.

Tzader would forbid the move . . . if he had a choice in Quinn's decision.

Disengaging his shields, Quinn tried again and passed through a gateway this time.

He shifted from viewing to engaging with the actual vision, a metaphysic change that allowed him to interact with the beings in this step into the future.

He stood still, allowing the visions around him to reshape and take form. Images fluttered between blurry and almost in focus. The stronger the emotion, the more defined an image would be.

Where was Larsen?

He shouldn't be able to ambush Quinn here, but nothing was consistent or static when probing the future.

Chanting came to Quinn from a distance, then grew in volume, but never louder than a normal speaking tone.

Quinn didn't move or breathe, to prevent alerting anyone to his presence, as he was an interloper in this dimension.

Nothing good ever came from being discovered somewhere you weren't supposed to be. And the less he interfered, the less influence he'd have on the outcome.

The mist slowly calmed and sank to hover at his knees, exposing ten figures dressed in gray robes. Torches lit the inside of a cathedral-like building. The figures all faced forward, to where a person draped in a bloodred robe stood on a stone platform in front of them.

A chill ran up Quinn's spine.

The place where they were meeting resembled what his education had taught him of the great hall in TÅµr Medb.

But it was the smell of decayed limes that confirmed he viewed a coven meeting of the Beladors' greatest enemy—the Medb.

You seek me, Belador?

Quinn forced himself not to react at the voice so close to his ear. He turned his head to face Larsen O'Meary. Quinn controlled his gag reflex at the sagging skin falling off the dead O'Meary. He couldn't allow an uncontained spurt of emotion to trigger a reaction and expose his intrusion to anyone else in this dimension.

Larsen said, *I wondered when someone would come looking for my spirit. I granted this connection and will allow you to witness this glimpse of the future only if you agree to protect my son.*

Agree to anything with a bastard who hadn't given a damn about his child? Quinn would love to interrogate the spirit—and choke him to death. But that would be redundant, and he would not risk alerting the Medb to his intrusion.

To do so would allow access to Conlan's mind.

Quinn would protect the young man first above all else.

If this really was a precognitive vision, getting an insight into Medb plans could be great news for Beladors, so Quinn nodded to encourage the spirit to continue.

Larsen turned his gaze toward the meeting in progress. His skin swayed with the movement.

Quinn did the same and willed the vision to turn slowly so that he could see everyone's faces clearly. He paused the motion when the chanting ended and the figure on the platform lowered the hood on her robe.

He shouldn't have been surprised at learning her identity, but one mistake and Kizira would know he was present.

This was new territory for him in mind probes and not the place he wanted to learn the consequences of making an error.

He reached for his deep point of peace to remain invisible.

The Medb priestess addressed her group. "I have seen a vision of breaching the Castle Treoir."

As a direct Medb descendant, Kizira had once told

Quinn that her visions were destined to become reality. She said, "I have seen the face of the one who will lead the charge."

Quinn's control quivered at the fierce urge to protect their warrior queen. Much as he wanted to return immediately to Tzader so they could figure out how to shield Brina, he couldn't.

Not until he had learned all he could from Kizira. He tried not to think about what would happen to Kizira if she attacked Brina. Even if Kizira was Medb, she'd once saved his life . . . and shared her body with him.

He forced his mind to be still again.

Kizira's voice rose with jubilation. "We have waited a long time for this opportunity and for the one who will hand us the key to our success. Step forward, brother, and tell everyone how we will triumph over the Beladors, who have persecuted you even though you bleed their blood."

A man in the center of the pack moved forward and lifted his hands to his hood as he spoke. "There is an Alterant who is ready to lead us to victory by breaching the warding of Treoir Castle. In return, we have offered this Alterant what no one else can, the end of being victimized by the Beladors."

When the hood dropped to the speaker's shoulders, Conlan's face—right down to the comma-shaped scar on his cheek—shook Quinn to his spine.

Conlan said, "When the time comes to take possession of Treoir, Priestess, I will deliver you Evalle Kincaid, who will destroy the inhabitants of Treoir Castle and open the gates for you."

In that split second, shock overrode his emotions. Quinn's control cracked.

Kizira's head slashed sideways, her sharp gaze slicing through the layers of the vision to reach him.

Her eyes widened. Recognition. Shock. Confusion.

In the next second, she dove into his mind with a rush of emotions. *What're you doing here? I miss you. If you interfere, you'll die. You shouldn't be here . . . you betray me?*

Her mind steadied and toughened as quickly as he tried to raise his mental shields against her.

Too late.

She was inside his mind, the last place he'd allow anyone.

And she was Medb.

Larsen laughed and howled. *Fools, all of you.*

Quinn called his spirit home, backing out of the mind lock with lightning speed. He gritted his teeth against the hot streaking pain that burst through his head and body.

The pressure built in Quinn's head and expanded, ready to explode. Ferocious pain stabbed the inside of his eyes at a blinding pace.

Conlan groaned and cried out.

Someone yelled at Quinn, but he couldn't make sense of the words. His head screamed for relief. Red hues burst behind his eyes . . . or was that blood?

At a distance, he heard Conlan howling like an animal trying to rip his leg from a steel trap.

Something hit him hard in the face . . . again . . . he put a hand up to stop the attack. Opened his eyes.

Tzader stood in front of him with sick worry in his face. "What happened, Quinn? Can you hear me?"

"I'm . . . I . . ." He crashed to his knees, unable to stand up. Warm liquid ran from his nose and ears. His vision had turned bloody.

Tzader was there with him. "Tell me what to do."

"Conlan . . . alive?"

"Yeah, but he's bad off. He'll need a healer."

"Gimme . . . minute." Bile rushed up Quinn's throat. Something drove a wedge down the center of his head. He gritted his teeth harder.

"Want lights?"

"No."

"Quinn, your nose, ears and eyes are bleeding. Tell me you aren't going to die from this."

"Don't . . . think so." Quinn held up his hand that he needed a minute, but it would take longer to quiet the hellacious pain in his head. He couldn't be sure Conlan wouldn't hear, so he spoke to Tzader telepathically though it doubled his misery. *Medb have a plan . . . to breach Brina's castle. They mentioned . . . Evalle.*

When Quinn squinted his eyes open, Tzader's blurry face was slack with shock, then his jaw flexed with anger. Tzader said, *They aren't touching Brina or Evalle.*

Quinn stopped short of saying Evalle would willingly help the Medb. He didn't give a rat's ass about a fucking vision. No bloody way she'd do that.

He took a couple of hard-won breaths, struggling to figure out how much to tell Tzader before he passed out.

Tzader was Maistir and had to act upon anything he was told.

Quinn wouldn't put him in a tighter spot with unconfirmed information.

When? Tzader asked.

Don't know. Quinn swallowed down the nasty taste in his throat. *Could be now or months from now . . . just don't know.*

What about Conlan being the traitor? Tzader asked.

Quinn questioned what to tell Tzader for a nanosecond, but much as he hated to use the vision against Conlan, there was no way he could shield this information. Evalle had only been mentioned in the vision, not present at the Medb meeting.

Quinn said between panting breaths, *Saw Conlan with the Medb . . . discussing how to breach Brina's castle.*

Sure it was Conlan?

Yes. Had the scar on his right cheek . . . like the one Conlan got in training . . . last month. Quinn heard disappointment in the silence. His stomach felt as though a rabid badger had climbed inside.

Tzader pulled out his cell phone. *Got to lock up Conlan.*

Quinn nodded and regretted the move when he almost puked. He clenched his teeth and said, *But a vision isn't hard evidence. VIPER can't hold him long, maybe not a whole day.*

I know. We'll do what we can to nail down answers fast. Based on what you saw we can also justify hunting for Evalle as part of our traitor investigation.

Quinn was actually glad that they couldn't find her

right now until he had time to think on that vision some more. Time to convince himself that Evalle was not going to be the key to the Medb capturing . . . and killing Brina.

But Kizira had shared with him that she was revered as one of the greatest Medb precognitives.

Was there any way Larsen had altered that vision?

Quinn shuddered at recalling her inside his mind.

She'd been in a future vision, which meant she couldn't get inside his mind now, right?

But what about that spirit that had killed the troll?

Quinn gave up thinking. If he could take his head off and shove it in a deep freezer right now, he would.

Conlan slumped in the chair with a whimpered groan.

Tzader had finished one call and was dialing another one. He glanced over and caught Quinn watching him. "Don't know which you need worse, a doctor or a healer."

"No, just rest." Quinn had no idea how long it would take this to pass though.

"Like hell. You're bleeding everywhere, Quinn!"

"Get Conlan a healer . . . I can't be unconscious . . . you gone . . . deal with Alterants . . ." Quinn groaned at the effort every thought took, but he needed Tzader to understand.

"Take it easy. I know what you're saying. I'll call in a healer to meet Conlan at headquarters. You don't want to be around anyone you can't trust while you're vulnerable and I'm out dealing with the Alterant problem. As soon as someone takes Conlan to VIPER holding, I'll get you to your hotel."

All Quinn could say was, "Yes."

Calmer now, Quinn clutched his head in his hands. He never allowed anyone to know where he stayed except Tzader and Evalle. He didn't want to waste a minute of Tzader's time, but he doubted he'd make it to the hotel room on his own.

A thud hit the floor. Probably an unconscious Conlan.

Quinn whispered, "What about finding Evalle?"

"Soon as I get you two settled, I'm calling the one person who might find her faster than us."

"Who?"

"Isak Nyght and his black-ops boys. Much as I despise bringing him into the loop, I think he'll locate her before we can."

Tzader never panicked, but he was clearly hitting a defcon level of worry to unleash Isak Nyght to hunt Evalle.

Quinn and Tzader had figured out that Isak had an interest in Evalle, which meant he didn't know she was an Alterant.

Because Isak's first priority was killing Alterants.

EIGHTEEN

Evalle hurried across the uneven concrete, where weeds sprouted through the cracks, glad her leg had healed so she didn't limp anymore. She kept an eye out for any movement in the wasteland of dark shadows that stretched between her and the door to the elevator she had in sight.

Sirens whined in the distance. Everything was normal at home. She could use some normal. In a few minutes, she'd be inside her underground apartment with Feenix, food and her bed.

Storm had offered her food and a bed, but not in that order based on what she'd read in his eyes. Or maybe she'd just misread him. They'd only known each other a few days and she had no plans to do anything with him, or any man, that involved taking off clothes. She should explain to him that he was wasting his time if that was any part of his motivation for sticking close to her.

She expelled a long breath and headed to the elevator that would take her down to her apartment. When she reached the door to her living quarters, she opened it slowly, listening for Feenix. He normally heard her coming and raced into the living room to meet her.

She had to be prepared or she'd end up knocked out if he collided with her.

Where was he?

Nothing appeared disturbed.

Houseplants filled corners and anywhere else she could shine a grow light on them. Her ratty furniture hadn't been reupholstered by elves during the night.

She moved quietly through the room in case an intruder had somehow overridden her security system, which was unimaginable. An intruder would need kinetic ability and the code, which she changed daily, to breach her system.

Only Tzader and Quinn knew the access to this place.

When she neared the kitchen and heard soft grunting sounds of concentration, she relaxed.

Feenix was safe.

One step into the stainless steel galley-style kitchen and she started smiling at the picture of Feenix sitting on the floor humming to himself . . . until she realized what he was doing. "Not my new pots!"

Feenix jumped up into the air, wings flapping and wide eyes flashing as bright as two orange turn signals. He made a strained honking noise.

Smoke curled from his nose in advance of blowing fire that could take out a concrete wall.

"Whoa, baby. Calm down. I didn't mean to yell." She knew better, but the only thing left of two pots from the set Quinn had just given her were the two wooden handles on the floor.

Feenix finally settled on the island countertop. His eyes drooped with worry. He tucked his wings and turned his head to look down at the mess on the floor, then back at her.

She glanced over at the box of scrap metal she'd left him that was only half eaten. He hadn't been hungry, just mischievous. But she couldn't lock up everything that looked silver when she was gone.

Or she'd be missing a stainless steel stove and refrigerator next.

She asked in a calmer voice, "What happened?"

His worried gaze searched the room for an answer, which might be tough, since his vocabulary was so limited. Then he smiled, as if he'd found the perfect word. "Ith a accthident."

Good call. He'd only been here two days when he'd startled her and she'd dropped a drinking glass, shattering it. He'd gone into a panic flying all over the place, making scary noises.

The blasted sorcerer must have tortured him when anything had gotten broken, which had to have been often, since Feenix tended to be clumsy.

When she'd finally gotten Feenix to come down to the ground, she'd spent an hour soothing him. She'd explained how accidents happen and it was okay when they did.

She was not up to explaining the difference between misbehaving and an accident right now. "We'll talk about it later, okay?"

"Yeth." He chortled and flapped his wings, dancing back and forth in his version of happy feet.

She made a quick sandwich, ate, then carried Feenix to her bedroom, smiling as he counted from one to eight followed by ten then nine. He almost had the numbers right.

Leaving the lights off, she put Feenix on the bed and stretched out next to him. She'd shower later. When she closed her eyes, a whirl of images spun through her mind of Storm appearing in the jungle and Storm holding her while she teleported . . . and kissing her.

But that last kiss stayed with her, the one where he'd whispered, "Sweet dreams." As if his deep voice, dark eyes, and firm lips had hypnotized her until all she could think about was kissing him again.

Her breasts ached, too.

Had he caused that?

Men didn't affect her this way.

Why him?

She wouldn't deny the feelings he stirred up in her body, but she would have killed a less resilient person in the tunnel today when she'd shoved Storm across the tracks.

When he'd plastered his body against her in the subway she'd tried not to react. But she'd been attacked in the dark. Shoved up against a wall and . . .

Her arms rippled, ready to change.

She closed her mind against the memories until her breathing settled down. She focused on Storm's kiss and felt herself melt.

But Storm wasn't a man who would be satisfied for long with kissing. She might not have had relationships—had never dated—but she knew where Storm thought things between them were heading and doubted she'd ever be able to open up that part of herself to anyone.

She should tell him the truth, that she couldn't give

him what he wanted, what any man wanted from a woman. She'd allowed him to touch her more than any-one else ever had, but some lines couldn't be crossed again in her mind.

And as an Alterant, she was forbidden from anything even remotely close to mating.

Even if she was willing to take the risk and could handle the idea of intimacy, sex could trigger a violent reaction, far worse than today's. She might shift and kill someone who tried to have sex with her.

Storm would have to understand that moving beyond a kiss required a level of trust she was incapable of giving. In fact, just thinking about it required too much effort until she got some rest.

Darkness filled in around her thoughts.

She'd almost fallen asleep when a voice whispered, "Trust is nourishment for a starving heart."

Evalle sat straight up and opened her empathic senses.

There was no one in the room except her and Feenix.

She might have been dreaming, but it was the same female voice she'd heard while hunting the Kujoo. Except the last time she'd heard the voice inside her head, not spoken out loud.

NINETEEN

Isak Nyght sat on the edge of his desk. He watched through the glass observation window between his office and the attached hangar, where six men loaded ammo into specialized weapons he'd designed.

He flipped the cell phone in the air, then caught it again and again, amused over the voice mail he'd just cleared.

Tzader Burke wanted something from him?

Isak had checked up on Burke, wanting to know who this guy was before he decided if he'd return the call or not.

His national defense contacts in Washington, D.C., had explained a few minutes ago that Tzader was connected high up the political food chain in D.C. So was Isak, because they knew he hunted nonhumans. Correction. He killed nonhumans, like those inhuman Alterants that turned from human to beast.

This yellow smog crawling just above the ground in cities was triggering the change.

Which meant he had bigger targets than Tzader Burke.

His contact had actually warned him to be careful, adding that word had reached D.C. that Tzader was not happy about the Nyght Raiders being in the Southeast, specifically Atlanta.

Tough.

Isak answered to no one and had his own ties higher up, but he only called in those favors for something significant.

Nonhumans were significant.

He could handle Tzader Burke without calling on D.C.

Isak punched the call back number, curious more than anything.

When the call connected, Tzader answered, "Hello, Isak."

How had he known who was calling? Isak blocked all form of ID on his phones. "What do you want, Burke?"

"To know if you've seen someone."

Isak grinned. "What makes you think I've seen anyone you know?"

"Because your Nyght squad misses very little that goes on in the city. I know you've been hunting in Atlanta."

"Then you know I don't hunt humans. You got a non-human you want to tell me about?" He waited through a short silence. "No? Guess there's nothing to talk about."

Tzader made a growling sound. "I see you earned the nickname 'prick' honestly."

"Now you're trying to flatter me."

"You can tell me what I want to know, or I can make it difficult for you to hang around Atlanta."

Isak said, "Yeah, yeah. I've got better ways to waste my time. File a missing person's report with Atlanta PD if you've lost someone." He started to slide his thumb over to end the call when Tzader said, "I'm looking for Evalle Kincaid."

This time the silence was on Isak's end. How did Tzader know Evalle? Isak's contact had indicated that Tzader handled special projects for D.C. but not exactly what those projects were.

"Still there, Isak?"

"I'm here. What do you know about Evalle?"

"More than you can imagine."

Isak extended and closed his trigger finger. Did Tzader know that Evalle talked to demons? The first time Isak had met the woman a demon had been preparing to eat her. He'd blasted the demon into bite-size chips. Why would Tzader call him unless he had some inkling about Isak's relationship with Evalle, a strange one at that. He'd had to kidnap her just so they could have dinner together.

Isak asked again, "How do you know her and why're you looking for her?"

"Can't share that. I just want to know if you've seen her on any of your surveillance equipment."

"Not in a few days." Truth, but Isak wouldn't have told him even if he had seen Evalle.

"Heard from her?"

That pretty much confirmed Tzader knew Isak and Evalle were acquainted well enough to talk on the phone. "Not a word."

"If you see her or hear from her, let me know."

"We're back to why should I?"

"Her safety depends on it. That's all I can share and not put her at further risk."

"I suppose I can let you know if I run into her," Isak said flippantly.

"Let me be clear. I'm asking for intel if you care about her safety. Other than that? Stay. Away. From. Her. Your ability to continue breathing depends on not crossing me when it comes to her." Tzader hung up.

Isak brushed the Off button on his phone and lifted the radio on his desk. He called up Laredo Jones, his right-hand man, who was in the hangar with his team. When Jones answered, Isak said, "Bring the team to my office. We're going hunting."

TWENTY

Night had overtaken Atlanta when Evalle rode her motorcycle away from her apartment and turned on Marietta Street, heading toward Grady Hospital to find her favorite Nightstalker.

A pocket of yellowish haze hung low over the sidewalks.

She'd never seen a fog like that.

Sirens screeched on the east side of downtown.

For a city that normally bustled with nightlife at nine in the evening, downtown roadways were eerily empty. She stopped at a cross street, just short of entering the fog that was translucent enough to see through.

The sulfuric stench burned her nose.

Reaching out empathically, she encountered hostility unlike anything human. Her beast stirred, interested in the battle.

That was new and something she needed to avoid.

She snatched her senses away from the misty cloud and searched for another route.

A new patch of fog had begun filling in the street behind her, floating her way.

Trapped.

Her palms were damp. That fog was not natural.

Could she hold her breath and drive fast enough

through the yellow cloud in front of her and reach clear air without shifting into her beast form?

If I sit here another minute I'm not going to have a choice.

Sucking in a deep breath, she rolled on her throttle and raced ahead but slowed when visibility dropped to ten feet in front of her. She couldn't risk hitting a pedestrian, with so little line-of-sight distance.

Fifty feet into the fog she started seeing fallen bodies, no . . . pieces of bodies. What had attacked them?

Across the street on her left, a teenage boy wearing a hoodie and carrying a backpack rushed along in the same direction Evalle rode. A woman in a business suit walked just as quickly toward him, both obviously in a hurry to get through the fog. But when the woman reached the boy, the woman slowed as they almost passed each other and swung her briefcase, knocking the kid sideways.

Evalle's lungs were crying for air, but she hit her brakes. She'd have to breathe if she got involved in that fight.

The kid jumped up and shoved the woman against the granite wall of the building along the sidewalk.

Crud.

Shoving down her bike stand, Evalle yanked off her helmet and gasped for air. Sulfur burned her throat. Her beast sent a tremble through her body. Before she could dismount, the woman had coldcocked the teenager.

As Evalle rushed over, the woman just walked away casually, as if she'd only stopped to ask directions of a passing stranger. When Evalle reached the young man he turned out to be in his early twenties.

She coughed from the sickening sulfuric air and bent down to give the kid a hand, asking, "You okay?"

He shoved up and swung a fist at her.

She caught his arm. "Whoa. Stop it."

"Screw you. Get your hand off me or I'll kill you." He swung another punch she knocked away. His eyes were crazy wild.

She let him go with a shove to create space between them.

This fog was affecting humans.

Her first thought had been to warn him to stay away from the fog, but this guy was out of his mind. Instead, she pulled her glasses off and let him have a look at something really scary.

His eyes practically popped out of his head. He turned and ran.

Any other time she'd protect her nonhuman identity, but with this kind of insanity going on no one was going to believe him if he told them about glowing green eyes.

He was lucky she hadn't shifted.

She paused, taking stock of her emotions. Her beast wanted to battle, but she had control of her urge to change. So the fog didn't bother Alterants?

A flash of energy swatted her skin.

She wheeled around to find a person in the last stage of changing into a beast.

The thing was hideous, with hair across its arms and legs. The distorted head on top of his shoulders had a mouth full of fangs, beaked nose, huge ears and patches of hair on his head, plus a single horn that stuck straight out of his forehead.

And brown eyes.

An Alterant? Not green eyes like hers or black like Tristan's eyes had been in his cage.

Was this a new type of Alterant?

Could this be what had been shifting across the country and killing? If so, the fog had to be behind the outbreaks.

The thing snarled and raised stubby arms with clawed fingers, coming for her.

Evalle took a quick look for humans. None . . . that were still alive. She lifted her hands and shoved a blast of kinetic energy at him.

He backed up a couple of steps and cocked his head at her.

He should have been knocked into the roll-off construction Dumpster twenty feet behind him.

She didn't want to kill him if she could figure a way to contain the beast and throw him into the Dumpster to hold him. Then she'd have Storm get word to VIPER. Capturing one of these things might help them figure out what they were, why the fog triggered their change and how to stop this from happening.

Based on her line of work, she reasoned that some preternatural being had created this fog to make the beasts shift, but why?

The beast stomped forward and lifted a fist he shook at her.

She laughed. "You don't scare—"

Something that felt like a bowling ball launched from a cannon hit her in the abdomen. The kinetic punch knocked her off her feet and slid her backwards ten feet.

She sucked in air and shoved up on her elbows.

A man in thrift-store clothes, an unkempt beard and ratty hair came riding up from behind the beast on a rickety bicycle. He rode past the beast without a glance, as if it didn't exist, but gave Evalle a long, curious look before pedaling past her.

He hadn't seen that beast?

But the beast saw the man on the bike and started after him.

That's it. VIPER would have to catch another guinea pig.

Evalle shoved up to a crouch. "Hey, Badass. You want to play? Bring it."

The beast stopped and swung eyes rotting with evil at her.

She lifted her dagger and waited for him to charge.

Didn't take long.

Leaping to her feet, she moved forward. In the first stride, she used her kinetic power to shove off the sidewalk, onto the wall, running horizontally for two steps that put the beast at her left shoulder.

He swung claws at her that extended six inches.

She flipped away from the wall and out of his reach at the last minute. Arcing over his head, she stabbed her dagger into the side of his throat, whispering, "Stay put" to the death spell on her blade.

When she landed on the ground and spun around, purple liquid spewed from his throat.

He howled, grabbing at the dagger, but that majik blade would not come out by any hand but hers right now.

Striking out wildly and banging his fist against the handle of the dagger, the beast lasted less than a minute before it collapsed. When the thing finally died, the body changed back into a female in her midtwenties.

The purple liquid turned into dust. Her heart had stopped beating, so no blood oozed out.

Evalle withdrew the blade that came out clean. When she looked back at the body it was deteriorating before her eyes, until the entire cadaver turned into a handful of gray dust that scattered away on its own.

Much as she appreciated not having to deal with a body, that was not a positive sign. With no way to keep track of dead beasts this could mean the number of Alterant-type beasts shifting was far greater than thought.

She couldn't be sure, but if that man on the bike really hadn't seen the beast, then this fog was also cloaking the beasts.

She crossed the street and got on her motorcycle with a new destination in mind before she went to see Grady. First stop was Five Points, so named because five streets met in downtown Atlanta at Woodruff Park.

A block away from the beast she'd fought, she burst out of the fog into the clear night and circled Woodruff Park until she found the blond-haired teenage male witch playing chess. She parked on the sidewalk and pulled off her helmet on the way to talk to Kellman. He and his twin brother, Kardos, lived on the streets. She and Grady kept an eye on the homeless pair of male witches, but Kellman had the unenviable task of keeping Kardos out of trouble most of the time.

She hoped Kellman could locate his sibling quickly.

"Have you not noticed the park is empty, Kell?" she asked when she got close to the concrete steps to the fountain, where Kellman sat across from an elderly African-American guy wearing a blue jogging outfit.

"Guess it has been quiet," Kell mumbled, distracted by studying his next move. "What's up, Evalle?"

"I need you to do something for me," she said.

Kell lifted a knight, still not looking at her when he asked, "Can it wait until we finish this tiebreaker?" He made a move and slapped the plastic timer that reset and started counting down for his opponent.

Evalle stepped up close. "Actually, no it can't wait. I need you to find Kardos, too."

Kell looked up, his blue eyes registering that he'd caught her tone. "This is serious?"

"Yes. You and this gentleman need to get off the street and inside a building like right now."

The old guy swung his sagging face up at her, eyes sharp as flint. "Why?"

She said, "There's a deadly fog seeping into the city. It smells like sulfur and it's causing people to go crazy. Insane to the point of being dangerous."

If the fog had crossed highways, which it probably had, the highways would be battlegrounds by now. That explained the continued whining of sirens.

The strong smell alerted her, but not fast enough. She

looked up to see the blasted fog rolling over the fountain. "It's here. You need to get moving, find Kardos for me and get him inside, too."

Always the levelheaded and polite one of the twins, Kellman sighed and told the old guy, "She's usually right about these things."

"Then you forfeit."

She would never understand men. "That's not fair and, besides, this is about keeping you both safe."

"No problem, Evalle. Joe's right, and I understand." But as Kell stood up, the fog rushed around them. His eyes went from serene to mean in a snap. He knocked the chessboard off the step, scattering pieces, and lunged at his opponent.

Evalle grabbed Kell before he could attack the old guy, who started growling something vicious. But she couldn't let Joe attack her and Kell either. Using her kinetics to swirl dirt like a small tornado, she whipped it up until dust flew into his eyes.

While the old guy lashed out blindly, Evalle dragged Kell out of the fog zone. Once he had taken a few breaths, she shook him. "Are you with me now, Kell?"

"Yes. I don't know what happened."

"I do. Told you that fog is dangerous. Can you find Kardos?"

"He's sleeping at the shelter."

"Is he sick?" She couldn't think of any other reason the born troublemaker would be inside when he normally roamed the streets at night.

"Sort of. Drank something nasty." He straightened the

navy blue golf shirt he wore, a donated shirt too big for his slender frame.

"He deserves the hangover. Go to the shelter and make him stay there until you hear this fog has passed." She lowered her voice and leaned in close to Kell. "It's causing some people to shift into beasts."

Kellman smiled with embarrassment. "Tell me about it. I'd never attack old Joe."

"No, I mean real beasts with fangs and claws . . . and some power."

That blanched his face. "Really?"

"Yes. Now where does Joe live so I can get him home?"

Kell told her he stayed in a vacant building close by, then gave his chessboard a pained look.

"You can't go back in that fog to get it," Evalle told him. "I'll find you another one."

"Don't worry about it. Take care of yourself, and thanks for getting Joe home." He took off for the shelter, running around the outside of the fog.

Evalle went back into the yellow haze and tugged old Joe backwards while he jerked and swung at everything, yelling that he was going to stomp some butt.

Take a number. She'd like to stomp some herself.

Once she had him in fresh air, he calmed down. She hated having thrown dirt in his eyes earlier. "Kell told me where you live. If you'll let me lead you, I'll find some water to clean out your eyes, okay?"

He agreed. Leaving her bike at the park, it took fifteen minutes to walk him two blocks and locate a newsstand that had water. She bought him a sandwich and another bottle of water for his dinner. When she had him settled with clear vision again and convinced to stay away from the fog, she rushed back the way she'd come.

Sweat soaked her short-sleeved shirt and jeans. Between the heat and this fog, the attacks were only going to escalate.

She swung around a corner and skidded to a stop in front of two men carrying heavy weapons.

Demon-killing weapons just like the one Isak Nyght had toted around when she'd first met him. He'd used his blaster to kill a demon she'd been trying to interrogate.

"Hello, Evalle," Isak said from behind her.

She turned around. "What's going on, Isak?"

Some men had a presence. Isak consumed space, owned the territory surrounding whatever piece of real estate he stood upon, whether he was in full battle gear or slacks and a dress shirt. Tonight he wore black cargo pants and a matching T-shirt with a weapon-packed vest over his supersized body. Those huge hands had held a delicate wineglass and cupped her face when he'd kissed her speechless.

His gaze took in everything around them and still managed to hold her in place when he said, "Word's out humans are shifting into beasts everywhere. We're here to keep the streets safe."

Take a breath. Isak doesn't know that I'm an Alterant. "Have you seen any?"

"Not yet. Saw the victims though." Isak looked over at his team. "Go ahead and I'll catch up to you."

That's all it took for her to end up alone in the dark with a man who had once kidnapped her in order to have dinner with her because she'd kept standing him up.

He'd mentioned not seeing any beasts. She asked, "What do you think these things look like if you haven't seen any?"

"Saw one overseas right before it killed my best friend. An Alterant. They look human, then turn into a monster that murders anything in sight."

She didn't want him killing any Alterant, but she didn't believe the thing she'd fought in the fog had been an Alterant. Not like her and Tristan. Isak and his men could help protect humans if they knew how to see the beasts in the fog.

"I've heard some reports on the attacks," she started, hoping he would heed what she was about to tell him even if she had to fabricate a little to be able to share intel. "Sounds to me like the fog hides the beasts. Maybe makes them invisible."

He let the weapon hang from the cord hooked to his vest and used a hand to scratch his chin, which was covered in short whiskers. Some men wore a five o'clock shadow for a sexy look. In Isak's case, he just hadn't taken the time to shave today.

That didn't change the fact that it still gave him an edgy attractiveness.

His eyes sliced down at her. "Invisible would explain why we haven't seen any in the fog even with our night-vision gear."

"But you have thermal imaging equipment, right?"

"Sure. But I won't risk killing a human by shooting without a clear visual of the beasts."

This was where she had to be careful. "Have you gotten a description of the beasts?"

"One of my teams out west took one down. The thing turned back into a human when it died, then it just vaporized."

"Did they say how tall the beast stood?"

"Yeah, the things are at least ten feet." Understanding dawned in his eyes. "We can pick up the heat signature and tell the difference between something that big and human."

She let out a breath of relief, but she had to go. "That's great. I've got to run, but it's good to see you."

He reached over and caught her hand, lifting it and inspecting the scrapes on her elbows. "Why is it every time I see you, you're banged up?"

"Just clumsy, I guess."

He pulled her hand up to kiss her knuckles, then let go and used a finger to lift her chin.

Her heart strummed with new energy. Isak wouldn't raise a hand against her—not as long as he didn't know she was an Alterant. She hadn't known him long, but in that short time he'd killed a demon that had considered her a meal, then helped her escape a sticky situation with law enforcement and offered to "take care of" someone if they were bothering her.

She had no one she wanted to have "taken care of" . . . except maybe Sen, but she doubted even Isak could go up against Sen and survive.

Isak's concern for her safety stirred up strange feelings and tugged at her emotions. Especially the night she'd shared a private meal with him and seen the charming side of this black-ops soldier.

He leaned down and surprised her with a tender kiss. His lips were firm and hot for the two seconds their mouths touched. When he lifted up, his eyes gleamed with keen interest.

Heat shivered over her skin.

She liked Isak, but spending time with him added one more problem to her unending list, and she had enough sense to keep her distance from a man so intensely sexual.

Or not, if she considered that she spent so much time with Storm, who had ruined her chance at a quick nap after *his* kiss.

She'd never had a man in her life who'd been more than a friend and had never wanted a relationship with any man, but now she had two showing decidedly male interest and . . . to be honest, she was starting to like the attention.

Storm and Isak were as different as two men could be except for when it came to their protectiveness around her.

Isak smiled with sly humor. "One of these days, I'm going to find out what's going on behind those dark sunglasses."

Let's hope not. She returned his smile. "We'll have to get back to that over the dinner I owe you." She hoped he wouldn't take that as an invitation to kidnap her again. "But I've got to run."

And she would run all the way to her bike, just as soon as she determined which direction he took. That way she could take a detour even if she had to circle back around. She didn't want him to see that she'd spray painted her beautiful gold bike black, or he'd ask more questions.

His radio crackled. He lifted it from his vest and keyed the button. After a quick exchange with one of his men, who had located a wide patch of fog, Isak put his radio back. "I've got to go, too. Where's your bike?"

"Just another block over that way." She pointed because it was in the opposite direction of his men. "I'll watch out for the fog."

"One more thing?"

"Yes?"

"Why is a man by the name of Tzader Burke looking for you?"

Uh-oh. She had zero acting ability but gave a casual shrug and tried to keep the worry from her voice. "I don't know. How do you know him?"

"I know *of* him."

Just how much did Isak know "of" Tzader? "How do you know he's looking for me?"

"He contacted me wanting to know if I'd seen you on any of our surveillance equipment."

If Tzader had reached out to Isak for help, then he was really worried. This would turn into the night of living hell if the Tribunal caught her communicating with Tzader or Quinn. "Why did he want to find me?"

"Didn't say. Do you want to be found?"

More than anything she'd have loved to have Tzader and Quinn at her side, but not at the cost of the Tribunal's wrath. "No."

"Okay."

Her heart stuttered at how quickly Isak agreed to shield her even when he didn't know why.

He asked in an overly curious tone, "How do *you* know Tzader?"

She had no idea what Tzader had said and couldn't deny knowing him.

Taking a step back to indicate she was leaving, she said, "I ran into him at the morgue a couple times. Not my type."

That relaxed the stern lines between Isak's eyes. "I don't like him stalking you. Next time we meet, I'll know everything there is to know about Tzader Burke, so you won't have to worry about him again."

She could not let Isak turn his formidable resources on Tzader. "That's not necessary. He's a friend, that's all."

Isak nodded and allowed her to leave without more questions. She wished that meant he accepted her explanation and wouldn't go snooping around about Tzader, but she knew better.

If she got out of this mess with the Tribunal, Isak would get that dinner she owed him.

TWENTY-ONE

Riding along the two-lane road behind Grady Hospital, Evalle had twelve minutes before she had to meet Storm at the MARTA train station. Flashing lights glowed from the front of the hospital and sirens screamed heading in from the interstate.

How were they going to stop this fog and all the killing?

She parked near the curb, cut the engine, lifted the visor on her helmet and glanced around. Most people avoided the dark corridor between the rear of the hospital and the interstate, especially around eleven at night.

She called out sharply, "Grady?"

"You rang?" He took form in front of her, smiling.

Oh, dear Goddess. He shouldn't have been able to take human form without having shaken the hand of a powerful being like her. But here he was, looking human. VIPER agents were allowed to trade a handshake for one minute maximum.

If anyone in VIPER found out what she'd done for Grady, Sen wouldn't have to wait on the Tribunal's decision to have her locked away.

Grady hadn't been able to do this yesterday—had it only been a day ago? She'd held his hand on and off for over twenty minutes so he could maintain human form at his granddaughter's wedding. Grady had died in the '80s, so he hadn't wanted to talk to his granddaughter, only smell the flower-laden chapel and hear her wedding vows spoken, because his human senses were sharper than his Nightstalker ghoul form.

So Evalle had broken a rule and held his hand longer than the allowed one minute, which could result in her suspension from VIPER. She couldn't bring herself to regret helping him after seeing his unbridled happiness last night.

Considering her current list of supposed transgressions, holding Grady's hand too long was a minor one.

"Stop lookin' at me like I'm a ghost," he grumbled.

"You are a ghost, sort of." She rubbed her tired eyes. "What else has changed after that handshake?"

"You mean besides me gettin' better lookin'?" He grinned, his teeth a soft white against his raisin-brown skin. He scowled at her. "Only lasts a few minutes when I do it on my own, so it ain't like I'm gonna be walkin' around all day like this."

She smiled, though it was a sad one. "I wish you could."

He angled his head, looking her bike over. "What the hell you do to your ride?"

The paint job on her GSX-R motorcycle would have been ugly even if she hadn't been in a rush. "I sprayed black over the gold to camouflage it so no one would recognize my bike, but I can clean off the paint when I'm ready. I covered the tag with pieces of sticky vinyl numbers."

Grady crossed his arms. "That because you got ambushed this morning?"

Not really, but she *could* talk to him about that. "Got

jumped right before the Tribunal meeting. I think they were working for someone else, almost like bounty hunters, but I'm sure I smelled Noirre majik."

He lowered his voice. "Glad you bein' careful, but don't know if that paint job will hide you. If those men that jumped you this morning are still around, they ain't gonna be happy about losing their prize for the Medb."

So the Medb had been behind her ambush. Grady had a point about the paint job, but she'd abused her Gixxer's beautiful finish for another reason—to prevent being spotted easily by VIPER, Quinn or Tzader.

Grady said, "I heard some of the Nightstalkers tried to warn you."

"I realized that later, but at the time I couldn't stop to talk to them. I was trying to not be late for that blasted Tribunal meeting."

"Those men were bounty hunters."

Grady normally bartered hard for a handshake before he gave up any information, but he seemed content with his current semi-human form, so she wasn't going to question this gift.

She asked, "Some of Dakkar's bunch?" She had a serious issue with Dakkar if he'd sent them. VIPER allowed Dakkar's people to track down bounties as long as they didn't interfere with VIPER business.

"Nah. Freelance mercs for the Medb. They're looking for Alterants."

Evalle needed help finding Tristan, but she had to be clever about how she asked questions or she'd get Grady caught between her and the Tribunal. He'd almost died at the hands of the Kujoo when he'd interfered a few days ago.

Okay, he was dead already, but the Kujoo would have done horrible things to him, and she doubted he'd fare any better if he ticked off the Tribunal.

She tapped her handlebar. "I wonder if the men who ambushed me were hunting just me or any Alterant."

"Could be both. Heard they were after a female Alterant, but they think she's with a male they're hunting for, too."

Who would that be? Evalle asked, "Did those men find any other Alterants, or are they still around?"

"Not a word on the bounty hunters since this morning." He lifted his head, sniffing, then looked at her. "You know about that stinkin' yellow fog come to town?"

"Saw it on the way here. Making people crazy. Have you heard about the fog anywhere outside of Atlanta?"

"Yep. It's on the West Coast, too. Humans think the Alterants are some kind of Bigfoot gone Frankenstein. They think someone's been experimenting and created these things. You better be careful."

"I haven't shifted into a beast."

"No, but I hear VIPER's declared open season on *all* Alterants."

"All? But not me, right?"

"Don't know. You be careful."

She had to get moving, but where was Tristan? Snapping her fingers, she realized how she could find out if Grady had any idea where Tristan had gone after he'd teleported into the subway tunnels. "Do you know anywhere the men from the Medb could hide underground, like around the MARTA rail stations in downtown?"

Grady looked away, his lips pooched out as if pondering. "Underground, you say? I heard once about tunnels the old Nightstalkers say the subway disturbed when it was built."

She wanted to laugh at his reference to "old" Nightstalkers. Grady had died thirty years ago when he'd slept exposed to the elements on streets near Grady Hospital. "Where are the tunnels?"

"What you got for me?"

She muttered, "Unbelievable," and pulled a bottle of Old Forester from her tank bag. She stuck it out to him. "Here."

He broke out a real smile for that, then looked at her expectantly. "That's it? No hamburger or french fries?"

She'd kill him if he weren't already dead. "I'm in a hurry. I had time to make one stop, and McDonald's didn't offer an Old Forester Happy Meal. I need information, Grady."

The old coot ignored her while he concentrated on opening his bottle. He downed a long drink, then sighed and wiped his mouth with the back of his hand. "Don't be lookin' at me like that. There's a place underground, or at least there was at one time, but these old guys are Methuselah-old, so I don't know if—"

"Grady!"

"O. K. 'Sposed to be a warren of tunnels humans weren't meant to access, but the subway cut through the tunnel system in a couple places. They run up and down like underground hills, so they go anywhere from near the surface to deep down and big open spaces like rooms. Been around since long before all this was built." He waved his free hand to encompass the city that sprawled around him.

"Why would someone build all those tunnels?"

"You're not the first nonhuman to inhabit Atlanta, Evalle. Long before the homeless died and turned into Nightstalkers there were thousands killed during the Civil War era that didn't cross over to the other side. And not all of them were soldiers. Atlanta couldn't have rebuilt if someone hadn't found a place for the lost spirits to go."

"They created a home for spirits?" She had this vision of a freaky halfway house for ghouls.

Any time Grady squared his shoulders and his voice turned instructional—like now—she wondered if he'd taught when he was alive. He had a voice that reminded her of Morgan Freeman, who could play any role from vagabond to president.

And Grady's enunciation and speech could shift from broken street talk to sound fluent as a university professor, which was how he sounded now.

"Hauntings progressed until it was a serious problem. People shied away from buying a house rumored to have haints or moving a business into a building that scared the workers. The spirits were just as upset about people, industry and progress disturbing their resting grounds. Someone got the wise idea to give them another place to reside. So the tunnels and cavelike rooms were built underground long before high-rise buildings and subways showed up."

"The ghosts just left?"

"I heard a pair of people, maybe exorcists, coaxed the spirits into going underground, but another rumor said they were tricked."

She started thinking about being stuck underground with a bunch of spirits. "Are they friendly?"

"Have no idea. None of the spirits up here will go down to the Maze of Death."

"You're kidding about that name, right?"

Grady had turned up the bottle again. He took a long slug and lowered it until his unyielding gaze met hers. "No, I'm not joking. Don't go down there. If those men that ambushed you are down there, leave 'em. They may not make it out again to be a problem, because we both know that some spirits are not nice. If that place is full of angry beings, especially former trained soldiers, it's dangerous."

Just my luck the Maze of Death is now on my bucket list.

She checked her watch—running late to meet Storm. "I got you. I have to go. Will you *please* stay out of sight while you work through whatever it is you can now do with your body?"

He looked hurt. "Why you want to be like that?"

"Because I don't know what Sen might do if he finds out you can take solid form on your own."

Grady sniffed and fisted his bottle in one hand. "He don't scare me."

The idea of what Sen could do to Grady scared her. "It won't help my case with the Tribunal either."

That changed his attitude. "In that case, I'll lay low, but if I find out they lock you up I'm gonna have to have words with Sen."

May Macha help her. "Catch you later."

She checked her rearview mirror as she pulled away and grimaced over Grady's still-solid form. Riding through the north end of downtown, she didn't encounter bodies lying around. This area appeared untouched by the fog. People were actually moving around. Did the fog just manifest itself in spots? Were people ignoring what they heard on the news because they didn't see fog around them?

Or did the newspeople know the fog was behind the killings?

In a couple turns she found a parking spot on West Peachtree Street near the North Avenue MARTA terminal.

Her bike had a warding. If anyone but her tried to ride it they were in for a nasty surprise, but did spraying paint over one section alter the warding symbols carved into the frame?

Tzader would know, since he'd had the bike warded as a gift to her, but she couldn't ask him right now.

At the stairwell she descended wide steps to the subway level and tried not to think about Grady's warning.

Maze of Death.

If Tristan was in there, she had no idea how she could pass through a concrete wall to find him or how to pull him out. She couldn't use the same gift from the Tribunal twice, so teleporting herself anywhere again was not possible.

When she reached the track level, Storm was leaning against a section of tile-covered concrete wall where passengers waited to ride trains.

He watched her coming toward him as if he saw only her.

He had on his usual dark T-shirt and faded jeans. His midnight black hair was pulled back from his face, accentuating the sharp angles and burnished skin his Native American blood awarded him.

Four women stood in a group pretending to chat while their gazes strayed to Storm, whose powerful shoulders pulled at his T-shirt when he crossed his arms.

Feral sexuality in an untamed package.

Women were drawn to the risk.

Men allowed all that unleashed danger a respectful distance.

Two strides from reaching Storm, Evalle noticed one of the women in the foursome giving *her* a thorough examination, clearly perplexed over Storm's smile for her.

Evalle had more to worry about than being snubbed. They didn't bother her. Not really. But sending them a little push of energy might rattle that bunch enough to wipe the snotty looks off their faces.

Storm *tsk*ed at her and warned, "No playing with the humans."

Evalle swung her gaze up at him and lifted her shoulders. "Don't know what you're talking about."

He chuckled. "Ready?"

She nodded and led the way to the service entrance, where Storm kept watch as she used kinetics to open and relock the door. Once they navigated their way back to the dark corridors, they stepped over the tracks and up onto the foot-high structure running alongside the rails.

That's where the trains pulled power to operate. She'd worried the first time Storm had stepped up on the shield that covered the power access, but it turned out to be stronger than it appeared.

Evalle checked over her shoulder to see that they were swallowed in the semi-dark area, then asked Storm, "Have you heard about the sulfur-smelling fog and Alterants shifting?"

"I saw some of the fallout on the news. The top end of I-285 is covered in wrecks. People were going crazy in some areas, shooting each other." He walked along for a moment. "Your Alterants might be dead."

"I hope not. I think I know where Tristan and maybe the other Alterants are down here."

"How'd you find out anything with only three hours to rest?"

Because I slept a half hour. "Saw a Nightstalker I know on the way here."

"Your friend Grady?"

"Yep. He said there's a warren of tunnels and rooms down here where spirits moved to live after the Civil War. Soldiers and civilian spirits. It's called the Maze of Death."

Storm didn't laugh, but he might as well have by the comical look he gave her when she glanced up at his silence.

"Hey, *I* didn't name the place," she said in self-defense. "Anyhow, we might have lost Tristan's trail because he teleported through the concrete wall into the maze. The only idea I have is to go back to the last spot you found his trail and see if we can find an access point nearby."

"Why go back if he's not there?"

"I'm considering dropping my mental shields to see if I can reach him through telepathy if Trey doesn't interfere. But I also still have two of the three gifts I got from the Tribunal. I don't want to use another one when I haven't found the Alterants yet, but those other two won't do me much good if I don't find them."

"What are you thinking about using for a gift?"

"Not sure. I might ask for a way to communicate with Alterants in the maze, but that could open the channel to a swarm of ghosts as well. I'm still working on it."

Storm walked along quietly for ten steps, giving her the impression he debated some thought until he said, "I have some intel, too."

Where had he been for the past three hours? "From a Nightstalker?"

"No. From Adrianna."

She muttered, "We know how you spent *your* three hours."

A smile teased his lips. "It didn't take three hours."

Evalle lifted her hand. "I don't need details."

He caught her hand, brought it to his lips and kissed her palm. "Adrianna and I have a purely business arrangement."

Pulling her hand back, she ignored the tingle that climbed up her arm and spread across her chest at his touch. "You made a deal with a Sterling witch?"

"Ever know one to give up information for free?"

"Not them. What'd you have to give her?"

"Told her I'd return the favor when she asked for it."

Evalle cringed at that idea. "*I'll* pay her back, since you asked her for me."

"Let's not quibble now." Storm turned his head, as if listening for a train, then turned back. "She's still with VIPER."

"Why? I thought they only brought her in to help with finding the Ngak Stone."

"I don't know why she's still here and didn't ask, but it probably has to do with the Alterants turning into beasts and the fog. Adrianna said VIPER has a hunt-to-kill order out on all Alterants."

Had Grady been right? She asked, "You mean the Alterants who are shifting and killing, right?"

"No, I mean you and Tristan, too."

"Why would they do that . . . wait. You said Tristan, too?"

Storm's jaw hardened. "The Tribunal found out Tristan escaped. They think you helped him."

"How did they find out Tristan was out?"

"Adrianna thinks someone spotted him in Atlanta on a MARTA security camera. She said he is nearby and she thinks Tristan is down underground in this area, so that fits with the Maze of Death intel you got. He has plans for the Alterants."

While Evalle appreciated the information, she could have used better news. "I figured out Tristan had other plans than mine when he left me standing in the jungle."

"That's not what I mean. Tristan might not hand over the Alterants to the Tribunal for *any* reason. He isn't going to work with you." He stopped and cocked his head to listen. "A train's coming."

"What do you mean? What exactly did she tell you about Tristan?"

"We've only got a minute to hide before the train reaches us."

She gave up and scouted ahead until she found an indentation in the wall two feet deep. Backing in, she called out to Storm, "Where are you?"

He appeared in front of her. "Looking for another spot."

The train clatter grew louder, and the engine headlight lit the edges of his clothes.

She could do this. "You can . . . share this spot."

"You sure? I don't want to end up drop-kicked into a MARTA train."

Lifting a sharp gaze at him, she snapped, "Then keep your hands out of trouble. Get in here before you're spotted."

He stepped forward and swallowed all the space.

She breathed in and out, in and out. This would work. She would be fine. No reason to go mental on him just because she couldn't see past his body to freedom.

Storm put his hands on the wall at each side of her head. "My hands promise to behave," he teased.

She looked up.

His lips curved in a smile as lighthearted as his tone, but his eyes reflected the animal caged inside his body.

Her heart pounded with him this close. The muscles in her chest twisted and tightened, shaking her body harder than the vibration from the approaching train did.

Storm inched his face closer to hers. "You smell like a fresh shower . . . sweet and tempting."

Why did she feel as though she was still naked from her shower when he said it that way? She watched his mouth say something else but couldn't hear the words over the train noise. Then he stopped talking and paused. The next look he gave her was one of internal resignation.

She mouthed the word, *What?*

He kissed her. His mouth settled on hers with a familiar feel, as though his lips had known hers a long time. He possessed her mouth, mated it to his, and turned her body into liquid compliance.

He tasted tempting. Dangerous temptation she should be backing away from at a high speed. Couldn't. Wouldn't.

His tongue explored, carefully at first, then with adventure in mind.

The train roared past, vibrating the wall at her back.

The rush of wind pushed Storm's body into hers, brushing her breasts that felt too full.

She shivered, breathing as hard as a runner at top speed when silence swept in behind the distant train with sharp abruptness. That's when she realized his hands were still on the wall, but she had stepped up on the balls of her feet and cupped her hands around his shoulders.

When she leaned back and dropped her arms, she licked her lips, tasting him again. If he kept this up she might lose her mind enough to step over that line one time.

She knew better. "We can't keep doing this."

He straightened away from her and ran a hand over his face in a frustrated motion. His voice reeked of disgust when he muttered, "I couldn't agree more."

On a logical level, she wanted his agreement.

On a female level, that hadn't been what she'd expected.

She clenched her hands and shoved past him. "Not like it was *my* idea to kiss you."

"Evalle."

Ignoring him, she kept stomping down the middle of the tracks.

"Evalle?"

"What?"

"Come here."

She spun around. "Now what?"

He was smiling, which confused and annoyed her in equal measure. He walked up to her. "I was irritated with *myself*, not you."

"I don't understand." Understatement. "And honestly, I don't care." Lie.

Which he called her on silently when he arched an eyebrow. "When I agreed with you, I meant I can't keep kissing you without . . . wanting more."

What kind of more? "So that kiss was"—she shrugged, searching for a word—"okay."

"I wouldn't say that."

She might drop-kick him again after all. She crossed her arms.

Mischief twinkled in his eyes. "'Okay' isn't even close. Kissing you is like a roller-coaster ride to outer space. The farther we go, the more I'm lost and the more I want to explore new territory."

He had an amazing ability to say things that lit sparklers in her heart and splashed bright colors across the ugly memories in her soul.

Calling the kiss "okay" would have been much easier to accept. He'd stepped all over her boundaries since the minute they'd met, but he always seemed to understand she had barriers he shouldn't try to breach.

She'd never enjoyed a man's touch until Storm.

She even missed him when he wasn't around her, missed the way his hands sneaked past her defenses without raising an alarm.

Isak had kissed her, twice now, but not like Storm kissed her. On the other hand, Isak didn't have the access to her that Storm had.

The more time she spent around Storm the easier he managed to infiltrate her emotions—and without using his majik, as he'd agreed after the first time.

He made her want that "more" part, made her consider tempting fate and taking a risk.

Unsure how to respond, she started looking around and changed the subject back to a real concern. "We probably should keep moving."

He ran his finger along her cheek. "We're about thirty yards from where Tristan's trail ended the first time we were here. I'll hunt for as long as you need me, but I want you to realize he has no intention of helping you by handing over the other Alterants."

That's what Storm had been saying when the train had showed up. "Adrianna told you that?"

The spell that had woven around them when the train had passed disintegrated with the edge to her question.

Storm took a deep breath and expelled slowly. "Yes, and I think her information's as solid as that Nightstalker you place so much belief in. What are you going to do if you find Tristan?"

She'd asked herself that since landing in the jungle inside Tristan's enclosure. "I'll figure that out when I find him."

"Not sure I like the sound of that. Thought the whole point was to get this bunch locked up again. Right?"

"Not exactly."

"Evalle."

She didn't believe any of them had gotten a fair shake, including Tristan, and she had never planned on just handing over the Alterants. "I can't condemn someone to a life I'd rather die than face. If they come in with me voluntarily I have Brina's support to protect them while we get the Tribunal to hear each of their cases. This would be a chance for real freedom for them, too, which should mean even more now that Alterants are being hunted."

"I agree with you in principle, but I'm not objective when it comes to your safety and freedom. I have no problem with handing them over to save you."

When had Storm become her champion? "I have a plan. If Tristan will just work with me, then all the escaped Alterants will have a chance to be treated fairly."

Storm didn't like hearing that. His scowl could scorch the walls. "Tristan screwed you once already with the Kujoo, then again by leaving you in the jungle. Why would you help him at all?"

"Tristan fell in league with the Kujoo because no one else had offered him any hope of freedom. I might have done the same thing in his shoes. He did leave me in the jungle, but not until you were there. He could have let the demons kill me or left me at the mercy of any animal with my knee crushed. But he didn't." She'd been thinking on that for a while. "I have to believe any person with a soul deserves a chance."

She felt Storm pull away from her emotionally. Why?

He asked, "You're so sure he has a soul?"

"Yes. He's not some demon."

Storm scoffed silently to himself, sarcastically whispering, "No, he's so much better than a demon."

She would have dismissed this as just another case of posturing if Tristan had been present. Storm and Tristan matched up like two rottweilers snarling over the same bone.

This would be easier if they could get along. She tried to smooth things over. "All I'm saying is that I'm willing to give Tristan a chance if I can find him."

A booming male voice behind her said, "In that case, this is your lucky day."

Evalle stepped back from Storm and turned to find Tristan striding up to her. "Where did you come from?"

"The Maze of Death."

"Where is that?"

"You'll see. That's where I'm taking you."

TWENTY-TWO

Fury and aggression swept around Evalle on all sides.

Storm's earlier teasing vanished. In one step, he moved slightly ahead of Evalle and told Tristan, "She's not going into the Maze of Death or anywhere else with you."

"She'll go anywhere I say," Tristan argued, moving entirely too far into Storm's space.

Evalle considered blasting them both against opposite walls. She stepped between them. "She's right here and not agreeing to anything anyone says right now!" She put her hands up on each chest. "Take a step back before I get testosterone poisoning."

She asked Tristan, "What makes you think I'm going anywhere with you after you just vanished this morning?"

Tristan held his hands out, palms up. "I stayed with you until this alley cat showed up. I had to get back to check on the other Alterants."

"You could have teleported all of us to Atlanta," she argued.

"No, I couldn't. I can only teleport one at a time."

Evalle had an even bigger beef with Tristan, now that she thought about it. "Why didn't you teleport me and you to that village or back here so we wouldn't have had to face those demons?"

Storm interjected, "Obviously his superpowers aren't so super."

Tristan cut a warning look at Storm and ground his jaw muscles.

She warned him, "If you aren't going to give me straight answers, I can't in good conscience go anywhere with you again."

Tristan finally told Evalle, "I *could* have brought you back here when I first escaped, but I couldn't have teleported again right away. That meant risking that you would call in someone before I had a chance to locate the Alterants. Your Belador buddies and those in VIPER would have swooped down to snatch them."

So Tristan couldn't transport a group, eh? She filed that away for later. "Okay. Never mind. We're here. You're here. Where are the other Alterants?"

Tristan shook his head. "They're not where I left them in the maze."

She checked Storm's face, since he was the walking lie detector.

He gave a little hike of his eyebrow, which she took to mean that he'd heard the truth but had reservations about accepting that as the entire truth.

What might have happened to volatile Alterants in a place like the Maze of Death? She didn't like the idea of being trapped with spirits from a hundred and fifty years ago, whom Grady had intimated were not necessarily friendly. "You left them in that maze for the past week with all those spirits? Maybe they freaked out and found some way to escape and got caught in the fog outside."

Tristan put his hands at his hips. "Teleporting is the only one way in or out that I've found. None of my three Alterants can teleport. I don't think they've left the maze."

She said, "So you know about the fog."

"I saw the yellow haze and all the crazies when I was topside." He grinned with malice. "That should keep VIPER busy."

Evalle chastised Tristan with her frown. "Did you get near the fog?"

"Hell, no. I don't want any part of something that could force me to change."

She kept it to herself about her encounter with the fog.

Storm asked Tristan, "Why'd you put the Alterants in that maze?"

Tristan just stared for an answer.

"I do not have time, Tristan," Evalle said. "If you want my help, then you're going to have to give both of us some straight answers."

Storm helped not one bit when his lips tilted with a smile.

Tristan gave him a look that promised they'd have a chance to finish their discussion some day when Evalle wasn't around to stop the bloodshed.

Storm's smile broadened in an easy-to-decipher message of any time and any place.

Tristan answered Storm's question, but he spoke to Evalle. "The maze was the only place I'd found where the Alterants couldn't hurt anything if they turned into a beast and no one would find them there. At least, I'd hoped no one would find them."

She sent a look of question to Storm.

He gave a little nod that Tristan was telling the truth. But from the closed look on Storm's face, he'd figured out something else Evalle hadn't picked up on yet. She stayed quiet to let him keep prodding.

Storm scratched his chin, pondering. "What do you plan to do when you find those three again?"

Tristan's jaw shifted with a grimace. "I'm going to give them a better chance than I had."

Tristan clearly wanted to save his fellow Alterants, which could mean he intended to work with her. Maybe.

Evalle asked Tristan, "Why are you here? You don't need me to find those three."

"That's true," Tristan agreed. "But I may need your help containing them and getting them out of there. I don't know what kind of mental or physical shape they're in since they've moved from where I left them."

"Oh, hell no, Evalle." Storm stepped in front of her. "He hasn't told you the truth since you met him. He turned a demon loose on you in Piedmont Park—"

Tristan interjected, "That was before we knew each other."

"—then he almost let the Kujoo kill you *after* you knew each other," Storm continued. "Then he lies to you when he escaped and could have teleported you when the demons attacked. Now he's here wanting you to walk into a concealed space where you have to fight three—or four—Alterants?"

Tristan deadpanned, "If I wanted to kill her I could have done it in South America."

Evalle took into consideration all that Storm said, but actually . . . "He has a point, Storm. I landed inside his spellbound cage with no way to use my powers against him and he didn't harm me there. If I want to find those Alterants, I have to go with him."

"Evalle, don't," Storm said in a voice so close to pleading that it surprised her.

"She doesn't have a choice," Tristan pointed out.

She'd rather not ever see the Maze of Death, but Tristan had given voice to her thoughts. She could either go with him or wait until the sand ran out of the Tribunal's hourglass. But the look of betrayal on Storm's face sliced past her need to appease the Tribunal and her trepidation over entering the maze.

She didn't want to part like this, so she told Tristan, "I need to talk to Storm."

"Make it fast."

Storm moved toward Tristan. She put a hand on his chest to stop him and felt his thundering heartbeat. Once Tristan had backed off, she told Storm, "Please don't call in Tzader or Quinn."

"If I agreed to that I'd double over in pain from the lie."

That surprised her. "Is it because of your ability to tell if someone is lying?"

"Yes." He brushed his palm against her face. "Don't go somewhere I can't get to you."

Guess that cleared up any question about whether he thought he could get to her in the maze. There went her safety net if Storm couldn't find a way in. "Then do me this favor. Give me two hours before you contact anyone."

"One hour."

"Ninety minutes."

"One. Hour."

She had to give him a reason that would overrule his concern for her. "Ninety minutes. If you call in Tzader and Quinn before I find these three Alterants, the Tribunal might twist it around to appear as though I called them in."

He nodded, unhappy about it, but he agreed to the compromise.

She moved close and lifted up to whisper, "Please understand. If you need me to face something like the Maze of Death to help with finding you-know-who"—she didn't even know the name of the woman Storm was hunting—"I will."

He nodded again, not any happier, but understanding swept his face, uncovering a gaze filled with caring that warmed her heart.

"Need to go," Tristan called over.

When she turned to leave, Storm pulled her back around and into his arms, kissing her before she could say a word.

Embarrassment heated her skin at Tristan watching them, but only for the two seconds it took for her to realize this was a new kiss. Her empathic senses burst awake and told her this kiss had a name and a meaning—possession. Any other time, she'd have shoved a man on his butt and straightened him out about the fact that no one possessed her, but her hands refused to untangle from their grip on Storm's shirt.

She rode a heady wave of feeling at the idea of a man like Storm wanting her this much.

When Tristan made a disgruntled noise, she smoothed her hands against Storm's chest and gave him a slight push until he lifted his head. "I have to go."

He dropped his forehead to hers. "Be careful."

"I will be."

She'd made three steps away when Storm told Tristan, "Bring her back with so much as a scratch on her and VIPER won't end up with enough of you to satisfy a pack of hungry rats."

Tristan smiled and hooked an arm around Evalle's waist. "See you, tomcat."

She closed her eyes, hoping she'd been right about Tristan having a soul, because he was her only way out of the Maze of Death. Sen wouldn't come unless the Tribunal sent for her, and even then he'd probably pretend he couldn't find her.

One way in. One way out.

TWENTY-THREE

Voices skidded through his mind, playing dodgeball with his thoughts.

Quinn kept his eyes shut tight even though the room was as dark as a moonless night and he had an ice compress over his forehead and eyes. He tried to thicken his mental shields to stop the onslaught of voices, but the effort almost sent him back to worship the porcelain god.

He had nothing else left to throw up.

Images flashed in and out from minds he'd linked to and probed. Images as garbled as the voices.

"Quinn?"

Had he heard that voice in his head or in the room? Couldn't have been in the room. No one could get in but Tzader.

No room service allowed since a bullet between the eyes wasn't on the menu.

Energy swirled in the room, whipping the chilly air to frost level. No, not now.

"Quinn?"

He gritted his teeth and tried to reinforce his mental shields, but they were weak, too shaky to battle any real power. "You shouldn't be here, Kizira."

"Then you shouldn't have called me."

Huh? He tried to lift up, but an invisible hammer pounded his head with vicious enthusiasm.

"I didn't call you, Kizira."

"I wouldn't have gone through all I did to be here if you hadn't. I risked leaving my bodyguards in charge of a project I'm responsible for."

Had he called her? He would have known that, right?

"You're in pain. I can help."

"No . . . don't. Go away. Please." His teeth chattered when the temperature dropped severely.

"I can drop the temperature even more to freeze the pain out of your brain."

"No." His thoughts tangled. How had she gotten in here? The mind probe. What had happened to him during that probe?

"You miss me." She hadn't asked, just spoken, as though saying the words would give them weight and value. "Remember the last time we were alone?"

All too well.

Good thing he'd stretched out still fully clothed. The last time he and Kizira had been alone they'd ended up naked.

Like he needed that image worming its way into his splitting head right now? She had to go. He was civilized only when he had all his faculties accounted for, and right now parts of his mind had taken a hiatus.

She spoke softly. "You were in my head today where you shouldn't have been, Quinn. Why?"

He frowned, and even that hurt. Had he reached into her mind during the probe, too? No. She'd climbed into his, fearless of what he might have done to her. She'd been in a vision of the future, not here today. What kind of connection had opened up by tapping the spirit of Conlan's evil father?

No matter what, Quinn had to keep her out of his mind.

He mumbled, "How was I in your head?" but the words might have come out, "Howz I in ure 'ead?"

She made a sound he recalled from their time alone when she'd get exasperated with him. "Can you at least sit up and talk to me?"

"Honestly . . . no. Had a . . . difficult day." When he heard the shirr of material heading his way, he opened his eyes again, but the room blurred.

Kizira crossed the room, her body appearing to flex and reshape as though she'd been caught in one of those warped circus mirrors. She moved silently, but her usual intense glow had dimmed to almost nothing.

He asked, "Why aren't you glowing?"

"You obviously have a volcanic headache, and as I recall, light hurts your eyes." The powder blue gown poured down her body, hugging curves and falling to her ankles. Her flame red hair—now a soft brunette—hung in a long braid over her left shoulder, falling past her breasts.

Beautiful breasts when she'd been naked.

He closed his eyes and indulged a moment of self-loathing at his mental track.

She'd stand out among all the women in contemporary clothes stalking around Buckhead outside his hotel because Kizira was like no other woman.

And she was his enemy.

He needed to keep that thought forced between the erotic images determined to crowd his mind.

The mattress depressed next to him when she climbed on.

"Kizira," he warned. He didn't want to use any kinetic power on her and frankly didn't know if he had it in him to raise a decent defense. Had to keep his energy focused on locking down the walls of his mind.

The ice pack disappeared from his head. The pounding kicked his skull. He released a noise that sounded pitiful to his ears.

Her cool palm covered his forehead.

He tensed, then groaned out a sigh of relief at the instant change from brutal pain to just a splitting headache. "Go, Kizira."

She hushed him. "Shh. Let me help you while I'm here."

Bad idea. But bloody hell, only a fool would refuse her help, especially when he needed to get back on his feet for Tzader and Evalle.

He'd let her do her majik, then he'd thank her and send her on her way.

"Do you miss me?" she asked again. Her words came to him soft as a caress, calling to him as dangerously as the sirens who lured sailors to their deaths. But he'd been the one who'd allowed disaster to happen last time.

Too young to think past the need to have her when she'd given herself so easily to him.

Not this time.

"Quinn?" She said his name as though no one had that name but him. "I'm asking a simple question. It's just me and you."

Why did her words sound like music? She wasn't singing.

Should he tell her he thought of her only twice a day? When he was sleeping and awake.

That he'd never touched anything as soft as her skin since parting ways or that he still remembered the way sunshine had come through the open window of the mountain hut and shimmered around her when she'd leaned over to kiss him?

He should lie, but he couldn't bring himself to hurt her, when she was easing his pain. "Yes, I miss you, but that doesn't change . . . a simple fact. I'm Belador and you're Medb." Sworn enemies. "You should hate me. I should never have taken advantage of you."

She kept soothing his head with her hand and laughed. The sound came and went as though fading in and out. "I was fully a woman when I met you."

"You were eighteen. I was older than you—"

"By two years only."

"—and should have kept my hands off."

She placed a kiss on his head, and gentle coolness spread across his forehead, dropping the headache to a moderate ache. He relaxed his shoulders for the first time in hours.

Kizira chided him in a cheerful voice. "Your memory must be failing, and such a shame to age so poorly at thirty-three."

He smiled at her jab. Some worry pressed at his mind . . . something he'd just had a grip on a moment ago.

Whispering in his ear, she told him, "*I* recall when we met that you fell to *my* charms, not the other way around."

"So you used majik on me then?" He couldn't recall, but he should. His memories bumped into each other in a confusing tangle.

"Only my personal charms," she assured him. "Now you wish me to think that only worked because you were so badly injured?"

Pieces of the memory poked at him.

He'd been alone on patrol in the mountains surrounding Chechnya and found a village destroyed by Medb warlocks. When he heard the scream of a woman being attacked, he intervened only to be captured by three warlocks who turned Noirre majik on Quinn before he'd been able to engage his mind-locking powers. He hadn't developed the skill much at that point. They beat him to his knees.

Then two warlocks had held him in place for the other one to torture so they could peel his mind open.

Quinn hadn't known at the time that the woman he'd saved, Kizira, was a Medb who had just been given her first task on her way to becoming a priestess. She was to capture a Belador and bring the warrior to her queen. A dangerous task for any eighteen-year-old woman, but Kizira had never been an average young girl.

She'd told him later that no warrior who fought so honorably should die by torture. So she'd interfered with the three warlocks, forcing them to stop hurting Quinn.

That had been a grave error on her part. The warlocks had been trained to kill any traitor in the Medb, no matter who.

To interfere with their handling of a Belador had sealed her fate without judge or jury.

They'd dropped Quinn in a heap of torn flesh and broken bones to turn on Kizira as one.

Quinn had rallied the minute they'd redirected their Noirre majik at Kizira. He'd opened his mind, reaching out in a rage of energy he used to quickly overtake the mind of two warlocks, dropping them where they stood.

The other one had been so intent on Kizira that he'd failed to notice the greater danger gaining his feet behind him. When Quinn had finished, all three laid scattered on the ground. He'd taken one look at a shocked Kizira and collapsed on top of the pile of bodies.

When he'd next opened his eyes, he'd found that Kizira had hidden him away in the mountains, where she cared for his battered body.

Just as she was doing now.

He held his thoughts for a moment before they spilled between the gaps in his mind. What had he been saying to her a minute ago? The words she whispered slipped inside his head and floated around. His mind fogged with pleasure from where her fingers rubbed his temples with circular motion. The pleasure seeped into his body as though carried on streams of rejuvenating oils.

Her voice whispered close to his ear. "Do you remember the bracelet I braided from your hair?"

"Huh . . . yes." He smiled at the memory. She'd worn the bracelet until the last day, when he'd suggested she might not want to go home with a Belador token of that sort. He'd told her the bracelet would only make her regret what they'd done.

She'd replied that she was keeping the bracelet to prove she didn't regret their time together.

A silly thing, but he'd been touched that she'd taken the keepsake with her.

It didn't matter. This was a mistake. He mumbled, "Kizira . . . can't be here."

Warm air rushed across his throat when she said, "I told you I'd come if you called."

Her words echoed in slow waves, bouncing across his mind. "Why . . . did I call you?"

Because you missed me. Remember? Her voice entered his mind gently, so much better than hearing sounds. *You do remember missing me, Quinn, don't you?*

Oh, yes. "I did . . . miss you."

Her hands moved to his neck and shoulders, rubbing deep into tired muscles while her voice massaged his mind. *You like to be touched and kissed.* Her lips brushed his, then disappeared.

The pauses between bouts of pain stretched longer.

He had something to do . . . something about . . .

Her lips brushed kisses along his forehead. Then her voice flowed into his mind on a soft hum. *I care for you, Quinn.*

I don't think . . . you should, he answered. Other thoughts flitted up, almost in focus, then backed away just out of his reach. *I'm not . . . I'm not . . . right for you.*

Yes, you are. Her fingers slid along his chest, stopping to delve into a tight muscle, loosening him inch by inch. *I want you, Quinn. Again. Like last time.*

Can't do that. Wrong. But he had a new ache that pulsed in his groin.

His belt unbuckled and his pants loosened at the waist.

She reached inside and caressed him.

He hissed, "Kizira."

That was supposed to sound like a warning, not a request.

She said, *I've missed you, too. Missed touching you most of all.*

The world lost shape, tumbled on its side and lay there.

Quinn tried to open his eyes. Couldn't.

Her voice and touch consumed him, binding him, filling him from the inside out. Her fingers . . . oh, her fingers . . . stroked.

His body took over, all attention shifted straight south. He tensed, ready to surge with the orgasm.

No control.

Couldn't breathe . . . waiting for her to move again . . . he ached . . . pleasure with teeth scraped his nerves. He couldn't move his hands to reach for her. Could do nothing but lie here, waiting . . .

Please.

I want you, Quinn, she repeated over and over. *Tell me you miss me.*

His muscles strained, everything tied to one part of his body waiting for release. "I miss you."

Her fingers slid along his length up an inch, then stopped, then up another inch. He shook with need.

Do you want me to help Evalle?

"What?"

I could watch out for her. Kizira's fingers stroked back down, her hand first hot, then cold.

His body clenched. He was panting. The edge was close, just a tip away.

Where is Evalle?

He struggled to recall. "She's gone."

But how do I find her?

"Don't know."

Pain shot behind his eyes.

Kizira whispered against his ear, *Think, Quinn. Where is Evalle?*

He swallowed, panting. Jagged shards of glass stabbed each of his eyes.

The pain subsided again and Kizira was kissing him. *I have what you want. What you need.*

He reached for her, surprised his arms moved. His hands touched bare flesh everywhere. She shivered and whispered seductive words, begging him to give her what she wanted.

Just ask. Whatever he owned was hers.

But he'd never told a woman that and didn't think—

Her fingers cupped him and he stilled. The delicate touch of her fingers drove him insane. Too gentle to push him into oblivion.

He ground his teeth. She kept teasing him, as if he could grow any larger in the tight skin sheathing him.

When she finally gripped him firmly, he made a sound deep in his throat, a primal need for release.

She said, *Tell me where Evalle is and I will give you anything you want.*

Somewhere from deep in his mind, a thought came charging forward, as if he'd commanded the very words to march into battle. "She's with Tristan."

That's all I needed to hear. Now I want to feel you inside me. She removed her fingers.

He wanted to snarl at her to go back and finish what she'd started, but it was as if someone had thrown a switch on his body. His muscles and limbs once again functioned.

His skin burned to rub against hers. He rolled her over, feeling nothing but her and sheets touching his skin.

They were both naked.

Just like last time.

Perfect.

The only thing stopping him from exploding when he finally shoved inside her was a basic male drive for control. Carnal need raced through his cells, burning him to take her. He struggled for a second with the sense this was not right, but her muscles clinched and his thoughts splintered. Pulling back, he slowly pushed into her again, shaking with his need for her.

She urged him, *Now, Quinn. Just like last time.*

Her nails dug into his shoulders.

Bloody hell, yes. He held her hips and drove deep inside her.

TWENTY-FOUR

That had to be the quickest teleporting trip in the world, which worked just fine for Evalle if not for the brief sick stomach.

Too bad it had been with Tristan and not Storm, her personal favorite as a full-time transport partner.

She opened her eyes and expelled a breath that came out as a white puff in the chilly air. "It's colder than I thought it would be."

"Creepy, huh?" Tristan said close to her ear.

"A kid's Halloween spook house is creepy. This is a twilight zone." She hadn't known what to expect with a name like Maze of Death, but not this. The hand-hewn dirt-and-rock tunnel that stretched in front of her glowed in spots where an eclectic mix of antique gas lanterns had been mounted.

She doubted any fuel lines ran to them.

Who would have been paying the gas bill?

Framed paintings hung along the walls at intervals, and an assortment of rugs covered the dirt floor in places.

Tristan angled his head toward the tunnel. "From what I could tell on my first trip through this place, someone moved personal effects down here. Guess it made the spirits feel at home."

"Wonder how they kept this from being discovered when MARTA built the subway system?"

"They've had over a hundred years to develop their spirit skills, and the subway only intersects it at a couple places." Tristan's fingers curled around her right side.

She cut her gaze over her shoulder at him. "Take your hand off me if you value it."

"You looked cold." His eyes dropped to her chest.

She refused to look down. "Keep looking down there and your nose is going to have a swift introduction to my boot. Last warning before you end up with a nub."

He withdrew his hand. "Thought we were working together."

"To a point."

"In that case, let's get moving."

She turned all the way around to face him. "Not until I get some answers."

"The Tribunal didn't put you on a time clock?"

She literally worked against the sands of time with no idea when the last grain would fall. "Speaking of the Tribunal, they know you escaped and they're blaming me."

No surprise in his face. "I heard, but I don't know how they found out."

"They caught you on a security camera in Atlanta and now VIPER has a hunt-to-kill order on me, you and the other three, along with every other Alterant shifting in the fog."

"Heard that, too. You should throw in with me."

"No!" What did she have to do to get through to him?

"Your chances are better by working with me to get all of us in front of the Tribunal."

"I'll have to think about that."

"While you're thinking about that, you can tell me what you *didn't* say in front of Storm when we were on the other side of the wall."

Tristan asked innocently, "Such as?"

"The location of the other three Alterants."

"I told you they aren't where I left them."

"Which is a sly way to avoid either telling me a specific location . . . or admitting you don't know where they are in here. Right?" If he'd been in the maze all the time she and Storm had searched for him, Tristan should have covered every inch by now.

"They're in this maze."

"Not good enough. I'm not moving until you give me *everything.* And I think you know exactly where they are, so the question is, why did you bring me, since you don't need my help to find them? If you want *my* help, I want the truth."

Tristan took in a deep breath of the chilly air, which came out in a white stream. "I left them in a room with two benign spirits and enough food to hold the three for a couple weeks. That's why I couldn't let you leave me in the jungle. I thought they were going to die because I couldn't get back. But when I got here, they were gone."

She could sympathize with him better now for having used her to escape if his story turned out to be true. "Where'd they go?"

"Into a large cavern deep inside here." The smug

cockiness normally inhabiting his face had given way to a haunted look he wore too easily.

As if he was more familiar with pain than happiness.

She pushed again. "And the reason you can't get them out of the cavern on your own is . . . ?"

"Because the Medb got here before me. Kizira found the other three Alterants and is holding them."

Of course the Medb had found the three Alterants.

Evalle rubbed the back of her neck. "How did you find this out?"

"From the spirits of a young Civil War soldier and old man who plays checkers. They live in the chamber where I left the three Alterants. After running into dead ends in this place all day—pun intended—I returned to their chamber. That's when the two spirits revealed themselves and told me where the Alterants were."

"So the spirits are working with Kizira?"

He shook his head. "Not even."

"Then how did Kizira get involved?"

"When I asked how I could find her, they said they told her to leave."

Evalle would have enjoyed watching Kizira sent packing. "She didn't blast them into Never Never Land?"

"This place is loaded with supernatural power that could cause a catastrophic chain reaction. Not even Kizira would want to be down here if it blew. She made them an offer. If they'd act as messengers if and when someone showed up looking for the Alterants, she and her men would leave as soon as she got what she wanted. The spirits are liaisons for now, but they don't like her being down here."

Evalle muttered, "I'm not so crazy about that myself. What does she want?"

"A specific Alterant."

She waited for him to say more, but Tristan liked to feed out one small piece of information at a time. "Who does Kizira want?"

"Me."

"She knew you were coming back for them? Does that mean she knew you'd escaped again?" Which would lead Evalle to believe that Tristan might have been playing her for sure and leading her into a trap. But it was too late to find a way out.

"No, she didn't know for sure I would be back, not until today. I figure she's had someone squatting here to see if I caved and told VIPER where to find the three escapees to keep them from starving to death, or maybe she thought I'd cut a deal with Macha or VIPER to trade the missing Alterants for my freedom, which *I* would never do."

Evalle flinched at the unfair strike to her conscience. "You said Kizira didn't know for sure that you would be back until today. How'd she find out?"

"Thanks to your friends at VIPER probably."

She had him now. "How do you figure that?"

"With VIPER hunting Alterants and word of me escaped, Nightstalkers would hear about it."

Grady hadn't known about Tristan escaping, but Grady had been laying low while working through his new ability to take human form on his own at times.

Unease squirmed along her neck.

If VIPER knew Tristan had escaped, did that mean the

Tribunal would send Sen after her before her time ran out? No, gods and godesses were slippery as eels to maneuver around, but their word was law. They said they'd send Sen only when her time was up.

If they wanted her, they could find her. She shook her head at him. "Way to go, Tristan. You use me to escape and now I'm an accessory to your jailbreak."

"Oh, give me a break. Like you wouldn't have escaped if you'd been in my shoes? I had three lives at stake."

She ignored his question, because the truth was, she'd have probably done the same thing. "If I help you get those three out of here, then I want you to agree to let me take them into the Tribunal so they have a chance at freedom, or no Alterant will ever be safe."

"My opinion won't matter much if you have to get them out of here for me."

He had no expectation of leaving here with her and the other three. She didn't want to admire him for being willing to trade himself. "How do you know Kizira wants you?"

"Because the soldier spirit gave me a message she'd left with him specifically if I returned looking for them. Kizira said she'd trade me for those three. I was going to wait to go into all this until we were closer—"

"—or until you had me so lost in here I would go along with anything."

"Same difference. If you get those three out of here alive, then just assure me they get a chance to plead their cases."

She'd considered everything that might have been driving Tristan's actions up until now except a selfless motive. "That's my plan. How long have you known these Alterants?"

"A week. The witch that opened the portal for the Kujoo was a freelancer, not Medb. I'd heard rumors about other captured Alterants and traded her some of my blood to find them. When I did, I released those three and found this place to hide them. I was coming back for them once I got my hands on the Ngak Stone . . . you screwed that up, too."

"I'm not going there again about the Ngak Stone. Why did Kizira let you go after those Alterants in the first place?"

"She didn't know. Once I had the ability to teleport I had freedom to pop in and out as I needed."

She still didn't trust him. "Why are you willing to take the place of those three Alterants?"

Tristan's wintergreen eyes turned hard as rock ice. "Because they trusted me to watch out for them and not use them. I'm the only one standing between them and death or cages. And, if they win their freedom, they'll watch over someone important to me."

Another new secret about Tristan, but he kept looking past her to the tunnel, clearly wanting to go.

"Fine. Let's go get them, but I'm not completely sold on your plan. We may revise it." She turned to head in the only direction offered and had an odd moment of feeling bad about tracking dirt on rugs. Some were the old braided styles, and others were expensive-looking designs.

"Revise my plan in what way?" Tristan stepped up next to her. The tunnel had an easy six feet of width.

"It may take two of us to get them out of here. I'll think of Plan B by the time we get there. Any chance Kizira has converted some of these spirits into dangerous ghouls, like that one you had attack me in Piedmont Park?"

He flinched this time at the reminder and muttered, "That was unavoidable at the time."

"Oh, really? Sort of like my having to send you back to South America?" Before Tristan could go off again on how he'd gotten the shaft, she said, "Just answer the question. What are we up against?"

"I haven't seen any rabid ghouls. I don't think the Medb want to piss off these ghosts, with all this energy concentrated into one place. I've met some benign spirits, but there's a few hostile ones down here, too."

She sized up the slashes in his jeans and shirt, which could have been made by claws. "What's your next step?"

"To ask the soldier spirit to take a message to Kizira that I'm ready to trade me for the hostages."

Evalle cast a wary glance at the strange mix of decorations along the tunnel. Junk furnishings had been placed alongside pieces Sotheby's would salivate to represent. She rubbed her arms against the chill that had settled in her bones, and not entirely from the temperature change. Working back through Tristan's plan, she remembered something he hadn't explained. "How am I supposed to get those three Alterants out of here if I can't teleport?"

"I'll tell you when it's time."

"That's if you live long enough to tell me."

"Then you better make sure I stay alive." He grinned, enjoying having the upper hand. For about five seconds.

An unearthly howl pierced the air. The guttural sound picked up volume quickly as it headed straight for them.

He yelled, "Ah, hell."

"What is it?"

"The spirit of some guy with a pitchfork who thinks everyone is trying to steal his pigs."

"Can he hurt us?"

"No, but the damn pitchfork can. Don't use your kinetic power in here."

"Why?"

"Been there, done that and got the claw marks to prove it doesn't work." Tristan swung around and cursed ghosts, tunnels and the day he was born.

She turned around and saw why.

The tunnel behind them had vanished, hidden by a brick wall that had formed right down to where it cut across the middle of a rug.

The bellowing got louder and echoed everywhere.

She spun back around, and the corridor they'd been walking through originally had now split into two directions. What the . . .

Evidently this maze changed shape and direction at the will of the ghosts down here.

Each length before her appeared identically black, endless and filled with the blood-curdling banshee sound of the spirit racing toward them.

With a pitchfork.

TWENTY-FIVE

In order to be heard over the bellowing spirit, Evalle yelled, "Can't I even throw up a wall of protective energy?"

They had to do something to stop the crazy ghost she expected to burst into view any minute holding a pitchfork like a weapon.

"Kinetics won't stop him," Tristan shouted. The high-pitched screeching could make a human's ears bleed. "Energy just ricochets and hurts like hell when it hits you."

Hesitation got you killed. She stared down the long corridor to where in thirty yards the tunnel split like a Y into two directions. "How do we tell which tunnel he's coming at us from?"

"We can't."

"Then what do we do?" Where was a ghost buster when you needed one?

"Run." He grabbed her hand and ran straight toward the split for the tunnels, dragging her with him.

She jerked her hand away and kept up with him.

Shrieking drilled the air with the power of a warning siren cranked to high in a small space.

Ten feet from the tunnel divide, Tristan veered off into the left vein.

Splitting up would be of no help if either one of them

got stabbed. She followed him. Fifty feet into the dark void, gas lanterns started appearing on the wall. Flames danced into view, lighting a passage draped in flowering vines.

Thick patches of clover covered the ground.

Peacefully silent.

Evalle swept a look over her shoulder, then back at Tristan. "Will he follow us?"

"I don't think so. The two times I saw him he was always running in one direction and only stopped once."

"What made him stop that time?"

"His pitchfork buried in my chest."

Was Tristan joking? No. There were three holes in his shirt. "What'd he do after his pitchfork got stuck?"

"Yanked it out and took off running again."

"And you healed." She put her hand over her stomach. That might not be so bad except for getting skewered. "Wonder what he died of?"

"His head hangs to one side like he fell and broke his neck while he was chasing whoever he thought had stolen his pigs."

"Is that the worst thing down here?"

"No."

Of course not. "Then what is?"

"Knowing what's down here will only make you jumpy, expecting everything to be a threat."

"Just once, I'd like a straight answer."

"I'd like to live a normal life," he said. "Maybe you'll get a straight answer when I get what I want."

In other words, never, but that wouldn't detour her

from trying to get as much out of him as she could. "Explain to me why Kizira wants you?"

"She doesn't want *me* so much as what I am."

"What are you that I'm missing here?"

"I told you. A Belador Alterant."

"Really? You're the one who keeps saying you aren't a Belador," she pointed out.

He made a grinding sound in his throat. "Fine. I'm an Alterant with Belador blood. Does that make it easier? Did you ever try to track down your father or pull your birth records?"

"No, I know it's a dead end."

Tristan shook his head. "You haven't even tried to trace your roots to find out your blood background, when you've been free to do so. And you say you really want to help all Alterants. Sure."

He paused at a crossing in the tunnels only long enough to make a right turn into another endless walk with the same outdoor look.

She stiffened at the censure. "Unlike *you* and most of the world, I can't go out in sunlight. I'm bound by my vows to do my duty, which includes being on a VIPER team. I've been doing everything I can on the Internet, but nothing on me shows up. I only have so many ways and time to search."

"I understand—"

"Really? I don't think so." She stopped and waited for him to turn around. "If we were a recognized race, the Tribunal would have to give us the same rights as everyone else. That's what I wish you'd realize."

"Not going to happen, Evalle. We'd have to be accepted into a pantheon. Who would take us? Macha?"

"I don't know." If she had all the answers, she wouldn't be stuck in the middle of this maze. "But I'd like a chance at life where I don't have to constantly dodge getting locked up. You can't just run, Tristan. Look what happened here. You had nowhere better to take three Alterants than to an underground tomb. How are they going to be safe anywhere else when they weren't down here?"

"You keep expecting me to put my trust in people like Brina, who screwed me in the first place, and the Tribunal, who don't give a rat's ass about any of us."

"I trusted you to bring me into a place I have no way to leave without your teleporting me back out. I did it because I want to find a way to help *all* of us. Show me a little faith by sharing what you know."

He gave her a withering look. "I am showing you trust by bringing you here. I'm making a leap of faith that you'll do as you say and not hand over those three and walk away with your freedom. And I wouldn't be doing this if I had a choice. That's more than you deserve after sending me back to the jungle when, if you'll recall, Brina didn't deny that I had been caged unfairly. I'm willing to do what it takes to get these three to a better place. My question is what *you'll* do when faced with the decision of your freedom over theirs."

She'd already told him her plan.

He could bite her boots. She was willing to fight to give these three a chance at life and freedom.

That had to be enough.

But she hadn't survived to this point by lying down

for anyone. "I don't have all the answers. I don't know if a pantheon will ever consider a bunch of half-breeds. But if you think enough of those three Alterants that you're willing to hand over your life to the Medb in trade, then why can't you care enough to fight for the chance to be accepted as a true race?"

He dropped his head, staring down at the clover hugging the soles of his boots. "I have a lot more at stake besides these three." He raised his head and his soul lay bare in his eyes. "When I can rest assured that everything that matters to me is safe, I'll fight. But I'm not trusting anyone with what's mine to protect until then."

He turned and strode away. End of conversation.

She followed him. Who was he talking about that he had to protect? Now wasn't the time to push him again, but she'd pry that clam open later when she had a way to keep it open.

He slowed as they neared another crossroads in the tunnels, then kept walking straight ahead where the path curved left, then right, then left for so long that Evalle thought for sure they'd gone in a circle.

Lights flickered along the corridor. She started to ask Tristan if he knew what that meant, when he held up a hand for her to stop and be silent.

She paused ten feet behind him and checked over her shoulder for brick walls, crazy guys with pitchforks or some new terror. When she turned back around, a figure wavered in front of Tristan, taking form little by little until it turned into a soldier, complete with a bayonet-tipped rifle, dirt-smudged Confederate uniform and a bloody rag tied around his head.

He looked to be in his early twenties until she took in his sad eyes, which had seen many years of hard miles.

Evalle remained very still to prevent disturbing the spirit. Nightstalkers like Grady were hard to rattle, but Grady was accustomed to dealing with humans and nonhumans.

She doubted that before meeting Tristan this soldier ghost had seen a human in the past hundred years. He'd probably never run across anything like Alterants or a Medb witch priestess.

Tristan asked the soldier, "Did you take my message to the witch?"

The young man nodded. He spoke in a sleepy voice. "She said iffin you don't show up in a half hour she's killin' hostages."

"A half hour from when?" Tristan asked.

The ghost stared off into infinity, then said, "Now."

Tristan's voice tightened with stress. "Where is the witch?"

"I kin show you, but she sent another message."

"What?"

"She's got a holt of four hostages. Says she's goin' to kill the new one last."

Evalle had opened her empathic senses to see if she could detect something from the soldier ghost. She only picked up weariness and a sense of being imposed upon.

When Tristan asked who the fourth hostage was, the soldier said, "Petrina."

Tristan roared, *"No!"* He raised fists with muscles bulging in his forearms. Bones popped . . . he was changing into his beast.

The ghost vanished.

TWENTY-SIX

Quinn grabbed at the air above his head.

Had to kill whatever was beating a spike into his skull with a sledgehammer. His fingers closed on empty air, hands hitting each other.

If he could just see it, but his eyes were shut.

He dropped his arms, fingers fisting the sheets.

Pounding started again, but this time it came from outside his aching head. He focused on the sound.

Someone was banging on the door.

What door? Why didn't he know where he was? He knew how to access anything in a mind, especially his.

Reaching deep inside, he searched for the center of his control and found it ravaged. A wasteland of scattered thoughts and mental shields that had once been his safe zone.

What had happened to him?

"Quinn!"

Had to open his eyes, but they felt glued shut. His lids quivered and strained, but he forced each one open.

Darkness.

Bloody hell.

"Open up, Quinn!" shouted at him from behind a door in another room . . . in his hotel suite. All at once, memory flooded into empty pockets.

Tzader was yelling at him.

Quinn rolled over and dropped his feet to the floor, sitting up on the edge of his king-size bed. Mistake of ginormous proportions. He grabbed his stomach and covered his mouth to stem the nausea.

Tzader couldn't come in because . . .

Quinn had hung one of his Celtic Triquetra blades on the hall entrance door to his suite.

A Triquetra he'd had warded to block entry, even from someone with Tzader's powers.

Lifting a hand that shook, Quinn kinetically flipped the Triquetra off to the side.

The banging noise disappeared, replaced by the sound of his door being shoved open.

Why did his head still ache? He could swear he'd slept soundly for a while. That should have taken the edge off.

Pushing himself onto wobbly feet, he reached instinctively for the belt on his . . . robe? What was he doing in his robe? He'd been in his dress clothes when he'd stretched out on the mattress with no intention of staying long.

The lights in the room flashed on, blinding him. He threw his hands in front of his face, but not before seeing Tzader barrel in.

"What's going on, Quinn?"

"Turn. Off. Those. Lights."

The room fell dark again with just a haze of light seeping in from the windows.

"Quinn? You okay?"

A question he couldn't answer yet. "I will be. Why are you here?" He hadn't intended for that to come out surly, but his head and stomach threatened to unhinge what stability he had.

Tzader said, "Been trying to reach you telepathically for the past half hour. Were you blocking me?"

"No." Quinn didn't think so, anyway. "What time is it?"

"Going on ten thirty."

"At *night*?" When he didn't get an answer, Quinn said, "I assume by your lack of response that I've lost quite a bit of time."

"Are you still having problems because of the probe?"

"Something has affected me, but I don't know what exactly. Any time in the past that I've had a bad reaction to a mind probe, a little rest was all it took to ease my headache and bring me back to normal."

Tzader crossed his arms. "How long were you out?"

"I remember lying down—fully clothed—and think I fell asleep after my headache went away. But your beating on the door woke me and I don't recall putting on this robe." A question about Evalle tugged at Quinn's memory. Somebody asking about Evalle . . .

"I knew probing O'Meary was a mistake." Grim worry tripped through Tzader's voice. "Any chance Conlan is accessing your mind?"

"I don't think so, but I've lost at least an hour, and I doubt I slept that whole time. This migraine was worse than any I've ever experienced. Maybe I just lost track of what I was doing. That happens even to humans." Quinn considered turning on low lights but couldn't muster the energy to try.

"But not you." Tzader's shoulders bunched with his

folded arms. Stress lines cut deep grooves at the bridge of his nose. "Any chance you can tap your subconscious and figure out what happened?"

"Maybe, but not until I've had some distance from this probing and get rid of this headache from hell. It's not a matter of enduring the pain, which I would gladly do to get some answers. But I pushed it once in the past and lost my ability to mind lock for weeks. That taught me to wait until at least the pain went away, which should be soon."

Holding his hand up, Tzader's gaze focused past Quinn, as if he was listening to someone reaching him telepathically.

Quinn took that opportunity to walk past Tzader into the living area and the bar. He waved his hand at a lamp in the corner to turn it on kinetically and the light flickered. What the devil? He pointed a stern finger at the light and it came on. When he reached his bar, he pulled out a cold longneck Budweiser, popped the cap off and downed half of it at one time.

Tzader walked over to him. "Never seen you drink beer, much less horse-piss beer."

"Lot of things we don't know about each other," Quinn pointed out. He, Tzader and Evalle had become close after escaping a Medb trap a couple years ago, but they still surprised each other at times. "When nothing else works I have a beer, and at one time this was top shelf for me."

"Does it cure the headache?"

"No, just tastes good."

Tzader chuckled. "Wait till Evalle finds out about the cheap side of your champagne tastes."

Where had that blasted thought about Evalle come from? Who had wanted to know about her? Quinn pushed around in his mucked-up mind for anything on her.

How does Evalle . . . do something? Something what?

He had a sick feeling the word he couldn't pull up in that question might be seriously important, like giving him the identity of who had asked.

Quinn said, "Speaking of Evalle . . . any word?"

Tzader let out a weary sigh loaded with exhaustion and frustration. "Trey just checked in. He's had Lucien, Casper and Devon searching for Storm and Evalle. Nothing yet."

"What about the fog?"

"All we've determined is that the fog seems to be primarily in the coastal states, which is one reason it took so long to finger the fog as the catalyst for Alterants shifting."

Quinn groused, "We don't have enough people to fight something that spreads this fast."

"Tell me about it. We could use Storm to track the beasts and Evalle to combat the Alterants shifting," Tzader said. "But Sen won't listen to any argument. Said it's out of his hands and if the fog makes her shift, she's dead meat just like the others. Hopefully, she won't run into the fog."

Quinn started to speak and a vision flashed in his mind, a fractured image, as if the transmission had been interrupted.

"What's up, Quinn?"

"Nothing." He waved off the moment, hiding the wheel of nervousness that started turning in his gut. He asked, "Has Trey found anything?"

"Not exactly. Trey's been in contact with our Beladors who work for MARTA monitoring security feeds on highways and subways. He's been sending out teams to hot spots. One of the security Beladors saw two people fitting Storm and Evalle's description in a MARTA station. Trey's on his way over to confirm if it was them in a downtown subway station, and he sent a small team to scour the other stations in the general area."

"You talk to Sen about the MARTA surveillance?"

"What do you think?"

Quinn smiled around sore jaw muscles that ached from clenching his teeth against the pain that had racked him for so many hours. His head had eased some, but he couldn't put his finger on what kept nagging him about Evalle. "I can only assume Evalle would not be in Atlanta if she was trying to evade the Tribunal, so she must be doing their bidding. Any idea what it might be?"

"Not yet."

"What about Brina? Where does she stand on this?"

"I'm waiting until I have solid information to go to Brina. All I can tell her right now is that Conlan's in lockdown but we don't have proof of his being a traitor. We can't accuse him of something he hasn't done yet."

"I agree. Any luck in trying to reach Evalle telepathically?"

"Nope. Not a sound from her. Trey can't reach her either."

"Since the Tribunal won't allow Evalle to contact us, she's probably blocking any telepathic communication we initiate," Quinn said.

Tzader nodded, reaching in for a beer from Quinn's refrigerator. "That's what I figured."

"Even our people might not be able to find her if she doesn't want to be found, especially if she's with Storm."

"True. Storm's another issue I'll deal with when we find her."

"He's probably helping her."

Tzader didn't look convinced. "Maybe, but Sen brought him in, which makes Storm not entirely trustworthy in my book. He's got a short-term lease on his apartment. Doesn't look as though he's planning to stay very long, so what's on his agenda?"

Quinn had to concede Tzader that point. "Any sighting of Tristan?"

"No. That's the only reason I'm a little relieved to hear that Evalle was spotted with Storm. Better him than Tristan."

A female voice whispered in Quinn's mind, *Where is Evalle?* Another memory of him answering questions in the dark fought to the surface. His lungs squeezed, making the next breath painful. Had he been talking to someone about Evalle? "We have to find Evalle."

"That's why I called Isak," Tzader said, not noticing the urgency behind Quinn's statement.

"Really think Isak will tell you where she is?"

"No, but he can lead us to her. I just got word on the way here that some of his men have been sighted."

Quinn didn't share Tzader's certainty over Isak Nyght. The chap was former Special Forces. He'd created a unique squad of former military special-ops soldiers he called the Nyght Raiders. A few years back he and his men had all

opted out of the military, disappeared for a bit, then surfaced Stateside, searching for nonhumans.

Isak could be more threat than help to Evalle if he figured out she wasn't human. Quinn pointed out, "Don't
you think it's odd that Isak hasn't realized Evalle's not
human?"

"Yes, and that worries me, because he will eventually."
Tzader put down his empty beer bottle and scratched his
head. "I'm starting to think we may have to move Evalle
somewhere away from here once she's clear of this Tribunal mess. Isak is obsessed with killing Alterants after
losing his best friend to one. He terminates them on
sight. If he doesn't know she's an Alterant it's because she's
managed to keep her bright green eyes hidden from him
behind her sunglasses."

A face smoked through Quinn's mind.

Kizira? He hadn't seen her in years except for a few brief
times and always rife with conflict. He'd had a glimpse of
her this past week when the Beladors had faced off with
the Kujoo . . . and he'd seen her in O'Meary's mind today.

But that had been a vision from the future, not a real
interaction. It might not even come to pass.

Quinn swallowed, hoping his wrung-out mind was
just dredging up random thoughts. "What do you want
me to do?"

Tzader gave him an assessing look. "I need you healed
up before you face a threat. It's too dangerous to put you
out on the street until you have full use of your kinetics."
He held up his hand when Quinn started to argue. "I
saw the light flicker when you tried to turn it on. You're

nowhere close to a hundred percent, which makes you vulnerable to an attack."

Quinn's voice dropped to an evil level. "Oh, I'd make something pay dearly if it attacked me in my present mood."

"But if you had to link with another Belador . . . you'd put him or her at risk."

The truth cut through Quinn's bravado, forcing him to think beyond his own need to strike at something. Where had that blatant aggression come from? Couldn't have been Conlan, because, in spite of what he'd seen, Quinn still believed in the kid. Everything he'd encountered in Conlan's mind had come from an upstanding young man and a loyal Belador.

No one should be convicted of a crime he hadn't committed yet and certainly not based solely on a vision. Quinn said, "Agreed. I'll call you as soon as I'm feeling top shape. Let me know the minute you locate Evalle."

"I will." Tzader gave him another questioning look but nodded and left.

Quinn suddenly felt unclean, as though he needed a shower.

On the way to the bathroom, a female voice whispered from deep in his subconscious. *Evalle is special . . . powerful . . . she is meant for greater things.*

Ice pumped through his heart.

His mind was screwing with him, because that had been Kizira's voice.

Dismissing the voice, he stepped into the bathroom and turned the shower hot enough to boil his skin red. When he dropped his robe he noticed a scrape across his shoulder. Now that his mind was returning to normal, he realized the skin on his back felt raw.

Why was that? He twisted his neck to look over his shoulder into the mirror.

Two sets of scratches raked his shoulders, as if . . .

Impossible. Even Tzader hadn't been able to get past Quinn's protective ward. Quinn hadn't been with a woman in the past two weeks.

But the scratches awoke another image in his mind with brutal clarity.

Excruciating pain and pleasure twisted in a sexual dance of erotic torture.

A woman's body stretched out beneath him, urging him on as he drove into her mindlessly. Her body had glowed softly in his dark room. Her milky shoulders tensed before she climaxed. Her face . . . *No!*

Kizira couldn't have been here.

He'd have known if she had.

He clutched his head with cold and clammy hands. When he opened his eyes his gaze caught on a thin swish of pale color against the vanity.

The bracelet made of his braided hair lay on the dark brown granite.

What had he done?

What had he allowed Kizira to do to him?

What had he told her about Evalle?

Quinn smashed his fist into the wall. Rage and betrayal roared through him.

No one was safe as long as Kizira could access his mind.

That meant one of them had to die.

TWENTY-SEVEN

Lights disappeared in the tunnel, which only sharp-ened Evalle's ability to see Tristan starting to shift into his beast.

The man seriously needed anger management.

She had to help him calm down. "Who is Petrina?"

"My sister!" Tristan raised his fists, shaking them at an empty tunnel where the soldier spirit had just vanished. He yelled, *"You're a dead bitch, Kizira!"*

Evalle stood very still, anticipating any sudden change or attack. She didn't want to end up a dead bitch, too.

Thunk . . . thunk, thunk.

She turned at the noise.

Bricks were piling on top of each other, forming a wall. She jerked around, looking past Tristan to where rough-cut beams that could be railroad ties began piling to form another barrier.

The Maze of Death residents were barricading her in with Tristan . . . who would be a full-blown beast in another minute.

Would being in this maze cause him to lose control of his beast?

"Calm down, Tristan," Evalle warned.

His neck thickened, veins sticking out. He swung his head back and forth, finally seeing the walls forming, and roared a vicious curse, then slammed his body against the stack of railroad ties. The wall didn't give an inch.

He started pounding the wooden barrier, his body still changing.

"Stop!" she yelled at him. "You're making it worse."

His shirtsleeves split when his arms lengthened. The back of his shirt ripped where his neck bulged. He'd be half again as big and twice as deadly within seconds if he didn't stop shifting into a beast.

"Tristan!"

He swung a face distorted with rage at her that would scare a demon.

Bones in his jaw cracked and muscle stretched to accept a double row of fangs. He snarled at her. Saliva dripped from his lips.

Not the controlled beast she'd met in the jungle.

She couldn't survive fighting him in her human body and doubted changing into her Belador battle form would make any difference. Not with his extra kick from the Kujoo highball.

Tristan dropped his head back and bellowed a blood-chilling scream. His fingers lengthened into sharp claws.

How could she reach him? What could make him stop when he was this far out of control? Didn't he realize he was wasting precious time they could use to save the three Alterants?

And his sister?

His sister.

She pointed a finger in Tristan's face she hoped wouldn't

end up snapped off by those fangs. "I will *not* help you save your sister unless you stop changing right now!"

That must have gotten through, because he stilled every movement but heaving, labored breaths.

Evalle pressed her point. "Take a look around at the walls closing in on us. I need you able to think."

Tristan's chest expanded and contracted quietly. He stared at her through green eyes burning with fury, as though she had been the one to hand his sister to the Medb.

Maybe he wasn't cognizant of anything in this form.

Maybe he wasn't as in control of his beast as he'd have her believe.

"Come on, Tristan, get a grip on yourself unless you want to leave your sister at Kizira's mercy."

Several tense seconds passed before he slammed a fist into the pile of railroad ties, then dropped his arms to his side. He finally began to change back and withdraw into his normal body.

She gave up the breath she'd been holding. For the first time since coming into this place, she enjoyed a moment of relief. Odd how facing down something she *knew* could kill her had taken her mind off the mere threat of what *might* be in here.

Returning to his normal body didn't completely take the edge off Tristan's anger. He stomped back and forth in front of her, growling when he wasn't spewing threats. "That bitch! I'm going to kill her if she hurts my sister. Rip her head off."

Evalle gave him a minute to vent in hopes it would help him calm down more, then said, "We can't do anything without your guide service. You scared off the soldier ghost who knows how to get us there."

Tristan stopped pacing and absorbed her words. "*Fuck!*"

"Shouting ran him off the last time, and it's wearing on what little patience I have left, so cut it out. Not to mention that cursing isn't helping your case either, since a Civil War soldier is from an era when they didn't talk like that in front of women."

That brought a wry twist to Tristan's lips. His eyebrow lifted in a derogatory arch. "I doubt he's concerned about offending the sensibilities of a woman wearing tight jeans, boots and a shirt short enough to expose her midriff. Not that I have any complaints about you being down to two buttons left on your shirt, but you're far from the image of a lady."

Had he just dissed her? "Fine. Go shout your head off and curse every ghost in here if that makes you feel better than saving your sister from the Medb."

That slapped the arrogance off his face, along with some of his color.

She hadn't intended to give him a verbal kick in the nuts, but she was running out of time and, at this point, so was Tristan.

And she'd had enough of his hardheaded attitude.

"You're right," he admitted, wiping an agitated hand across his blond hair, raking the short hairs out of shape. "We have to find the soldier's chamber, and fast. I wish he'd at least have had a sense of time so we'd know when Kizira might start killing Alterants."

"I agree, but we have one small problem. What about these walls?"

"Hell. You willing to suffer trying to knock these railroad ties loose with kinetics?"

Not really, and she didn't think that would improve their situation anyhow. "I could handle the pain and we'll heal eventually, but using any power at this point might tick off these ghosts even more. Can you teleport us to other areas down here?"

"I've only teleported in and out of the maze at the couple places where the subway intersects these tunnels, so I don't know if we could actually teleport outside the maze from here. If I tried to teleport us from here and the maze shifts something solid into an area I remember as being an open landing, we'd die. It'd be like hitting a solid wall at mach speed."

She saw no other way out. "We're screwed."

"I can go first. If it works, I'll come right back for you, but it's going to take me a minute or two before I can teleport again."

"Wait a minute. You're going to leave me *here*? What if you hit something solid and splatter? I'm stuck down here forever."

He shoved his hands to his waist and leaned toward her. "What's *your* idea, then?"

"I don't know. Let me think." She removed her glasses and rubbed her tired eyes, then put the glasses back on. What had he just said? "You need a minute or two to teleport a second time even for a short distance? That's why you didn't shift to fight the demons that attacked us in the jungle, isn't it? You were saving your energy to teleport from one continent to another when we reached the next village."

He crossed his arms and gave her his silent routine.

Confirmation, as far as she was concerned, but . . . "Was that another side effect of your Kujoo cocktail?"

Still no answer. Fine. Taking a look around, she said, "The ghosts did this to us. Why don't you ask them nicely to let us continue? Apologize for disturbing their home."

A small muscle flexed in his jaw while he thought. He finally grumbled something, then stared at the railroad tie wall and said, "I'm sorry I disturbed you. If you'll let us pass, I will respect your home."

Nothing happened.

He glared at her. "Happy?"

"Do I *look* happy?" She dealt with Nightstalkers all the time, Grady in particular. Sometimes they just wanted to show off what they could do and show you who ran things in their world. She turned slowly as she spoke to the ghosts. "You have an interesting home. Nothing built above ground is anything like this."

Tristan's sigh suggested she was a moron.

A gas lantern took shape on one of the walls, and a rug appeared beneath her feet.

The look on Tristan's face *now* was priceless.

She cleared her voice and said, "I've been admiring all of the maze. Do you have anything else to show us?"

Nothing happened.

Crossing her arms, she waited patiently as railroad ties began disintegrating. Once there were only two left, she stepped past Tristan and said, "*Now*, I'm happy."

He caught up and passed her, moving in a hurry. "This way."

Evalle kept up with him, but five minutes later she had her doubts that he knew where he was going. Every time he reached a new choice of direction in the maze, he'd shoot off without hesitation, then hit a dead end, backtrack and do it again.

Stress bounced off him in stronger waves at each wrong turn.

The ghosts might let them move forward, but only one could show them how to find Tristan's sister and the Alterants.

Evalle called out, "Tristan, wait. I have an idea."

That he stopped immediately confirmed he had no clue where he'd been going. He strode back to her, breathing hard. "Make it fast."

Who did he think he was to order her around after she'd just gotten him out of ghost jail? But she couldn't afford to waste time straightening him out. Storm had given her ninety minutes and they were down to the last thirty of that.

She held her patience in a tight fist. "What made the soldier talk to you the first time?"

Tristan huffed a breath that clearly said he didn't have time for twenty questions, but he also squinted, thinking. "I'd only sensed that the area was benign when I originally left the Alterants there—I hadn't met any spirits. When I couldn't find any sign of the three Alterants, I returned to the chamber and walked around, talking to myself."

"Really?" she asked, hiding a smirk.

He shrugged sheepishly. "Sometimes I think better

out loud. That's when I actually met the spirits inhabiting that space. An old guy showed up first playing checkers, then a little while later the soldier appeared."

"What happened then?"

"The soldier asked me why I was unhappy. I explained that I'd lost three people down here. That's when he told me about Kizira and her protectors holding the Alterants." Tristan's shoulders drooped in defeat. "I know I was on the right path to find that chamber until I pissed off the soldier and he disappeared."

She'd noticed something else about the maze while they'd been walking this time. "The tunnels have changed behind us and around us. I'm thinking the spirits are just showing us this is their territory. They removed the wall so we could move forward again as long as we weren't a threat. I think they're now changing the maze constantly to stop us from going forward or backward."

"You're probably right, but how does that help?"

"Let's give talking to them another shot."

"I don't have time to stand around talking to ghosts."

"I don't either, but we can either lose another minute or two running through endless turns of this maze, or we can take a stab at finding your soldier again."

Time whispered by while he made up his mind. "What have you got in mind?"

"My empathic skills are picking up everything from anger to frustration to the urge to maim and kill from you."

"All that and no crystal ball? Want to guess my weight next?"

"I don't want to hurt you, but that's still on the table for getting me into all this."

"You got yourself into this by sucking up to the Beladors." He hooked his thumb in the waistband of his jeans and shifted his weight to one leg.

"You're an asshole. You know that?" Evalle expected an airslap for the curse, but none came. Sadly, that just confirmed no Belador could reach her here. "I'm trying to help you save your sister, and you're not helping."

That silenced him. He drew a deep breath and ran his hand through his hair, scratching his head. "You're right."

"Why are you fighting me at every step?"

"Because I don't want you here."

"Tough."

He shook his head in wonder. "If I'd had your deal with the Beladors, I wouldn't be in this situation, but you have this screwed-up sense of honor instead of hardened survival skills, or you'd have turned me in as soon as you got back to Atlanta."

Did that mean he felt guilty? Had he been screwed over so many times in his life that he fought everyone like a wounded dog? "I meant what I said about giving all of us a chance. You ready to do this or not?"

He squared his jaw and nodded.

"You taught me about healing from what you learned while in the jungle. I've spent my time in the city dealing with Nightstalkers. They might be dead, but the spirit still has emotions and feelings. The ghosts down here responded to me a few minutes ago, but they're not responding to you and I think it's because you're generating aggressive energy."

"I'll play your Dr. Phil game. What do you suggest we do?"

"Calm down completely. Close your eyes and think about how much your sister means to you and how much you want to save all the hostages."

Seeing that light up some embarrassment in Tristan's face encouraged her to counsel him further. "Once you stop sounding like you're going to rip out throats, talk calmly again about looking for the hostages. I'll keep an eye out to see if anything happens."

He didn't appear completely onboard with the plan, but he did close his eyes. Seconds later, his arms dropped to his sides in a semi-relaxed state.

Evalle opened up her senses fully. Tristan's aggression bled away grudgingly, and in place of that he started emitting pulses of concern and worry. He spoke softly, wondering aloud where he could find his sister and the Alterants.

He'd rambled for almost a minute when a form shimmered near them.

First a barrel appeared, then a stool supporting a shrunken elderly man who wore overalls and spectacles. He hunched over as if studying something. As soon as a faded checkerboard with red and black discs arranged on the squares took shape on top of the barrel, the old guy moved a red checker to an empty spot.

He raised expectant eyes at Evalle. She forced a mild expression, not wanting to react at seeing his throat slashed open.

Tristan held very still.

"Your move," the old guy croaked out in a froggy voice.

Me? She glanced over at Tristan, whose amused expression said *This was your idea.*

Did the old guy want a real challenge, or just to win?

Before she made a wrong move, literally, she asked the ghost, "Do you know a soldier?"

"Yes."

"Would you ask him to come here?"

"Depends."

"On what?"

"If you play a right nice game."

Since he hadn't threatened her with a sharp object, she stepped over and lifted a black checker. The poker-chip-sized disc felt light and soft, not like the plastic ones set up outside on tables at a Cracker Barrel restaurant where she'd eaten once.

His crinkled gaze watched the board expectantly, waiting for her to place her chip.

Which move would bring the soldier back?

Which move would cause the checker player to vanish?

TWENTY-EIGHT

Evalle turned the black chip in her hand, debating on the right spot on the checkerboard.

Tristan had become mute the minute the old guy's spirit had appeared, but she sensed how much he wanted her to make the correct move.

His sister's safety depended on it.

The sister he'd obviously wanted to keep a secret.

She slowly lowered the black chip to a spot that left her ghost opponent an easy jump with his red chip.

She slid her gaze sideways to see how Tristan judged the move. Sweat beaded on his forehead in spite of the chill that surrounded them.

No confidence there.

The old guy's hand moved fast as lightning.

He jumped two of her black chips and cackled as he lifted his winnings off the board. "I'm hard to beat."

That had to be a positive sign, right? She asked the ghost again, "Would you ask your soldier friend to come here?"

"He can't play. No good with checkers."

Tristan's anxiety ramped up.

She shot him a warning look and he calmed down. Evalle smiled warmly at the ghost. "If you'll call the soldier so we can talk to him, I'll move another chip."

The old guy's eyes rounded with such excitement that she hated that she didn't have time to play a whole game with him. If Grady had been here, he would have taken the time to entertain this man, but Grady wouldn't have been happy down here.

In the next few seconds something must have happened between the ghosts, because the soldier's image wavered into view on the other side of the checker player.

Tilting her head slightly toward the spirit, she used her eyes to tell Tristan he had a connection to the soldier and had better fix this mess.

Tristan said to the Civil War ghost, "Sorry I yelled earlier. I need to talk to you."

She gave Tristan a silent attaboy for apologizing again but noticed the soldier didn't speak. Maybe he had to take a fully corporeal form to communicate.

What was he waiting for?

The old guy said, "He's here. Your move."

So the old guy had to be appeased first, huh? She placed another black chip. Her two-hundred-year-old opponent won three of her chips that time. He laughed and slapped his leg.

That must have done the trick, because the young soldier's form solidified. He stared at Tristan. "Why you so unhappy?"

Tristan answered in an even tone. "I'm looking for my three friends again, *and* my sister. Do you know where they are?"

"She done told me."

"Will you lead us to them?"

"I 'spose . . . if you promise to make *her* git out."

The soldier had to mean Kizira. Evalle glanced at Tristan, who told the ghost, "If I can help my friends and sister escape the witch, she'll have no reason to stay. And we'll leave, too."

"Alrighty," the soldier said. "I reckon that'll work."

The checker player asked Evalle, "'nother game?"

She swallowed her misery over having to disappoint him, even if he'd probably asked that question repeatedly for a hundred and fifty years with no positive results. "I'm sorry, but I have to go."

"Okee dokee." He started setting the board as if she'd agreed.

The soldier began floating backwards into a dark tunnel.

"Evalle," Tristan called softly.

"I know. Let's go." She stayed close to Tristan, who followed the shimmering shape of the soldier's now semi-transparent, and glowing, form. Their moving beacon took a path through a narrow walkway that began dropping in elevation, then turned right, then left, and continued to descend.

No furniture. No plants. No maniacal pitchfork guys. So far.

Tristan stumbled a couple of times, which indicated he didn't share her exceptional night vision.

She stepped ahead of him, whispering, "Follow me. I can see changes in the terrain. I'll let you know when to step over or around something."

When she reached a landing type area the soldier stopped moving forward and turned to face Tristan as if

Evalle didn't exist. "The witch poisons our world . . . I ain't goin' no further. She ain't allowed to come this way with you. She knows we'll stop her."

That worked for Evalle.

The soldier added, "Follow the lanterns. You'll find her."

Evalle asked the soldier, "Can we get back to where we started today?"

His sleepy eyes finally noticed her. "I reckon it's possible."

What kind of answer was that? "Do we still have time before she kills a hostage?"

The soldier stared straight through her to the point Evalle thought he'd zoned out, but then his eyes focused. "Mebee a quarter hour. You're 'bout two stone throws away."

The soldier began fading until he turned into a glow of light the size of her hand and blinked out.

Tristan wouldn't be any more motivated than right now to talk, and he couldn't afford to leave her behind.

Evalle put a hand on his chest to stop him when he made a move to leave. "We've got fifteen minutes. I want two of them."

Tristan argued, "He might be wrong about when she's going to start killing people."

"Then you need to talk fast. Why did Kizira bring your sister here?"

He took too long to answer. "I don't know, maybe some kind of insurance that I wouldn't try to trick her. We're wasting seconds."

"Before you go off half-cocked again, we need a plan. We can't just waltz into a nest of Medb warlocks and Kizira."

"I'm trading myself for the hostages. You're getting them safely out of here. *That's* the plan."

"If that's your whole plan, it's time to tell me how I go through several feet of concrete to reach the subway again, wise guy."

He shook his head and scoffed at her. "Thought you'd already have this figured out. I'll tell the Alterants to go with you if you swear you'll do two things. First take my sister somewhere safe, get her out of Atlanta and don't tell anyone she's associated with me. Second, make sure that Tzader cuts a deal for you to accompany the Alterants to the Tribunal before he tells Sen where you are."

She wasn't agreeing to anything now that she knew Tristan had a sister in here to rescue. "Still listening."

"As for getting through concrete, the minute you're far enough away from Kizira, call Tzader or Quinn telepathically and first make sure they'll protect these Alterants then tell them to bring in Sen, who can teleport in where we entered and take you out. Tell everyone my sister is an innocent bystander, that she was dragged into this by mistake."

"*That's* your plan for me to escape?"

He pulled back. "Yes. Why? What's wrong with it?"

"I can't use telepathy in here. I've been battling to keep my mental shields in place to block out any Belador telepathy since I got back to Atlanta. The minute you brought me into the maze the attack on my shields stopped. I lowered them to see if anyone's voice came through. Haven't heard a peep."

"Maybe the Tribunal won't allow anyone to contact you."

"Nothing would stop Tzader or Quinn from trying to find me, and Trey has been trying to reach me nonstop. He's so powerful that his telepathy thumps against my shields. Trey's like a supernova of telepaths. If he can't get through, no one can."

Tristan had that sick kicked-in-the-balls expression again, but it was his own fault this time. He should have discussed this with her earlier.

She cocked her head, arms crossed. "Here's *my* plan. I say we rescue the hostages and get out of here using your teleportation once we make it back to the access wall. *If* you can find the right spot again."

His body practically vibrated with the need to head toward the hostages. "I'm sure I can find one of the places to teleport out if the ghosts don't block us."

"Sounds like they'll help us if it means Kizira goes, too."

"The question is what you intend to do when we land on the other side?"

"You give me the three Alterants—"

"Here we go again."

"Let me finish. I *will* have Storm go to Tzader, since I can't be seen, and Tzader will contact Brina about the Alterants. She's already agreed to guarantee their safety and a chance to speak to the Tribunal. I can't tell you all that transpired at the Tribunal meeting, but Brina will help if it means me showing up with three Alterants." Evalle had worded that carefully, because Tristan had it in for Brina. He didn't need to know the Tribunal would punish Brina if Evalle failed.

"What about me and my sister?"

If the Tribunal wanted to pin the responsibility for his escape on Evalle, she would argue that they failed to forbid her from helping him escape.

Use their own twisted logic on them.

And hope Brina could make it stick.

She told Tristan, "I won't say a word about you or your sister, but in return I want your help with finding out more about Alterants." Something pinched her arm. She jumped, spinning around to find nothing there.

A hollow laugh bounced around her.

Why couldn't these things have been demons? She could kill those. "Think it through, Tristan. There's already a neutralize order out on all of us. With the massive Alterant problem across the country right now, VIPER will probably bring in Dakkar. He's a mage that runs bounty hunters. He'll find out you have a sister. You'll never be safe, and neither will she."

"There's not going to be anything to discuss if we lose those hostages."

She didn't say a word.

"Fine. If you can get those three hostages to the other side of the wall in the train tunnel safely—without VIPER killing them—I'll go along with you."

She was running tight on time, but she had to believe that Storm would be there to help her with this. He wouldn't let anyone from VIPER draw down on them. "Agreed. Get moving."

Tristan took off as fast as a gunshot, with her right behind. The lanterns the soldier had promised appeared along the way.

When a glow filtered out through a garage-door-sized opening in the wall on her left ten steps ahead, Tristan slowed and crept up to the opening.

Evalle tucked her back close to the wall of rock and sidestepped until she was next to his shoulder. She couldn't call out to Tzader from here, but she should be able to speak telepathically with Tristan, since it had worked in the jungle. *You know I won't shift into my beast state, but you can, which will give us an edge.*

He told her, *No, I can't either. If I shift it might trigger the other four to lose control and change.*

Evalle angled her head to the left to see his face. *Four?*

Chagrin over having to share something significant bathed his face. *My sister is an Alterant, too.*

Two in one family? What—

Can we discuss genetics and heritage later, Evalle? Tell you what. If we get out of here alive and I can put my sister somewhere safe, I'll explain how I think Alterants are connected. We aren't anomalies. You're right. We should be a recognized race, and I think I know enough to prove it. Satisfied for now?

I'm good. More than good. Her heart raced from adrenaline and hope. She'd face an army of Medb for the chance to get that information from Tristan. *How do you want to work this?*

Stay here until I need you, and follow my lead. Tristan stepped away from the wall and entered the room.

Tristan! she hissed at him.

Don't distract me right now.

Evalle slid to the edge of the entrance, taking in the

open space that soared thirty feet high. The hollowed-out chamber stretched as wide and long as a concert hall, but the only music playing here tonight would be death throes if their half-assed plan went bad. Torches blazed around the room and on each corner of a stone slab twenty feet across. Three knee-high, round bands of flames positioned on the ground in front of the platform provided half the light in the room.

Three men in ragged and dirty clothes had each been imprisoned in three fire circles.

Those had to be the escaped Alterants.

They all looked to be around mid- to late twenties. One had dark brown hair that mopped around his shoulders and could have been a center in basketball with his height. The next guy had frizzy, carrot-red hair, a medium build and skin so white it almost glowed. The shortest guy wore a dangly little earring in one ear. He had curly black hair and a Haitian face.

And none of them had green eyes, but they did have one thing in common. Terror.

Tristan stopped in the center of the room.

The three men started shouting for him to free them.

Kizira appeared out of thin air, floating inches above the stone slab. Flames shot up in front of the stone, then spread out until it formed a wide moat of fire surrounding her.

Evalle suffered her first real doubts about escaping the Maze of Death alive.

The Medb priestess waved a hand at the three men, silencing them and setting the bar for her witch powers.

Tristan addressed Kizira. "I'm here. Release the Alterants *and* my sister."

"Nice to see you again, Tristan. I missed you." Kizira had a debutante's voice that scraped across Evalle's nerves.

"Can't say the feeling's mutual, Kizira. Where's my sister if you want to deal?"

"Our last bargain did not end successfully. You still owe me for that one."

Evalle fingered her dagger at the sour note in Kizira's accusation. That priestess had tried to use Tristan a week ago in a fanatical plan to kill all the Beladors.

The scary part was that it had almost worked.

But Kizira had abandoned the Kujoo and Tristan the minute things had gotten dicey.

Tristan countered, "I fulfilled my part of the agreement and got shipped back to South America when you disappeared on us. The failure was not on my end. Release these Alterants and I'll come to you willingly. You don't want to cross me."

The pale blue robe and hood gave Kizira a saintly look, but any sweet image ended there. She had the heart of a snake, too small to be anything but deadly. "I agreed to exchange these three Rías for you. Your sister's not part of that deal."

Evalle cocked her head. *Rías?* What did she mean by that distinction?

Tristan replied, "Then *make* it part of this deal. My sister is of no use now that I'm here."

"But I want something else in trade for her."

"I have nothing else to offer you but me," Tristan said as though it was obvious.

Kizira laughed, a tinkling sound of delight. "Oh, that's not true. You have something lurking nearby that I want as much as you want your sister."

"What?"

"Evalle Kincaid."

TWENTY-NINE

Evalle froze. *Kizira wants to trade Tristan's sister for me? Is Kizira bluffing about knowing I'm here?*

Tristan hadn't given Kizira an answer yet.

He might be willing to exchange his life for those other three Alterants, but he had no reason to risk anyone to save Evalle.

Especially not his sister.

Kizira called to Tristan, "I have made you a fair offer, Tristan. Evalle for your sister."

He said, "Show me my sister." Then he came into Evalle's mind. *I can only shield my mind from Kizira and talk to you at the same time for seconds. If I can get my hands on my sister, you take her and find your way back to the subway wall. When you run late, Storm will figure a way to get someone to you.*

Evalle blinked. He wasn't throwing her to the Medb?

Evalle! We have a deal?

She nodded even though he couldn't see her. *Yes, but what about you and the other three?*

I'll try to get them out, but if you and my sister can escape, that'll have to be good enough. Just promise me you won't hand her over to the Tribunal no matter what.

Like she could do that to Tristan at this point? *I promise. Do you think Kizira knows I'm here in the maze?*

I don't know. I didn't tell her.

Evalle believed him.

Kizira said, "I'm tired of waiting, Tristan. Hand over Evalle. I know she's close by. Call her in here."

Guess that answered my question. Evalle gripped her dagger.

"Don't know what you're talking about. She's not here," Tristan bluffed.

Evalle peeked again. Kizira rose high in the air. "Don't waste time trying to fool me. Her friend told me I would find her with you."

Evalle almost snorted at that. Stupid witch. Evalle could count her friends on one hand, and none of them would help Kizira find her.

"Who told you we'd be together?" Tristan asked.

"Vladimir Quinn."

Evalle swung around, slamming her back to the wall. Her heart cramped. Quinn would never betray her. How would he even know she was here with Tristan?

Because word was out that she'd helped Tristan escape.

Quinn wouldn't believe that I intentionally released Tristan. He wouldn't.

"You're lying, Kizira," Tristan argued. "Evalle's thick as thieves with Tzader and Quinn. You know that. Why would those Beladors hand her over to a Medb?"

"Because VIPER is hunting all the Alterants with a kill-on-sight order, even Evalle. I owe Quinn from a past debt and offered to keep her safe. He also knows that I'm her best chance at freedom."

Evalle didn't buy that. Why would Quinn think she'd be safe with Kizira?

"And Evalle?" Kizira called out. "If you want proof that I spoke to Quinn privately today, he was in the Ritz on Peachtree in downtown Atlanta in a room the same number as today's date. I was curing Quinn of a severe headache. Even with my soothing skills, he was in no shape to come after you himself, and he didn't want Tzader caught between loyalties."

Air backed up in Evalle's lungs.

Quinn had a system of hotels he stayed in, and on Thursdays he stayed in a room based on the date. He changed to a different hotel every day as a safety precaution, but he'd told her and Tzader yesterday he'd be at the downtown Ritz today.

He'd said no one knew his system except Tzader and Evalle.

Kizira had been in Quinn's hotel room. Soothing him.

Evalle understood that reference with no problem. She couldn't believe Quinn had slept with this murdering witch. The first time Evalle had met Quinn she'd found out he'd had history with Kizira, but never had she questioned his loyalty to the Beladors.

Or to her.

Did he really think she'd walk into the Medb camp for any reason? If so, he didn't know her as well as she'd thought. Even if she believed Kizira, Evalle knew Tzader wouldn't agree.

A soft female voice whispered next to Evalle's ear. "Believe who you trust and trust who you believe."

She sucked in a sharp breath at the bodyless voice. The same voice that Evalle had heard earlier tonight in her apartment and for the first time this past week. If Tristan had been standing here she could have asked him if he'd heard it, but Evalle had a feeling he wouldn't have.

Who kept trying to reach her?

Evalle whispered, "Who are you?"

No one answered.

Kizira called out again, "If you don't come with me, Evalle, the fog will grow across North America until it covers everything in a week. Do you want all those deaths on your shoulders? Or to lose Tzader and Quinn? Because you know they'll be on the front lines. Come willingly and I'll clear the air. Literally."

The beast stirred inside Evalle.

She should have known that wacked-out witch was behind the fog. But would Kizira really spare mere humans or anyone who mattered to Evalle? Even Quinn?

"I'm through waiting, Tristan. Tell Evalle to come forward or I'll have to hurt one of your friends."

Tristan warned in a deadly tone, "Hurt one of them and expect to pay a price. Make this easy on everyone. Let these three and my sister leave. I'll stay."

Evalle tensed at his challenge. She peeked around the corner.

The witch flicked her fingers and a bolt of lightning shot toward the redheaded Alterant.

Tristan whipped his hands across his body, throwing a kinetic field of power to block the lightning bolt.

The block worked like a champ.

Kinetic energy hadn't bounced back at Tristan. The

maze spirits wanted Kizira out of here. They must have cleared this area from any backlash.

But the witch had used the strike of lightning to divert Tristan's powers.

She waved a hand and snarled out a hairy-sounding chant.

Two creatures rose from the moat of fire around Kizira. The scaly creatures had heads the size of fifty-gallon barrels, with teeth and jaws that looked as if they could crush cars. Fire raced up their red-orange scales and crawled along four arms that grew from each of their undulating serpent bodies.

Six long tentacle-like claws curled in and out at the end of each arm. The creatures continued to rise and coil into shape. When their tails came into view, the last ten feet curled up and over with a scorpion pincher.

"Last chance, Tristan," Kizira warned.

"What good am I to you dead?"

"You'd be surprised what I could do with a dead Alterant, like, oh, bring Evalle to me and I'll show you." She called out another chant and flames roared to life around the tallest of the three Alterants.

Tristan charged the flaming circle, but one of the serpents lunged at him. He twisted around to throw up a field of energy to hold the thing off.

The other two Alterants lunged, but their fire circles flamed up, stopping them. They roared, shifting into beasts.

Evalle stepped from cover and raced into the room.

No one was dying to protect her.

The fire must have broken Kizira's silence spell over the tall Alterant. Amidst his screams of pain he cried out, *"Petrina . . . not . . . here."*

The smell of charred flesh gagged Evalle. She shoved a blast of kinetic energy to knock the burning Alterant from his circle. The flames went with him.

He stopped struggling, dead.

Tristan yelled in Evalle's head, *Kizira lied. My sister's not here. Run!*

Evalle said, *No way.* She made a decision she hoped she wouldn't regret. *Link with me and we'll kick her scrawny butt.*

But when she opened her mind to link with all the Alterants, she only connected with Tristan. His beast power raged through her body, but he had his shift under control.

That allowed her to keep her beast in check.

Kizira screeched and flew across the top of her creatures at Evalle.

"I really hate the sound that witch makes," Evalle muttered. She'd seen Tristan throw a lightning bolt back when he'd been with the Kujoo. Drawing on his powers, she whipped her hand at Kizira.

Their combined powers created a shaft of energy that blasted the witch as if she'd been shot from a fireman's hose, knocking her back fifty feet into a wall of rock.

The second creature had gone after the other two Alterants, who had shifted into nasty-looking beast forms. Those two fought the creature from where they were caught in the circles.

Evalle threw a blast at the creature to back it off.

One of the Alterants charged out of the fire circle, howling as he rolled to put out the flames streaking up his body. The other Alterant did the same while Evalle kept the creature pushed off of them, but she couldn't keep doing this and help Tristan.

She screamed at the two Alterants, "Run!"

They tried, but the creature whipped between them and the exit. The Alterants attacked it as a team. One latched onto the serpent's arm. When the serpent dove his head down to bite the offender, the other Alterant jumped and dug his fangs into the serpent's neck.

Stomping her boots to release the hidden blades, Evalle turned to help Tristan.

The first serpent had Tristan pinned down on his knees, caught between the ground and the field of kinetic energy he used as a shield. He'd be crushed in seconds. The thing's tentacles had latched onto the power and lengthened, snaking around to find an opening.

Evalle blasted a wave of power at the beast. It whipped its head around toward her. Eyes of hell blazed with yellow centers. Foam poured around his fangs. He snarled and turned back to Tristan.

That hadn't worked. Tristan needed more power on his side of the energy. Evalle took a step toward him.

The ground beneath her feet started swirling and sucking her down into a sand pit.

She searched for Kizira.

The Medb priestess hovered again, chanting, head back in a trance state. Lightning crackled and fingered away from her body. She was feeding power to her creatures.

Evalle pushed and kicked at the funneling sand, but it kept dragging her down. She started gaining and broke a boot free to step away from the sand when she felt a hard draw on her energy from Tristan.

She lost her footing and was back to pedaling against being swallowed by the swirling sand. She looked to Tristan, needing his power.

He roared and shoved up against the serpent, knocking the creature back. Then Tristan whipped out a length of power that sparked and glowed. When the serpent roared back to life and dove at Tristan, he swung his six feet of sparking power across the serpent, cutting off its head.

The head flew past Evalle, purple liquid gushing all over Tristan and the floor, bubbling in the flames.

The sand pit sucked Evalle faster and faster. *Tristan!*

Had Kizira wanted to kill her after all?

Evalle clawed at rushing sand and air, sinking to her waist, then her chest. Sand reached her chin . . . her nose.

Her gaze shot up, searching for any help.

Tristan dove toward her as she sank beneath the surface.

His hand clamped around her wrist with iron force.

Evalle couldn't breathe. Tristan came into her mind. *Stay with me. Kizira's still in her trance. Hold on. I'm taking all your power.*

When he drained her power this time, it was as if her insides had been turned inside out.

She had no strength left to fight.

What had happened to her power?

He yanked her up once and had her head free. She sucked air, wheezing for every breath. Her lungs burned.

Ah, crap. Kizira came out of her trance right then. She raised her arm to attack.

Using the power of two Belador Alterants, Tristan threw a series of lightning bolts, shoving her back.

He wrenched Evalle's arm, dragging her clear of the pit.

Kizira shouted a mouthful of undecipherable words and raised her arms, pointing at the ceiling.

Throw another lightning bolt, Evalle told Tristan.

Can't. I zapped everything you and I had left in that last attack. He looked over to where the two Alterants were ripping arms from their creature and yelled, "Get out of here."

A rumbling sound started across the ceiling and grew.

The ground shook beneath Evalle, throwing her backwards.

She struggled to her feet. Tristan hooked an arm around her waist and started dragging her to the opening.

Rocks began falling, crashing down in front of their exit.

One hit Evalle on her shoulder. She yelped.

A baseball-sized chunk bounced off Tristan's temple, drawing blood. He flagged against her. The other two Alterants howled, pelted by more and more stones.

If she didn't get out of here, the last two gifts the Tribunal had awarded her would be of no use. But what would stop that bitch from raining rocks down on them and contain her long enough for them to get away?

Evalle could not use any of the three gifts to kill unless she had no other choice, and she still had to justify wielding the power.

Would the Tribunal consider saving the three Alterants as an acceptable reason to kill Kizira?

"Turn me around," Evalle ordered Tristan and added, "Now!" before he could argue.

When he did, she covered her head with her arms, ready to call upon the Tribunal powers.

THIRTY

Evalle flagged against Tristan as he shifted her to face a wild-eyed Kizira. The witch's hair lifted with all the static energy firing from her.

Killing her was tempting, but Evalle did have an alternative, so lethal force couldn't be used. She spoke in a voice hoarse from the dust and fires. "By the Tribunal power gifted me, I command the rocks from the ceiling to unite as one above my head and form a wall that will not touch me."

Rocks hung in midair, then immediately changed direction. All sizes and shapes started banging together as if magnetically drawn to each other.

Kizira paused and stared at Evalle, mouth gaping.

Evalle grinned. "Didn't expect me to have that kind of power up my sleeve, did you . . . *bitch*?"

She figured even Brina would call Kizira that right now.

Kizira railed and threw fireballs at the wall forming below her in midair, but the gaps were closing down to openings smaller than Evalle's fist. Harmless sparks pinged through the holes.

She laughed at the last vision of Kizira until she noticed Tristan and the two Alterants staring at her.

Tristan asked, "Where did you get *that* power?"

Evalle shrugged. "I would say I have friends in high

places that loaned me a trick, but they aren't friends, and I can't do it again. I'm not sure how long that will hold her or if she's any better at teleporting around this place than you are, so we need to roll."

Tristan started toward the exit, which was now blocked by rocks that had made it to the ground. He lifted his hands to use his kinetics, and two small stones tumbled from the top.

Evalle had nothing to give him until her power regenerated. What could have drained her this way? Linking with Tristan? "How many Alterants does it take to get out of a hell party?"

One of the Alterants in beast form trudged over in front of Tristan and started shoving rocks aside as if they were foam balls. When he finished, he swung his head around at Evalle, then Tristan.

She recognized him by his exotic Haitian eyes . . . that were still brown. She smiled. "That's what I'm talking about."

"Thanks, Webster," Tristan agreed.

Evalle gave a quick check of the other Alterant, whose eyes were blue.

Blue and brown eyes.

Why had Kizira called them Rías? These Alterants looked like the one that had shifted in the fog, but these two had their beasts under control.

Does that mean *any* Alterant could be taught to control his or her beast?

Tristan headed out through the opening with her stumbling along beside him. At some point in the last few minutes, Tristan had unlinked with her. She could feel her energy finally seeping back through her limbs.

She stepped out of his hold and he let his arm fall away. "Why am I so drained? I'm never like this."

Tristan covered several long strides before he answered. "I think it's got something to do with that cocktail the Kujoo gave me that the witch made up with their blood mixed in."

She ran back through the fight with the Kujoo. "They were immortals. Are you . . ."

"No. I'm not."

But the downside of his extra abilities, like teleporting, was the drain on his powers. Her powers must have been drained by linking with him . . . just like when Beladors had the benefit of her night vision when they linked with her.

That's also why he wouldn't have shifted into his beast form to fight the serpents. He wouldn't have been able to teleport soon if he had.

Could Tristan get all four of them out of here now? "Are you going to be able to teleport us, even one at a time?"

"I think so. If we can get out of here without another fight with Kizira or the ghosts, I'll be back to a hundred percent soon."

"Our kinetics didn't backlash so I'm guessing the spirits are doing whatever they can to move us along. I just hope Kizira has a healthy respect for the maze's ability to change shape, too." Evalle looked back, checking to make sure that those two behind her were staying caught up.

Yes, but they were hanging back, as if reluctant to walk with her and Tristan.

Were they returning to their normal bodies? No.

She kept her voice low and asked Tristan, "Are those two going to be able to shift back to human form?"

He gave a negligible glance over his shoulder, then faced forward again. "Sure. They can do it in less than a minute. When I brought them to the Maze of Death, I showed them how to make the change and keep control."

"Then why don't they change back?"

A smile touched his lips. "I don't think they want to walk around you as a human male in all their swinging glory. You didn't notice how once the fight was over they kept their bodies turned away from you? That much adrenaline running through a man's body makes him hard as a two-by-four after the fight's over."

"Oh." Her face heated at finally understanding. "What's the red-haired guy called?"

"Aaron."

"No last names?"

"Not necessary."

Or he just wasn't sharing that. She asked, "What did Kizira mean when she called them Rías? Why aren't their eyes bright green like ours? And why couldn't I link with them? Don't they know how?"

Tristan slowed at the next turn and took the tunnel on his left.

Unless the ghosts were screwing with them again, this tunnel looked familiar even to Evalle. This one had vines on the walls and clover on the ground, so the next one they intercepted should have antiques, paintings and rugs.

Tristan finally answered, "The two behind us are not Belador Alterants. I don't know what she meant by Rías. I never heard that term when I was around her."

"Then what are they?"

"I have an idea."

She curled and uncurled her fingers. "But you're not going to tell me."

"Not until I have my sister in a safe place. Think I missed the fact that you're now short an Alterant for your meeting even if I hand over those two?"

Actually, she hadn't stopped to consider that, but he was right. She had to show up with three, which meant convincing Tristan to go in with her.

She'd have an easier time convincing Kizira to enter a convent.

With VIPER hunting all Alterants, Evalle had to figure out how to reach VIPER headquarters alive. Now that she thought about it, the Tribunal hadn't made a provision for her to contact anyone once she had the three Alterants.

Why not?

Because everyone expected her to fail.

That's why they would only order Sen to find her once the top of the hourglass emptied. If they weren't all busy battling the fog.

Evalle muttered, "Kizira said she was generating the fog. I hope I didn't make a mistake by not going with her."

Tristan shook his head. "She was lying about stopping

the fog. She'd have taken you and me, killed those two behind us and let the fog go. She wants specific Alterants and must believe that fog is going to flush them out."

Evalle let go of some of her guilt. She had to get word to Tzader and Quinn so they could alert VIPER . . . but why hadn't VIPER stopped the fog already? They had to know it was not part of the natural world.

"I just realized something, Tristan. VIPER would have figured out something supernatural was behind the fog by now, but it was still growing when I came down into MARTA."

"So?"

"If VIPER hasn't found a way to stop the spread . . . that means even the deities might not be able to fix this."

He didn't say anything for a few steps, but real worry fed into his gaze.

She gave voice to what she believed he was thinking. "If that fog covers everything in a week, there will be no place safe for any Alterant, even your sister."

She wanted him to work his way through the unsaid part—that he, his sister and the two behind them might be safer within VIPER's network than out on the streets. Tristan knew far more than he was sharing about a lot of other things as well. "What does the Medb want with us?"

He thought on his answer for a moment, but he didn't seem to be avoiding her, just pulling his thoughts into sync. "I think the Medb know something about our history and they plan to use Alterants somehow to capture Brina's island. I pieced that together from a few things I picked up around Kizira when we were with the Kujoo."

Tzader had told her no immortal could get inside the castle to touch Brina, but could an Alterant harm the warrior queen?

She could not fail Brina and put the Belador warrior queen at risk of repercussion. Showing up with fewer than three Alterants would be failure no matter how anyone tried to spin it with the Tribunal.

Analyzing what Tristan had said, Evalle asked, "Why do the Medb think an Alterant can breach the home of an immortal?"

"I have a feeling the Medb know something about the way we're evolving."

"Wait a minute. Evolving? Are we going to change into something more hideous than a beast?"

He lifted his shoulders. "Don't know. The Medb know a lot about us, too much." He shook his head. "I don't have all the answers yet, but I think Belador Alterants have the most to lose in this battle . . . and in the hands of the Medb we might end up being the most dangerous creatures in this world."

That sort of information would only support the case against allowing Alterants freedom.

Tristan added, "And those two behind us are considered disposable by the Medb. She'd have killed all three whether I showed up or not. I think she was trying to grab me and you, then she'd have figured a way to lure my sister out of hiding."

"Tell me what you know about how all Alterants are connected."

"Not yet. I'm not giving up that bargaining chip until I have to, in case my sister needs it."

Evalle dodged a vine that reached out for her. These spirits had too much time on their hands. "If you don't share information, how do you expect me to help Belador Alterants and any others like those two behind us?"

"I've already handed you a lot. I'll give you more when I can. I told you, we'd talk about this once we get out of danger."

She'd let it go for now and hope that once she found a place to keep them safe, she could talk Tristan into going in with her in spite of what Adrianna had told Storm about Tristan not throwing in with Evalle. That did give her a moment of worry, but Adrianna was not infallible.

Evalle still had the last Tribunal gift left, but she couldn't use teleportation again because no request could be duplicated.

And truthfully, she didn't want to force them to join her.

Free will meant everything to her. She wanted these guys to *choose* to go with her. Once they were all out of here, she felt certain all she had to do was explain her plan to those two behind her to convince them of their best chance at freedom.

If Sen showed up with the hourglass first, the decision would be out of Tristan's hands.

Speaking of time, she was past the ninety minutes Storm had agreed to wait for her. "We've got to hustle."

Tristan took a look at his watch and signaled the other two with a wave of his hand to pick up the pace.

The ghosts must have been ready to get rid of them, because no one so much as said *Boo* on their way to the subway access wall.

When they reached the spot where Evalle had entered the maze, she told Tristan, "I probably need to go first and make sure Storm knows I'm alive before you bring those two out."

For once, Tristan didn't argue. "Good idea."

Webster and Aaron stood a few feet away, their backs turned to them, but Webster was already shrinking back into his human body. He called out in a voice not quite human yet, "We going to Deca—"

Tristan cut him off. "Not yet. I'll take her out and be right back."

Webster growled and nodded.

Evalle allowed Tristan to put his arm around her waist once more to teleport. A blessedly short trip, which allowed her to throw up mental shields against receiving any telepathy the minute her feet hit hard ground again. She pulled out of his grasp and searched in both directions for Storm, then grumbled, "Crap."

"What's wrong?"

"Nothing." But she'd thought Storm would cut her ten minutes' slack. She turned to Tristan, immediately calculating the best way to slip him and the other two Alterants out of the subway area before a threat to all of them showed up. "Webster and Aaron both need to change before they get to this side."

"They're already shifting as we . . . speak." Tristan stumbled to the right and grabbed his head.

"What's wrong?"

"Teleporting . . . it's . . . never mind."

She knew. Teleporting drained his powers, which weren't back up to full speed yet. "Can you get the other two out for sure?"

"Yes."

"How long will it take?"

"With this short of a jump, one, maybe two minutes."

She gave her watch a quick glance. Storm had expected her almost fifteen minutes ago. "Hurry up then before any VIPER agent or Belador finds out we're here. By the time you get back, I'll figure out where we can go in order to be safe, unless your sister has a secure location."

"No, she doesn't."

"What about clothes for Aaron and Webster?"

"I've got that covered." Tristan shook off his momentary debilitation and stood with his back straight, as though he prepared to teleport, then looked at Evalle. "Thanks for fighting at my side."

"Like I had a choice?" But she smirked and lifted her chin in a small salute. "Once we make it to a secure location, I'll have Storm or Tzader bring your sister so she'll be safe, too, just like I promised."

He hesitated, then nodded right before he faded into a swirl of motion and disappeared.

"Evalle?"

She jumped around to see a man in a hoodie running toward her. But she'd recognize the moves of that body anywhere. Storm jogged with the same fluid gait in human form as when he shifted into a black jaguar.

He was alone, which meant he might not have called anyone yet.

She smiled, genuinely happy to be out of the maze and even happier to see Storm.

"What the hell happened?" he shouted at her from ten feet away.

That killed her smile. She yelled back, "I've been a little busy dodging pitchfork-wielding ghosts, fire serpents and an insane priestess. *Don't* yell at me for being late."

He stopped two steps short of her.

She was vibrating with so much adrenaline that she only picked up on a flood of intense emotion wafting from him. She'd been too battered over the last hour and a half for her empathic sense to narrow down specifics, but anyone could hear the anger riveting his voice.

"That's not what I meant to say first," he said, changing to his other voice.

She just realized he had this other voice, the one he'd used sometimes around her. Like when he'd soothed her after a demonic ghoul had stabbed her leg with Noirre majik two days ago, and to calm her while teleporting with him today.

"What did you mean to say, Storm?"

"I was worried when you ran late. What happened?"

She didn't need her empathic side to understand honesty. Giving him a tired smile, she said, "I'll tell you everything as soon as we have time, but I only have two Alterants right now."

Taking a step forward, he said, "Two?"

"The Medb killed one."

When he closed the distance between them to inches,

he lifted a hand and pushed hair behind her ear, smoothing his hand against her cheek. One touch and pleasure rippled out from her center.

He gently tested a spot on her neck that felt raw. "Is that why you look like you've been in a rock fight?"

She nodded, trying not to smile and expose her emotions even though he could read them blindfolded. He'd been upset about what had happened to her. Again. When would that stop surprising her? She'd only known him a week, hardly long enough for the flutter of emotions he stirred up in unguarded moments.

She added, "But we won the rock fight."

"We?"

"Tristan and the other two Alterants."

He nodded, his eyes still taking in all of her. "I need a moment alone with Tristan when he gets here."

Storm said that so amiably that she had to run the words back through her mind before she grasped his meaning. "Now, Storm."

"Have you taken a look at yourself?"

She dropped her chin to peer at herself and had to admit an insurance adjuster would declare her body totaled. But her injuries would heal, even faster if she took the time to draw on her inner Alterant.

And she fully intended to do some practicing on her own. Anything she could use to prove Alterants could control their beast with some training.

But one look at Storm's face said he planned to unleash all that pent-up anger on one person. "This was not Tristan's fault."

Not entirely.

"He took you into that hellhole. I warned him what would happen if you came back like this."

She had no idea if Storm could harm someone as powerful as Tristan, but her heart did a silly wiggle at his declaration. To distract him from focusing on Tristan, she asked, "You didn't call Tzader or Quinn?"

"No, but they've been looking for me, which I'm betting has to do with everyone hunting Alterants and trying to find you."

He had that right. Trey's telepathic thumping had started against her mental shields as soon as she'd landed on this side of the wall.

"Thanks for waiting." She lifted up and touched her lips to his and smiled at the shock on his face. "I know we talked about this, and I can't just kiss you when-ever—"

He cut off her words with his mouth. His hand went into her hair, which had fallen loose during the battle. Kissing Storm started healing her aches and pains almost as fast as drawing on her internal powers.

She held his face between her hands and kissed him back, shocking herself at the bold step, but he felt so wonderful . . . so right. She could have died in the maze and still wasn't free of the Tribunal.

This moment belonged to her.

Storm wrapped his arms around her and pulled her close, lifting her off her feet.

Adrenaline had to be behind her next move. She teased her tongue against his. One of his hands slid down, then back up under her shirt, skin to skin. Another hand cupped her bottom, pulling her against him.

Against a very aroused part of him.

Her mind leaped back to the last time an aroused man had touched her . . . driving a stake of pain through her moment of pleasure.

She tensed, then shivered and pulled back, staring into his eyes.

He watched her through eyes smoldering with feral hunger.

"Storm." Her fingers dug into his shoulders. She loved the feel of being in his arms . . . and hated the fear that flashed to the surface of another hand touching her skin.

He exhaled a ragged breath and dropped his forehead to hers, muttering, "I am six kinds of a fool for letting this happen here."

"I . . . uh . . ."

He withdrew his hand. "Right idea. Wrong time. My bad, not yours."

She mumbled, "Umm." Her body had turned into one twisted and frayed nerve.

He set her away from him gently. "But once this Tribunal job is over and you're free, we're going to find somewhere private to finish this conversation. Dinner as a minimum."

Her brain caught up to her body and jammed the pieces of what he'd said into a cognizant thought. She had never allowed any man to touch her since the attack. Not like that.

But strangely enough, she wanted to know what it would feel like to let Storm.

He had nothing in common with the man who had attacked her, but allowing Storm this intimacy hadn't been the brightest idea on her part.

He'd think she was leading him on if she kept pushing him away. Could she let this go further now that Tristan had shown her how to tap her Alterant without shifting?

No one could flip a switch to erase a rape, but she was tired of being alone.

What about when she'd thrown him across the subway tracks earlier when he'd pinned her against a wall to protect her? And she'd made him feel bad about kissing her this time when it was her fault for kissing him first.

Any man would take that as an invitation, especially one as virile as Storm. Confusion cluttered her mind. She'd sort through her conflicting emotions later once she had some rest.

"Evalle—"

"Hey, we're good." She would not show an emotional vulnerability to anyone, not even Storm.

He wiped a hand over his mouth and shook his head. "Serves me right."

"What?"

"Nothing." He angled his head to look past her. "How long does it take Tristan to teleport?"

She'd forgotten everything around her. A dangerous lack of attention in her line of work.

"No more than . . . a minute . . . or two." She lifted her watch into view. It had been almost ten minutes.

Tristan had told her the other two Alterants had been

shifting while he'd teleported her to this side. She grabbed Storm's arm. "He should be here."

"Think he has a problem?"

"No. Adrianna was right. The bastard lied to me. He said he had a couple places to teleport out of there. He's taking the other two Alterants out a different way. I'm going to kill him."

"That's the spirit."

THIRTY-ONE

I sak moved through his communications center, eyeing
the multiplex of computer screens being watched for
any sign of Evalle Kincaid.

She'd been right about using thermal imaging to target the beasts, but she hadn't just guessed at that. She'd
known the fog was cloaking the Alterants.

What else did Evalle know that she wasn't sharing?

If she moved around this city, his men would find her.

His radio spurted a crackle noise, then, "Jones to base."

Isak cued the mic on his radio. "What have you got?"

"Found a black Gixxer with a bad paint job. Gold
underneath. Once I peeled vinyl off the tag it read EVL-
ONE."

Evalle's tag and her Gixxer had been gold the last time
he'd seen her. Isak said, "Location."

His man gave him the coordinates in downtown
Atlanta, saying, "Her bike's close to the North Avenue
MARTA station. That would be my bet for locating her."

"Stay with that bike no matter how long it takes her to
return. Let me know the minute it's mobile."

"Will do, but she handles that thing like a Daytona
pro. She'll spot me tailing her without a team *if* she
doesn't lose me first."

"Understood."

"Want me to tag the bike?"

Isak considered sticking a transmitter on her motor-cycle and dismissed it as quickly. She might have a way of picking that up. If so, she'd abandon the bike and take off on foot, which would make it far easier for her to disap-pear. "No. The team is spread out across Atlanta. If we get a confirmed sighting of her, I'll alert everyone to meet up. She might have left the bike as a decoy. I'll put eyes on every MARTA rail station. You just stick with her if she surfaces."

"What if she's with someone or something else?"

Isak caught Jones's "something else" reference to a nonhuman. The first time he'd met Evalle she'd been in the grasp of a demon he'd blasted with a custom-designed six-shooter. One of his many Nyght weapons. He hadn't nailed down why Evalle dealt with nonhumans, but she was different.

She'd had a silver aura the first time he'd met her.

Tonight it had been gold.

He hadn't known many auras to change and had never seen one like hers. Had she forgotten that he could see auras, or did she even know hers was different?

Nothing had turned up to confirm her as nonhuman . . . yet. He hoped that didn't change.

For now, he wanted to find out who was after her and what else she knew about Alterants. He'd made the offer once before to make her disappear if she needed his help.

She'd declined.

If she had Tzader Burke on her trail, she might recon-sider.

Isak keyed the transmitter and told Jones, "Pick your spot and snatch her. If a human interferes, stun 'em. Kill any nonhumans."

What was Evalle up to that had Tzader Burke searching for her? She'd dodged that question tonight.

He wanted another shot at a straight answer. The best way to do that would be to talk to Evalle before Tzader found her.

THIRTY-TWO

Storm stepped onto the up escalator at the subway station behind Evalle. She moved as though her muscles were pulled tight beneath the windbreaker he'd brought her to wear when the weather had turned vicious.

Her silence needled his guilt. Taunted his control.

Nothing rattled his steel reserve like she did.

He'd pushed the kiss too far, but he could fix that.

Greater problems existed, based upon what he'd learned earlier tonight.

His spirit guide could be a source of knowledge . . . or frustration. When the witch Adrianna hadn't been able to answer all of his questions, he'd gone to his apartment so he could call upon his ancestors. A withered female shaman who wore her years etched in her ghostly face had answered his questions with mixed messages he'd had to unscramble.

The shaman had spoken of several things, including the female Ashaninka witch doctor, who, she said, was not today's worry. But he hadn't been able to decipher if that meant the witch doctor he hunted would be tonight's worry or next week's worry.

Precise time had no more relevance in these conversations than precise meaning.

Except for one warning his spirit guide had given him.

She'd said Storm would lose Evalle before he won her.

Out of instinct to protect her, he lifted his hand to place at the small of Evalle's back, but he pulled away before touching her. If he'd kept his hands to himself downstairs, she wouldn't be so tense right now.

Where had all the years of learning how to stalk a skittish prey gone?

You didn't put moves on a woman who had been hurt by a man.

Especially when he'd caught the signs of sexual abuse.

But finding her beaten to hell and running late on top of the spirit guide's warning had left his jaguar teetering on the edge of violence. Tristan had been wise not to return after dropping off a battered Evalle.

Storm shouldn't have touched her with a dangerous animal raging inside him. At the sight of Evalle injured, his animal had reacted violently with a primal objective, demanding blood . . . or sex.

Had Tristan been there, Storm might have relieved his need for blood. Without that, his control had stretched until it was paper thin and taut as tight wire cable.

Evalle had picked a hell of a moment to take the initiative to kiss him for the first time.

Nice way to fracture what trust she'd allowed you, idiot.

When Evalle stepped off the top of the escalator and moved to the side, Storm was a step behind her. Thunder and howling rain waited for them outside the North Avenue MARTA terminal. The earlier thunderstorm had picked up strength, pounding watery fists against every surface.

Would something as simple as rain destroy the yellow haze attacking part of the country?

Evalle paused short of walking out into the downpour and turned to Storm, stopping him with a hand on his arm. "I think I know where Tristan is going."

Between the roar of rain battering the concrete roof and the clatter of foot traffic going in and out of the station, this wasn't the spot for talking. He guided her over to a wall that protected them from sheets of rain.

Storm spoke loud enough for Evalle but kept his head turned away to shield his words. "Where do you think Tristan's headed?"

"To get his sister."

"Have any idea where she lives?"

"Not specifically, but we might get close enough to track him. When we were on the way out of the maze, one of the other Alterants started to ask Tristan if they were going to . . . something that sounded like Deck-A. Tristan cut him off. I think the guy might have been saying Decatur."

"That doesn't narrow it down much and, unless you can teleport again, we can't follow him."

"I don't think we need to teleport. Tristan's power isn't constant. He has to regenerate after drawing heavily on it. The battle with Kizira weakened him."

Storm let his gaze slip past her to keep an eye out for threats. "You think he couldn't get the other two out of the maze?"

"No, I think he *did* get them out, but that he can't just jump again. He can only teleport one person at a time, and it takes a toll on him. Also, he would want to avoid the fog. I think he may use the subway to transport all three of them to Decatur. If that's the case, you could track them from the MARTA station where they exit."

Storm would have to shift into his jaguar for any hope of carrying a scent in this rain. "How far ahead of us do you think he is?"

"Maybe not that much. The other two Alterants were shifting back into human form when Tristan teleported me out. He still has to get them out and dressed in clothes, then onto a train. Plus, they have to change trains in town."

"You sure enough to go to Decatur?"

"I don't have another idea and no time left with VIPER hunting us and this fog expanding."

"What specifically happens when you're out of time?"

"They'll send Sen for me. The Tribunal turned an hourglass over. When the last sand runs out, the hourglass will lead Sen to me."

How was he going to get her somewhere safe from that? He couldn't, but if they found that pack of Alterants, the Tribunal would have to let her go, according to their ruling. "How far is Decatur?"

Thunder boomed. The rain pounded harder.

Evalle grimaced. "In this weather, maybe twenty minutes if traffic doesn't bog down to a stop, but it shouldn't be too bad this late at night."

He gave her a look that suggested she'd forgotten how bad traffic could be anytime in Atlanta, especially when it rained.

"Traffic was nil when I came through. Kizira said the fog was going to continue to expand."

"That confirms VIPER's suspicion that the Medb are behind the fog."

"If they know that, why aren't they stopping it?"

"I don't know. Wonder if the rain will help?"

"I doubt rain will make a difference. In fact . . ." She looked at him, then down, as her voice trailed off.

In spite of lecturing himself about keeping his distance, he couldn't feel all that distress coming from Evalle and not touch her. He put a finger under her chin and lifted until their gazes met. "What's worrying you?"

She tried to sound cavalier, but concern bored deep into her voice. "You mean besides not showing up with three Alterants, trying to make sure the two I might take in get a fair deal if I do talk them into it, or the end of the world in general?"

"What's worrying you about *me*?"

"That the fog might cause you to lose control of your jaguar."

Should he tell her why his jaguar wouldn't hurt her? That he'd marked her with his scent before the Tribunal meeting so that he could find her? "I know my jaguar won't harm you. If I lose control . . . let's just say you should have enough power to stop me." Only because he'd never fight her. "And I won't blamc you."

"I would never . . ."

"Kill me?" Storm finished. "You will if you have to."

"No, I couldn't."

He would do whatever he could to prevent putting her

in that position, but she *would* do the right thing no matter what. He knew that. "Time to go hunt."

She chewed on her lip, indecision weighing her down until she finally gave up. "I know it's raining, but we should take my bike instead of your truck. Glad you brought this." She zipped up the gray rain jacket he'd had in his vehicle.

A frisson of worry fingered up his spine at the idea of her exposed on the Gixxer, and he wasn't thinking about rain. Some threat hovered around her that he couldn't pin down. "Don't you need a vehicle for transporting the Alterants if you get them?"

"The Tribunal gave me no instructions on how to bring in the Alterants."

"They expect you to just wait somewhere once you have them in hand?"

"Actually, I don't think the Tribunal expected me to deliver the missing Alterants, but I have a plan. Once I have the Alterants ready to go in with me, I'll have you contact Tzader and he'll send Brina. She'll work out the details with the Tribunal."

He kept his attention divided between watching Evalle and any threat. "*If* VIPER doesn't spot us first. We need to get out of here before someone does recognize either one of us."

"That's why I said to take my bike. I bet they already have your sport ute under surveillance. I painted my bike black and altered the tag. With us riding two up, I won't be as obvious."

"Okay."

"But I don't have a helmet for you, and you have to ride behind me."

He wouldn't let her ride on the back without full-body armor to protect her anyhow. "I don't mind hugging up close to you."

She pushed her soft eyebrow up in a smartass way that relieved some of his guilt from earlier. He didn't worry about her anytime she dropped into cocky mode. "How does you hugging close to me negate the lack of a helmet?"

Storm gave her a half smile. "You really think a cop wants to stop a bike in this downpour? And we still have a couple hours until daylight. We're both in dark colors. If I pull up my hood, they may not even notice."

Her eyes took note of his head and shoulders. "If we wreck you won't live through it without a helmet."

He leaned down and kissed her quickly on the forehead. "Then don't wreck. Let's get moving."

THIRTY-THREE

Evalle cruised her motorcycle into Decatur and located the city parking deck close to the MARTA station Tristan would have exited from if he had come this way. She was betting heavily on guessing right. Evalle found a corner spot and climbed off. Removing her helmet, she swiped wet hair off her face.

Storm couldn't have been any more soaked if she'd dumped him in a lake. When he pushed the hood off his head, wet black hair clung to his neck. He stuck his cell phone in her tank bag, then peeled off his soaked hoodie, wrung out the water and started using the jacket as a towel.

Using both hands, he wiped water and damp hair off his face. "Let's go."

"Storm, if I ask you to back off and stay out of sight, will you?"

"I'm not leaving you."

"I don't want you caught or shot." She'd seen what Isak's demon blaster could do to an enormous demon. Storm wouldn't stand a chance.

"Let me worry about that."

"No, I need this promise from you or you can't help me."

"We can talk or we can track."

She crossed her arms and said nothing.

He scowled and uttered something in a strange language. She didn't need a translator to interpret pissed off, but she wasn't budging without his agreement.

Storm said, "Okay, okay. I promise. Now let's go."

No one loitered on the sidewalks running along the front of eclectic retail shops and restaurants between the parking deck and the MARTA station. That still didn't lower her anxiety when they reached the subway station and Storm stepped behind bushes to strip down and shift.

The black jaguar emerged, blending into the obsidian night except when he turned bright yellow eyes on her. He stalked around the station for a minute, sniffed one spot twice, then turned to Evalle.

She asked, "Got it?"

He gave a nod and took off along McDonough Street with her right behind.

Storm hung close to the walls. When he reached an older neighborhood surrounded by woods, he padded up to a two-level brick apartment building. Judging by the simple window and door trims thick with paint, the structure had probably been new in the '80s.

Evalle waited at a spot where she could see both entrances to the apartments while Storm searched around the building. When he headed back to her, he nodded.

The Alterants were here.

But the real confirmation had just stepped out from the far entrance behind Storm.

Tristan held an umbrella for a young woman he had his arm around. She had brown hair—nothing like his blond locks—and wore hers in crazy curls piled on her head. When she lifted her head, Evalle saw a blink of bright green eyes. Neither Tristan nor his sister had Evalle's night-vision eyesight, or they'd have been wearing sunglasses to hide their eyes in the dark.

Evalle waved Storm off to the left before he reached her. He could meld into the dark pocket of thick bushes surrounding the corner of the building.

When he hesitated, she mouthed the words, *You promised.*

Storm conceded and backed into the dark, watching.

She called out to Tristan when he got within twenty feet of her. "Don't be a fool thinking VIPER will not get you."

His head jerked up, green eyes shining in the night. He shoved his sister behind him. "Get out of my way, Evalle."

"I can't go back empty-handed, and you have nowhere to run. Stand and fight with me, just like I did with you today."

He handed the umbrella around to his sister. "You're wrong. I can take us far away from here to live safe."

"The only way you could do that is by flying, and I heard people in the subway station talking about Hartsfield being covered with the fog." Big lie, but he wouldn't know that.

Tristan's sister stepped up beside him with a hand on her hip. "That's just bullshit."

He scowled at her.

Evalle looked his sister over. An attractive young woman, if someone liked petite and mouthy. "I guess you're Petrina."

The young woman gave her a duh look. "I guess you're the ass-wipe that wants to use us to buy your freedom."

Snotty little twit. Evalle ignored her. Tristan drove the decisions for his group. "The Tribunal will give Sen freedom to hunt you himself. His philosophy is the only good Alterant is one that is never seen again. And that doesn't even take into account the Nyght Raiders."

"Who?" Tristan asked.

"A black-ops group run by a man who lost his best friend to an Alterant. They've had a kill-on-sight policy for much longer than VIPER. You're putting your sister and the other two at more risk than you realize." She looked around. "Where are those two?"

Petrina started to mouth off again, but Tristan squeezed her. He said, "They're busy."

Evalle changed her tactic. "You can risk your life and your sister's, but it's unfair to jeopardize Webster's and Aaron's without giving them a chance to have their say."

Tristan snapped at Evalle, "You're holding me up. Move aside. We're leaving."

"When we were in the maze, you said you'd share information and help me once your sister was safe."

"She's not safe yet."

"Neither of you will ever be if you don't work with me."

Indecision finally entered Tristan's face.

Evalle jumped on her opening. "Let me at least take Webster and Aaron with me if they agree. Give me enough information to plead for the three of us. I won't go anywhere without them, and they'll be safe from the fog if they're at VIPER headquarters."

Maybe Brina could argue that Evalle had brought in two of the three escaped Alterants that were still alive. How could the Tribunal expect Evalle to deliver a dead Alterant?

Petrina said, "She's lying."

Evalle shook her head. "You know I'm not, Tristan. I won't accept freedom unless the Tribunal gives it to all three of us."

Rain streamed down his face while he debated. He wiped water from his eyes and finally said, "If Webster and Aaron agree to go—"

Petrina grabbed his arm. "No!"

He gave her a hard look that silenced her, then finished saying, "You're right. I can't make that choice for them. If they agree to go with you, then I'll tell you enough to support your case, but if I find out you've lied to me at any time, I'll make you regret using them for as long as you live."

The weight she'd been toting on her back for days lost a few pounds.

Petrina's gaze shifted to her right, where Webster and Aaron came walking up from across the street.

"Hi, Evalle," Webster called, grinning.

"Hi, Webster." She started to speak to Aaron, but she smelled sulfur. Then saw the leading edge of the fog creeping up behind Tristan and his sister. Webster and Aaron would be in the line of fog in another few steps when they joined Tristan.

Webster called over to Tristan, "Thought we were meeting at the subway station."

Before Tristan could answer, Evalle said, "The fog is coming. We have to get out of here."

Tristan spun to look behind him, and just that quickly the fog began to circle them.

A growl rattled from the bushes.

Storm. Evalle looked at him and shook her head, pleading with him not to attack.

Tristan said to Webster and Aaron, "Stay close to me and hold your breath if the fog catches us." When the other two Alterants joined Tristan, he turned to Evalle. "The only way out is behind you. You can talk to Webster and Aaron on the way if—"

A man's voice boomed through a loudspeaker from behind her, *"Evalle, back away from the Alterants! We've got them in our sights."*

She turned and saw nothing, which meant Isak's black-ops team was invisible in the night. When she looked back at Tristan, his face had twisted with rage.

He shouted at her, "It's a trap. You lied to me!"

"No, I didn't. I tried to tell you about the Nyght Raiders."

"Bullshit. You were just buying time until you had us all in one spot. You knew I wouldn't agree to go with you and leave my sister. I can't believe I listened to you."

"That's not true!" She caught Storm moving from cover, where fog smoked around him. She shook her head again.

He growled viciously, padding back and forth, ready to leap.

The sulfur stench burned her throat on her next breath, and yellow haze fingered closer to Tristan's group.

The voice behind the loudspeaker said, *"Evalle. Back. Away. Now."*

When she looked over her shoulder this time, seven men had emerged from cover in full battle gear, holding Isak Nyght's mega blasters. In fact, Isak led the group.

She called out, "Isak, stop. Don't shoot."

Webster and Aaron roared, and she knew without looking that they were starting to change into beasts.

But the damage had been done the minute Isak saw Tristan's and Petrina's green eyes.

In that moment of thunder rolling, Storm snarling and Isak shouting, everything felt as if it happened in slow motion as she realized she had a way to save others even if it meant the end of her last hope.

She had one Tribunal gift left.

Speaking the words that would seal her fate, she called out, "By the Tribunal power gifted me, I command Kizira's fog to disappear—" She thought fast, adding, "—and never return."

The fog vanished.

Aaron and Webster hadn't shifted much. They looked at her as they returned to human.

"Move now, Evalle!" Isak called through the bullhorn again.

She stared at Tristan. "I did not set you up."

He gave a look past her shoulder, then back at her. "Going to be hard to prove that once we're all dead."

"I know. Get out of here."

His eyes narrowed with suspicion.

Putting more power into her voice, she ordered him,

"Go, because the only reason he's not shooting yet is to keep from killing me. The minute he decides I'm a threat to humans, too, that will change. I could call Tzader, but he won't get here fast enough to stop Isak."

Tristan told Webster, Aaron and Petrina to walk away single file behind him. He backed up as they did, keeping his eyes on Evalle.

She could see his confusion and inner debate over what he should do, but they both knew he was out of options.

And so was Evalle as she watched her only chance at freedom disappear into the woods across the street. She turned to find Isak's team moving forward, but they had thirty yards yet to cover.

Isak called to her without the bullhorn. *"That was a mistake, Evalle."*

She nodded her understanding.

Storm snarled and she jerked around to him. "Don't come out here. You promised. If you break that promise, I bet it will hurt you as much as lying, but it will hurt me more."

Energy flushed the rain away from her in a short blast.

Sen appeared in front of her holding the hourglass . . . empty. "I don't see three Alterants with you."

"What the hell is that?" Isak yelled, no longer using his bullhorn and heading toward them.

Sen turned with an annoyed expression. Red laser dots peppered his head and chest. He lifted his hand, pointing a finger toward them, a clear sign of aggression to a black-ops team.

A blast of power exploded from one of the weapons.

Sen flipped his palm up, stopping the round in midair inches from his hand.

What was this guy? Evalle expected Isak's men to unload everything at that, but they had all turned into living statues, locked in whatever position they'd been in when Sen had lifted his palm.

She asked, "How long will they stay frozen like that?"

Sen turned back to her with a negligent shrug. "Until I leave, and they won't remember any of this."

What she wouldn't give to have that kind of power, especially with Sen still holding the empty hourglass.

He glanced around with a smug smile. "As I was saying, I don't see three Alterants with you."

"There's a good reason why."

"Like I give two shits?"

From the corner of her eye, Evalle saw Storm step from the shadows, eyes glittering with deadly intent. He dropped into a crouch, getting ready to attack Sen.

A suicidal move.

She yelled, "Don't!"

Sen didn't even turn around or move a muscle, but she knew he was the one who sent a wicked blast of power that knocked Storm against the apartment building. Bones cracked viciously when his body smashed against the bricks. A sickening sound rattled from his lungs as he slid down into a boneless heap.

Blood trickled from his mouth.

She lunged for him, screaming, "*No!*"

But her body halted in midair. Sen held her there for

a minute, long enough to make her realize Storm's chest hadn't moved. He wasn't breathing.

When the world started spinning, her arms and legs functioned again. She beat her fists in every direction, trying to hit Sen, whose laughter rolled through the swirling colors.

She called up her kinetics. Useless.

Storm couldn't be dead.

That couldn't be the last vision of him she'd carry with her to a lifetime of isolation. The Tribunal would listen to nothing she had to say. No provision for failure.

Oh, dear Goddess. Failure.

If she'd thought her heart couldn't take another hit, she'd been wrong.

What would the Tribunal do to Brina?

What would that do to the Beladors?

THIRTY-FOUR

When the teleporting ended, Evalle ignored Sen, who stood next to her with arrogant pleasure. She barely noted the plush grass beneath her feet and black sky filled with shooting stars and two moons.

The most beautiful and deadly part of this parallel universe were the two gods and one goddess positioned on a shining gold dais this time. An arch of diamond-shaped sparkling lights curved above their heads.

Water dripped off Evalle's nose and soaked her clothes. That might be why she couldn't get her eyes to clear, but she doubted all of the water on her face was left over from being drenched.

Was Storm really gone?

Defeat devastated her. She wanted to curl up somewhere and hide, but not with Brina's fate still in jeopardy.

Pele addressed Evalle. "You come before us with not one of the three escaped Alterants?"

"About those," Evalle started in.

Ares interjected, "Four, counting the one you helped escape."

Denying she'd played a role in Tristan's escape would be futile. "Of the first three, one was killed by the Medb."

No sympathy to be found on that dais.

"I used my last gift to keep them from being killed,

and I destroyed all of the fog when I did. I saved millions of lives—"

Ares said, "You were told to deliver the Alterants. The fog had not reached the point of harming millions of lives—"

Evalle argued, "But I ran up against the Medb while trying to bring in the Alterants. Kizira took credit for the fog and said she planned to expand it across North America."

"And," Ares shouted to let her know she'd made a huge mistake by interrupting him, "we suspect that only the creator—who you say is the Medb—or someone associated with that pantheon could disperse the fog. If that is the case, you may now explain how *you* were able to wipe away a sentient fog that no deity in the VIPER coalition could affect."

Trying to save the world had cast her as being in league with the Medb? She'd give the Tribunal credit. "I don't know. It had to be your power, because I used the gift you gave me."

Wrong suggestion. Every regal face on the dais hardened with insult.

Loki spoke up. "I call Brina of Treoir."

No! Evalle tried to reach the warrior queen telepathically. *Don't come to the Tribunal meeting, Brina.*

But Brina's holographic image took shape between Evalle and the dais. Brina said to Evalle, *I must come when summoned.*

I failed big time. Those words cut her heart with the sharpness of a razor against raw skin.

I know. I heard about Tristan escaping.

That was an accident, Evalle pled. *Tristan has information on the Alterants that might sway the Tribunal if they'll just let me explain, but they're blaming me with the fog because I used my last gift to make it go away permanently.*

You shouldn't have been able to do that when VIPER deities could not influence the fog.

I have no idea why it worked. Maybe it was the power of all three of these in the gifts or the fact that I was in the fog when I called on the gift, or maybe Kizira just lied about being responsible for the fog . . . I don't know, but I swear I'm not with the Medb, Brina.

Brina nodded, then spoke to the Tribunal. "I ask that you allow Evalle a chance to explain—"

"That was *not* our agreement, Warrior Queen," Ares charged. "You accepted the terms, and I see no Alterants or the one known as Tristan, freed at her hands."

The dark heavens surrounding them shook and rumbled with the force of his declaration.

Pele agreed. "No deity among the VIPER coalition has been able to stop the fog from spreading. Yet your Alterant destroyed something *she* now tells us was created by the Medb. Based upon her own testimony, she is aligned with your enemy and yet you defend her?"

Brina answered, "No one has proof of who was behind the fog. The Medb could have been lying to her."

Pele's impatience was evident in her refusal to debate the fog issue further. "Regardless, this one"—she pointed at Evalle—"has answered beyond any doubt that her loyalty lies with seeing her fellow Alterants remain free."

The goddess directed her attention to Evalle. "Is that not so?"

Not the way Pele stated it.

Evalle would not stand here and have her loyalty called into question. "I am *not* involved with the Medb. I am loyal to the Beladors. I have no idea why the gift worked, but even with what you're accusing me of I would use it again to protect humans across this continent."

"As well as Alterants?" Loki challenged softly.

Evalle considered all that had transpired and figured this would be her last chance to speak up for Alterants. "Would I like to see all Alterants who've done nothing wrong be free? I never said those specific words, but as one myself, I can only answer that question as yes. We should have the right of every other free being. I left here with the goal of bringing those three escapees back to face judgment that I *thought* would be fair."

Evalle paused to consider her next words. When no one on the dais stabbed her with a lightning bolt, she added, "I told the other Alterants that I believed a fair and just Tribunal would have given each of them the chance to plead his case to remain free. And Tristan has information that sheds light on the origin of Alterants and will answer many questions."

Brina turned halfway around at that declaration, gave Evalle a questioning look, then resumed her quiet pose.

Evalle went on. "He believes he can show that we are not anomalies of nature but a race to be recognized."

"We would hear this Tristan, but"—Loki made a show

of looking around the room—"he is not here." A sarcastic laugh feathered his taunt.

Ares spoke with the power of a gun blast. "We have heard enough. The task was not performed. Judgment is due."

Brina spoke up. "Can Macha not—"

"Macha?" Loki chided. "What more would you ask of your goddess when she has been generous to offer sanctuary to this Alterant until now? There is no challenge to this judgment when the Alterants are not a recognized race and have not been accepted into a pantheon . . . unless you wish to inform this Tribunal of such a change in their status?" He angled his head in question. "No? I thought not."

Evalle stared at the back of Brina's quiet hologram with horror.

Pele nodded as though a silent discussion had just ended between her and the two gods. Her lyrical voice rang out with unquestioned authority. "Brina of Treoir, you are held accountable for this failure."

Evalle shouted, "No! That's not fair."

Ares pointed at Evalle's feet, and the lightning bolt she'd been worried about struck the ground an inch from her toes. Energy stung her skin. Ares said, "Speak another unsolicited word and the next one will go through your heart."

Brina spoke in Evalle's mind. *Do not make this worse by arguing. I doubt they will do anything more than suspend me from standing at Tribunal meetings with sanctioned Beladors for a while. That would leave a warrior under judgment at the mercy of the Tribunal with no support, but there are worse things in our world.*

Evalle calmed at that, but now it was her fault other warriors would not benefit by having Brina at their side to face a trio of heartless deities.

When Brina spoke, Evalle understood why warriors followed this woman into battle. "Evalle may have failed you, but she did not fail me or her Belador tribe. I do not believe she has anything to do with the Medb. I will always stand by my warriors in any battle, even those sent to battle upon uneven ground."

Loki gifted Brina with a gorgeous smile. "Your reward for believing in a genetic mishap is to remain with us forever."

"You know I can't do that," Brina countered, suspicion coloring the end of her words.

"Oh, but your hologram can."

"What? You can't—" Brina lifted her hands in defense against an invisible threat . . . and turned into a translucent statue locked in that position.

Oh, dear Goddess. What had Loki done? Evalle looked to the grinning god, opened her mouth to curse him a thousand ways when he said, "You wish to speak, Alterant?"

She caught the warning and clamped her lips shut. Brina had cautioned her not to antagonize the Tribunal. Evalle shoved her fisted hands behind her back, sure that Sen would notice the movement, but the bastard had to be enjoying this too much to interrupt.

Evalle nodded, then answered Loki in a respectful voice, when she'd rather rip his throat out. "I have nothing to say for myself, but I don't see the point in freezing Brina's image when I'm the one who failed."

Pele covered her mouth and laughed. She cut her eyes to Ares, then Loki, who both erupted in laughter.

What could be so funny about that? What would have united those three on any front?

Evalle sent a quick glance at Sen, who seemed mildly confused.

When the laughter died, Pele said, "Loki did not *freeze* Brina's image. He captured her hologram and locked it into a timeless prison. A part of Brina's essence travels with her in the hologram to allow her use of power outside of Treoir Isle."

Did that mean . . . they had actually locked away part of Brina's power? What about the Beladors?

Full all-out panic shook Evalle. What had she done to her entire tribe?

"Evalle of the Beladors, you are hereby sentenced to VIPER imprisonment for as long as you shall draw a breath."

VIPER? What about the jungle like Tristan had been sent to?

She turned to Sen, who whispered, "I promise that you will live a long life."

THIRTY-FIVE

Could there be any lonelier cellmate than honor?

Evalle sat on the edge of the cot in her suffocatingly small space, heart thumping in beat with the pain stabbing her chest. She'd thought the basement of a simple two-bedroom house had been a claustrophobic cage for the first eighteen years of her life.

She hadn't known the true definition of cage until getting dumped in a ten-by-ten room with cold rock walls. Smooth gray stone covered the floor.

No door. Unnecessary with teleporting.

No window. Nothing to see this far beneath the mountain that held VIPER headquarters in north Georgia.

No way out. All she'd ever wanted was freedom.

She hugged the windbreaker around her, glad Sen had no idea how much she cherished the jacket Storm had given her. Now that she'd dripped dry, she could smell him on the cloth.

Her heart bled a little each time she inhaled his scent.

One of the four stone walls started changing. A wooden door with black hammered-metal attachments formed.

The door swung open to admit Tzader.

The sight of him threatened to pull her loose at the seams. She would not cry. No one had seen her shed a tear since the age of fifteen.

She couldn't think about not seeing Storm. That would cut loose the river of misery waiting to flash flood through her.

She swallowed down the hurt.

When Sen had grudgingly admitted that VIPER rules allowed her one visit by a single person, Evalle had given him Tzader's name. She didn't know if Quinn had truly betrayed her to Kizira, but the witch had gotten her information somewhere.

Tzader walked in and stood just inside the door that closed behind him. The hard angles of his face shared nothing of his thoughts.

Did he hate her for what had happened to Brina?

"Z, I'm, uh, sorry . . ." That sounded so useless. What could sorry do to free Brina?

"Not your fault, Evalle."

"Yes, it is my fault. They locked Brina's hologram form in some kind of clear statue."

His neck muscles flexed. "I know."

"They captured her essence . . . they . . . what *did* they do to her? What will happen to the Beladors?"

Worry crowded Tzader's gaze. "Brina can't leave the castle at all, even if it's under attack. Her hologram originates from wherever her physical body exists. If she moves more than a short distance from the spot where she last transmitted her hologram, her body would begin to deteriorate. She wouldn't die, but she'd feel as if her bones were being crushed."

"What will Macha do?"

"Nothing yet." He crossed his arms. "With a part of

Brina's essence cut off from returning to her body, the Belador powers have a chink in the armor. We don't have the ability to link with each other or communicate through telepathy."

How could she have harmed the tribe this way? Probably just as well that she would never see them again.

Most of the Beladors had barely tolerated her half-breed status before.

Tolerance would give way to open hatred at harming their warrior queen.

Evalle covered her eyes, then pinched the bridge of her nose, anything to keep from breaking. "That means if Macha retaliates in any way and breaks faith with the VIPER alliance, our warriors will be extremely vulnerable. They could be taken out by single attacks."

"Exactly."

Evalle shoved to her feet, ready to fight the enemy . . . but the enemy was her. "Can't you tell the Tribunal that it was a mistake to take me in, that I'm not really a Belador and Brina shouldn't be punished just for getting stuck with me . . . and—"

She shouldn't shout at Tzader. He hadn't done this to her.

Tzader walked forward, closing the gap between them. "That would be a lie."

"It's true. I let you all down, Tzader. I won't let you waste time trying to save me when Brina needs your help more."

"No you didn't let us down, and I'm not going to allow anything to happen to her . . . or you. I won't leave you here."

Of course Tzader would try to get her out of this box. Honor ran through his veins, and his heart bled loyalty.

Tzader said, "I'll send everyone after Tristan and those Alterants. I know you wouldn't have helped that bastard escape."

"I know you don't want to hear this, Z, but you can't hand the Alterants over to the Tribunal."

Tzader could have backed down an army of Medb warlocks with the fierce look on his face. "Stop defending them! Not *one* of those Alterants hung around to help you."

"I know, but listen to me. Kizira is trying to capture Alterants." If nothing else, she had to give Tzader anything he could use to free Brina and protect the Beladors.

"We figured out the Medb were behind the ambush on you."

She nodded. "They want certain Alterants. Me, Tristan and who knows how many more, but not all the Alterants have Belador blood. Tristan has information about Alterant origins and thinks the Medb plan to use the green-eyed ones to breach Brina's castle." Which just turned into a much more dangerous situation with Brina's hologram held hostage by the Tribunal.

Tzader's sigh carried a world of troubles. "Where did you hear that?"

"When Tristan was around Kizira and the Kujoo, he heard enough to believe the Medb know something important about our background that they can use to their advantage. You have to find him and try to help him so he'll help the Beladors."

"Why would you believe him, Evalle?"

"I think I could have talked him into coming with me to face the Tribunal, but Isak Nyght showed up."

Tzader's cocoa-brown skin lost two shades of color. He slapped his hand to his forehead. "Ah, hell."

"What?"

"Quinn probed Conlan O'Meary's mind—"

"Why?"

"Because Brina wanted proof of Conlan either being the traitor helping the Medb or not." Tzader made a disgusted noise. "When Quinn was inside Conlan's mind, he encountered Kizira and learned of plans to do just as you said—use Alterants to breach Treoir Castle. The Tribunal learned about Tristan's escape and handed Sen orders to kill any Alterant without question."

"I know."

Pausing, Tzader's chest rose and fell with a sigh of deep regret when he said, "I had no idea where you were, and Quinn had heard your name mentioned when he entered a vision in Conlan's mind. I wanted you found as quickly as possible, so I contacted Isak for help."

Did he think after all he'd done for her that she'd hold that against him? "What happened is not your fault, Z. Isak knew I was in Atlanta. I ran into him while I was searching for Tristan. When he saw glowing green eyes standing with me, he sighted down on a target. Could have happened no matter what."

Tzader accepted that with his usual stoic quiet, but she knew he wouldn't forgive himself for bringing Isak into the mix.

She needed to tell him something else. "You've piqued Isak's interest. He may go digging around on you."

"I'm not worried about Nyght."

She was. "Please be careful and watch your back."

"I will." His throat muscles flexed with a swallow. "I have to leave soon, but I'll make them let me come back."

Sen had said one visit meant one visit.

Even Tzader might not be able to bully his way back in.

Panic scurried through her with sharp rat claws. "Do me a couple favors just in case . . . it takes a while."

"Anything."

"Storm was with me when Sen came for me. Sen hit him with some kind of power that might have, um—" She took a breath. She could not say the words she didn't want to hear spoken. "I was in Decatur—"

"I know. Trey's team must have shown up right after you left. Isak's men were standing around looking confused."

Her heart leaped with hope. "Did he find a—" She stopped before asking Tzader if anyone had found a dead animal at the scene. She'd told Storm she wouldn't share that he could shift into a jaguar. She wouldn't betray that trust even now.

"Storm must be fine."

"Why?"

"Sen told me Storm quit. I've had people trying to find Storm since you were brought in, but he's gone."

Gone or dead? Had Storm survived that attack after all, or had Sen removed the body and made up the story about Storm quitting?

Tzader said, "About Storm—"

"He's a good man, Z. I know you're not sure about him because Sen brought him in, but he's an ally."

Tzader thought on that. "Why'd they let Storm help you when we couldn't?"

"They didn't. When the Tribunal had me teleported to Tristan's spellbound cage in South America—"

Tzader cursed in Gaelic.

"—Storm found me on his own. I'm not entirely sure how he did it, but he did and he refused to leave me while I searched for Tristan and the other Alterants."

"In that case, if he hadn't quit I'd thank him," Tzader said. "Sen blew me off when I asked about Storm. Said he was jacked up over you being locked up. Sen thinks he'll be back in a day or two once he cools down. Storm's one of their best trackers, so VIPER won't let him get away."

That sounded like a story Sen would fabricate to cover why Storm had left if Sen didn't want to deal with explaining a dead agent.

But Evalle wanted what Tzader said to be true with every part of her being no matter how little chance she believed he'd had of surviving Sen's attack.

Sen would have made sure Storm could not help her again, no matter what.

Thinking of that blasted Sen, he might pull Tzader out any minute, too. She needed Tzader to do a couple more things.

"In case you can't come back to see me, please give this to Nicole." She reached around her neck and untied the leather thong holding Nicole's amulet. She wouldn't think about how this could be the last time she ever saw Tzader. When she held the amulet out to him, he reluctantly opened his hand. "And make sure that Feen—"

Her voice broke. She'd thought she could say his name.

Tzader wrapped his arms around her. When he spoke, his voice sounded as if he'd eaten rusty blades. "We won't abandon you."

She pulled in a shaky breath, determined to get this out. "I know." She licked her dry lips, searching for the strength to make sure her baby was cared for. "Take Feenix . . . to Nicole . . . so he won't be alone. Tell Feenix . . . tell him—"

Her baby would go berserk when she didn't return.

The first tear charged down her cheek.

Tzader hugged her. "We'll take him to Nicole's tonight as soon as I finish all the VIPER meetings. We'll tell him you love him and take care of him *until* you get back. I swear it."

More tears rushed to join the first one, but she squinted her eyes tight.

The door to her cell opened on its own.

She pulled back from Tzader and tried to smile. "Thank you for all the times you've been my friend and believed in me."

"Don't talk in the past tense. I *will* find a way to get you out of here. Quinn and I won't stop until we do."

Should she tell Tzader about Kizira's claim that Quinn had shared information about Evalle? Not without proof. Evalle could only live with so much guilt, and she'd hurt enough Beladors for one day.

She trusted Tzader to know who his allies were.

She couldn't spend forever in here thinking Quinn had betrayed her to Kizira.

Tzader stepped away, looking back once more before he walked out.

The door swung shut and dissolved into a rough-cut rock wall again.

Her heart dropped with the sudden empty ring. Her watch emitted a loud tick . . . tick . . . tick every time a second passed.

Sen's doing, no doubt. He wanted her to be aware of every second she spent in this cage.

He'd made sure she'd spend all those seconds in agony thinking about Storm and everything she'd lost in one day.

THIRTY-SIX

The watch had become Evalle's nemesis. She tried to stomp out the noisy thing, but the timepiece was indestructible, so she put it beneath the thin mattress on her bed.

The blasted thing ticked louder.

She finally gave up and put the watch back on her arm, where the sound of each second ticking returned to a normal level that echoed off the hard walls.

Energy began forming inside the chamber.

Evalle backed up to the wall facing where the door had appeared last time, but no door took shape.

The energy gathered power until an explosion of light ended with a woman who glowed from head to toe in an angelic dress of sparkling white pearls.

But that was no angel giving her the death stare.

Evalle hadn't expected another guest so soon, and never this one. "Good morning, Goddess."

Macha slid a perturbed look down her narrow, but perfect, nose. "You have caused our tribe a great deal of trouble, Evalle."

The Celtic goddess over all the Beladors took time out of her busy schedule to come here and state the obvious?

Or had Macha dropped by to turn Evalle into a smoldering block of charred Alterant for getting Brina in a jam?

Macha started to pace, took one look at the cramped cell and shared her disgust in a loud sniff. "I should destroy all the Alterants as they become known, and I would if I thought that would solve my problems."

Not feeling the love right now.

Evalle considered everything that had happened and decided that if Macha wanted to toast her for speaking up, she had nothing left to lose. "What's the point of this visit, Macha?"

The goddess studied her as if Evalle had surprised her and proven more interesting than a wounded roach. "My point is simple. If I challenge the Tribunal's ruling against Brina, I put the entire Belador tribe in conflict with VIPER. The risk is too great for that."

Evalle noted that Macha hadn't mentioned the ruling against her. "I understand the predicament we're in."

She probably shouldn't have used "we" in that sentence based on the way Macha's gaze scolded her.

The goddess said, "Tzader came to me and shared everything he'd learned by Quinn probing a possible traitor's mind, as well as what you told him."

Had they decided Conlan O'Meary was a traitor?

Or had Macha decided Evalle was a traitor after she'd dispersed the fog?

As Grady liked to say, "No good deed goes unpunished."

Evalle said, "I assume you heard how I used a gift given me by the Tribunal to destroy the fog, too."

"Yes."

"Do you believe I'm aligned with the Medb?"

"If I did, we would not be having this conversation."

That sounded like confirmation that Evalle *could* have ended up as Alterant charcoal briquettes.

But the goddess had more to say. "More importantly, I believe what you told Tzader."

That was good, right? "About what specifically?"

"That the Medb are trying to bring these half-breed Belador Alterants into their fold and use them to harm Brina. I can't allow that, nor can I allow Brina's hologram to remain in Tribunal custody."

The goddess said nothing about throwing her help Evalle's way, but if she freed Brina's hologram form, Evalle would be thankful for one blessing. "I'm glad to hear you can fix some of this."

"Some? I'm a goddess. I don't fix *some* of anything. I will not be held at the Tribunal's mercy for any reason." She touched her flowing golden-auburn hair with a beautifully manicured nail, and her hair shifted into an even more perfect shape. "Listen carefully, as I do not repeat myself."

Not a lot inside this box to distract me, but whatever.

"Only a deity can approach the Tribunal regarding the viable status of a race. As such, I will open a dialogue with the Tribunal to formally decree that you have given me cause to believe Belador Alterants should be recognized as a viable race. That once the Alterant origin is clearly established and proof of their loyalty to my pantheon has been delivered to the Tribunal their race will be established and protected under the laws of our world."

Evalle's jaw hung slack.

"Do close your mouth." Macha paused, then continued. "In the interim of establishing this race, I will offer amnesty to any Alterant who comes forward willingly to swear allegiance to me and does not harm a coalition member, a Belador or a human while the origins are being researched."

Evalle cut her eyes around the room, searching for this to be a trick.

"Are you paying attention?" Macha snapped at her. "I will not return again if we do not come to an agreement."

"I'm paying very close attention, but what about Brina? Saving her comes first." Evalle nodded to double stamp her words. Hope and reservation struggled for equal space in her heart.

"Brina will be freed once this clears the Tribunal."

Evalle had learned hard lessons about the devious ways of gods and goddesses, which spurred her to pin Macha down more precisely. "I have the feeling what you're talking about involves me doing something, but I'm not going to be a lot of help in this cell."

"Tzader led me to believe you were bright. Did you think I came here to exchange fashion tips?" Macha sniffed at Evalle's ragged clothes.

Didn't get a chance to pack for this trip.

"Once I open the charter for a new race with the Tribunal, that decision supersedes their judgment, as you will then become responsible solely to me and my laws."

There was a loophole in Tribunal rulings?

Macha angled her head and pursed her lips as though she'd heard that thought. Then she continued, "I am designating you as my coordinator for this undertaking with the Alterants. You will be released under my custody and responsible to me while the Alterant race status is being documented. You will continue to serve as a Belador agent for VIPER and will be protected from anyone in the VIPER alliance harming you."

Did that mean Sen couldn't screw with her again?

Part of Evalle wanted to demand that Macha show her where to sign on the dotted line, but another part—the one tired of being used as a pawn in everyone's personal games—had her hesitating to jump up and shout.

Macha said, "If you need some time to think about it, go ahead. You have the rest of your life to ponder while I'm gone." She lifted her hands.

Evalle feared she would teleport away. "Wait. Please."

"Does that mean you've come to a decision?"

Deals with a god or goddess were irrevocable. Evalle didn't want to lose this chance or spend the rest of her life away from all that mattered to her—Tzader, Quinn, Grady, Nicole . . .

What about Storm? No one would search for the truth behind his disappearance if she didn't.

Feenix's face swam through her mind, sealing the decision.

Evalle would face much worse than the fine print in a goddess's contract to hold Feenix again. "I'll do it."

"Big surprise," Macha said under her breath, then went on instructing her. "Do not speak of this to anyone, and do not fail me, Evalle. Brina is far more forgiving than I am."

Macha lifted her hands in a swoosh of movement, vanishing.

End of meeting.

What now?

Evalle would like to think she'd just gotten a reprieve, but she had a strange feeling that she might have only stuck both feet into quicksand.

Once Macha departed, Evalle paid attention to her empathic senses, which had been busy deciphering the meeting. She fingered what had been nudging her to take notice at the very end.

Macha had given off a potent emotion. Exhilaration.

Why had she been so excited over this agreement?

Or had all this been nothing more than a cruel way to punish Evalle for getting Brina into trouble by coming in here to offer Evalle what she most wanted?

Then disappearing and never coming back.

Honor might be a lonely cellmate, but hope was a vicious mistress that would kill her over and over every minute she believed she would be freed.

"Faith is not a learned skill . . . but the blossom on the vine of hope," the soft female voice whispered in the silent room.

Evalle asked, "Why won't you tell me who you are?"

No one answered.

THIRTY-SEVEN

We need to talk, Tristan.

The telepathic contact broke Tristan's concentrating on where to take his band of Alterants tomorrow. After facing off with that black-ops group and walking away from Evalle, he had no doubt Tzader Burke would unleash the fury of the Beladors on him.

Tristan's only regret in all of this was leaving Evalle to face the Tribunal. When the black-ops team had burst on the scene, all Tristan had been able to think was that she had betrayed him.

In hindsight, he began to have his doubts.

At least he'd taught her how to survive in whatever place the Tribunal would send her so she wouldn't die of an animal attack or snakebite.

You need my help, the male voice said again.

Really? Tristan leaned back in the hotel room office chair and looked out the glass at Hartsfield-Jackson Atlanta International Airport. *What makes you think I need anyone's help?*

Because you're on the run from the Beladors and VIPER. I can offer you refuge.

If you're speaking to me telepathically, then you're one of the Beladors.

Yes, I am. Or at least I was until they decided to treat

me like a criminal. You can't run far enough to protect your sister.

Tristan's eyes shot to the second bed in the room where Petrina slept. Exhausted, but safe. He relaxed back into the chair. *If I believe what you say, then the Beladors are after you, too.*

True. There's only one place safe enough to hide, and I'm in that spot with full protection.

That sounded tempting. Tristan had his doubts about his ability to keep Petrina and the other two Alterants safe. He couldn't link with Webster and Aaron in a fight, and he didn't want Petrina in a risky situation.

The voice said, *Don't panic at what I'm about to tell you.*

Tristan laughed. *I doubt you could say anything that would panic me.*

Excellent. I have people waiting outside your hotel, watching the same airplanes take off and land.

That drove Tristan to his feet. He searched the ground below his window but saw nothing. *Where are they?*

Close enough to keep watch over you. Wait a moment . . . I understand you've changed clothes and are wearing a pale yellow button-down shirt.

Tristan touched his shirt as if the damned thing had told on him. *Who are you?*

We can meet in person to allow you to decide for yourself. My people will not bother you. They'll make sure no Belador or VIPER agent comes near you, but they will let you depart the hotel only upon my authority.

Should he trust this guy to meet him?

The airport was still jammed from all the damage

caused during the fog. He couldn't fight a team of powerful beings alone if this guy had people in place to prevent him from leaving. Tristan said, *I'm not agreeing to anything, but I'll meet you.*

Splendid. I believe you'll find my offer exceptional. Expect a car downstairs in ten minutes. Your sister and the other two will be safe while you're gone. If I wanted you captured you would already be sitting in front of me. I want to work with you, not be your enemy. Until we meet . . .

Tristan felt the presence seep out of his mind.

He stood up and wrote a note for his sister with instructions to stay in the room until he returned or contacted her telepathically.

If neither happened by tomorrow morning, he told her to contact Tzader Burke telepathically and ask for Belador protection.

Evalle trusted Tzader to be an honorable man.

Tristan hoped his trust in Evalle was as well placed.

THIRTY-EIGHT

Kizira waited on her platform in her red robe dyed with the blood of dragons. She chanted the words that would cast the torch-lit hall under a shield of privacy. Gazing at the ten men dressed in gray robes, she counted nine of them as her most trusted warlocks.

But the tenth addition might prove to be her most valuable weapon. Twin snakes of conflict and loyalty twisted through her. Cathbad had compelled her loyalty, but her soul fought for freedom to choose which Beladors died and which one—Quinn—was spared.

She finished chanting and lowered the hood of her robe. "I have seen the breaching of the Castle Treoir in my visions." Her face squirmed with a smile while murmurs of excitement surged through the room. "I have seen the face of the one who will lead the charge."

When silence fell once more, she was ready to present their newest member. "We have waited a long time for this opportunity and for the one who will hand us the key to our success." She gave a pointed look at her new disciple. "Step forward, brother, and tell everyone how we will triumph over the Beladors who have persecuted you even though you bleed their blood."

Conlan O'Meary lowered the hood of his robe. "There is an Alterant who is ready to lead us to victory by breaching the warding of Treoir Castle. In return, we have offered this Alterant what no one else can, the end of being victimized by the Beladors. When the time comes to take possession of Treoir, Priestess, I will deliver you Evalle Kincaid, who will destroy the inhabitants of Treoir Castle and open the gates for you."

Shocked silence hung in the air, then the warlocks cheered.

When Conlan lifted his hand, the warlocks quieted. "The Alterant Tristan has agreed to meet me, but he's careful. I like that trait in someone I'll be working with. Once we have Tristan in place, we'll use him to bring Evalle in. I told you, Kizira, I understand how Beladors operate."

THIRTY-NINE

A stiff breeze cut across the top of a thirty-story building that towered over Peachtree Street. Tzader had stood here long enough for the sun to set and turn downtown Atlanta into a sparkling jewel.

Evalle had been in that hole since this morning.

He wanted justice, but he would settle for satisfaction.

When energy charged through the air he didn't turn to welcome the presence that arrived.

That might appear as though he were pleased to see her.

"Are you not happy to see me, Tzader?"

Swinging around, he leaned against the waist-high parapet wall, then crossed his arms and his legs. "Depends."

"I've kept my part of the bargain. Evalle has been released from her cell and Brina's hologram is free."

He'd have enjoyed the relief those words gave him if not for the nasty taste of having had to bargain for what Macha should freely give. But he'd sworn loyalty to Macha as a child and owed her a level of respect. "Thank you."

His father had once told him that few might understand Macha, but she made no decision about the Beladors that was not honorable and in the interest of protecting the tribe. He'd warned Tzader not to judge her too quickly, because time played a role in understanding many of her decisions.

No matter how many times Tzader told himself that, it didn't change the fact that he couldn't see the reason behind the corner Macha had forced him into.

She smiled, her eyes changing from silvery blue to the color of sunlight striking blue-green Caribbean water. Her radiant red hair never seemed to remain still or even the same color, always busy finding a more flattering shape.

"What did you tell Evalle?" he asked.

"Just what we'd agreed upon. She's to become my coordinator of Alterant research and pursue locating the missing Alterants." Macha became impatient, tapping her foot. "I could have sent someone to find Tristan instead of freeing Evalle."

"And risk Evalle falling into Medb hands?"

"We both know the chances of Evalle escaping were zilch."

Tzader had considered several possible ways to have Evalle freed, but every option had put him and Quinn fighting VIPER, Macha and the Beladors.

That would have left him no way to protect Brina.

If not the best choice, this had been the only one that protected all he held dear from danger.

Macha sighed heavily. "Even with Evalle free, we must be vigilant to protect Brina. I'm not entirely certain we can stop the Medb from finding a way to breach the castle as long as Alterants are running around loose."

"I will always protect Brina. You know that." He could only stomach so much of this, but he had to keep his end of this bargain or Macha would take away everything she'd given. But he didn't have to stand here acting as though she really had his best interest at heart. "That's not what you're here to discuss."

"You're right. You share a certain amount of responsibility in what happened to Brina. She trusted Evalle based upon your ties to the Alterant."

He'd conceded that point when he'd almost lost his mind upon learning that Brina's hologram form had been captured.

But he wondered how much of this happenstance Macha had orchestrated. He'd known the goddess a long time and had never trusted her as completely as his father and Brina's father had.

Look where that trust had gotten their fathers. Killed.

And Brina stuck in a castle until she produced an heir. "What about Brina? Does she get a say?"

Macha said, "The last time I saw Brina, *she* broached the subject of it being time for her to produce an heir."

Okay, that surprised him based on the reception he'd gotten from Brina. She wanted to have a baby now . . . with someone else? All he could get out was, "I see."

"She recognizes the need more than ever to have a child and protect the future of the Beladors, especially in the face of all that has just happened."

"Then remove my immortality so I can marry her."

"I can't go back on the oath I gave to your father. You speak of marriage? Must I remind you to give me your vow as your part of our bargain? Or shall I return Evalle to the cell in VIPER and prevent Brina's hologram from leaving the castle?"

No. He'd relive this moment a million times over from here on out. The words stuck in his throat, but he had negotiated in good faith and had no choice but to do his part. "I vow to not pursue Brina's hand in marriage anymore and to do nothing to prevent her from marrying another."

The muscles in his fingers tightened into balled fists inside his crossed arms. How could he stay in this world and allow another man to touch Brina?

Macha waved her hand in exasperation. "You make it sound like I've given you a death sentence. Are you so selfish as to make Brina wait forever for something that is impossible?"

He'd never hold Brina back from having a life with someone else if she wanted another man, but letting her go was ripping him apart inside. "Of course I want her to be happy. I told you I wouldn't pursue her. Are we done here?"

"Not quite. You agreed not only to let this relationship go but also to convince Brina that she is free so she can move on without guilt. She was very upset after your last meeting and doesn't know what to say without hurting your feelings."

Hurt his feelings?

What a ridiculous description of losing the most important person in his world. "I'll convince her."

FORTY

Evalle strode along the last hallway to her underground apartment, bruised from head to toe, heart to soul. Sen had teleported her to where she'd left her motorcycle in Decatur.

He hadn't said a word, but there'd been no way to mute the raw hatred in his eyes.

And no way he would have given her a straight answer about Storm, so she hadn't wasted time asking. She didn't need him to find answers. Tzader had said he'd let her know when anyone heard from Storm.

She opened the door of her apartment and stepped inside. "Feenix . . . I'm home."

Where was he?

Thump, thump, thump . . . then the flap of wings.

Her heart caught in her throat when he came flying at her. She normally stepped aside so he could land in the beanbag and slide across the floor for his NASCAR finish.

She just stood there.

His orange eyes blazed in surprise. He angled away, circled the room and came back to her open arms, tucking his wings as he landed.

She pulled him in close, hugging him, hurting and happy at the same time.

Feenix patted her face and pressed his nose into the curve of her throat.

She shook with the effort of holding back a sob that she couldn't let free. Her insides were shredding with hurt. Storm had to be alive.

If he was, where was he?

He'd found her in South America.

He'd found her near where she lived.

Feenix said, "Mine."

Her heart was sandwiched between misery and joy. "You're mine, too, baby."

Her gargoyle lifted his head and chortled with delight. "Mith me?"

"More than you'll ever know." She gave him a kiss on his scaly forehead and lowered him to the floor. "Let me grab a shower and we'll watch reruns."

Anything that felt normal.

The shower helped, and so did fresh clothes. She put Storm's windbreaker back on before climbing into bed with a bowl of popcorn for her and a handful of lug nuts for Feenix.

Feenix puttered around the room, flapping his wings every time he reached the count of ten. He even counted in order, ending with nine and then ten once she explained he could count either horn as nine or ten.

She opened her laptop and booted up her email. The minute she started tapping on keys, Feenix flapped his wings rapidly, lifting up in the air.

He flew over the end of the bed and settled next to her, where he'd left his pet alligator earlier. *"Nathcar!"* He gave her a toothy smile worth any deal she'd had to make with Macha.

She tweaked his toe and got the deepest giggling sound she'd ever heard. "We'll watch the NASCAR rerun as soon as I finish a couple emails. Okay?"

He clapped his hands. "Ithe cream."

That counted as yes from Feenix.

Turning back to her laptop, she scanned through the usual notices from VIPER before she found the ones that mattered. Her email service was protected by some uber-security operation run through www.Beladors.com, which meant no spam. She opened the first one from Quinn that had come in yesterday:

> *The morgue believes you are on a leave of absence. You may return at your leisure.*

She hated that her first thought was to question if he had done that out of his usual sincere concern for her . . . or out of guilt if he really did talk to Kizira about her. She could use a couple days to sort things out in her head.

She needed some Feenix time.

When Tzader had contacted her telepathically on her way home, he'd told her to check her email for a message from him, which they'd discuss tomorrow after she got some rest. She found Tzader's email that said:

> *Quinn encountered a threat to Brina during Conlan O'Meary's mind probe so we took him into temporary custody. Conlan disappeared*

> *from the holding facility. Contact me immedi-*
> *ately if you hear from O'Meary. Don't meet him*
> *under any circumstances without me or Quinn*
> *present. We need to talk first.*

What had Quinn seen in O'Meary's mind that would make Tzader think O'Meary would contact her?

Quinn had sent a more recent email:

> *I am exceptionally pleased you have returned*
> *unharmed. We'll speak soon.*

How could something a crazy witch said change the way Evalle thought about one of her two closest friends?

It shouldn't. It wouldn't.

She refused to feel suspicious about Quinn. He'd earned her trust and had yet to give her reason to question it. She'd tell him what Kizira had said and he'd explain how there was no way possible for Kizira to have gotten that information from him.

She stared at her inbox, willing an email from Storm to be waiting for her.

None.

Feenix rubbed her arm.

She smiled over at him, but his eyes were sad. He put his head on her shoulder.

Did this little guy have empathic ability?

Or could he hear her heart cracking with a new fracture every minute she didn't hear from Storm?

She patted his face. "We'll watch NASCAR next."

He grinned at her and plopped down on the pillow beside her, grabbing his stuffed alligator to hug.

Starting tomorrow, she had to take care of Alterant business. Macha had handed her the chance to prove Alterants should be a recognized race. Evalle would tell Tristan as soon as she found him. She doubted he'd make it out of this country, since the airport really was shut down after all. He should be more open to working with her once he found out she had Macha backing.

Life was good.

All she had to do was find Tristan and Storm.

She turned back to her computer to send Storm an email and a new one popped into her inbox—from Storm. She froze, staring at the blinking message, then clicked on it. The message had been sent from his cell phone several hours ago. She hadn't seen any of his clothes when she'd gone back to search after being dropped at her bike, but now realized she hadn't seen his cell phone when she'd unloaded her tank bag. Had Storm retrieved his things . . . or had someone else?

Her heart thumped like crazy. She opened the email and read:

> *Evalle*
> *I'll be in touch.*
> *Storm.*

Building a unique world with rich details often requires using unusual names and terms. These are sometimes fictional as well as being drawn from actual mythology.

Below is a list of pronunciations.

Asháninka	[ash – AH – neen – kah]
Batuk	[bah – TOOK]
Belador	[BELL – ah – door]
Birnn demon	[beern demon]
Cú Chulainn	[KOO-ku-lin]
Ekkbar	[ECK – bar]
Evalle	[EE - vahl]
Flaevynn	[FLAY – vin]
Gixxer	[JICKS – er]
Kizira	[kuh – ZEER – ah]
Kujoo	[KOO – joe]
Loch Ryve	[lock reeve]
Medb	[MAEVE or MAVE]
Nhivoli	[neh-VO – lee]
Nihar	[NEE – har]
Noirre	[nwar – EH or nwar – A]
Treoir	[TRAY – or]
Tzader	[ZA – der]
Vyan	[VIE – an . . . first part rhymes with BYE]